the
LAST GARDEN
in ENGLAND

Also by Julia Kelly

The Whispers of War
The Light Over London

the
LAST GARDEN
in ENGLAND

Julia Kelly

G

Gallery Books

NEW YORK   LONDON   TORONTO   SYDNEY   NEW DELHI

G

Gallery Books
An Imprint of Simon & Schuster, Inc.
1230 Avenue of the Americas
New York, NY 10020

This Gallery Books Canadian export edition January 2021

GALLERY BOOKS and colophon are registered trademarks of Simon & Schuster, Inc.

For information about special discounts for bulk purchases, please contact Simon & Schuster Special Sales at 1-866-506-1949 or business@simonandschuster.com.

The Simon & Schuster Speakers Bureau can bring authors to your live event. For more information or to book an event, contact the Simon & Schuster Speakers Bureau at 1-866-248-3049 or visit our website at www.simonspeakers.com.

Interior design by Jaime Putorti

Manufactured in the United States of America

10 9 8 7 6 5 4 3 2 1

The Library of Congress has cataloged the hardcover edition as follows:

Names: Kelly, Julia, 1986– author.
Title: The last garden in England / Julia Kelly.
Description: First Gallery Books hardcover edition. | New York : Gallery Books, 2021.
Identifiers: LCCN 2020018853 (print) | LCCN 2020018854 (ebook) |
    ISBN 9781982107826 (hardcover) | ISBN 9781982107833 (trade paperback) |
    ISBN 9781982107840 (ebook)
Subjects: GSAFD: Historical fiction.
Classification: LCC PS3611.E449245 L37 2021 (print) | LCC PS3611.E449245
    (ebook) | DDC 813/.6—dc23
LC record available at https://lccn.loc.gov/2020018853
LC ebook record available at https://lccn.loc.gov/2020018854

ISBN 978-1-9821-7112-4
ISBN 978-1-9821-0784-0 (ebook)

For Dad, who gave me his love of gardens

Therefore all seasons shall be sweet to thee.

—SAMUEL TAYLOR COLERIDGE

the
LAST GARDEN
in ENGLAND

· PROLOGUE ·

JANUARY 1908

Her steps in sturdy walking boots are steady on the stone path despite the ice that crunches underfoot. All around her, snow-covered branches bend and bow, threatening to break. All is quiet.

She walks deeper into this winter garden. Stark and beautiful, with its clusters of silver birches broken by dogwood, bloodred stems violent against mournful grasses bending in the wind. Pure white hellebores—the Christmas rose—dot the border. It pains her to think that, in a month, the first green heads of snowdrops will burst forth through the snow in elegant white blooms before purple crocuses with vibrant yellow stamen follow. She will not see these heralds of spring. Others will have to read the signs that this garden is ready to relinquish its crown.

She stops at the edge of the stone path, sorrow clawing at her like a feral beast desperate to break free. She wipes away a half-frozen tear. She should not be here, yet she could not leave without once again seeing this place of love and loss.

No. She won't stay long. Only the length of a goodbye.

WINTER

· EMMA ·

FEBRUARY 2021

*E*ven if Emma hadn't been looking for the turnoff, Highbury House would have been hard to miss. Two brick pillars topped with a pair of stone lions rose up from a gap in the hedgerow, harkening to a time of carriages and riding to hounds, hunt balls and elaborate house parties.

She turned into the gravel drive, steeling herself to meet her clients. Normally she wouldn't take a job sight unseen, but she'd been too wrapped up in the restoration project at Mallow Glen to travel down from Scotland for a site survey. Instead, Emma's best friend and the head of her crew at Turning Back Thyme, Charlie, had gone ahead and done the measurements, while Sydney Wilcox, Highbury House's owner, had arranged a series of video chats to explain the project: to return the once-spectacular gardens to their former glory.

The short drive opened up into a courtyard, around which the U-shaped house was built, but its elegance was marred by piles of construction debris.

Emma parked behind a steel-gray Range Rover and climbed out, slinging her heavy canvas workbag over her shoulder. The high-pitched whine of power tools filled the air, followed by a volley of barks. Out of the corner of her eye, she caught a flash of red. A pair of Irish setters bounded through the front door, straight for her.

She threw up her hands to fend off the smaller of the two dogs, who still managed to rear up on its hind legs, planting its paws on her shoulders and licking her face. The other danced around her feet, barking encouragement.

She tried to push the dogs away as Sydney burst out of the doorway, half jogging across the courtyard. "Bonnie, get down! Clyde, let Emma through!"

"They're fine," said Emma, hoping she sounded at least a little convincing as Bonnie managed another lick. "You'd be surprised how many of my jobs start like this, especially in the country. Everyone keeps dogs."

"I really am so sorry. We spent so much time and money training them, and we still ended up with two of the most ill-behaved dogs in all of Warwickshire." Sydney grabbed Bonnie's collar and hauled her away while Clyde went to sit obediently at his owner's feet.

"Don't pretend you aren't as bad as her," Sydney chided Clyde, her voice reminiscent of good schools, lessons at the local riding club, and Saturday cricket on the village green.

Straightening, Sydney reached up to reclip her curly red hair.

"I'm sorry about that. These two follow the builders around all day long. Someone must have left the door open. Did you have any trouble getting up here? Was there traffic on the M40? Sometimes it's a nightmare. Did you find the turnoff okay?"

Emma blinked, wondering which question to answer first. A cheery chaos seemed to swirl around the owner of Highbury House. Emma had noticed it on their calls, but in person, surrounded by a pair of dogs, in the shadow of a house under construction, it was an entirely different experience. Finally, she said, "I didn't have any problems finding the house."

"I'm so glad you arrived when you did. It rained this morning, and I told Andrew that it wouldn't do for your first real look at the garden to be in the middle of a rainstorm. But then it cleared, and now here you are!" Sydney turned toward the house, gesturing for Emma to follow. "You'll have to forgive the noise."

"Are you living here through the construction?" Emma raised her voice to ask as she peered around the entryway draped in drop cloths. A ladder stood next to a grand staircase bracketed by a hand-carved banister, and the scent of fresh paint hung in the air, although the walls looked as though they had only just been stripped of wallpaper.

"We are," a man's voice came from over Emma's shoulder. "I'm Andrew. It's a pleasure to meet you in person."

Emma shook Andrew's hand, letting her eyes slide between the husband and wife. He towered over sprightly Sydney, his Clark Kent glasses sitting on the bridge of his nose and his short brown hair combed neatly to the side. He wrapped his arm around his wife's waist as though it was the most natural thing in the world, looking down at her with a healthy mixture of amusement and adoration.

Even standing amid the dust of a half-finished house, the Wilcoxes exuded polish, education, class. They were a golden couple, which— experience had taught her—made them all the more likely to be huge pains. However, they were paying customers who wanted a restoration project, not a brand-new garden, and they hadn't even flinched when Emma had given them a quote.

"Andrew let me convince him that we should be on-site through the restoration work." Sydney bit her full lower lip. "It's been a bigger project than even we expected."

Andrew shook his head. "Six months they said."

"How long has it been going on now?" Emma asked.

"Eighteen months, and we've only done up one wing of the house. There's so much still left," said Sydney. "Darling, I was just going to take Emma for a tour of the garden."

"I don't want to bother you," Emma said quickly. "I've been working off Charlie's specs. I'm sure I can find my own way."

"I insist," said Sydney. "I'd love to hear your first impressions, and I have a few ideas."

Ideas. All her clients had ideas, but so few of them were good. Like the man outside of Glasgow who insisted he wanted a tropical garden in the middle of Scotland despite her warnings that it would require intensive work to maintain. He'd called her six months after Turning Back Thyme had packed up and moved on to another job, complaining that every single one of his banana plants had died over the winter and wanting them replaced for free. She'd politely referred him to her contract, which stated she was not responsible for neglect on the part of the owner.

At least Highbury House would be different in *that* regard—a respite from all of the contemporary design projects she took on to keep the business afloat. A historic garden of some importance that had lain virtually abandoned for years, the Wilcoxes wanted to see it bloom again just as it had when it had been created in 1907.

Although they took up time and research well beyond her modern projects, Emma loved nothing more than sinking her spade into a restoration. She'd done battle against poured-concrete patios and cursed stretches of lawn previous owners had laid down because it was "easier" than doing any real gardening. In one particularly egregious instance, she'd ripped out a half acre of artificial lawn installed in the 1970s and re-created the eighteenth-century French knot garden through which ladies in powdered wigs had once strolled. She could make long-forgotten gardens bloom out of pastures and paddocks. She could rewind the clock. Make things right again.

Still, she couldn't live on challenge alone, and since Sydney would be paying her bills for nearly a year, she would humor Sydney's ideas. Within reason.

"I'd be glad of the company," she said, putting as much enthusiasm as she could into her voice.

"Are you coming, darling?" Sydney asked Andrew.

"I would, but Greg said something about floor joists earlier," he said.

"What about them?" Sydney asked.

Andrew gave a half laugh and pushed his glasses up. "Apparently we don't have any in the music room. They've rotted straight through."

Emma's brows rose as Sydney's mouth formed an O.

Andrew waved a goodbye, darted around the ladder, and disappeared through one of the doors off the entryway.

"I'm afraid that's been happening a lot recently." Sydney pointed to a pair of French doors that had been stripped of their paint and looked like they were waiting for a good sanding. "The easiest access to the garden is just through here."

Emma followed her employer out onto a wide veranda. Some of the huge slabs of slate were cracked underfoot and weeds pushed up through the gaps, but there was no denying the view's beauty. A long lawn rolled down a gentle hill to trees lining a calm lake. She squinted, conjuring up the old photograph she'd found in the Warwick Archives showing the garden during a party in the 1920s. There had once been a short set of stairs down to a reflecting pool surrounded by two quarter circles of box as well as a long border that ran the eastern length of the property. Now there was nothing but a stretch of uninterrupted lawn that held none of the charm that surely would have imbued Venetia Smith's original design.

Excitement pricked the back of her neck. Emma was going to restore a Venetia Smith garden. Long before she'd become famous in America, the Edwardian garden designer had designed a handful of gardens here in Britain. Emma owed her career to a BBC program about the restoration of Venetia's garden at Longmarsh House. At seventeen, she'd insisted that her parents take her there on holiday. While most of her friends were thinking about where they might go to university, she stood in that restored garden and realized what she wanted to do with her life.

As they descended the veranda steps, Sydney gestured to the western edge of the lawn. "There isn't much of the shade border left."

Emma walked to one of the gnarled trunks that made up the long straight path that ran the length of the great lawn. The cold, rough bark felt comfortingly familiar under her hand. "The trees along the lime walk look as though they've been well maintained."

"That would be the garden service. Dad kept on the same company that Granddad employed. They do what they can to keep things tidy," said Sydney.

Tidy but nothing more.

"This whole stretch would have been much more vibrant when it was first created," said Emma.

"Even in the shade?"

Emma smiled. "It's a common misconception that shade gardens are dull. I haven't found an archival photograph of how it looked when Venetia planted it, but she loved color, so we can assume she used it."

"I bought a couple of collections of her books and diaries after our last call," Sydney said. "She wrote so much, I almost didn't know where to start."

"Her diaries are my favorite. She published a few between the wars, but about twenty years ago someone bought her old house in Wimbledon and found two from her very first projects," said Emma.

"But not Highbury."

Emma shook her head. "If they had, we'd have a built-in project plan. The tea garden is through there?" she asked, nodding to a gated passageway between the lime trees.

"Yes," said Sydney.

The neatness of the lime walk dropped away as soon as they crossed into the tea garden. An enclosed room with walls of brick and yew, it would have been created as a sanctuary for ladies to gossip among soft pastels of whimsical flowers. Now it was chaos.

"The gardeners don't make it into the garden rooms much," said Sydney, a touch of apology in her voice. "Dad said it was expensive enough to do the lawn and the parts you can see from the house."

It showed. A stand of dead gaura twined with Queen Anne's lace, all dried-up and falling over itself. Several sad clumps of roses heavy with hips had become scraggly from too many winters gone without a good hard pruning, and Emma doubted they threw off more than a dozen blooms in June. Everything else was an indiscriminate mix of long-dead flowers and weeds.

"I can help you find a crew to maintain the gardens when I'm done here," she said.

"That bad, is it?" Sydney asked with a laugh.

"If I were your dad, I'd ask for my money back. That entire patch looks like it's just weeds," she said, pointing to an odd gap of packed earth where a single bindweed-covered teak bench sat forgotten. "There was probably once a gazebo or a pergola of some sort there."

"It was one of the casualties of the Great Storm of '87. I know we lost some trees on the edge of the lake and in the ramble. I found receipts for the tree surgeons in Granddad's records," said Sydney.

"Did you have any luck finding anything from the year the garden was created?" Emma asked.

"Not yet, but don't worry. Granddad never threw anything out. I'm still pulling boxes of papers out of the study, and I haven't even tackled the attics yet. If there's something there, I'll find it," said Sydney.

Emma followed Sydney through a yew hedge into the lovers' garden, which featured bare clumps of ground and struggling tropicals Emma was certain Venetia wouldn't have had access to in her time. Beyond that, the children's garden was little more than a collection of wildflowers and four large cherry trees in desperate need of pruning, and the lavender walk was wildly overgrown but thriving. The sculpture garden was now mostly lawn and a few broken, weather-scarred statues. Next was a mismatched garden Emma still couldn't place the purpose of, despite her research, and what was supposed to be a white garden that had self-seeded into what she was certain would be a multitude of colors come spring. Down they walked into what Emma guessed was a long-defunct water garden, the low trough in the middle of it now choked with non-aquatic weeds. It all struck her as . . . sad, an indistinct mess of sprawling neglect.

"And that," said Sydney, as they walked down a path between the water garden and the white garden, "brings us to this."

At first, all Emma saw above the tall brick wall were the reaching tops of trees and long canes of a climbing rose fighting for supremacy and sunlight. However, as they walked around the gently curving wall that formed a circle of brick, they came to an iron gate rusted brown and orange. Vines twined around its bars, and stems shot out rudely. Everything in this garden seemed desperate to escape.

"This must be the one Charlie warned me about," she said.

"The winter garden. When I was little, we only came up to the house two times a year—for Granddad's birthday and on Boxing Day—but I remember Dad walking me around the gardens every time. In the depths of December, this would be the only bit that seemed alive," said Sydney.

"You've been inside?" Emma asked, wrapping her hands around the iron bars and trying in vain to see beyond the thick foliage.

"No, it's been locked for as long as I can remember."

Emma ran her finger over the huge keyhole cut into the iron. "And I take it there's no key to the gate, then."

Sydney shook her head. "Another thing I'm hunting for. Andrew suggested getting a locksmith in, but I've called two and they both said that the condition and age of the gate means they might have to cut it off its hinges to get it open. Doing that just feels . . . wrong."

"Wrong?" Emma asked, pulling back.

"I couldn't in good conscience destroy part of the garden's history while I'm working so hard to restore the house. And . . ." Sydney paused. "There's just something about the winter garden. It feels so abandoned."

The entire garden was a living example of neglect, but Emma saw her point. She guessed Sydney was around her age, and the idea that someone could leave this garden untouched and untended for thirty-five years made her shiver. It was so . . . sinister? Solemn?

Secretive.

Nothing about this job was going to be easy. There were no plans, there was little archive material, and much of the original structure of the garden had been lost to time. But while that might have scared off some of her competitors who preferred the ease of designing a contemporary garden to their clients' exact specifications, Emma couldn't help the hint of excitement that fizzed through her when she looked at the hopeless mess. This was what made slogging through payroll and ordering and appointments with her accountant worth it. Highbury House was the sort of project she loved.

"Well, we could get a ladder and try to scale the wall," Emma suggested.

"Andrew had a go at that," Sydney said. "He got up there and realized that there was nowhere to safely put a ladder down the other side."

"When was this?" Emma asked.

"Right after we sold our company. We offered to buy the house from Mum and Dad. Granddad had left them some money, but most of it went to fixing leaks in the roof and trying to heat the place so the damp didn't set in. It had become a bit of a millstone over the years, but Dad never had the heart to sell it," Sydney said.

Emma offered her a small smile. "And now you've decided to put it back together again."

"That's right. We're Sydney and Andrew Wilcox, saviors of old houses."

"And their gardens," Emma said.

"I hope that the scale of the project hasn't scared you off," Sydney said.

Even if the size of the Highbury House project had been intimidating, Emma still would have taken it. Mallow Glen had run over by a month because of three different issues with suppliers, forcing her to sacrifice a smaller job doing up a cottage garden in Leicestershire while prepping for Highbury House. Losing that additional injection of money into the business hurt, but Highbury would be a much bigger prize.

"It is tricky," she admitted. "We just don't have that much to go on in the way of original documentation or photos, so I've drawn up plans based on Venetia's other designs from the same era."

"I'll work on those boxes, I promise," said Sydney. "Now, what happens next?"

"The crew arrives. You've already met Charlie, but there's Jessa, Zack, and Vishal, too. They'll start by clearing away the overgrown vegetation so we can really see what we're working with. I should be able to show you final plans this week."

Sydney clasped her hands in front of her, looking for all the world as though she was about to break out into song like the heroine in a musical. Instead, she said, "I cannot wait."

Neither, Emma thought, *can I.*

Emma shifted the groceries she'd picked up from one arm to the other and pulled the keys out of her pocket. The letting agent had offered to walk her through Bow Cottage, but she had politely declined. After a day of following Sydney around, she was craving the peace and quiet of her rental.

After just two attempts, she managed to open the red front door and switch the hall light on. She let the door swing shut behind her and let out a sigh of relief before setting about searching for the kitchen in her home for the next nine months. She would deal with the luggage crammed into the back of her car later. First she needed a cup of tea and to charge her mobile.

She found a good-sized sitting room right off the entryway and a small study next to it. Across the hall was a dining room with a big plank-topped table that she would use for drafting rather than entertaining. Next door was the kitchen: basic but pretty, with gauze curtains hanging in the wide windows that looked out over a brick patio and lawn of dwarf ryegrass with a mature *Magnolia grandiflora* at the back. She slid her grocery bags onto the counter, plugged in her dead phone, filled the electric kettle that stood ready, and began stocking her temporary refrigerator.

She'd just put yogurt and milk away when a message chimed through. She winced when she saw how many texts she'd missed, including several from Charlie asking her if she wanted him to bring anything the next morning when they met on-site and then teasing her for letting her phone run down yet again.

As she kept scrolling, she saw she'd missed a call from Dad. She dialed him back and put the phone on speaker so she could continue to unload her provisions.

"You all right, Emma?" came her dad's voice, his South London accent out in full force.

"You sound chipper," she said with a smile.

"I've been waiting by the phone all day to hear how your first day went."

"Hello, love!" called her mother, somewhere in the background. "I'm glad to see you aren't neglecting your loving parents."

"Your mother says hello," said Dad, tempering his wife's greeting.

Emma sighed. "Sorry I didn't call earlier. My phone died."

He laughed. "Your phone is always dying. How was the garden?"

She placed bread out on the counter. "Sad. The current owners, Sydney and Andrew, bought it off Sydney's parents, who inherited it from her grandfather. It sounds like Sydney's parents did what they could to keep the place standing, but anything else was beyond their reach. You can imagine the state of the garden."

"That bad?" he asked.

"In some places it's been dug over entirely, but others are just wild. There are four morello cherry trees that look as though they haven't been properly dealt with in thirty years. And then there's the bottom of the garden. It's all a mess, and there's one garden room I can't even figure out the theme of."

"Sounds as though you've got your work cut out for you," he said.

"I do. The place must have looked beautiful even just five years after Venetia finished it." Except she doubted Venetia Smith ever saw her work come to fruition. As far as Emma knew, she'd never come back to Britain once she left.

"I'm sure it was." The line went muffled, and she could tell Dad had done his best to cover the microphone on his mobile. She braced herself for the moment he came on again and said, "Your mum wants to speak to you."

Before she could give some excuse—she was tired, she needed to get dinner on—she heard the shifting of the phone from one hand to the other and Mum came on. "Have you heard anything from the foundation?"

"Hello, Mum. I'm doing well, thanks for asking."

"We're waiting on pins and needles here, Emma. You *need* that head of conservation job," said her mother, ignoring her.

"Need" wasn't the way Emma would put it, but she tried her best to shove her annoyance aside. Mum wanted the best for her, and to Mum a stable job at the prestigious Royal Botanical Heritage Society was the best a girl from Croydon without a university degree could hope for.

"I don't know yet. They said they'd call *if* I progressed into the next round of interviews," she said.

"Of course they'll want to bring you in again. They couldn't find anyone better to head up their conservancy efforts. And you could have a steady paycheck for once in your life."

"I have a steady paycheck," she said. *Most of the time.*

"Didn't you spend last summer chasing down that horrible couple who refused to pay you?" her mother asked.

It would have been more accurate to say that her solicitor chased the couple who'd refused to pay the last half of her fees and tried to stick her with a bill of £10,000 for rare plants and hardscaping they'd insisted she work into their garden's design.

"They paid in the end," she said with a sigh, remembering the legal fees that had cut into the money she'd recovered.

"After you threatened legal action."

"That doesn't happen very often," she said.

"Admit it, love. Turning Back Thyme is a good little business, but it isn't exactly paving the streets with gold."

"Mum—"

"If you took the foundation job, you could finally buy a house. Prices aren't so bad if you go far enough south of the Thames. You could have your own garden, and you could be so much closer to your father and me instead of roving all over the place," said Mum.

"I like moving around," she said.

"Your father and I didn't pay all of those school fees for you to be homeless," her mother pushed.

"Mum! I'm not homeless. I live where I work. Besides, *if* the foundation offered me the job—which they haven't even done second interviews for—I'd still have to figure out what to do with my company. That isn't an easy decision."

"You could sell it."

"Mum."

"Would that be such a bad thing?"

The denial didn't come as fast as it should have. She loved Turning Back Thyme, but owning a business alone was hard. She lived with the near-constant stress of wondering if this was going to be the year things came crashing down. A few bad jobs—or a stretch of no work—and it wouldn't just be her livelihood on the line, but her entire crew's.

If all she had to do was design, it would be heaven, but it was so much more than that. She was also accounting, HR, payroll, marketing, sales all rolled into one. Some days she'd stumble from working on a site to a night spent over her laptop, processing the piles of digital paperwork that came with running a small business. Then she'd fall into bed, only to wake up with a gasp from the recurring nightmare of logging in to the business's bank account only to find a £75,000 overdraft.

It was days like that—and conversations like this—that made her wonder if she was kidding herself that she could do this for the rest of her life.

Clearing her throat, she said, "I need to make dinner and get ready for tomorrow."

"You have so much potential, Emma."

I didn't raise you to dig around in the dirt all day.

You were supposed to be better than this.

You threw everything away, Emma.

What a disappointment.

Emma couldn't unhear those words thrown at her during every single fight they'd had when Emma had turned her back on university and chosen this life. A life that Mum, who had risen above her working-class roots, hadn't wanted for her.

"I need to go, Mum," she said lamely.

"Send us photos of the house you're staying in," her mother said, her tone shifting to cheerfulness now that she'd gotten her shots in.

"And the garden, too!" her father shouted in the background.

"I will," she promised. She hung up and turned back to her groceries, trying to shake off the creeping doubt that Mum was right.

· VENETIA ·

TUESDAY, 5 FEBRUARY 1907
Highbury House
Sunny; winds out of the east

*E*ach new garden is like an unread book, its pages brimming with possibility. This morning, as I stood on the step to Highbury House, I nearly trembled with excitement. Every garden—every hard-fought commission—feels like a triumph, and I am determined that Highbury House shall be my greatest effort yet.

But I am rushing my story.

I rang the bell, setting a dog off barking somewhere in the house, and waited, tugging at the lapels of my navy wool coat that looked so smart against the white of my shirt. Adam had approved of my appearance before sending me off on the train with a promise that he would look after the house and garden while I was in Warwickshire.

I glanced around, wondering at how stark Highbury House looked stripped of the wreaths and garlands that had merrily hung on doors and windows when I visited in December. Mrs. Melcourt, the lady of the house, was out visiting that day, but Mr. Melcourt spoke to me at length before letting me walk the long lawn and tired beds of a garden so lacking in imagination it saddened me. He purchased the house three years ago and now, having done over all the rooms, he's turned his attention outside. He commissioned me on the recommendation of several of my past clients whom he no doubt wishes to impress. He wants a garden imbued with elegance and ambition, one that will look as though it has been in the family for years rather than being a new acquisition funded by the recent inheritance of his soap fortune.

The huge front door groaned open, revealing a housekeeper starched into a somber uniform of high-necked black with a chain of keys hanging off her like a medieval chatelaine.

"Good morning," she intoned, her measured voice laced with Birmingham.

I gripped the cardboard tube of papers I'd carried up from London a little tighter. "Good morning. I am Miss Venetia Smith. I have an appointment with Mr. Melcourt."

The housekeeper assessed me from the brim of my hat to the toe of my boot. Her mouth thinned sharp as a reed when she spotted the mud I'd acquired performing one last check of my roses that morning.

"I can remove them if you like," I said archly.

The housekeeper's back stiffened as though I'd poked her with a hatpin. "That will not be necessary, Miss Smith."

The woman led me to a double drawing room and gestured to me to wait just outside the door. I could see that the room was undeniably grand, with a half-open set of pocket doors that could divide the hand-tooled wood-paneled walls. At one end, a carved marble fire surround stood watch over a roaring blaze. Overhead, a large chandelier glinted with electric lights in dozens of glass cups, illuminating tapestries and paintings. Yet the grandest ornament of all sat at the center of the room: a tiny blond woman in a white wool day dress belted with a slash of black. Across from her were three children, sitting in a row, their nanny watching over the eldest girl as she read out, "Pussy said to the Owl, 'You elegant fowl! How charmingly sweet you sing!'"

"My dear," said the woman in white, who I presumed was Mrs. Melcourt.

The child stopped at once. From the armchair rose the barrel-chested Mr. Melcourt, wearing a suit of inky black.

"Miss Smith," the housekeeper announced.

"Thank you, Mrs. Creasley. Please show her in," said Mrs. Melcourt.

Mrs. Creasley stepped back so I could take her place.

"Miss Smith, I trust your journey was not too difficult," said Mr. Melcourt with a curt nod of his head.

I watched, fascinated by the way his Adam's apple bounced against the stiff collar of his shirt. Was every member of the household a prisoner to starch?

"It was very pleasant, thank you," I said.

"My wife, Mrs. Melcourt," said Mr. Melcourt.

I gave a shallow curtsy, which Mrs. Melcourt returned with a slight nod. She did not rise.

"Are those the plans?" Mr. Melcourt asked eagerly.

I lifted my cardboard tube. "They are."

"I trust that corresponding with Mr. Hillock was helpful," he said.

"He's a very knowledgeable man." A good head gardener can be a great asset in executing a new design. Long after I leave Highbury, Mr. Hillock will be charged with maintaining the spirit of my creation.

"Would you like to see the latest drawings?" I asked.

Mr. Melcourt nodded. Mrs. Melcourt managed only a small smile, sent the children away, and rose to join her husband's side.

As I unrolled my plans on a rosewood table, I studied my employers over my steel-rimmed spectacles. I don't strictly need them for anything other than detailed sketching, but I've found that people vastly underestimate a bespectacled woman, most often to my advantage.

"We will start with the overall vision for the grounds. You told me that you wanted to combine formal and natural styles for a sense of elegance and surprise. The great lawn is your formality." I pointed to the rectangular shape that represented the long stretch of grass that already existed at Highbury House. "The view from your veranda down to the lakeside is beautiful, but it is missing something to draw the eye. A sense of drama. We will cut stairs into the slope and create a small wall edged with plantings. The stairs will lead down to a wide, shallow reflecting pool and then an uninterrupted stretch of lawn all the way down to the lake."

"Will you remove the trees at the edge of the lake?" he asked.

I shook my head. "You have mature beech, birch, and hawthorn trees that will lend the property a sense of history. You'll find that the most formal parts of the garden are also those nearest to the house, where you are most likely to entertain." I glanced up at Mrs. Melcourt. "Perhaps your guests will picnic or play croquet on the lawn and then wander the long border that will run along the eastern edge of the lawn or the lime walk and shade borders opposite. As they approach the lake, the garden will naturally transition to a looser, wilder style."

Mr. Melcourt's lip curled. "Wilder."

"Mr. Cunningham and Mr. McCray both hesitated when I suggested such a move, but I can assure you that they are pleased with the result," I said, mentioning two wealthy industrialists who were members of the same London club as Mr. Melcourt.

I held my breath, because this was the telling moment. Would the Melcourts be the sort of clients who thought they wanted new, beautiful, and innovative but really sought the comforting familiarity of the strictly manicured, formal spaces of the previous century's gardens? Or would they allow me to give them something so much more—a lived-in, lush piece of art more vibrant than any painting?

"McCray did mention that you have some radical ideas," said Mr. Melcourt. "However, he told me that the effect has won him nothing but praise."

When his wife raised no objections, I smiled. "I'm glad to hear it."

Quickly, I pulled free a detail of the long border next, showing him how tall columns of clematis would tower over roses, Echinops, campanulas, allium, and delphiniums in soft pinks, whites, silvers, and purples. I showed them how walls of hedge and brick would create garden rooms of varying themes just to the west of the shade border. I warned them that some elements of the garden would take time: the lime trees would need to be carefully pleached each year by tying in flexible young shoots to give the impression of walking between two living walls. We talked about which pieces from the Melcourts' growing collection would look best in the sculpture garden, and where the children might play.

A distant bell rang in the house, but the Melcourts hardly looked up.

"I've maintained the kitchen and herb gardens to the side of the house. There's no need to move them, and the orchard is already mature and producing fruit for you," I said.

"But so close to the house," murmured Mrs. Melcourt.

I understood the lady's objections immediately. "At the moment, you have only a yew hedge separating the kitchen garden from the rest of the property. I would recommend building a wall between the kitchen garden and the garden rooms to create a greater sense of separation between the gardens for work and for pleasure. I can show you if you like."

A man's heavy footsteps raised all of our heads as a newcomer joined us. Unlike Mr. Melcourt's, this man's tie was slightly askew, and even from where I was standing I could see the splatters of mud on the cuffs of his trousers.

"Matthew!" Mrs. Melcourt exclaimed, her coolness transforming into real affection.

"Hello, Helen. You look lovely today," said the gentleman, kissing her on the cheek before shaking Mr. Melcourt's hand.

"Miss Smith, may I present my brother, Mr. Matthew Goddard," said Mrs. Melcourt.

"How do you do, Miss Smith," said Mr. Goddard, taking my hand. It was warm in spite of the frozen temperatures and unexpectedly rough for a gentleman.

"I must confess, Miss Smith," Mr. Goddard continued, "I came to Highbury House on the hope of meeting you today. I'm a great admirer of your work."

I jerked back a fraction, breaking our connection. "You are?"

"I visited Longmarsh House last year. The gardens are exquisite," Mr. Goddard said.

I relaxed a little, remembering Longmarsh and Lady Mallory with affection. A widow with a passion for nature and a difficult property situated high on a hill, Lady Mallory had been my first major patron after my father's death. The project had been wildly ambitious, requiring building terraces into the hills and creating seven levels of planting. I had made mistakes along the way, as any new designer might, but when I finished, Lady Mallory had declared it her own Hanging Garden of Babylon.

"It is kind of you to say so, sir," I said.

Mrs. Melcourt glanced between us, as though looking for something. Finally, she said, "That is great praise indeed, Miss Smith. Matthew is a talented botanist and has an eye for these things."

My stomach dropped. Nothing gives me less pleasure than finding an amateur lurking around one of my commissions. Often he is the gentleman of the house who, having been born into wealth, decides that he should cultivate a hobby. He reads extensively about plants and even tries digging a hole from time to time, but the bulk of the work is given over to his oft-harried gardener. Winter pruning when the wind snaps the skin on your face raw. Digging drainage ditches in the hot sun. Dibbling and planting hundreds of bulbs on hands and knees to create bluebell meadows for April. The gentleman gardener wants no part of it, and so he has no practical knowledge of gardening, no matter how much he insists that his opinions should be taken into consideration.

"Miss Smith is just showing us what she has planned for Highbury, Matthew. You should join us," said Mr. Melcourt.

Mr. Goddard made a half bow. "I would never want to impose."

I just managed to keep my smile. "It would be no imposition."

Mrs. Melcourt called for a maid to fetch everyone's things. Despite the sun, the February day was bitterly cold, so we bundled up tightly.

On the veranda, I quickly pointed out where the reflecting pool, lime walk, and borders would be. Mr. Goddard listened intently, his gloved hands clasped behind his back. He asked a question here and there, but nothing more.

Then we walked down to where the edge of the lawn met the house. "There will be a gate here," I said, gesturing beyond the kitchen garden, where now only stood a gravel path. "If we step through here, this will be the first of the garden rooms."

"What is this one's theme?" Mr. Melcourt asked.

"The tea garden. A gazebo will provide some shelter for you and your guests from the sun or sudden changes in weather."

For the first time since I began describing the garden, Mrs. Melcourt's lips curved up. "How thoughtful." Then her eyes slid to me. "Will there be roses in this garden?"

"I thought to grow them against the pillars of the gazebo," I said, pointing to the plans I'd brought with us.

"They'll be Matthew's roses, of course," said Mrs. Melcourt.

"Helen, I'm sure Miss Smith has her own suppliers." Mr. Goddard cast me an apologetic smile. "I merely dabble in breeding roses. Please do not feel obligated to change your plans."

"He's too modest. I would be very pleased if you were to use Matthew's roses." Despite the veneer of politeness, I knew that it was more order than request.

I bristled. The roses I'd planned for the tea garden were a pale pink moss rose variety called 'Madame Louis Leveque' that had been developed not a decade ago. They would not be difficult to replace with something similar, but I did not appreciate Mrs. Melcort's interference.

You must remember that a garden is a collaboration. My father's long-held advice echoed in my head. *It should be the very best of you* and *your clients, but never forget that it is nature to whom you must defer at all times.*

And so, biting back a sigh, I said, "I'm sure we can come to an agreement on a suitable rose for the tea garden."

"And the others, in the other rooms?" asked Mrs. Melcourt.

"Perhaps you could provide me with an inventory of your stock," I said, trying my best not to grit my teeth.

Mr. Goddard sent me an apologetic look. "It would be best if you came to look for yourself. Wilmcote is just six miles away."

"Now that's settled, what of the other rooms?" Mr. Melcourt said.

I breathed deep, determined to regain control of my plans. "From the tea garden there will be the lovers' garden done all in vibrant colors with your statue of Eros at the center, then the pastel children's garden with cherry trees, followed by the all-white bridal garden. After that will be a water garden to encourage contemplation. Mr. Melcourt, I'm given to understand that you are something of a poet?"

He beamed. "I had a volume published just last year."

Adam researches our clients well, so I already knew this. Still, I mimicked surprise and said, "It may please you to know, then, that I have planned a poet's garden with nods to many great poets. From there, a sculpture garden to feature your collection, a winter garden, and a lavender walk. At the bottom, a gravel walk lined on the southern side by trees. Beyond those trees, before you come to the lake, will be the ramble. I'll construct paths and plant it through with spring-blooming bulbs before it gradually fades into the wood, stretching to the lake's edge and giving way to Highbury House Farm's fields."

I watched the three look between the plans and the rather uninspired, repeated boxes of bedding plants and lawn that made up the garden now. I wanted them to see it as I did. To understand what it could be.

"It will be surprising, unexpected." I glanced at the rings on Mrs. Melcourt's fingers and the pearl tiepin centered at her husband's throat. "And impressive. The garden will tell a story that your guests will be able to enjoy over and over again."

A look passed between husband and wife. Finally, Mr. Melcourt said, "I think you have quite the task ahead of you, Miss Smith. We shall look forward to seeing it come to life."

· BETH ·

Dearest Beth,

It still feels strange to address you as "dearest," but I think I'll come to like it. We have been on the march these past two days, which is why this letter will reach you a few days late. I hope you won't think I'm neglecting you already.

Even in February the sun sits higher in the sky than it does back home, and I find myself missing the mist of an English winter. So strange to think that just a few weeks ago, the men in my unit and I were all complaining about the sticky mud clinging to our boots during drills. The war is more real than I could ever describe on paper—not that the censors would allow it.

I think every day about the last time we spoke. Maybe I should feel guilt over asking you so abruptly to be my girl, as the American GIs would say. I hadn't planned to do it over the telephone, but I wanted to hear your voice.

Knowing that you're at home, waiting for me, gives me the strength to face whatever might be ahead of me in battle.

With all my affection,
Colin

The train shuddered to a stop in Royal Leamington Spa Station, and up and down the line people began to pour out onto the platform. Beth clung to the handrail, doing her best to balance the canvas bag slung over her shoulder and avoid tipping over as she stepped down. When her practical, low-heeled shoes hit the cement, she exhaled.

At last.

The train ride from London had taken twice as long as it should've, inconsistent service being a hallmark of wartime travel. And that wasn't even counting the early-morning leg of her journey up from the agricultural college where she'd done her training. But now, she was almost to Temple Fosse Farm, which would be her home for the foreseeable future.

Rebalancing her bag, she started to make her way down the platform, looking out for Mr. Penworthy. She had no idea what he looked like or if he would be able to single her out from all the other travelers. She should have changed into her uniform in the Marylebone Station loo like her land girl's manual recommended, except she'd known that this train ride would be the last time she'd wear her own clothes in . . . well, she didn't know how long.

Her life was about to become all soil and crops and weather and harvest. She'd heard during her training that the isolation of rural life could be difficult for city girls like her, but she'd spent her childhood on a farm. She was sure it would be like returning home. Besides, in some counties, the land girls arranged dances in neighboring villages and towns on the occasional evening. She hoped Warwickshire would be so well organized.

The crowd on the platform began to thin as people made their way to the station lobby. The wind lifted her brushed-out blond pin curls, and she was patting them back into place when she spotted an older man standing by the waiting room door, woolen flat cap clasped between his hands and olive-green waxed jacket hanging loose from his shoulders. She let her hand fall to the strap of her bag and, swallowing down a bubble of fear, walked straight up to him.

"Mr. Penworthy?" she asked, her voice shaking a little despite her false confidence.

He looked over as a man might examine a cow for sale at market. "You're the land girl then?"

She nodded. "My name is Elizabeth Pedley."

"That's a long name for such a little thing," he observed.

"My parents called me Beth, and I might be little but I'm strong."

His mouth twitched. "Is that so? The last girl they sent us wasn't much to write home about."

"What happened to her?" she asked.

"Still working the farm. We can't afford to be too picky. It was Mrs. Penworthy's idea to get a second girl up." He passed a hand over his head and stuck his cap on. "It's best to agree with Mrs. Penworthy when she gets an idea into her head. Come on now. It'll be dark soon."

He reached out to take Beth's bag, but she held on to it, resolute.

He grunted. "Suit yourself."

Beth followed the farmer down the train station's steps and out to a horse and cart that was tied up on the gate. "Have you ever ridden in a cart?"

"Not in a long time," she answered honestly. "My parents owned a farm."

"They don't have it anymore?"

"They died." A beat stretched between them as it so often did when she talked about being an orphan. "I lived with my aunt in town until I turned eighteen and joined the Women's Land Army."

"Fuel is kept for farmwork now, so a cart it is," said Mr. Penworthy.

She nodded, grateful he didn't offer her any platitudes about being so sorry for her loss.

When Mr. Penworthy let down the gate for her, Beth hauled up her bag into the back of the cart.

"Will you be wanting to ride in the back or up front?" he asked.

"Up front, please."

"Suit yourself," he said again.

She climbed up and settled herself in. Mr. Penworthy did the same, and then took up the reins. With a click of his tongue, the horse set off.

If Beth had thought they would talk on this journey to the farm, she was mistaken. The road was rutted, and the February air had a wicked bite to it. She spent half the time trying to stop her teeth from chattering and the rest of it with her hand clamped on her cap to keep it from falling off. By the time Mr. Penworthy turned off the road at a sign with

"Temple Fosse Farm" painted on it, her fingers felt as though they were about to fall off.

As soon as the horse and cart slowed, the side door of the farmhouse burst open. "Len Penworthy, what are you doing letting that girl ride all the way from the train station in only that thin coat?" demanded a tall woman with a canvas apron tied around her. "She'll catch her death."

"That will be Mrs. Penworthy," murmured Mr. Penworthy.

Beth's eyes cut to him, but she was surprised to see no annoyance or weariness in his expression, only affection.

"Now, you must be Miss Pedley," said Mrs. Penworthy, who bustled up to her.

"Please call me Beth," she said.

"Beth it is, then."

The older woman steered her by the shoulders straight into the kitchen. A huge black iron stove emanated warmth from one corner, and an array of vegetables midchop rested on the table. The scent of stew, something rich, wafted up to her, and Beth nearly whimpered. It had been so long since she'd had a good homemade meal.

"You sit right down here, and I'll make you a cup of tea," said Mrs. Penworthy.

Her husband made to sit down at the other end of the table, but Mrs. Penworthy threw over her shoulder, "You go tell Ruth that she's to come meet Beth."

Mr. Penworthy gave a deep sigh. "I'll see if she'll come."

As soon as he was out of the room, Mrs. Penworthy said, "You mustn't mind him. Farming isn't for everyone, and Ruth has had a hard adjustment to it. Still, she might make it easier on herself if she realized she wasn't in Birmingham anymore."

"I hope that I find it easier. I've lived with my widowed aunt Mildred in Dorking since I was ten."

If Mrs. Penworthy thought anything of Beth living with her aunt rather than her parents, the farmer's wife didn't say anything. Instead, she asked, "And will she not miss you back in Dorking?"

Beth hesitated. "I think she is glad to know that I'm doing my bit in the war."

"Feeding starving Britain?" came a sharp question. Beth looked up as a woman with an hourglass figure and a cloud of perfect red curls floating around her shoulders walked in. Even with clothing coupons rationing what everyone could buy, this woman was well-dressed in a cream ribbed turtleneck and a tweed skirt. On anyone else, it might have seemed dowdy, but she looked as though she was about to serve her guests a round of drinks after a long day's hunt.

"Be nice, Ruth," said Mrs. Penworthy.

Ruth's eyes cut from the farmer's wife to Beth and back. Then a smile cracked her face. "I'm only *teasing*, Mrs. P. I'm Ruth Harper-Greene."

Beth frowned at Ruth's double-barreled name. Girls like Ruth usually ended up secretaries or worked on switchboards, where their crisp accents would be best shown off.

She shook Ruth's hand. "It's a pleasure to meet you."

"Let's all have a cup of tea," said Mrs. Penworthy cheerfully. "I'm afraid it's just chamomile, but needs be in war."

Mr. Penworthy did not rejoin them until dinner, which, though comprising solely root vegetables, was easily the best meal Beth had had in months. Afterward, Ruth showed Beth to their room.

As soon as the door was closed, Ruth flopped on the bed. "What an absolute bore. I swear that if something interesting doesn't happen soon, I'll scream."

"The Penworthys seem very kind. I'm sure I'll like it here," Beth said.

Ruth pushed up on her elbow and shot her an assessing look. "Yes, well, you've likely never spent time in London. Or even Birmingham. Warwickshire is something of a disappointment, to say the least."

Beth pursed her lips and set about unpacking her things.

"Oh, I've offended you," said Ruth, getting up to catch Beth's line of sight.

"You haven't offended me," said Beth. "I'm just happy I'll be of some use."

"Yes, well, we all have to be *useful*, don't we?" snorted Ruth as she reached into a drawer and pulled out a crumpled packet of cigarettes and a match.

"Please don't smoke in here," said Beth, a little sharper than she'd meant.

Ruth looked up, the cigarette hanging from her mouth. "The mouse has a bite."

"I'm not a mouse. And I would appreciate it if you would not smoke in this room."

"Why not?" Ruth challenged.

"Because my aunt Mildred smokes, and I never could stand it." Beth turned around fully to face her roommate, her arms crossed over her chest. "We don't have to like each other, but we do need to bump along together. It would be easier if we agreed upon that from the beginning."

Silence stretched between them. Not having had much practice, Beth'd never been very good at gauging this sort of interaction. Maybe she'd gone too far. She didn't want to make an enemy out of her roommate within the first few hours of meeting her. But then Ruth took the cigarette from her lips and slowly slid it back into the packet.

"I'm sorry. I can be a horrible child when I don't get my way, and these last months, nothing seems to have gone my way," said Ruth.

"You mean being a land girl?" Beth asked.

Ruth laughed. "You're not just a pretty face, are you, Bethy?"

"Don't call me Bethy. It sounds horrid."

"I hate it here, Beth. I hate the work, and the early hours, and that there's not a damned thing to do for fun. I hate that I hate it because Mr. and Mrs. Penworthy have been nothing but kind and patient with me, and I've been utterly beastly."

"Why don't you apply for a transfer? Or become a Wren or a WAAF," said Beth, even more convinced than ever that the navy or the Royal Air Force's women's auxiliaries would suit Ruth far better.

Ruth flopped back onto her bed again. "The Wrens won't have me because I was kicked out of the ATS."

Beth couldn't help it when her eyes flicked to Ruth's stomach. "Kicked out?"

"Not because I was pregnant or anything like that, you goose," Ruth laughed. "I drank on base and stole an officer's car. Thought I'd be able to toddle off down the road and find some fun, but I crashed it into the gate instead. Silly of me, really. After that, none of the auxiliary branches would take me. Becoming a land girl was my very best option out of a lot of rubbish. Conscription waits for no woman."

"And now you're stuck here," said Beth.

"Until I can find someone to marry me, although not even that's enough. I'll need to get pregnant, too, before they'll let me go."

"It doesn't sound like the quickest plan," Beth said.

"What about you? Do you have a beau?" Ruth asked.

"Actually, I do." How odd that sounded.

Ruth flipped over on her stomach and grinned. "Oh, do tell."

Beth drew in a breath. "His name is Colin. He grew up on the next farm over from my parents. When I moved to Dorking, we began writing to each other. It was silly, really—we were only ten—but eight years later, we're still writing."

Still writing and somehow . . . sweethearts? She wasn't entirely sure how it had happened. One day, just after Christmas as Beth was waiting for her instructions from the Women's Land Army, Colin had rung her at her aunt's house.

"I've been thinking. We like each other, don't we?" he'd asked.

"Of course we do. We've been friends for ages," she said with a laugh.

"Will you be my girl?"

She'd bobbled the telephone receiver, barely catching it before it crashed to the floor. "What?"

"Think about it. You're off to your training soon. I'm being sent to Italy in just a few days. Wouldn't it be better if we both had someone waiting for us?" he asked.

"But, Colin, we barely see each other."

"But we write. We speak on the telephone sometimes," he said.

"But do you actually love me?" she asked.

"More than any other girl I've ever met," he said. "Besides, who would love a farmer's son like me except the girl I've known all my life?"

Pity pricked at her conscience. "That's ridiculous, and you know it, Colin. You're a good-looking man."

But despite her reasoning, by the time she hung up, she somehow had a beau.

"Do you have a picture?" Ruth asked.

Beth reached into her case for the sketchbook she'd lain carefully on top of her clothes. From it, she drew a photo of Colin in his uniform, wholesome and still such a stranger to her.

Ruth scrutinized the photo with such an air of expertise that Beth blushed.

"Not bad," Ruth finally announced. "What's his regiment?"

"First Battalion, East Surrey Regiment."

"Where he is now?"

"Somewhere in Italy. He can't say more than that."

"It must be nice knowing that there's a man looking forward to your letters," said Ruth, a little wistful. "Between the air base and Highbury House, I'm determined to land one."

"What's Highbury House?" she asked.

"Then they haven't told you yet?"

"No."

Ruth grinned. "Then I think I'd better let you find out on your own."

The next morning, she and Ruth both groaned as the alarm on Ruth's bedside table rang at half past four. By five, they were dressed and finishing breakfast at Mrs. Penworthy's big kitchen table. At half past five, Mr. Penworthy was giving Beth her first lesson in being a land girl.

They were spreading slurry on the fields, a messy, smelly job even with the help of the tractor that Mr. Penworthy drove. Halfway through the morning, Beth had muck splattered all over her Women's Land Army–issued gum boots and halfway up her breeches. She had shed the two wool jumpers and jacket she'd worn out that morning and was down to just a shirt. A blister was forming between her thumb and index finger.

The strangest thing was, despite all of the discomfort, she loved it. She was outside. Each breath was cold and crisp—if laced with the scent of manure. Her muscles burned, but Mr. Penworthy had let them stop long enough to admire the sunrise coming up over the barren trees at field's edge. She felt vital and useful for the first time in a long time.

Ruth, however, was miserable.

"Can we not stop for elevenses?" Ruth called out.

Mr. Penworthy frowned from atop his tractor. "Elevenses? It's half ten."

"Soon enough," grumbled Ruth.

"We're nearly done," said Beth, looking back over the three quarters of a field they'd already raked over.

Mr. Penworthy tugged at his cap. "There's another field to do after this one."

"Another?" Ruth screeched.

Beth let out a long breath. "Mr. Penworthy, didn't Mrs. Penworthy say that she might start painting part of the barn today?"

The farmer stared down at her for a long moment before nodding. "Off you go, then, Ruth."

Ruth dropped her rake and made for the edge of the field as fast as her mud-caked boots could carry her.

Beth went back to raking, but Mr. Penworthy didn't start up the tractor again.

"You're not tired, then?" he asked.

She stopped, holding on to the top of her rake. "I'm exhausted. I don't think I've ever worked as much in a single day as I have in this one morning."

"Will you be wanting to go paint the barn as well?" he asked.

"If that's what you need me to do. If you need me to stay here and rake slurry, I'll stay here and rake slurry."

For the first time in their brief acquaintance, Mr. Penworthy smiled. "Up you come, then."

"Up?"

He nodded to the tractor. "You'll have to learn to drive it at some point. We'll be planting out beetroot and wheat soon."

She was going to learn to drive? Colin wouldn't believe it, after all of his letters teasing that she'd lost her country ways living in town.

Excitement sparkled through her as she hauled herself up while Mr. Penworthy moved over for her. She nearly slipped because of the mud on her boots, but made it onto the wide bench seat.

"Right," she said, putting her hands on the steering wheel.

"What have you driven before?" he asked.

"Not a thing," she said with a grin.

He let out a breath. "What do they teach you city folk?"

She laughed in surprise. "Dorking isn't exactly a city."

"Even worse, lass," he said.

"Well, I'm learning now."

He grunted, then launched into the basics. Ignition, clutch, gas, break, gear shift. He patiently explained how to press down the clutch, shift gears, and get the behemoth machine moving. He made her recite it again and again until the sequence rolled off her tongue smoothly.

"All right," he said, sitting back. "Give it a go."

Beth sucked in a breath, aware Mr. Penworthy was gripping the edge of his seat. She pressed the clutch firmly to the floor, turned the ignition, put the tractor into gear, and slowly let her foot off the clutch. It gave a great rumbling roar. She jumped back, lifting her foot. The beast of a machine shuddered violently and went quiet.

"Well, you've stalled it."

She looked over at the serious, resigned expression on Mr. Penworthy's face and all at once began to laugh. She laughed and laughed, holding on to her sides. She could hear the farmer's low, dry chuckle that sounded as though he was blowing dust off his humor.

"What's this? Farmer Penworthy laughing along with a land girl? I never thought I'd see the day," a man called out.

Beth's head snapped up to see a large man swathed in the greatcoat of an army officer standing on the edge of the field.

"Captain Hastings," bellowed Mr. Penworthy. "Stay there." He nodded to Beth. "Down you go."

She scrambled down the side, landing on two solid feet in the soft earth and manure. The officer watched them as they trekked to the side of the field. It wasn't until she was half a dozen yards away that she realized why the man seemed so broad. He had only one arm pulled through a sleeve. The other was anchored to his neck by a sling, his coat hanging over it.

"You have company," the man said to Mr. Penworthy as they stopped in front of him.

"Miss Pedley, this is Captain Hastings," said Mr. Penworthy.

"Graeme Hastings, of the Second Battalion, Royal Scots Fusiliers. It's a pleasure to make your acquaintance, Miss Pedley," said Captain Hastings.

"And yours, sir," she said.

"You must be new?" said Captain Hastings.

"Yes, I arrived yesterday. Mr. Penworthy was just teaching me to drive the tractor."

"And?" Captain Hastings asked.

"I stalled it on the first go," she admitted.

He laughed. "We all do. Don't believe anyone who says otherwise. You'll get it."

"Aye, I think she will," said Mr. Penworthy.

A glow spread through her chest at the praise. She could—*would*— do this.

"May I ask what happened to your arm?" Beth said.

"Oh, this?" he asked, glancing at the bandage as though seeing it for the first time. "Walked into a German bullet. Quite clumsy of me, really."

She couldn't help but smile. "I take it the doctors set you straight about doing it again?"

Captain Hastings barked a laugh. "Yes, the nurses scolded me until Tuesday and back. Can't say I'll be seeking out a repeat experience. It's rather shattered my shoulder."

"I'm sorry to hear that," she said, sobering.

"Oh, we'll have none of that. It earned me a very nice convalescence, and the good company of my friend Mr. Penworthy."

"Captain Hastings has an interest in farming," said Mr. Penworthy.

"Is that so?" Beth asked.

"Actually I don't know a thing about it, but I like walking in the fields. There's nothing like being cooped up inside to make you feel like an invalid, and the doctors seem to approve of the exercise so long as I'm careful." Captain Hastings turned to Mr. Penworthy. "Will Miss Pedley be taking on your deliveries to the big house?"

Beth looked at the farmer, whose lips twitched again. "Might be" was all he said.

"Which big house?" she asked.

"Highbury House. It's been requisitioned as a convalescent hospital. They specialize in bones, which is how I ended up there. Now"—Captain Hastings tipped his peaked cap—"I must be going. The sheep are rather put out when I don't do my rounds in a timely fashion. Farmer Penworthy. Miss Pedley."

He rambled off as though he didn't have a care in the world, bandaged arm or no.

"He seems like a nice enough man," she said.

"Captain Hastings is better than most. I'll say nothing against the men at Highbury House. They've all done their bit for Britain. Still, some of them can be . . ."

"Louts?" she offered helpfully.

He snorted. "Louts will do very well, Miss Pedley."

"I will consider myself warned," she said.

Mr. Penworthy smiled again. Aunt Mildred wasn't a cruel woman, but she wasn't a warm one, either. Beth had had a roof over her head and meals on the table, but little else. No kindness, no approval, no love. Colin had been her one lifeline for so long, and now he was at war. Beth could have sat in the glow of the farmer's smile for hours.

"Back to the tractor, then," said Mr. Penworthy. "You'll try again until you get it right."

And back to the tractor Beth went, but not without casting one last look at the disappearing figure of Captain Graeme Hastings.

· VENETIA ·

MONDAY, 18 FEBRUARY 1907
Highbury House
Raw

*P*apa used to tell me that the harsher the day of planting, the more vigorous the bloom. If today's weather is any indication, the garden at Highbury House will be healthy indeed.

I arrived at the house yesterday and have already settled myself into the old gardener's cottage at the southern edge of the property. Mrs. Melcourt offered to give me one of the guest bedrooms in the eastern wing. However, upon learning that the gardener Mr. Hillock lives above the village shop his wife runs, I insisted on the cottage.

I said that I needed to keep a close eye on the many plants I would propagate from cuttings and seeds here at Highbury. In truth, I'm used to my freedom. I live with Adam, but he leaves me be when I am working.

This morning, my first day of real work at Highbury House, I bundled up against the weather and ventured out. On my last visit two weeks before, I'd left Mr. Hillock instructions to clear the grounds where the garden rooms will stand. Mr. Hillock's men have also cut into the lawn to create the borders, and cartloads of earth have been delivered to improve the soil.

Mr. Hillock met me at the gated entrance to the tea garden. We were discussing the lime trees that would be delivered later that week when I heard a *hallo* from the veranda. I looked up from under the brim of my wide gardening hat and saw Mr. Goddard wave before he came loping down the steps.

"You've already met the brother, then," said Mr. Hillock, pushing his felt hat back on his head with a thumb.

"Yes, when I came from London earlier this month," I said.

"He's a talent for the roses. He brought me a few varieties when Mr. and Mrs. Melcourt bought Highbury House. Said he wanted me to let him know how they got on."

"And?"

Mr. Hillock scrubbed a hand over his whiskered chin and, just before Mr. Goddard came to a halt in front of us, said, "They're growing like weeds."

"Miss Smith, Mr. Hillock. It's good to see you both. I was just stopping in to see my sister on my way to Warwick for some business, but she isn't here." Mr. Goddard looked around him. "You're making quick progress."

"The sooner the architecture of the garden is in place, the sooner I'll be able to begin directing the planting," I said.

"It looks as though you've already begun." He nodded to the heavy leather gloves that were tucked into the pocket of the apron covering my long brown skirt. They were coated in mud, as were my heavy garden boots.

"There are a few good buddleia growing near the greenhouses. I was pruning them back earlier to make moving them more manageable later," I said.

"When will you begin planting?" he asked.

"April, maybe earlier if the weather is favorable," I said.

Mr. Goddard cleared his throat. "I wanted to apologize for Helen. Half of the time she tells me I'm wasting my time growing roses. The rest of the time she expands upon my horticultural genius."

"The relationships between brothers and sisters can be complicated, as my brother Adam would surely agree. I would be happy to do what I can to incorporate some of your roses in my design," I said.

He placed a hand to his heart. "It would be a great honor to play a small role in any design of yours, Miss Smith." Then he bowed and left.

It wasn't until hours later, when I was soaking my aching feet in a bath of salts and dried lavender, that I had cause to think of Mr. Goddard again when I heard a sharp rap at my door.

Hastily I dried my feet and jammed them into a pair of old slippers. I opened the door a crack, peering around.

A maid stood on the doorstep. She dropped into a curtsy. "Evening, miss."

"Hello. What's your name?" I asked.

The girl dipped her chin. "I'm Clara, Miss Smith."

"Well, Clara, what can I do for you?"

"Mrs. Melcourt bids you come to dinner. If you wish," said Clara.

If I wished. Was it a request or an order? And was the invitation willingly given or prompted by Mr. Melcourt, who seemed more interested in my work at Highbury House than his wife? For, while I might be a gentleman's daughter, I knew that the lady would not be accustomed to inviting professional women to her table.

"Please tell Mrs. Melcourt I should be delighted to come to dinner," I said.

I moved to close the door when Clara fished a letter out of her neatly pressed pinafore pocket. "Also, this came with the afternoon post, miss."

I accepted the letter with thanks. She bobbed another curtsy and practically scrambled down the path. I wondered if she would race to the kitchen to tell the other maids of the eccentric woman covered in a day's worth of dust who was going to dine with the master and mistress that evening.

I slid my finger under the letter's seal. The message was written directly onto the back of the paper folded into an envelope.

Dear Miss Smith,

I hope you won't feel it's impudent of me to invite you to visit my nursery this Friday morning at eleven o'clock. It's rare that I meet someone who shares my passion for plants, and I should welcome the opportunity to show you my collection.

Yours,
Matthew Goddard
Wisteria Farm, Wilmcote

I stared at the letter for a moment. Impudent? What could be less impudent than an invitation to view roses?

I shook my head and set the letter down to go in search of my third-best dress and a pair of shoes fit to be seen.

· EMMA ·

*E*mma stood with her hands on her hips, staring at what had once probably been a beautiful trough of water dotted with waterlilies. "We'll need to dig it out entirely, repour, and reline it," she said.

"It doesn't look like there was a water feature," said Charlie, making a note on his phone.

She frowned. "I've never heard of Venetia using pumped water in her gardens, but without plans—"

"It's impossible to know." Her friend nodded. "Have you got Sydney digging into the family archives?"

She gave a laugh. "You know me well."

"I don't think I've ever seen you let an owner off the hook on a restoration."

"In the end, it's their garden. They have to care, too. Come here, I want to show you something."

"It would be nice if Sydney could find a long-lost diary and cache of Venetia's letters," said Charlie as they set off down the overgrown yew-lined path that formed the top edge of the water garden and the mysterious room next to it.

"With a neat description of where everything was planted, and why. We can dream."

"You know, we've definitely done gardens in worse shape," he pushed.

"You might not feel that way after you see this," she said as they broke through a gap in the yew and caught sight of the wild mess of brambles and branches over the top of the winter garden's brick wall.

Charlie let out a low whistle. "If it looks this bad from out here . . ."

"I can't even imagine what's inside," she finished.

"What do you know about it?"

"Sydney says it's a winter garden," she said.

"Then why is there a twenty-foot buddleia growing out of the middle of it? That's not a winter plant," he said.

"Because buddleia will seed anywhere it can. It gets even better," she said, leading him around the curve of the wall until they got to the gate. "According to Sydney, this has never been unlocked in her lifetime."

"Sinister," said Charlie, giving the gate a shake. Rust shed bright orange against his dark brown skin. "It's well made, but there's no way it was treated like this for more than one hundred years."

She squinted, trying to see past the tangle of branches. Even in late February, thick greenery obscured the view. The tangle of climbing rose and the bright red bark of dogwoods were easy to spot. And was that a hellebore struggling out from under an unpruned camellia? It was hard to tell.

"This looks like at least twenty, thirty years of growth. Someone's probably used a ladder to hack at the worst of it when it's started to creep into the rest of the garden. Look at the cuts to that dogwood," said Charlie, pointing up at the oddly slanted tree.

"Sydney said the gardeners cut things back once a year." Charlie shot her a look, and she added, "I'll have her bring a new team in before we leave."

"So how do we get into the winter garden? And what do we find when we get there?"

And why had it been locked for so long?

Charlie knocked back the faded Mets ball cap he'd picked up on a trip years ago and scratched his forehead. "From most to least destructive?"

"Sure," she said.

"We get a blowtorch and cut the gate open," he said.

"I love playing with a blowtorch as much as you do, but that's off the table. The owners are very much on the side of restoring history, not destroying it."

"We get a cherry picker and hack a path in to get a ladder down there. Machetes at dawn," he said, thickening his Scottish accent for effect.

She glanced over her shoulder at the gap in the gate. "Maybe, but the plants could be valuable."

"There's got to be another way."

"Yeah, a key, but until that turns up we'll have to figure it out," she said.

"Hey, you heard about that Royal Botanical Heritage Society job?" Charlie asked.

She froze. "What?"

"They're looking for a head of conservancy."

"Okay," she said slowly.

"You'd be good at it."

"Why would I need a job? I have Turning Back Thyme," she said sharply.

He held his hands up. "Hey, hey, I just thought it would be a good fit for you."

"I've spent six years building this business."

"Come on. Don't pretend like you haven't had days where you want to pack it all in. I know you get stressed. I know you don't usually love the client side of the business," he said.

Or logistics or personnel or taxes or . . . the list could go on and on.

"I love our clients," she said firmly.

Almost on cue, her mobile began to ring. She pulled it out of her back pocket and made a face. "Will Frayn."

"The influencer's husband?" Charlie asked. "Didn't he call last week?"

With a sigh, she swiped to answer. "Turning Back Thyme, this is Emma."

"Emma," boomed Will's voice. "Gillian's here, too. Let me put you on speaker."

"Emma," Gillian cooed into the phone, "we miss you."

"What can I help with, Gillian?" she asked.

"There's a problem with the garden," Gillian said.

The garden consisted of a series of traditional English borders planted to create an ombré effect, going from deep purple to lilac to pale white, all connected by a weaving path of switchbacks that ended in a redwood deck surrounded by cherry trees. It would look good this spring, but it would be truly stunning in a few years when everything had a chance to grow in.

"Did your gardeners have trouble with the handoff notes I left?" she asked.

"Oh, it's nothing like that," Gillian said.

"What's the matter, then?"

"Nothing's blooming!"

"It's a real problem," Will jumped in. "Gilly has a shoot tomorrow, and there isn't a single flower."

Emma pressed the tips of her fingers to her forehead. "It's February. Nothing in that garden is going to bloom until at least April, but the trees will start budding out soon."

"But, Emma, what's the point of having a garden without flowers?" Gillian asked.

"Gardens have cycles. You need to work with the seasons, which is why I suggested succession planting. Then you would have had something interesting to look at most of the year," she said.

A few feet off, Charlie snorted.

"What do we have?" Will asked.

"A lot of late-spring- and early-summer-blooming plants. It will look incredible in June." She'd warned the Frayns about this very thing. However, when they heard that succession planting would have meant staggering the flowers' blooms throughout the season, slightly reducing the impact of having full beds in flower all at once, they'd pushed back. Since they were paying the bills, Emma had been forced to acquiesce.

"I need it to look great now. We've sold an ad campaign around this," said Gillian, panic starting to enter into her voice.

"What's the company?" Emma asked.

"It's an organic meal subscription box," said Gillian.

"Talk about how gardens have seasons and so do vegetables. If you eat what is in season, you lower your carbon impact. If they're organic, they'll love the idea of seasonable and sustainable food," she said.

Whispers on the other end. Finally, Gillian said, "We can do that."

"Good luck with the shoot," said Emma.

When she turned around again, Charlie burst out laughing.

"I'm going to get 'Gardens aren't just about flowers' tattooed on my forehead one of these days," she muttered.

"I bet the Royal Botanical Heritage Society doesn't have to deal with Gillian Frayn." When she shot him a dirty look, he shrugged. "I'm just sayin'."

She couldn't help but smile. "Come on, let's go mark out the long border."

"You got it, boss."

· STELLA ·

FEBRUARY 1944

*S*tella slammed the door of the larder so hard the clock on the wall trembled and threatened to fall to the floor.

"Mrs. George," she barked at Highbury House Hospital's head cook. "This is the second time in as many weeks that you've made off with my milk."

"Miss Adderton, please," Mrs. Dibble, Highbury House's housekeeper and a member of the regular staff like Stella herself, said with a gasp.

Mrs. George, that miscreant in blue serge and white linen, slowly wiped her hands on her apron while the two junior cooks who reported to her watched in wide-eyed fascination, a potato and a knife frozen in each of their hands.

"Miss Adderton, think of what you're saying. Are you really accusing me of stealing?" asked Mrs. George.

"I'm sure Miss Adderton wouldn't—"

"I'm not accusing you," Stella cut off Mrs. Dibble. "I'm telling you that I know you stole the milk from the larder again. And eggs. There were six in the green bowl this morning. Now there are just four."

The four chickens that Mrs. Symonds had let her keep in a corner of the kitchen garden weren't laying as much as they had just six months ago, and eggs were becoming more and more precious. And real milk that wasn't powder in a can was practically liquid gold. Stella didn't even want to think of the criminal acts she would commit for a taste of real cream in real coffee.

"This hospital doesn't need your eggs and milk. We have our own rations," said Mrs. George.

"And what about the time I caught you in my flour, red-handed?"

The woman dropped her eyes to the pile of carrots in front of her. "That was a biscuit-making emergency. I had every intention of replacing the flour I used."

"A likely story," Stella muttered.

"Excuse me, Miss Adderton," said a meek voice from across the room.

Stella spun around on her heel to face Miss Grant, the diminutive junior cook who couldn't have been more than nineteen. "What?" she demanded.

Miss Grant opened and closed her mouth like a fish out of water.

"What is it, Miss Grant?" she prompted, trying to soften her tone.

"I broke the eggs this morning. I backed into the counter and I must have hit it just the wrong way because the bowl tipped over and two eggs rolled out and fell onto the floor, and I'm very sorry, miss." The truth poured out of the young woman like a waterfall until at last she was spent and her shoulders slumped forward.

Mrs. George shot her a scathing look.

Oh, why doesn't the bloody floor open up and swallow me whole?

Mrs. George said Stella scared her cooks more than the Germans frightened the wounded soldiers upstairs—and now Miss Grant would scurry away from her even faster. For as much as she disliked having her kitchen overrun by cooks from Voluntary Aid Detachment, she disliked it more when those cooks wouldn't talk to her.

She touched a hand to the synthetic silk scarf she wrapped around her hair to keep it out of the way and straightened her shoulders, preparing to make amends as best she could. "Miss Grant, accidents happen."

"I'll replace the eggs. I'll . . . I'll find a way to do it," promised Miss Grant.

But she couldn't by that evening, when Stella needed them. They were to make a custard, which she would be serving Mrs. Symonds; Father Bilson, the vicar at Highbury; and his wife, Mrs. Bilson. Mr. Hyssop, a solicitor from one village over, would round out the party. This long into the war, few people had illusions that any dinner party would come close to the ones they'd had before 1939, but Mrs. Symonds was one of the few holdouts. To not serve pudding—even in wartime—was unthinkable.

"I'll make do just fine with four eggs, Miss Grant," said Stella.

The young woman nodded several times in quick succession and scooted off down the hallway.

"But, Miss Adderton, Mrs. Symonds ordered a custard specially because it the vicar's favorite," Mrs. Dibble said, her hands twisting before her.

"I'm afraid Father Bilson will just have to be happy with a different sweet," said Stella, flipping through her mental list of recipes to try to figure out what she could make with four eggs, a bit of milk, and not much else.

"I'll go tell Mrs. Symonds," said Mrs. Dibble.

"Do that," said Stella to the retreating housekeeper's back, knowing that the news would incur her employer's disapproval. Not that Stella received much else from Mrs. Symonds these days.

Mrs. George gestured to her other assistant. "Miss Parker, go see to Miss Grant."

The taller girl set down her knife and half ran from the room.

When they were alone, Mrs. George began, "Miss Adderton."

She put her hand up. "I'm sorry to have upset Miss Grant. I will apologize."

"We must share these facilities, tight as the quarters might be," said Mrs. George.

"They wouldn't feel quite so tight if you would keep a tidier work space," Stella said, sweeping her eyes over the countertop covered in carrot peelings.

Before she could continue her attack, a knock on the kitchen door cut her off. Stella marched over, wrenched it open, and froze. Standing in front of her was her sister, Joan, with her nephew, Bobby, in tow.

"Hello, Estrella," said Joan, deploying the pet name Joan always used when she wanted something.

"What are you doing here, Joanie?" she asked, taking in Joan's deep blue wool coat with a wide black felt lapel, which showed off her creamy skin and rich auburn hair to their best advantage. A smart little black hat Stella had last seen her sister wear to Joan's husband's funeral sat perched at a rakish angle on the crown of her head. The lipstick smeared across her lips was a brilliant vermilion—just a shade too bright to be respectable.

"Aren't you going to ask us in? It's freezing out here." When Stella didn't move, Joan put a hand on Bobby's head. "You don't want your nephew to catch his death in this cold, do you?"

Stella stepped away from the door.

"What a lovely big kitchen you have here," said Joan, looking around and nodding a hello to Mrs. George and the other cooks, who'd slunk back in.

"It isn't mine. Why aren't you in Bristol?" She looked down at Joan's hand that clutched a small battered brown case. "And why do you have luggage?"

Immediately Joan looked contrite. "You're going to be angry with me."

"What have you done?"

"It's just that I didn't want to write to you only for you to say no—"

"Joan . . ." Her tone was warning.

Joan sucked in a breath. "I need you to take Bobby."

Stella blinked. "I beg your pardon."

"Your nephew. I need you to take him. The bombing's started again," said Joan.

"So evacuate like you did at the beginning of the war," she said.

"I have a job now at the munitions factory. I'm a vital worker," said Joan.

News to Stella. Joan had always run from work like it was a rash, but she supposed that had been before Joan's husband had died.

"Besides, I can't evacuate with Bobby again," Joan continued. "I'll go crazy if they send me out to the countryside, but you're here. You can take him."

Stella looked at her nephew, who gazed up at her with enormous hazel eyes and then dipped his head.

"I can't, Joan. I'm a cook. I work all day."

She was running Highbury's kitchen on her own with no help, volunteering twice a week with an Air Raid Precautions unit, and spending long hours every night hunched over the little desk in her room, toiling away at her coursework. Trying her hardest to make something of herself.

But as she looked down at the thin little boy in his little school coat and trousers with a tie that looked almost comically big on him, guilt welled up in her. How could she say no to her nephew?

"How long?" she asked.

"Oh, Estrella, thank you!" her sister cried, throwing her arms around Stella.

"I haven't agreed to anything yet. I'll have to ask Mrs. Symonds first, and—"

"Ask me what?"

Stella stiffened and turned to find Mrs. Symonds, perfectly pressed as always, walking through the door.

"Well, this is quite the scene. Mrs. Dibble told me that there was to be no custard tonight, but I didn't expect it was because you were having a party, Miss Adderton," the mistress said.

"This is Bobby, my nephew, and my sister, Joan," she said.

Mrs. Symonds looked between the two of them, as though trying to find a resemblance between mousy Stella and brashly glamorous Joan. "Your sister?"

"It's such a pleasure to meet you, Mrs. Symonds," said Joan, her hand outstretched.

Stella wanted to crawl out of her skin. A cook's sister approaching a lady for a handshake. Joan, a domestic's daughter and a domestic's sister, should have known better.

Mrs. Symonds looked at Joan's hand and flicked her gaze around the room, as though searching for someone to blame. "Can anyone please explain?"

"Joan lives in Bristol and is worried about air raids. She's concerned about Bobby's safety, so she's brought him here. It's quite the surprise to all of us," said Stella, hoping her employer could read between those incredibly broad lines.

Something flashed in Mrs. Symonds's eyes, and she fixed her gaze on Joan. "And where did you anticipate that Bobby would sleep, Mrs. . . . ?"

"Reynolds, ma'am," said Joan, some of her earlier boldness faltering in front of the lady of the manor. "I had thought that maybe Stella could make room for him. She told me that she has a room to herself."

"Did she? Well, I suppose we shall have to find a cot for Bobby, then, won't we?"

"He won't be a bother. He can help me do little jobs around the kitchen," said Stella.

"Don't be ridiculous. He's a child," said Mrs. Symonds.

"He just started school in Bristol this year," said Joan.

Mrs. Symonds strode forward before coming to a halt before Bobby and bending a bit at the waist. "How old are you, Bobby?"

Bobby's little hand grabbed on to the skirt of his mother's coat, watching this new lady with rapt, silent attention.

"Go on, Bobby," said Joan, shaking his hand off. "He can be a little shy to start, but once he gets going he's a proper chatterbox."

Mrs. Symonds paid the mother no mind, her gaze fixed on the boy. "I have a little boy, too. His name is Robin, and he has a whole room full of wonderful toys. Would you like to see them?"

"Yes," whispered Bobby.

Yes, ma'am, Stella scolded silently.

"Good. And maybe we can arrange for you to go to school with Robin as well. Do you like school?"

Bobby nodded.

"I'm very glad to hear that." Mrs. Symonds straightened. "I will bring him along with Robin tomorrow and see that he's registered."

It was a generous gesture—placing a child at midterm could prove tricky to anyone but a lady of Mrs. Symonds's influence—but still Stella couldn't keep from grinding her teeth. It was so high-handed and nonchalant, sweeping in and making the decision for Stella.

"Now, why don't you let Mrs. Dibble take you to visit with Robin and Nanny? I'm sure that your mother and your aunt have many things to speak about," said Mrs. Symonds.

Bobby looked to his mother, who nodded. "Off you go. I'll see you again before I leave."

As soon as the boy was gone, Mrs. Symonds turned to Stella. "Now,

Miss Adderton, there is the matter of the menu. We agreed upon it hours ago."

"Yes, ma'am. Only there was an accident with the eggs and—"

"An accident? I shouldn't have to remind you how precious food is these days, Miss Adderton. You should know that more than most."

"It was my fault, Mrs. Symonds," said Mrs. George. "I do apologize, and I've told Miss Adderton that I will replenish her stock from my own allowance."

Stella's eyes narrowed, wondering what the woman was up to.

"Your fault, Mrs. George?" asked Mrs. Symonds.

"Yes, I was moving things around and dropped two of the eggs. It will be nothing to replace them, I assure you," she said.

"You were moving things around?" Mrs. Symonds asked, her tone dangerously even. If Mrs. George had been an ally, Stella might have warned her that this was when her employer was at her most dangerous. Ladies never raised their voices, but the bite of Mrs. Symonds's glare could make a general cower.

Mrs. George at least had the good sense to fold her hands behind her back and look contrite. "Again, I apologize."

"Mrs. George, I would remind you that you and the hospital that you work for are guests in this house. I expect my property to be treated with respect. That includes the contents of my kitchen. There is no cause for you or any of your cooks to handle any of the food for Highbury House. That is meant to feed me, my son, and our staff. Have I made myself clear?"

Mrs. George's expression hardened like stone. "I understand you perfectly, Mrs. Symonds."

"Good. And I expect the commandant will as well," Mrs. Symonds said as she marched out of the room.

Behind Stella, Joan sucked in a breath. "Not an easy one, is she?"

"I would say she hardened after her husband died," Stella started.

"But . . . ?"

"She's been just like that ever since I arrived at Highbury House. Come on, we'll take Bobby's things up to my room."

· DIANA ·

*D*iana Symonds's nails bit into her palms as she climbed the stairs from the basement kitchen to the ground-floor servants' passage, let herself out of the hidden door in the paneling next to the grand stairs, and walked straight into her morning room. Keeping her chin lifted as the door shut behind her, she moved methodically from window to window, closing the rose-gold embroidered curtains. Only once the room was plunged into semidarkness did she drop onto the sofa and let her head fall into her hands.

She hated arbitrating squabbles between her cook and the staff of the convalescent hospital that had taken over her home. But then, very little of the dream Murray had promised matched the reality.

They'd only just finished redecorating Highbury House when Germany attacked Poland and Prime Minister Chamberlain declared war. Less than a month later, Murray had come home on the train from London and told her he'd volunteered as a doctor in the army. She'd held their son Robin and wept, but Murray had convinced her he was doubly obligated to serve—first as a doctor and second as a gentleman. Then he'd promised her that he would keep himself safe.

"What would be the use of living in a building site for three years if I can't come back to enjoy the home I built with my beautiful wife?" he'd asked with a laugh before kissing her. And because life seemed to bend to Murray's genial will, she'd believed him.

How naive she'd been.

Diana pushed her hair back off her face and stood. Just as diligently as before, she opened the curtains, stopping only to check her face in the mirror and straighten the fine plum cashmere cardigan that she'd learned to treasure since the government had issued clothing coupons. She'd learned all sorts of things since that awful day when two khaki-clad officers had driven into the courtyard to tell her Murray had been killed en route to a field hospital.

She let herself out of her morning room's sanctuary and made for the entryway that joined the house's two wings. Down the corridor, two nurses in white uniforms with red crosses emblazoned on the bosom stood with their heads close together, giggling. The moment they spotted her, however, they scurried away.

She ignored them. When the government declared it was requisitioning Highbury House mere weeks after Murray's funeral, it had taken the Voluntary Aid Detachment mere weeks to occupy most of the main house and its outlying buildings, leaving only a small suite of rooms in the western wing for the family. Still deep in mourning, Diana had emerged one day to find that the home she'd lovingly restored had transformed into wards of neat rows of hospital beds, a surgical suite, and accommodation for nurses and doctors.

It had all happened without her because Murray's sister, Cynthia, had traveled down from London to become the commandant of the new Highbury House Hospital. Still raw from the shock of her husband's death, Diana had viewed Cynthia's taking charge as a kindness. Soon, however, she saw what it really was: a way for Cynthia to force her way back into the childhood home that had passed to Murray upon their mother's remarriage. Yet if her sister-in-law had hoped Diana would remain in her suite swathed in black crepe and sadness and never show her face in the hospital, she'd been sorely mistaken.

Diana strode through the ground floor, past the east drawing room, long gallery, and ballroom. Each had been made into a distinctive ward and was lined with two rows of white enameled beds.

At first Matron McPherson, who ran the medical side of the hospital, had tried to keep Diana out of the wards with a sharp "Mrs. Symonds!" every time Diana appeared.

Finally, Diana had had enough. "This is still my home, and I will go where I please," she had argued in the middle of her ballroom, eight wounded men watching her from their beds with a degree of respect.

"I cannot have people traipsing through my wards," Matron had shot back.

"Never mind that; it isn't appropriate, Diana," Cynthia had said in a rare moment of agreement with the matron. "The men aren't used to female company."

"They're surrounded by women," Diana said.

"Nurses," Matron corrected her.

"You're a woman," Diana pointed out. "And so are you, Cynthia."

"I am the commandant of this hospital," said her sister-in-law, as though the term unsexed her.

"I will come and go freely in my own home," Diana said firmly, refusing to be moved until both Matron and Cynthia relented. The world might be at war, but she would not be ordered about like an infantryman in her own house.

Now, as she walked into B Ward, Sister Wharton, the senior nurse on staff, looked up from observing a junior nurse administer a shot to Private Beaton, who was fast asleep.

"Mrs. Symonds," Sister Wharton said with a nod.

Diana slowed. "Sister Wharton, how are your patients today?"

"Some are better than others. He's asked me to thank you again for helping him write to his mother." Sister Wharton nodded at Private Beaton.

The man's right hand had been ripped to shreds by shrapnel. He hadn't yet mastered using his left, and he didn't want to alarm his mother by writing to her in a different hand. Diana had lugged Murray's old typewriter to the ward and set it up on a little table by Private Beaton's bedside. His dictation had been the first of three letters she'd typed that day.

"I hope his upcoming surgery is a success," said Diana. "I was wondering if you knew where Miss Symonds might be."

"I believe you'll find her in her office," said Sister Wharton.

Diana did not point out that Cynthia's office should be called the billiards room. That was one battle she'd lost. Instead, she thanked Sister Wharton.

At the billiards room door, Diana drew in a deep breath before knocking, trying her best to ignore the bitter taste of having to knock on doors she owned.

"Yes?" came a thin voice from the other side.

Diana twisted the brass doorknob and stepped inside to be greeted by the back of Cynthia's head. With blond hair that was beginning to streak with silver, it would have been easy to think that the woman who dressed in demure pastels and high lace collars might be soft and compassionate. Five minutes with Cynthia, however, and anyone would have been disabused of that notion. Cynthia was made of flint and dogma.

Cynthia swung around in Murray's old desk chair, her sharp, birdlike features pinched with thinly veiled annoyance. "My darling sister-in-law, how good of you to stop by. Do you find yourself at a loss for things to do?"

"You know that I have more than enough work to keep this house running on a quarter of its staff, with or without forty-three patients, three doctors, six nurses, six general service members, a matron, a quartermaster, and yourself in residence."

"So you often tell me." Cynthia sighed. "What is the matter today?"

"We would have no need to speak every day if the staff and patients would give a care to this house and my family living in it," said Diana, taking a seat before she'd been invited to.

"If this is about the flooding in the green bedroom—"

"That has been repaired. It was fortunate that Mr. Gilligan was able to turn off the water to the sink as quickly as he was, otherwise it would have seeped through the ceiling," she said.

Cynthia's lips thinned as she shuffled some papers on her desk. "Yes, well, that was an unfortunate accident."

"It was entirely preventable," Diana pushed.

"I spoke to the nurses on the second floor about minding that the patients aren't throwing cricket balls inside, but you must understand that the men can become bored."

"Perhaps you would extend that warning to the rest of the house. Mrs. Dibble found that the silk wallpaper in the blue bedroom has been damaged after someone bounced a rubber ball against it," she said.

Cynthia hesitated but then frowned, picked up her pencil, and made a note in the little book she kept close at hand. "I will speak to Matron."

Diana let out a breath. "Thank you."

"Is that all?" asked the older woman.

"It is not. Earlier today one of your cooks broke several eggs belonging to the house. As you know, I am to have the vicar and a few other people to supper tonight."

"Surely Father Bilson will understand if his custard is made with dried eggs."

"I cannot serve Father Bilson a custard made from dried eggs," said Diana.

"Why not? I'm sure that it's nothing he hasn't eaten at his own table."

"That is not how things should be done."

Cynthia made an exasperated noise, but again the pencil went up. "I will see to it that they are replaced. How many?"

"Two." When Cynthia looked up at her, she pressed on. "But that is only a symptom of the real problem."

"And that is?"

"This is not the first time that my cook has dealt with the damage or disappearance of rations since the hospital arrived at Highbury. The VAD explicitly promised that you would keep to your own rations and leave ours alone."

"Ours? I'm a member of this family, too, lest you forget," said Cynthia.

Lest she forget? How could she when Cynthia mentioned it so often? But it was Diana whom Murray had left the property and all of its contents to, *not* his sister.

"The hospital cooks are not to touch the family's rations," Diana said slowly. "That is food your nephew eats." *It is food you eat night after night because, while you want to rule over the nurses, you won't eat with them.*

"I will speak to Mrs. George," Cynthia finally said.

"Thank you," Diana said.

Cynthia glanced down at her notebook. "Before you go, I wanted to talk to you about the night nursery. Is it really necessary for Robin to sleep there?"

"Where is he supposed to sleep if not in the night nursery?" The hospital had already requisitioned the day nursery for four patient beds.

Cynthia looked up. "Well, he could sleep with you."

"No," said Diana.

"Or you could send him out to school," Cynthia said.

"He's not yet five."

"I took the liberty of writing to Mr. Keen at Charleton Preparatory School, and he said that, given the extraordinary circumstances we are living under, he is prepared to take boys as young as seven."

"He's only four."

Cynthia waved her hand. "A small matter of making arrangements. With Robin away at Charleton, he would be well prepared for Winchester just like his father—"

"I am not sending Robin away to school," said Diana.

"Diana, be reasonable," her sister-in-law said.

"I am."

"If this is about his ailment—"

"His asthma," she corrected. "No, it is not."

"He has always been a sickly boy."

"He is not sickly any longer," said Diana. "He is healthy and in little danger so long as he keeps his inhaler with him."

"He's so thin," said Cynthia.

"Please feel free to take the matter up to the Ministry of Food who issues his ration book."

"Robin is a Symonds, Diana. Symonds boys have been going to Winchester for decades."

"Robin is my son, and I will decide what to do about his education. He stays at home," she said.

"Is that really wise, considering? All of these men coming and going from the hospital, and some of them can be quite rough. And then there is the issue of space. I have a third of my staff living in cold attic bedrooms, a third in barely habitable cottages, and a third down the road in the village. The Royal Army Medical Corps wrote last week that we're to expect more men by midmonth, and the surgeon is demanding that we find him another room for a surgical suite because the old storeroom is too poorly lit. If Robin were to go, we could have the night nursery, too."

"No," she bit out.

"We all must make sacri—"

"You will not tell me about sacrifices," Diana said fiercely. "You will not dare."

Her sister-in-law folded her hands one over the other. "I understand that you are still mourning my brother's death."

Diana pushed herself up out of the chair. "Please remind Mrs. George that she and her cooks are to stay out of Miss Adderton's way."

Diana was halfway to the door when Cynthia called out, "I thought you should know, we have a chaplain in Ward C. I thought that you might like to meet Father Devlin." Cynthia hesitated. "Perhaps you could speak to him about Murray."

A long pause stretched between them as Diana clenched her fists. Finally, she said, "Cynthia, my request to stay out of my rations extends to matters of my personal life as well."

For once, Cynthia was silent as Diana shut the billiards room door behind her.

Still seething, Diana made her way to the mudroom off the kitchen—too small a space for the convalescent home to commandeer—and pulled on Murray's old waxed jacket and a well-worn pair of leather loafers. She wrapped her hair up in an old scarf that she kept on a hook by the door and gathered up her trug and secateurs.

She threw open the side door to the kitchen garden and crunched across the gravel to the gate. It wasn't raining, but she could smell it in the air. It was her favorite time to be in the garden, with the urgency of impending weather hurrying her along.

She was not a great gardener by any means. But then, none of the women in Murray's family had been. Murray's grandfather, Arthur Melcourt, had brought in a woman named Venetia Smith to do the design.

Even decades later, the effect was breathtaking any month of the year, and Diana was determined to be an excellent caretaker of the grounds. However, after four and a half years at war, she was beginning to admit that bare competence was more realistic.

When Murray was alive, six gardeners on staff were led by a head gardener named John Hillock. After the declaration of war, though, half of the young men had enlisted, with the others called up one by one. Then Mr. Hillock, who had worked on Venetia Smith's designs under the direction of his father, had died of a heart attack while dividing bleeding hearts in the lovers' garden. Now two men who were too old to fight came up from the village every other day to tend to what they could, calling on a pair of young boys to do any heavy lifting they couldn't manage. The garden had taken on a loose, shaggy quality, with faded blooms that desperately needed deadheading. Even the yew had become more wild shrub than wall as it waited for a much-needed trimming.

Still, Diana loved the garden because it was fully her own. For a time, Murray had taken an interest in the redecoration of the house, but he'd left the grounds to her, saying it was a good hobby for a lady. Now, when everything became too much, she could hide in the garden rooms and pretend that her home wasn't overrun, her husband wasn't dead, and life wasn't slipping through her fingers.

That afternoon, she made for the water garden. She liked its cool calm, even in the depths of winter. She should clean the pond out before the spring, but that task was for another day when she wasn't expecting company. A war wasn't an excuse to let standards slip, and if she became dirty, she would have to endure a cold bath before her guests arrived.

She set about pruning the late-flowering clematis, cutting the long vines back to a healthy bud and pulling away the old growth from the plant. The pieces went into her trug, destined for the great compost heaps near the greenhouses at the bottom of the property.

After ten minutes, an uneven shuffling came from the other side of the garden wall. She straightened just as a large man in a uniform walking with the help of a pair of crutches rounded a gap in the brick wall.

"Mrs. Symonds, I presume?" he asked through huffs and puffs.

"You wouldn't happen to be Father Devlin, would you?" she asked, sliding her secateurs into Murray's coat pocket.

He smiled. "Miss Symonds told you about me, did she?"

"You'll find that there aren't many secrets at Highbury House these days." She gestured to a teak bench. "Would you like to sit down?"

"I would, thank you," he said.

She watched as he slowly eased himself down and propped his crutches next to him.

"What is it, if you don't mind my asking?" she said, nodding to the crutches.

"My hip. I'm afraid I rather shattered it. Very inconvenient."

She smiled a little. "Shattered bones seem to be a specialty of this house. How did it happen?"

He looked sheepish. "I'm afraid I've no story of derring-do."

"We have rather enough of those around here."

"Quite. The truth is, I fell off a tank, and the ground broke my fall. And then broke my hip."

"How inconsiderate of it," she said.

"I thought so, too. So what did our dear commandant Miss Symonds tell you about me?"

"She suggested that I might like to talk to you," said Diana.

"Well, we're talking now, so you clearly didn't object to the idea."

She raised a brow.

"Ah, I see. It was one of those 'Speak with the man of God' suggestions. Do you think you need to talk to an old army chaplain?"

"No. I don't," she said.

"You know, I find that some people who don't need to talk just need a friend."

A friend. How long had it been since she'd had one of those? She'd never been the most popular girl. She was far too focused on playing her harp and a touch too shy for even the singers and other musicians she accompanied. But all of that had changed when she'd become engaged to Murray. He was like a whirlwind, sweeping into a room and collecting people up in his wake. The early years of her marriage had been awash in parties, and his friends' wives had become her friends.

But how long had it been since she'd seen Gladys or Jessica or Charlotte?

When she didn't respond, the chaplain leaned back, folding his hands in front of him. "I will admit that I could use some company myself. The most disturbing thing about landing yourself in a convalescent hospital is realizing that you're now surrounded by all manner of sick men."

"I would have thought that being an army chaplain would have prepared you for that," she said.

"Oh, it does. But every once in a while, it is good to spend some time in the land of the living, too."

She gave him a hard look, but then shrugged. If the man wanted to sit out in a half-wild garden and watch her prune a plant, that was his prerogative.

She gestured at the clematis. "I'm going to continue my work here."

"Please do. I wouldn't dream of disturbing you," he said, tilting his head back to soak in the weak sunlight.

With a shake of her head, Diana set about mastering the clematis once again, but as she did, she found that a little bit of the fury that had driven her out into the garden had passed.

· EMMA ·

MARCH 2021

*T*his one, too!" Emma shouted down to Charlie. She was perched on a ladder, looking at the structure of a tree in what Sydney called "the ramble." It had been a long time since anyone had given the trees any love, and a few of them needed to come down, either because they were rotting or to open pockets of air and light to the forest floor.

"Got it," Charlie yelled back.

"How many is that?" she asked as she descended.

Charlie tallied up the morning's notes. "Seven if we include that elm near the cottage."

"I hope the Wilcoxes need firewood," she said.

Rustling in the yew branches behind them had them both turning just as Bonnie and Clyde raced up.

Charlie immediately dropped to his knees and rubbed Bonnie's ears. "Hello, gorgeous girl," he cooed, his Scottish accent wrapping around each "r."

"When are you going to get a dog?" she asked.

"I could ask you the same thing," he said.

"I move around too much for a dog. At least you have the narrow boat."

Charlie grunted as Sydney burst through the clearing.

"Oh, good, you're both here. I was going through some things and, well, I think I found something exciting!" Sydney said in a rush.

"What is it?" Emma asked.

Sydney just grinned and retreated.

It could be anything, Emma reminded herself as she and Charlie followed Sydney back through the garden, into the house, and over drop cloth–covered stairs to the finished wing of the house. She always asked owners to dig through any papers that came with a house, but finding something new and significant was rare.

"I was excited after talking to you, and poor Andrew and I have been spending every night up in the attic going through boxes. Granddad might have been a pack rat, but at least he was somewhat organized. The boxes are all marked 'House & Garden,'" Sydney chattered as she opened the door into a study with a large mahogany desk in the center and bookshelves lining two sides. Several containers sat in the middle of the room, their tops open.

"I was disappointed at first. It seemed to be a lot of receipts for roof repair and a new Aga in the seventies, but then I came across this." Sydney pointed to a cardboard tube and an ancient-looking file folder. "Do you want to do the honors?"

Emma picked up the tube, uncapped the top, and slid out a sheaf of rolled-up papers. Sydney and Charlie cleared the desk, and she laid them out.

"These look like the house's blueprints," she said.

"They aren't originals. I think they're from the late 1930s, just before the war. You can see where an architect moved a wall on this floor to create a larger bathroom," said Sydney, pointing to the blue ink.

Emma flipped through the pages. There was the entire house in view, then each floor, including the cellar, where the kitchen, pantry, and an old-fashioned stillroom had been. But when she flipped to the next page, her breath caught in her throat. On the large yellowing sheet of paper was a pencil sketch of the garden with "Highbury House" written across the top.

Her eyes went wide. "That is Venetia Smith's handwriting."

"You're sure?" Sydney asked hopefully.

"She's sure," said Charlie. "She's been obsessed with this woman for as long as I've known her."

"Longer," she murmured. "I should be wearing cotton gloves." Not that that was going to stop her from examining the plans.

"When I first saw them, I was confused because the way the garden is laid out didn't look anything like it does today," said Sydney.

"This is what Venetia would have replaced. It's a formal garden." She pointed to the symmetrical beds laid out in a knot pattern. "There might have been a low border of bedding plants here, or it might have been hedged in."

"Ah, that makes sense. But take a look at the next sheet," said Sydney.

Lifting the garden plans, Emma found a thin piece of nearly transparent tracing paper. Carefully she lifted it and laid it over the original plans. She lined up the two sketches of the house, the kitchen garden, and the orchard and then stepped back. "There."

"That's it," said Charlie. "That's the garden."

"And it's labeled!" said Sydney.

"The tea garden, the lovers' garden, the children's garden, the bridal garden," Emma read.

"Oh, that's why it's all white," said Sydney.

"Look. The one next to the water garden is a poet's garden," said Charlie.

"There's a book of poems in the library by my great-great-great-grandfather Arthur Melcourt. He was the one who commissioned the garden," said Sydney.

"Maybe Venetia was trying to flatter him into agreeing to the rest of her designs," she said.

"Why would she need to do that?" Sydney asked.

"She was ahead of her time. There were a very small number of designers in England who created the English border garden look that we are all familiar with now. Venetia would have been considered a bit of an artist, a bit of a revolutionary," she explained.

"How is Arthur Melcourt's poetry?" Charlie asked.

"Pretty terrible from what I remember," said Sydney.

Emma carefully lifted the page to reveal another drawing. "This looks like it might have been made a bit further along in the project. You can see she added a series of paths to the children's garden."

"They look like the Union Flag," said Charlie.

"A playful nod to the Melcourt kids maybe. And it looks like there's something here in the winter garden," she said, pointing to a circle. "Maybe a pond or a small paved area."

"This must have been a working drawing. You can see where she rubbed out some of the pencil," said Charlie.

"Hold on." Emma lifted the sheet up to the light. "Something's written here above the winter garden. It's so faint . . ."

Charlie and Sydney leaned over her shoulder, peering at the spot. After a moment, Sydney said, "I think that says Cecil's garden."

"No, it's got too many letters," said Charlie, pushing his ball cap up to scratch his forehead.

"Celeste," said Emma. "Celeste's garden."

"Who was Celeste? And why is it written in someone else's handwriting?" Sydney asked.

Emma's gaze flicked back to the faint writing. "I don't know about a Celeste. And you're right. Someone else wrote that in."

"Is it anywhere else?" Sydney asked.

Methodically Emma sifted through the sheets, revealing details of all the major parts of the garden. Some of the details even had planting lists and diagrams of the borders. The children's garden—overgrown with self-seeding wildflowers now—had once held impatiens, foxgloves, poppies, and gerbera daisies. Down the side of the poet's garden's detail was a list of flowers with their corresponding poets. A detail of the winter garden was drawn on a smaller sheet of paper that looked as though it had been ripped from a notebook.

"No 'Celeste' on this one," said Sydney. "Did she have a sister?"

"Just her brother, Adam," Emma said.

"What about her mother?" Charlie asked.

Emma screwed up her lips trying to remember. "I think her name was Julie or Juliet or something like that."

Charlie pulled out his phone for a quick search. "Her mother's name was Juliet. Middle name Caroline."

Emma stared down at the faint pencil markings. *Who is Celeste?*

"These are still good, right?" asked Sydney, interrupting Emma's thoughts.

Emma looked up. "Do you know how rare it is to find such an important collection of drawings?"

"No idea," said Sydney cheerfully. "Tech is my world."

"These drawings should be in an archive somewhere, or at least preserved correctly," she said.

"*If* you want them to be placed in an archive, either on loan or as a donation. It's your choice, Sydney," said Charlie.

"But first we want to keep them here, right?" Sydney glanced between them. "You can use them to make sure that you're restoring Highbury House's gardens exactly as they were."

Emma nodded, even though proper preservation should have been her first priority. To be one of the few people in the world to know about a new set of Venetia Smith drawings was simply extraordinary.

"Well, maybe we can hold on to them until the time is right, and then you can help me find the right people to take care of them," said Sydney with a sly smile.

"There's a man I know, Professor Wayland, who would probably write ballads to you if he knew that you had original Venetia Smith drawings, especially for a garden we know so little about," said Emma.

"Just wait until your friend sees this, then," said Sydney, handing over the file folder.

Emma's heart beat a little faster as she opened up the file. Instead of Venetia's handwriting, she was confronted with a letter written in another—bolder, slashing—hand. She flipped it over. It was signed *Adam Smith*.

"This is from Venetia's brother. He acted as her man of business when she was working in the UK," she said.

Charlie leaned over her shoulder and began to read, "'Dear Mr. Melcourt, please find included in this letter the bill of sale for thirty-six four-year-old limes intended for planting along the lime walk.'"

"The next one starts, 'Dear Mr. Melcourt, Please find included in this letter the bill of sale for twelve bare-root peonies of three varieties.'" Emma looked up at Charlie. "There are peonies in the tea garden."

"So this stuff is helpful?" Sydney asked.

"It's incredible," she said. "It's about as close as we can get to knowing what Venetia planted without having a treatise from her on the subject."

A knock came at the study door, and Andrew pushed it open, bearing a tea tray. "Hello. Why do I feel as though there's a party I haven't been invited to?"

"Oh, Andrew, you're a star. Would you put that tray over there?" Sydney pointed to a sideboard. Emma was about to warn about liquids anywhere near the drawings and receipts when Sydney said, "We might need to have tea standing up to keep it away from the documents."

While Andrew took milk and sugar preferences and poured tea, Sydney filled him in. When they were all settled with mugs in hands, Andrew said, "You should ask Henry if his grandmother did any sketches of the garden."

"Oh, that is a good idea. Henry Jones owns Highbury House Farm. His grandmother, Beth, was a land girl on another local farm near here. She ended up becoming an artist of some acclaim in the sixties, doing paintings of Warwickshire landscapes."

"We should be seeing Henry at the pub quiz this week. You'd be very welcome to come along," said Sydney.

"Oh, no, thank you," said Emma quickly. "If you still want to go for historical accuracy in re-creating the garden, I'm going to need to scrap most of my plans."

"Yes," said Sydney firmly. "Let's bring the garden back to the way it was."

"It's going to delay the project," Emma warned.

"This house is one giant delay," said Sydney.

"She's not wrong," said Andrew.

"Okay, then. I'd better get started. I'm going to spend some time going through these," said Emma.

"Do you want a hand?" Andrew asked. "I'm not promising that I'll know what I'm looking at, but I like systems."

"Sure," said Emma.

"Maybe you could help me with a couple of questions about access to the property, Sydney. We're going to need to bring in a lot of compost to improve the soil," said Charlie.

"There's access via the farm road and the gate at the back near the greenhouses. I can show you," said Sydney.

"Perfect," said Charlie.

When Sydney and Charlie left, Emma and Andrew settled into a companionable quiet. As Emma began to read through Adam Smith's letters, she almost forgot Andrew was there. Between the letters and the drawings, it was easy to lose herself.

She was reading a three-page list of plants when Andrew cleared his throat. She looked up. "Did you find something?"

"Not unless you're interested in the irrigation system installed in the kitchen garden in 1976," he said.

"Not really."

"I thought not. No, I just wanted to say, I hope you aren't too thrown by Sydney's invitation to the pub quiz."

"Thrown?" she repeated.

"She wasn't just being polite about inviting you. She'd be genuinely delighted if you came. If you wanted to."

"I didn't mean to be rude," she hurried to say.

He laughed. "Trust me, you weren't rude. Just know that you're always very welcome."

For a moment, she considered what it would be like to walk into a village pub and find friendly faces waiting for her. A tiny part of her liked the idea that someone might have a drink ready for her. That she might be a part of something. But that was where danger lay. She didn't socialize with her clients—even those she liked—because it just made it harder to unpick her temporary life and move on at the end of a job.

"Thank you," she finally said. "I'll keep that in mind."

· VENETIA ·

FRIDAY, 8 MARCH 1907
Highbury House
Rain overnight; overcast

This morning, I borrowed a horse from Mr. Melcourt's stables and rode to Wilmcote after overseeing the final marking of the lime walk. The trees were delivered yesterday, and I've already written to Adam to ask him how he had possibly found thirty-six four-year-old limes in such short order. He will only tease me and remind me that he can work his own magic with paper and a pen.

I will admit that I am finding my employers as challenging as much of their ilk, but not so much that I cannot abide them. I dine with the Melcourts every night unless I beg off with a headache. However, Mrs. Melcourt remains high-handed. Just two days ago, she spent both the soup and fish courses espousing her brother's virtues.

"Mostly he is a collector, but he sometimes sells plants to a very select group of gardeners, such as Mr. Johnston," she told me, the diamonds on her fingers glinting in the candlelight as she dipped her silver spoon into broth. "Do you know Mr. Johnston?"

"I don't have that pleasure," I said.

"He is a wealthy American who just purchased a house near Chipping Campden, although the rumor is his mother gave him the funds. I can't imagine how Matthew met him."

"Has Mr. Goddard ever considered going into the horticultural business?" I asked.

Mrs. Melcourt looked up sharply. "My brother is a *gentleman,* Miss Smith. He has no interest in trade."

She did not, I noted, look to her husband, whose fortune had been built on the back of his father's business acumen that was so shrewd there is a bar of Melcourts Complexion Clearing Soap in my bath back in Wimbledon.

I spent most of my ride to Mr. Goddard's home this morning thinking about how the younger Mr. Melcourt and his wife seemed intent on washing the newness from their money. I was so engrossed I nearly missed the sign for Wisteria Farm. However, when I looked through the gate, there could be no mistaking I had arrived: a huge wisteria clambered over the front of a two-story farmhouse, ready to explode into leaf and bloom.

"Miss Smith!"

I twisted in the saddle to see Mr. Goddard emerge from a gap in the hedgerow some hundred yards away.

"The entrance to the nursery is just a little further down the road. Shall we walk?"

I let him hold my horse's reins so I could slide down. We walked the animal to a wide wooden gate that led into a yard lined on two sides with greenhouses, with a barn squared off to the lane. Everywhere I looked were roses. Climbing up the wall around the yard, their bare stems waiting for the spring. In terra-cotta pots large enough to hold three plants at a time. In a border leading to another garden. In the greenhouses, where long rows of plants sported neatly wrapped grafting joins.

"Welcome to my laboratory," he said with a smile. "It's a shame it isn't later in the year so you could see the roses in bloom," he said.

"The yard alone must be spectacular in June."

"It is, if I might be so bold. Still, I think there's something beautiful about a garden in winter," he said.

"Everything is stripped back and exposed. You can see the structure of the garden," she said.

"Precisely. Although that also means there's little to hide a garden's flaws."

"How did you come to grow roses?" I asked as we walked into one of the greenhouses, a rush of seductive warmth washing over me.

He passed a hand along the back of his neck and looked around him at the tables filled with lines of plants in various stages of growth. "Like many young men, I had something of a feckless youth. My mother and father always hoped I would amount to something, but I seemed determined to prove that aspiration wrong. I intentionally did little at Cambridge except for irritate my tutors. And one night I was caught in a rather embarrassing state," he said.

"How embarrassing?" I asked.

"Enough that I'm not certain my sister would approve of my speaking to a young lady about it."

I raised a brow. "I'm a confirmed spinster of thirty-five, Mr. Goddard."

"Surely you're not— That is to say, you don't look—"

I put the poor man out of his misery with a smile. "Thank you, but I'm quite happy with my age. It is rather liberating. For instance, today I was able to borrow a horse from your brother-in-law and ride it several villages over to visit a gentleman to discuss roses. No blushing debutante could do the same."

He nodded and then stopped in front of a row of pots to check the place where he'd grafted a scion stem to a rootstock. "This is 'Souvenir de la Malmaison'. Do you know it?"

I shook my head.

"It's a bourbon rose that throws off exuberant flowers in blushing white that almost seem to overwhelm the bush that they grow on, and the scent . . . it's sweeter than perfume."

"Sweet enough to be a welcome accompaniment as a group of ladies take tea outdoors together?" I asked.

"Perhaps," he said with a smile before moving to the table behind us. "Or maybe you'd like a shot of crimson for dramatic effect. 'Madame Isaac Pereire' could be just what you need."

I thought of the lovers' garden I had planned to create directly to the west of the tea garden. I wanted to shock a visitor walking from the calming, feminine plantings of pale purple heliotrope, light pink echinacea, and creamy peonies into a room almost obscene with color. Rich red roses, deep purple salvia, and the red flowering spikes of persicaria. Banana plants, Japanese maples, dahlias, tulips—I wanted it to make people gasp.

"Maybe it will be easier to start with what I need," I said, drawing out my notebook from my skirt pocket. It fell open to a bird's-eye view of the entire garden.

"And what would that be?" he asked, turning the notebook so that he could get a better look. The very edge of his littlest finger brushed the side of my hand. Heat flushed my cheeks, and I cleared my throat.

"I need jewel tones for the lovers' garden, the palest pinks for the children's and tea gardens, and pure white for the bridal garden."

He tapped the page where I'd written "Poet's Garden" and said, "A clever homage to my brother-in-law's hobby. I think you'll find Arthur is always most amenable when he believes the person he's speaking to fully appreciates his place in the world."

"Are you not fond of Mr. Melcourt?"

Mr. Goddard laughed. "Quite the contrary, I think he's the perfect match for my sister. Helen can be one of the most stubborn, determined women I've ever met. She has certain ideas of how the world should be, and she finds it very irritating when all of us don't fall neatly into line."

"She seems to expect great things from all those around her," I admitted.

"I will confess that it becomes tiresome sometimes. I'm rather set in my bachelor ways, so I sometimes chaff when I'm summoned to Highbury House for long dinners. I dare say you'll have seen it for yourself: never a quiet night of cold meats and simple wine at my sister's table."

"I have," I said. "My own life is rather quiet by comparison. My brother, Adam, moved to Wimbledon two years ago when I began to travel more often for my work. We often find ourselves happy to picnic on a second meal of whatever Cook made for lunch rather than sit through an entire five courses."

"You will find no such concessions to economy or practicality at Highbury. Tell me, Miss Smith, have you ever crossed roses before?" he asked.

"I—I can't say that I have," I said, stumbling over the abrupt change in subject. "I've crossed other plants. My father used Gregor Mendel's experiment with pea plants to teach me about recessive and dominant traits."

"Roses operate in much the same way. Colors, scents, foliage, flowering patterns—all are traits that may be passed down through generations. If you'll come with me," he said, gesturing to a glass-and-wood cabinet.

"I've been collecting and drying out pollen from various roses I wish to use as the stud." He unlocked the cabinet with a small key that hung from his watch fob and held open the doors. "Would you care to choose one?"

I peered around him and found myself confronted with dozens of roses stripped of their petals. Each of them sat on a small piece of card, carefully labeled in pencil.

"'Souvenir de Madame Auguste Charles', 'Alfred de Dalmas', 'Shailier's White Moss', 'Gloire des Mousseux'." I straightened. "I don't know what to choose."

"What do you need for your tea garden?" he asked.

I closed my eyes and envisioned the garden as it would be in five years—ten, even. Densely planted with exuberant but elegant blooms bending their gentle heads. A faint breeze dancing through the air, rustling the lime leaves just a few feet away.

"I think I should like the pale pink color of 'Alfred de Dalmas' with the fullness of the blooms of 'Gloire des Mousseux'," I said.

"A good choice," he said, reaching for the paper marked 'Alfred de Dalmas'. "We'll use this because the stud usually influences the color of the bloom."

"Usually?" I asked.

"One can never be certain. Roses are sometimes more fickle than a bored lover." Red rose high on his cheekbones. "That is to say, 'Gloire des Mousseux' is such a richer pink, I would worry that Alfred's delicateness would be lost."

He led me out of the greenhouse to the next one, carrying the piece of paper as we went. Whereas the structure we'd just left was full of tables, this one looked like spring had been trapped under glass. Flowering rosebushes grew merrily in terra-cotta pots. Many of them wore brown paper tied up with string.

"Here we are," he announced when we reached a bush free of paper. Several blooms were just beginning to open and reveal their many bright pink petals. "'Gloire des Mousseux'."

"It's beautiful," I said.

"She's a favorite of mine. Now, if you care to do the honors?" He reached into his pocket, pulled out a fine-tipped paintbrush, and handed it to me. He showed me how to remove the petals and the stamens before sweeping up the pollen to dab it carefully onto the pistil. Then he dove into his pocket to pull out paper and twine to preserve the integrity of the cross. We repeated it five times with five different blooms before he declared our work done.

"And now, we wait," he said.

I handed him back the brush. "The only problem is that I don't have much time to wait. Mrs. Melcourt is already asking about whether the borders on either side of the great lawn will be ready in time for a party next spring."

"And it will take far longer than that to see if our experiment has worked," he said. "It's a good thing, then, that this rose isn't for them."

"It isn't?" I asked.

"If you can make do with planting out 'Alfred de Dalmas' in your tea garden, I can supply you. You can think on what you need for the other gardens."

"'Madame Isaac Pereire' will be perfect for the lovers' garden," I said.

"Then you shall have it. And this rose"—he gestured to the flower we'd just crossed—"whatever it might be, will be yours to do with what you wish."

I found myself strangely touched by his thoughtfulness. "No one has ever made a rose for me before."

"Think of it as a present—a reminder of your time in Warwickshire."

A strange emotion lodged in my throat so that I could hardly swallow around it. "Thank you," I managed.

"It is my pleasure, Miss Smith. Now, shall we venture inside and see what my housekeeper has managed to find for us in the kitchen? I can't promise it will be more than simple fare."

"That sounds delightful."

He offered me his arm. "If you'll indulge me, I'll tell you over lunch about an extraordinary gentleman that I met the other day. A Mr. Lawrence Johnston who is intent on turning the fields around his new home into a gardener's paradise."

"Your sister mentioned his name. She said that you had supplied him with some roses."

"Yes, and I was fortunate enough that he showed me his plans. I thought you might find him interesting because he, too, is designing a series of garden rooms," he said.

"I should very much like to meet him," I said.

"Then I'll arrange it," he said, holding a side door to the house open for me.

Inside, his housekeeper fussed us into a small dining room warmed by a rolling fire. Mr. Goddard and I sat down across from each other—bread, cheese, meats, and pickles between us—and soon were lost in conversation.

I can honestly say that I've never had a better meal.

· EMMA ·

*T*he discovery of Venetia's plans transformed Emma's project. For two weeks, she had sifted through every relevant piece of paper she could find, taking photographs and notes. The question of who Celeste was nagged at her, but still she worked to adjust her own plans to match Venetia's. Then came the difficult part—canceling and placing new orders, sourcing large numbers of plants, and figuring out a way to make it all come in on budget and on time for Sydney and Andrew.

Her days weren't any less stressful as she directed the crew in the necessary work to clear the mess of plants from the garden and prepare the garden rooms to be planted out. She came home every day bone-tired, and more than a few nights, she fell asleep next to her laptop at Bow Cottage's dining room table.

Finally, one afternoon when everyone seemed to be busy with their respective jobs, Emma set aside her gardening gloves and made the short walk from Highbury House to the farm next door in search of its owner. Her sturdy boots sucked mud with each step she took up the farmhouse's drive, and deep grooves from tractor tires were half full of standing water. Even now, mist crept under the collars of her waxed jacket and her cream fisherman's sweater to settle into her bones.

Sydney had told her that Henry Jones came from a long line of farmers who had worked Highbury House Farm. The property had once belonged to the house's original owners, the Melcourts, before it was sold to the Joneses in the 1920s. It had weathered a world war, industrial agriculture, and countless other changes and remained in the family to this day.

The farmhouse came into view. She ran her hands over her temples to find that her wispy brown baby hairs had started to pull free from her ponytail. She tugged the band free to retie it, catching sight of the dirt under her nails, despite the gloves she wore religiously while working. Henry Jones would just have to face the reality that a woman who worked in dirt all day might be dirty.

The sky had already begun to turn inky, so she wasn't surprised when she saw farm equipment standing idle in the yard a hundred yards or so away from the house. Not seeing anyone around, she made for a redbrick building with lights on in the ground-floor windows.

As she approached, she could hear music—something with a good beat and some brass behind it. It only got louder as she approached, and when she knocked on the pale green door, she wasn't surprised at the lack of response.

She pounded the side of her fist against the door as the mist turned to a steady rain. After a moment, the music lowered. She stepped back. The door swung open, revealing a man sporting a James Brown with the Dramatics T-shirt over a white thermal. His dark hair was messy and all bunched up on one side, as though it had spent all day under a hat.

"Hi," the man said.

"Hello, I'm looking for Henry Jones," she said.

"You found him."

"I'm Emma Lovell. Sydney Wilcox may have mentioned me."

His expression brightened. "The gardener. She did mention you. You wanted to see if I had some of my nan's old drawings?"

"That's right."

"Shit, sorry. I shouldn't be making you stand outside in this rain. Come in," Henry said, making way for her.

"Thanks." Noticing he was only wearing socks, she asked, "Do you want me to take off my boots?"

He rubbed his hand over the crown of his head, mussing his hair even more. "Do you mind? Normally I wouldn't ask, but Sue's just been through and done the office. She'll kill me if I tread mud over the floors less than twenty-four hours after she'd cleaned."

"Who is Sue?" she asked, toeing off her boots.

"She keeps the accounts for the farm. Occasionally she gets tired of my mess and does a cleanup. Come through here," he said.

Emma followed him down a short corridor and into an office with two desks. One was neat as a pin. The other was . . . not.

Henry took a seat behind the messy desk, moving a stack of seed catalogs off a spare chair and shoving some forgotten tea mugs to the side. There was a laptop on this desk, but it was half buried under a stack of paper, including what looked like a chemical analysis report, an old edition of the Saturday *Telegraph*, and a paperback book bent open at the spine.

"I'm guessing you can tell which side is Sue's," he said over the sound of a classic soul song.

"I think so. Charlie, who heads up my crew, and Sue would get along."

"He's the neat one, then, huh?" Henry asked.

"Comparatively, although I'm not as bad as you."

Henry laughed. "No one's as bad as me. Now, tell me more about what you're hoping to find in my nan's drawings."

She explained a bit about her project and what she was hoping to find in his grandmother's old sketchbooks. "Drawings can sometimes fill in the gaps between intention and reality."

"Wouldn't photographs be more helpful?" he asked.

"Yes, ideally, but this was 1907. It was still pretty rare for people to document a garden really closely unless they knew it was significant. Venetia Smith didn't become famous until years later."

"She wrote books, right?" he asked.

"Pardon?" she asked, leaning in to hear over a series of horn blasts from the music.

He snatched up his phone and lowered the volume on the speaker set on a bookshelf. "Sorry about that."

"What was the song?" she asked.

"Jackie Wilson. It's called 'The Who Who Song.' Dad used to drive up to Stoke-on-Trent to dance Northern Soul at the Golden Torch before he took over the farm from Granddad. Soul, Motown, Stax. He listened to all of it when he did the accounts, and I just sort of kept doing it after he died."

That explained the James Brown shirt.

"I asked if Venetia Smith wrote books. The name sounds familiar," he said.

"That's right. She moved to America, got married, and lived there until she died. Highbury House was her last British commission."

"Well, it's decades later, but Nan was at Temple Fosse Farm during the war, and she used to do deliveries up to the big house. She didn't get serious about her art until the fifties, after my mother was born."

"Sydney said that your grandmother was a well-respected artist," she said.

He grinned. "She wasn't well-known enough for me to pack in farming and live a life of luxury, but she did sell to some galleries in London for a while. She used to take me up to visit her old favorites in the early nineties. A friend of hers used to travel all the time, so we would stay at her flat in Maida Vale."

"I'm hopeful any sketches might give me some clues," she said.

He leaned back in his chair. "My sister, Tif, and I cleaned out her house after she died. Tif didn't take much—she lives in London so she has less than zero space. I ended up with the lot of Nan's things. I'm sure I have at least a few of her sketchbooks."

Emma sat up. "Could you dig them out? I hate to take up your time when you're obviously busy, but . . ."

He laughed. "But you're going to anyway. Don't worry about it. I'm always happy to help Sydney and Andrew."

"Have you known them long?" she asked.

"About a year since. I would see Sydney's grandfather, Rob, around a fair bit. He wasn't a talkative man, but we'd say hello."

She frowned. "I would have thought you'd known each other longer. Sydney mentioned a pub quiz."

"Have you been recruited to Menace to Sobriety yet?"

"I beg your pardon?"

"It's the team name. I come along most weeks, although unless the subjects are about farming, classic soul music, or British military history I'm not particularly helpful," he said.

"I would be gardening, garden writers, historic gardens, so you've got a more diverse knowledge base than I do," she said.

"We need to bribe the quiz master to start gardening. Even out your chances of getting some questions you could ace when you come along."

"Oh, I'm not coming to the quiz," she said quickly.

"Why not?"

"It's not really my thing."

He cocked his head to one side. "You don't have to drink, if that's what you're worried about. You don't really need to help with the questions, either. The same team wins every week. We never stand a chance."

"I'm usually exhausted in the evenings." The excuse sounded as lame as it was.

"I get that. Farming means early hours. If you do ever change your mind, though, you know where to find us," he said.

She didn't actually, but since she'd only seen one pub in Highbury so far—the White Lion—she could make a pretty educated guess. Not that she would be going.

Her phone chirped. She glanced at it as a text from Charlie flashed up:

Rosewood's sent the wrong order. Everything's got to go back.

"Dammit," she cursed softly. Any more delays and she was in danger of running so far behind on this project that she'd cut into all of the grace period she'd built into the contract.

"Trouble at work?" Henry asked.

She shoved her phone into her back pocket. "Nothing I can't handle."

"Is the business just you?" he asked.

"Yeah. I started it after I got tired of working for other people."

He gave a low whistle. "That is impressive going it alone."

"Thanks, I think," she said.

He flashed a grin. "It's a compliment. Want to give me your number? I'll look around for those sketchbooks this weekend and give you a shout when I find them."

He grabbed his phone off his desk and held it out. She hesitated. It had been ages since she'd given her number to a man, but they weren't sitting in a bar or even on the opposite ends of a dating app. This was work.

She tapped in her number, and when he took the phone back, he shot her a quick text.

"Now you can message me if you ever need anything," he said.

"From a farm?" she asked, a smile tugging at her lips.

"You never know. You might wake up one day and think, 'I could really use Henry's hay baler.'"

"I'll keep that in mind. Thanks," she said when she reached the front door of his office.

"Maybe I'll see you around at the White Lion. It's tradition to buy new neighbors a drink."

"Is it?"

"Sure," he said.

She found herself considering his offer. A simple drink with a nice man who had an easy way about him sounded appealingly novel, but almost immediately she dismissed the idea. Forming bonds with anyone in Highbury would only make it tougher when she inevitably left.

"Maybe sometime," she said.

Out in the rainy farmyard, she pulled her collar up closer around her neck. Even though the mud clung to her boots harder than ever, she couldn't help but feel a little lighter.

· BETH ·

19 March 1944

Dearest Beth,

Reading your letters makes me want to be back on the farm again. I'm glad to hear how much you are enjoying your work. It warms this farmer's heart to know that you'll soon be as comfortable in the field as anyone.

I have forty-eight hours' leave coming to me, and I'll be spending it with Clifton, Macintyre, and Bates. I can't say yet when I will have enough leave to make the trip back to England. When I do, though, we'll go anywhere you want: tea, dinner and dancing, whatever. It's strange to think that it will be our first date.

With all my affection,
Colin

"Now, you're sure you know where you're going?" asked Mrs. Penworthy as Beth once again checked the leads on the horse and trap.

"Down the Fosse Way, left at the bridge over the river, and then two miles south until Highbury Road. It will be the big house on the left, half a mile down," said Beth.

"And don't forget the grand gates were taken down—"

"For scrap," Beth finished with a smile.

Mr. Penworthy lugged over the second wooden box bound for Highbury House. "Will you leave her be? The girl's smart."

After a little more fussing from Mrs. Penworthy, Beth climbed up onto the seat of the cart, flicked the reins, and turned to wave goodbye.

On the road, she couldn't help herself from grinning as the cold wind whipped at her hair. Her free time tended to be spent going to the cinema with Ruth and two girls who worked on a dairy farm in Combrook, and she rarely found herself alone. When she did, she felt guilty if she didn't use it to keep up with the steady stream of letters from Colin every few days. However, with reins in hand, she had nothing to do but enjoy the peace of her own company.

Her good mood carried her all the way to Highbury House. She pulled past the gap in the wall where the iron gates would have once stood and turned into the service entrance, just as Mr. Penworthy had told her she should. She hopped down from the cart and tied up the horse before letting down the gate and stacking the two boxes on top of each other.

Carefully she maneuvered around the cart to the kitchen door. She could hear the clatter of pans and the rush of water. Wedging the boxes between the door and her stomach, she knocked.

A moment later, the door swung open, revealing a woman in an apron with her chestnut hair caught up in a snood. The woman squinted at her and then looked down at the boxes. "No Mr. Penworthy today?"

"No, he couldn't get away," she said.

The woman stepped aside. "You'd better come in, then."

"Where would you like the boxes?" Beth asked.

The woman nodded to the big worktable in the middle of the room. "Right there's fine. I've just put on the kettle. Can you stay a minute?"

Beth hesitated but nodded.

"Good, I'll fix you a cup of tea."

"Oh, you don't have to do that," she said quickly.

"I'll need to go through the delivery and give you a list for next week. You might as well have your tea while I do it. They'll be leaves from this morning used again, but at least it's hot." The woman began pulling down stoneware mugs. "What's your name?"

"Beth Pedley," she said.

"I'm Stella Adderton. How are you liking being a land girl?" Miss Adderton called over her shoulder.

"Oh, I like it very much."

"The work isn't too hard, then?" Miss Adderton asked.

"It's not too bad when you get used to it, but there's a lot to learn," she said, rubbing at a chapped spot on her hands absentmindedly.

Miss Adderton placed a mug in front of her. "I don't suppose you enjoy dried milk, do you? No, of course not. Who does?"

She watched Miss Adderton reach into a delivery box and rummage around before pulling out the bottle. "Ah, here we are."

"We sent milk?" Milk was meant to be rationed.

"Mr. Penworthy has been supplying Highbury House for so long he never asks Mrs. Symonds to pay for real milk. I don't think it violates the rationing rules because it's a gift well before the milk would ever see the market." Miss Adderton paused. "I haven't shocked you, have I?"

Beth laughed. "No. It seems to me there are far worse ways that people cheat rations."

"That's the spirit," said Miss Adderton, dropping a tiny dollop of milk into each of their mugs. "What's your name again?"

"Beth Pedley."

Miss Adderton passed her a mug. "I like you, Miss Pedley."

That simple statement tore at Beth, and she stared down at the mug clutched between her hands, afraid that if she looked at Miss Adderton, she would start to cry. She couldn't remember the last time anyone her age had been this easy with her.

"Please call me Beth," she managed after a moment.

"And you'll call me Stella," said Miss Adderton with a nod. "It's much better than being 'Cook.'"

"I hope you don't mind me saying, but you look far too young to be a cook," Beth ventured.

Stella sighed and began unpacking grit-covered leeks from one of the wooden crates. "I grew up in Highbury and was the most senior kitchen maid before the war started. One by one, all of the other girls left to join up. I went, too. I wanted to be a WAAF because I think flying around the world would be grand."

"What happened?" Beth asked.

"I was deemed medically not fit for service—asthma, just like Master Robin—so that dream died." Stella offered her a half smile. "Anyway, it all worked out because now my nephew, Bobby, is staying with me."

"Do you like working at Highbury House?" Beth asked.

"I like the money from my wages. I like that I can have a dash of milk from time to time that others might not have. And on Wednesdays and Saturdays, I put on a uniform and work for the Civil Defense unit and feel as though I've done something in this war. But no, I don't think I like working at Highbury House at all."

"Why don't you leave?" asked Beth.

Stella smiled. "One day I will."

"It sounds as though you have a plan."

"I take correspondence courses. I can do shorthand and take dictation. I'm working on typing now, but I don't have a typewriter, so I have to use a chart and pretend."

"Will you go to London?" Beth asked.

"To start," said Stella. "Then wherever I can go. I collect postcards and photographs of all of the places I want to go someday."

"Where is first on your list?" Beth asked, fascinated.

"Tahiti. There is an island called Moorea. I'd like to go there." Stella's face fell. "It's more complicated now that I've got Bobby, of course."

The cook looked so sad Beth rushed to change the subject.

"And what of Mrs. Symonds?" she asked.

"What about her?"

"Mr. Penworthy spoke very highly of her."

Stella snorted, glanced over her shoulder at the door, and then dropped her voice. "She's very grand. When the government requisitioned this house right after her husband died and the hospital moved itself in, Madam tried her very best to go on as though nothing had changed. She still entertains. Still dresses for dinner, even on nights where it's just her in her morning room because the hospital put beds in the formal dining room. She spends time with the soldiers, I'll give her that, but more often than not she's in the garden."

"The garden must be beautiful," said Beth.

Stella shrugged. "If you enjoy gardens. You can see them on your way out if you like."

"Oh, I couldn't," she said.

"No one will know, if you're worried about that. Mrs. Symonds went up to London this morning to take care of some business, and the patients will pay you no mind. You can just let yourself through the side gate from the kitchen garden."

"Well, maybe, if you're sure it'd be all right," Beth said.

"I will say one thing for Mrs. Symonds," said Stella. "She loves her son. Master Robin is a sweet, handsome boy, although he doesn't have the size of his father. He was sickly when he was very young, but maybe he'll grow into himself one day." Stella put her palms on the worktop. "Well, this seems to be all in order. You'll have to thank Mr. Penworthy for giving us cauliflower. We haven't seen that since last year."

"He asked me to tell you that more will be coming. We've only just taken up the first heads."

Stella nodded and then stooped to scribble a few things on a scrap of paper. "This will do for next week."

Beth reached for the paper, but Stella grabbed her hand and flipped it over, exposing one of the cracks in her skin that had been nagging at Beth for the last few days.

"That has to hurt," said Stella.

"It mostly stopped stinging yesterday. Now it's only uncomfortable when I hold a pencil," Beth admitted.

"Writing letters?" Stella asked.

Fewer than I should. She was managing just one to Colin's three.

"I sketch, too," Beth said. "Just for fun."

"Well, we can't have chapped hands keeping you from that. Wait one moment."

Beth sat obediently in front of her empty mug until Stella came back with a small package wrapped in clean cloth. "Here. This will help."

"What is it?" Beth asked, unwrapping a corner to expose a hard ball of creamy wax.

"Beeswax and olive oil heated up and then cooled together. If you rub it on your hands whenever you wash and dry them, it will help," said Stella.

"Thank you," she said sincerely.

Stella waved it away. "It's an old trick you learn when you first start working in a kitchen. A few days of plunging your hands in and out of hot water, and you'll want to cry. If you come again next week, you can tell me if it helped."

"I'm sure it will," said Beth.

She said her goodbyes to the cook and let herself out the kitchen door. She fully intended to climb up into her cart and head off again, but the gate to the kitchen garden caught her eye. After a moment's hesitation, she loaded the empty crates she'd taken from Stella into the back of the cart and let herself through the gate into the kitchen garden.

An iron gate that must have been overlooked in the scrap collection connected the kitchen garden to a yew hedge. Beth opened it, wincing at the squeak, and glanced around. No one in sight. She scurried down the column of yew and found herself in a circular garden with a statue of a winged god in the middle. Though it was barren now, she could tell that in the spring it must be lush.

She found a gap in the overgrown hedge and followed it to another garden, and then another. She itched for a watercolor palette and some thick paper, but a bit of pencil would have been enough to commit the space to memory. She could see why Mrs. Symonds would want to spend time here. In these garden rooms, one could find something close to peace in a time when none was to be had.

Beth rounded a corner—this one constructed from brick—and found herself staring at another gate. If the garden rooms she'd just walked through were still dormant with the winter season, this one was audaciously alive, awash in greens and silvers and reds.

Glancing over each shoulder, she tried the gate. Locked. She stood there, her hands wrapped around the bars, wishing that she could enter. To see life springing forth so vigorously in the first weeks of March felt almost . . . obscene.

She was about to leave when something caught her eye under a bush just to the right of the gate. She crouched down and snaked her hand through the bars, just managing to grasp it—a toy train, the paint slightly chipped but otherwise in good nick. Tilting her head, she could see other toys stored under the same bush. A smile touched her lips. This must be Mrs. Symonds's son's playground.

Voices drifted to her from somewhere nearby. Quickly Beth replaced the train and hurried out of the garden the way she'd come, shutting the gate quietly behind her.

· STELLA ·

*S*tella hurried down Church Street, her hand clapped on the crown of her head to keep her green felt hat from blowing away. She was not supposed to be out and about at this time of day. She *should* be in the kitchen, trying to coax a final rise out of the stubborn brown bread she was baking for the household staff's tea. In her own quiet, worrying way, Mrs. Dibble was as much a stickler for tradition as her mistress, and she had refused to let meals around the servants' table fall by the wayside even if Highbury House boasted only a fraction of the staff it had before the war. However, the strict tradition meant that if Stella didn't have tea on the table by half past five, her timings would all be off for Mrs. Symonds' dinner. And now, pulled away from her duties, she would almost certainly be late.

It was Bobby, of course. Half an hour ago, a hospital clerk had clattered down the servants' stairs and announced that the village school was on the telephone. There had been a fight.

Stella rushed up the school's steps, her disbelief still fresh. Bobby had been in a fight? Her meek little nephew, who only spoke when spoken to?

Inside, Stella stopped at a pitted pine desk manned by an ancient man.

"Can I help you?" the man asked.

"Could you show me to the headmaster's office?" she asked.

The man stood and slowly began to shuffle down the hall. "You'll be the other boy's mother then."

That was just what she needed. The mother of another child, raging or fretting or crying, wasting her time when she had a job to do.

"Here you are," said the man.

She thanked him and let herself into the door marked "Mr. Evans, Headmaster." As soon as she was inside the small reception area, her eyes fell on Bobby, who had a plaster over his right eye and—was that Robin Symonds under all that dirt?

"Bobby, what happened?" she asked, even as she threw an appraising glance at Robin. He had no visible injuries, just a torn shirt collar and his share of smudges. *Thank God.*

Behind her, a door creaked open and a voice called, "Miss Adderton, would you care to join us?"

She swallowed hard, as though she'd been the one caught misbehaving.

"Are you all right?" she asked her nephew.

He nodded, his eyes still downcast. "Yes, Aunt Stella."

"Good. Don't you dare move." She hesitated and then dropped a kiss to his forehead.

Her nephew didn't protest. He didn't do anything.

She straightened and braced herself as she turned to the headmaster.

"Miss Adderton, I'm Mr. Evans. Would you take a seat?" the man asked.

Her grip wrapped around her handbag strap a little tighter when she saw Mrs. Symonds sitting in front of the headmaster's large oak desk.

Mrs. Symonds twisted to watch her take the chair next to her, her eyes giving nothing away from under the brim of a neat, dove-gray hat.

Mr. Evans crossed his hands on the top of his leather blotter and fixed both of them with a look. "Mrs. Symonds, Miss Adderton, as you can imagine, we are very careful at Highbury Grammar not to allow any fighting in the schoolyard."

"Of course," she murmured. Mrs. Symonds said nothing.

"This is not a place for roughhouse and play. I know we have taken both Robin and Bobby earlier than is usual, but they are expected to behave as the older boys do." He paused. "I've already spoken to both boys individually, but I'm going to ask them to come in and tell us what happened. They must understand that actions have consequences."

Consequences. Stella knew what that meant. Smacks on the hand with a ruler. Lashes on the bottom with a cane. "Consequences" were one of the reasons she'd been glad to leave school as early as she could.

Mr. Evans rose, returning a moment later with a hand planted firmly on each boy's shoulder. He steered them beside his desk and then resumed his seat.

"Reynolds, why don't you tell us what happened?" the headmaster prompted.

Bobby's face screwed up in thought.

Robin jumped in with a bright, animated voice. "We were arguing over who could run faster."

"Symonds," the headmaster cut him off.

"It's true," said Bobby in a quiet voice. "We all ran to the edge of the schoolyard and back."

"Robin, you ran?" Mrs. Symonds asked.

"I've been practicing, Mum! I'm really good and I didn't need my inhaler once," said Robin.

"Robin and I beat everyone," said Bobby.

"And then it was only Bobby and me left," Robin jumped in.

"Symonds," Mr. Evans warned again.

"Let him speak," said Mrs. Symonds in a quiet, firm tone Stella knew only too well.

"We bet a sixpence that we could run fastest," said Robin.

Stella bit her lip. She knew for a fact that Bobby didn't have a sixpence to bet because, although Joan had packed Bobby's ration book in his little case, she hadn't left a cent to help pay for things like his books. Those fees had come out of Stella's savings.

"I was winning," said Bobby, a hint of pride in his voice.

"Then I tripped him," Robin finished, matter-of-fact.

"You tripped him? Why would you do that, Robin?" his mother asked.

Robin shrugged. "He was winning."

"That is *not* a gentlemanly thing to do," Mrs. Symonds scolded.

"He didn't trip me, I fell down," said Bobby quickly.

"No, you didn't. I tripped you, and then you punched me," said Robin, as though that explained everything.

"Two teachers had to pull the boys apart from one another," said the headmaster.

"I'm very sorry, Mr. Evans. Bobby is usually such a well-behaved boy," said Stella.

"And so is Robin," said Mrs. Symonds.

"I'm afraid the boys will need to be punished," said Mr. Evans.

"If you think that you will be responsible for doling out that punishment, you are sorely mistaken, Mr. Evans," said Mrs. Symonds, her voice polished as steel.

Mr. Evans sighed. "Mrs. Symonds, there is nothing to be gained from leniency in these sorts of affairs. Boys must learn—"

"I will not tolerate you or anyone else striking my son." Mrs. Symonds glanced at Stella. "And given that I believe what is fair is fair, neither will Bobby face that punishment."

"Mrs. Symonds, both boys—"

"Will be punished, you have my reassurance. Now, if that will be all."

Sputtering, Mr. Evans half rose from his desk, but by then Mrs. Symonds had already gripped her son's hand and was leading him out. Stella bid the headmaster a hasty goodbye and grasped Bobby by the elbow.

"Are you truly okay?" she whispered as she helped Bobby ease on his coat and collect his satchel out in the reception.

"Yes," said Bobby, more cheerful than she'd heard him since he'd arrived at Highbury House.

"Do you like Master Robin?"

"We're friends. He lets me play with his toys, and I help him run. He doesn't have to stop anymore. Nanny doesn't know, but we're going to show her."

Outside, Stella found Mrs. Symonds waiting with Robin, who was crouched down, examining a bug crawling on the brick wall of the school.

A lump rose up in Stella's throat again. It wasn't fair, but she knew what was expected—even if Robin had been the one to start the fight.

He was to the manor born, and Bobby was just a little boy with a cook for an aunt.

She put a hand on her nephew's shoulder. "Bobby, you must apologize to Master Robin and Mrs. Symonds."

"We're friends," said Robin. "I'm going to teach him how to throw a cricket ball."

"It's true, Aunt Stella," said Bobby.

"Well, in that case, it will be even easier for you to both apologize to one another, won't it?" asked Mrs. Symonds.

The boys muttered hurried, insincere apologies. They weren't sorry for what they'd done. They were just being boys.

Stella was about to grab Bobby's hand and say their goodbyes before walking the long way back to the house—alone—when Mrs. Symonds said, "Robin, why don't you run ahead with Bobby? Miss Adderton and I would like to talk."

Bobby broke free from Stella's grasp, laughing as he ran down the pavement with Robin, their friendship newly solidified. Her hand fell away. A child in a cook's care did not harm the heir of the house. She should've reminded Bobby of that, but Stella hadn't thought it was necessary. The separation between people like Bobby and people like Robin was so great, the rules felt self-evident.

Mrs. Symonds cleared her throat. "Miss Adderton," she started slowly, "I believe I owe you an apology, even if my son doesn't seem to think that one is necessary."

"You? Owe me?" she stumbled in shock.

"I understand the very difficult position that Robin put you in by acting so disgracefully with Bobby. I can assure you that he will receive a fitting punishment." Mrs. Symonds tilted her head as she watched the boys meander off down the road. "I think that some time spent weeding in the garden would suffice. Two weeks after school should do it, I think. Robin does so hate the wet, and this is such a wet time of year."

"Could Bobby join him?" Stella asked.

A slight smile touched Mrs. Symonds's lips. "I'm certain there are more than enough weeds in Highbury for two punishments."

Mrs. Symonds began to walk, glancing back at Stella as though she expected her to join. Stella frowned deep. The stuck-up, stuffy lady who demanded preposterous things like a cheese soufflé for a Sir Something or Another and his wife wanted to walk with her.

Cautiously Stella followed, and Mrs. Symonds slowed her pace to match Stella's.

After a few silent minutes, Stella ventured, "If you don't mind my asking, Mrs. Symonds, do you object to the cane?"

"In schools, in homes, anywhere. I know it's frequently used, but I don't ever wish Robin to know it."

Why? Stella wanted to shout. Why, when in so many other ways Mrs. Symonds seemed traditional to her very core?

"It was my late husband Murray's wish," said Mrs. Symonds, as though reading Stella's mind. "He experienced a particularly brutal beating at his preparatory school. I had no desire to send Robin to such a school, much as my sister-in-law might disagree with me."

"I see," Stella said carefully.

"How is Bobby adjusting to life in the country?" Mrs. Symonds asked.

Stella sighed. "He's clung to me. I think he is shy."

"He doesn't seem to be shy around Robin."

He isn't old enough to have the good sense to be.

She peered down the pathway to the two boys zigzagging, their arms stretched out like Spitfires. "No, he doesn't."

"You have asthma, don't you? That is why you can't serve?" Mrs. Symonds asked.

"Yes," she said, preparing herself for the judgment.

"I've never seen Robin run before without becoming winded."

"Maybe his lungs have grown stronger," she suggested.

Mrs. Symonds made a noncommittal sound. "Has your sister indicated how long she wishes Bobby to stay at Highbury?"

As though it were anyone's decision but Mrs. Symonds's.

"No. Joan isn't much of a letter writer unless she wants something. I've only had two letters since February." She paused. "I hadn't seen her since her husband's funeral."

"And yet still you took her son," said Mrs. Symonds.

"Where else would he go?"

But even as she said the words she knew that they were only part of the truth. Yes, Bobby had no other family besides her. And yes, he was just a child. Yet it wasn't as simple as all of that. If she could, she would be gone from Highbury. She'd take herself off to London, New York, Shanghai—she didn't care where, so long as it wasn't Highbury, where everyone knew her and there was no escape.

What she would do when she got there, she still didn't know.

"This war has brought so much unhappiness, we must do anything we can to shield our children from it," said Mrs. Symonds.

When she glanced over and found that Mrs. Symonds was gazing at her son, her eyes were blank—almost as though she wasn't there.

"Master Robin looks very much like his father," said Stella.

"He does."

"Mr. Symonds was a kind man," she offered.

"He was," said his widow with a nod. "Some decency left the world the day he was killed, and the world needs decency right now. The convalescent home, for instance. He would have been delighted that the house had become a place of rest and recuperation for so many men. All I can see is the invasion of my home. I did ask Cynthia to speak to Mrs. George about respecting your needs, by the way."

Stella jerked back in surprise. "You did?"

Mrs. Symonds shot a smile—tiny but sly—at her. "Some battlefields must not be lost. Given the state of rations these days, I am happy to declare the kitchen one of them."

Stella was struck by the warmth of Mrs. Symonds's gesture.

"If I might be so bold, madam, I think Mr. Symonds would want you to be happy."

Something in the air shifted, and she could see Mrs. Symonds's back straighten.

"Miss Adderton, you overstep," Mrs. Symonds snapped. And once again, the walls were in place, the boundaries clear. One of them was the employer, and one of them was the cook.

"I do apologize. I— It's only that I—" She tried to string together the right words.

"I expect dinner will be served at half past seven, as usual," Mrs. Symonds said before marching off and leaving Stella very much on her own on the last strip of pavement before the village gave way to the road to Highbury House.

SPRING

· EMMA ·

APRIL 2021

*D*ue to necessary cuts across the foundation, we have decided to place the Head of Conservation position on hold indefinitely. This is in no way a reflection of the selection committee's feelings about you as a candidate. Indeed, please accept my personal apology . . .

Emma gave the email from the Royal Botanical Heritage Society's executive director one last scan and then locked her phone. After almost three months without a word, she wasn't exactly surprised that the position had been effectively eliminated, but it still stung that they had made her wait so long to find out. She *knew* she'd been a good candidate.

The more she thought about it, the more she could see the potential good she might do with a budget and the weight of the Royal Botanical Heritage Society behind her. It didn't exactly help that she'd checked Turning Back Thyme's business account that morning and realized that if Highbury House had any more delays, she was going to have less money in reserve than she liked at the end of the year. And that wasn't even taking into account the advance payment on her taxes her accountant would soon be hounding her to make.

"You don't need a job. You have a company," she muttered, stuffing her phone into the canvas bag on the front seat of Charlie's American-style pickup truck and cutting the ignition. Martha Reeves and the Vandellas stopped singing about a heat wave midverse, plunging the truck into silence.

She would do what she always did. Head down. Move forward. Don't look back.

Emma thrust open the truck door and braced herself for the cold, pounding April rain that stung her face as she ran the short distance to Highbury House's front door. The thirty clematis that she needed for the long border and the tea gardens would be fine in the bed of the truck, but if water made it through the flap of her bag, she was screwed.

Like magic, the door swung open, and she hurtled past a very dry Sydney and Bonnie and Clyde, practically skidding to a stop on the black, white, and gray tile of the entryway. Gone were the drop cloths that had littered the space when she'd first arrived, and the scent of newly applied paint still hung in the air. Highbury was making progress, and so was she.

"I saw you drive up," said Sydney.

"Thanks," she said, holding her bag out as she tried to wring out her hair one-handed. The dogs danced around her, thrilled as always.

"Bonnie, Clyde, down. Where's Charlie?" asked Sydney, peering out at the truck.

"He's patching up his narrow boat. The roof sprung a leak," she said.

"He lives on a narrow boat?" asked Sydney, frowning.

"He stays on it when he's on jobs near the Grand Union Canal, otherwise he'll take a cottage like I did."

"Does he like it?" Sydney asked.

"When the weather's nice."

"It's England . . ."

"And the weather's never nice for long. I know. He bought it at the height of the summer, and all he could talk about was motoring up the canals in the sun." Fun-loving, easygoing Charlie was brilliant at troubleshooting and logistics but wasn't exactly a forward planner.

"Let me get you a towel," said Sydney.

Emma didn't protest as her employer led her downstairs to the basement. It was often easier to agree with Sydney than try to persuade the woman that she didn't need or want any help. Surprising herself, though, she'd quickly become accustomed to going along with the other woman's whims. The fact that Sydney seemed to delight in making people's lives just a little bit easier, brighter, or more welcoming didn't hurt, either.

"Have you been down here before?" Sydney called over her shoulder.

"No, not yet."

"This used to be the servants' domain." They reached the bottom of the stairs, and Sydney pointed to the left. "The kitchen is that way. We still have the wine cellar, but sometime in the last fifty years someone installed a washing machine and a drying rack in the old stillroom."

Emma followed Sydney into a spacious utility room with a washer and dryer, a Welsh dresser, and a set of cabinets built into the wall. Sydney opened one of the cabinets and pulled out a neatly folded ivory towel.

"Thanks," said Emma.

"I was just going to put tea on, if you want to join me."

Given the rain, she wasn't eager to get out into the garden. "Sure."

"Wonderful!" Sydney lit up so brightly that Emma felt guilty she hadn't accepted the woman's offers of tea more often.

Emma squeezed water out of her long ponytail as she walked up the corridor to the kitchen. When she crossed the threshold, however, she stopped short.

"Wow."

This had to be the most beautiful kitchen she'd ever seen. A huge central island of stone-gray-painted wood and granite with a set-in gas cooktop sat in the middle. On the far wall a huge hunter-green Aga dominated, a conventional oven set in next to it. There were generous counters, a deep Belfast sink that looked like it could fit either Bonnie or Clyde, and cabinets done in a slightly lighter shade than the island. Emma knew they were virtually underground with only a tiny set of windows near the ceiling allowing natural light in, but somehow the space felt airy. And to top it all off, a bouquet of forget-me-nots spilled out of a blue-and-white jug with casual elegance.

"This is incredible," she said.

Sydney blushed. "Thank you. Cooking is a passion of mine, and I wanted to make sure we had a usable kitchen when we moved in."

"It looks more than usable. I want to cook in here, and I don't even like cooking."

Sydney laughed. "Andrew said the same thing when he saw the architect's plans. Let me get the tea on. Why don't you take a seat?"

Emma rounded the island to where Sydney had pointed and found a set of black bar stools tucked under the ledge. She pulled one out, watching Sydney fill the kettle and flip it on before pulling out a teapot, teabags, and two mugs before heading to the refrigerator for milk.

Sydney put a slice of lemon drizzle cake in front of her just as the water came off the boil. "If you want it. It's just something I've been experimenting with."

"Your own recipe?" she asked.

"A lemon drizzle cake with pistachio and poppy seeds," Sydney said as she poured the water into the pot. "I don't think I have it quite right yet, but I'm not embarrassed to feed it to you."

"It's been ages since anyone gave me anything home baked. Thank you," said Emma.

"How have things been progressing? I know I haven't been around much this week."

She straightened. They usually had this conversation in the garden, where she could show Sydney and Andrew all that the crew had accomplished.

"We wanted to start on planting the long border two days ago, but the rains have been so heavy, the ground is a mud pit," she said.

"Good for the garden, bad for the gardener," said Sydney.

"Something like that. Charlie and Zack spent some time working on the pleached limes. It's going to be a few years before they look their best, but the heavy prune will pay dividends. Jessa and Vishal have been working on the gazebo."

"An indoor activity," said Sydney, pouring tea into the mug in front of Emma and nudging the milk toward her.

"Thanks. Exactly. They'll do as much as they can until it has to come outside to be constructed."

"And what about the winter garden?" Sydney asked.

That was the question that had been nagging at the back of Emma's mind since she'd seen the garden. What was behind that impenetrable wall of brick? What was hidden?

"We've cut back the climbing roses where they were jutting out into the rest of the garden. Other than that . . ." Emma shrugged. "We'll let it die back and see if it's any easier to assess a safe way down into the garden without damaging anything valuable."

"Plants or people," said Sydney.

Never a huge fan of too much sweet with her tea, Emma took what she intended to be a polite bite of the lemon drizzle cake. Flavor exploded on her tongue, and she looked up sharply at her employer. "This is so much better than I thought it would be."

Sydney laughed. "Oh, thank you."

"Sorry, I meant—"

"I'm just teasing," said Sydney, popping a piece of cake into her mouth. "I only tease people I like. ·

"I meant to text you yesterday. I've found some more photographs of the garden," Sydney continued.

"When from?" Emma asked, her attention immediately diverted.

"Well, they were tucked away in an old visitors' book, and all of the entries are addressed to Claudia and John Symonds. I checked the family Bible. Arthur Melcourt died in 1921. The house would have passed to his eldest daughter, Claudia, because his son was killed in World War I. She was married when she inherited, but she divorced her husband, John Symonds, in 1923."

"You have a family Bible?" Emma asked as she watched Sydney cross the room to a small table.

"On a stand in the library. I don't think anyone's touched it in years. It weighs a ton, but all of the family history is written in the front pages." Sydney held up a yellowed envelope. "Here we are."

Emma took the envelope and pulled out a series of photographs. Most of them were posed group shots with people standing in various parts of the garden.

"That looks like the shade border, doesn't it?" Sydney asked, pointing over Emma's shoulder at the top photograph.

"It does. I was right in thinking that Venetia used astilbe—false goatsbeard—in the shade border. It was something of a signature in her later shaded gardens, but I didn't see it in the receipts or in her initial plans. It's possible that she reused existing plants from Highbury's grounds."

"Economical," said Sydney.

She shuffled the photograph behind the others and peered down at a group of women taking tea in a gazebo. "I should show this to Jessa and Vishal. They'll be happy to know their design doesn't look far off." She peered a little closer. "And those look like roses climbing up the posts of the gazebo. Charlie owes me ten pounds. He thought clematis and jasmine; I thought roses. Both were in a plant list on the tea garden's detail, but Venetia didn't leave any plans for the borders."

"So these help?" Sydney asked eagerly.

"They do," said Emma.

"Good."

Emma leaned back as best she could on the bar stool. "Can I ask, why are you so intent on restoring the garden as it was? Most people would think it easier to knock everything down and turf it."

"Shouldn't your gardener badge be revoked for saying a thing like that?" Sydney teased.

"I'm serious. Most people don't care."

Sydney thought for a moment. "Have you ever loved a place so much that it sunk into your bones?"

Emma shook her head. "Ever since I started working, I've never stayed in one place long enough."

"I don't think it's necessarily the amount of time you spend somewhere. It's about a feeling. I don't remember a time when I didn't love Highbury. Maybe it's because it's been in the family for so long. Granddad inherited it from his mother, Diana, when Dad was about ten. Apparently Granddad had always been a little strange, but he only became moodier and more difficult after his mother's death. My grandparents' marriage hung on for a couple of years, but finally Grandmama took the kids and left him.

"Dad thinks Granddad was probably depressed, but I guess they didn't talk about these things back then. Anyway, Dad grew up, and I think he tried his best to have some sort of relationship with Granddad for my sake. Twice a year, Mum and Dad would bundle me off to Highbury for a visit. Each time was awkward, but I still managed to fall in love with this place. It was like a Victorian fairyland to me, even as I got older and could see how shabby it had become. I think it was too much house for Granddad, but he refused to let it go."

"And you want to bring it back to life," said Emma.

"It deserves to be filled with people and love and laughter again. And the garden, too."

Emma picked up the photos. "If you don't mind, I'll show these photographs to Charlie, and we'll incorporate them into our plans. We'll start planting the garden rooms and borders as soon as the rain eases up."

"Have you had any luck with Henry?" Sydney asked.

Emma shifted in her seat, thinking about how often she'd checked her phone the week after they'd met. "We talked, but he hasn't been in touch," she said. He was a source of information, that was all. But that didn't explain why she'd started listening to Motown albums since meeting him.

"I'll talk to him and get a progress report. Or better yet, you could ask him yourself. He'll be at the pub quiz tomorrow," said Sydney.

"I—"

"And before you tell me that you're busy that evening—again—just know that it's a no-pressure situation. We won't make you do an initiation rite or anything like that. You can ask Charlie. He came a couple of weeks ago."

And Charlie showed up to work with a sore head the next day, claiming he'd gotten caught up in a discussion with a philosophy professor from Warwick University and hadn't noticed the bartender swapping his empties.

Still, Emma returned Sydney's smile. "I appreciate that, but I'm not sure I'm free."

"One of these weeks I'm going to catch you in the right mood at the right time, and you're going to come and love it."

"One of these weeks," she echoed. Maybe a little time at the pub would do her good after all.

· BETH ·

12 April 1944

Dearest Beth,

You don't know how much I look forward to your letters. They remind me there's someone besides Ma and Dad waiting at home for me, praying I return.

The little drawings you've done of all of the land girls and the Penworthys are very good. I feel like I almost know them. My favorite is Stella, chasing after the Bosh with a rolling pin. If we had women like that on the front, this war would be won faster.

It's strange that you've met so few of the soldiers at Highbury House, but maybe that's for the best. I'd like to keep you all for myself.

With all my affection,
Colin

The spring sun shone down strong and hot enough that Beth took off her cap as she crossed through the gate of Highbury House Farm. Last week, the farmer here, a Mr. Jones, had called on Mr. Penworthy, asking if he could have loan of her because she knew how to drive a tractor. Her employer had allowed her to go, but with strict stipulations.

"She's a good one, our Beth. As good as any of the men I've had work here," she'd overheard Mr. Penworthy say from around the corner of the barn where she was scrubbing mud off the tractor. "I won't like it if I hear any word about her being mistreated."

Beth's heart had swelled twice its size, and she'd smiled brightly the next time she'd seen Mr. Penworthy, causing him to mutter something about cheerful girls.

Apparently she was not the only one on loan that day. In Mr. Jones's farmyard, she saw a dozen land girls in a semicircle. She hurried to the edge and nodded hello to Christine and Anne from the dairy farm in Combrook and Alice, a girl who'd just turned eighteen and had come to help with the sheep in Alderminster. She'd seen them last at a country dance at the end of March, each one dressed in their best, imitation stocking seams drawn up the back of their calves with eye pencil and lips coated in the precious lipstick they saved for when the men from RAF Wellesbourne Mountford were allowed off the air base. Now these same girls were scrubbed clean, dressed in bulky green sweaters and loose-fitting, durable trousers. Without their makeup and with their hair pulled back, they all looked startlingly young, but, Beth supposed, that was because they were.

"Welcome to Highbury House Farm, ladies," said Mr. Jones, casting a skeptical eye over each of them. "I don't know what it's like on your farms, but I want to make it clear that I won't tolerate any whinging here. If you can't do the work, I'll send you back. Is that clear?"

"And what work will we be doing?" a strapping girl with a crooked grin asked. The posh cut to her vowels drew some looks, and even Beth cast her an extra glance. Yet this girl leaned forward as she spoke as though she couldn't wait to get stuck in.

Mr. Jones grunted. "Clearing land at the big house. We have a week to prepare and plant it."

Beth's heart sank at the idea of all that beauty sacrificed to the war effort. Each time she made her deliveries for Mr. Penworthy, she risked a little peek at the garden. She didn't dare go as far as the lake because of the risk of being spotted by the hospital or household staff, but she loved the garden rooms with their surprising little nooks and crannies. She'd asked Stella about them, but her friend said she had far too much to do every day to spend time in the garden.

"Which of you can drive?" Mr. Jones asked. Beth and Christine put their hands up. "You'll find the keys in the ignition. The rest of you can walk."

Beth walked over to one of the two tractors and climbed up into the cab.

"Mind if I join you?" called a voice from the other side.

Beth peered over the seat and saw the posh woman staring at her, hands on her hips. "Climb up."

The woman hauled herself up as Beth pressed the clutch and turned over the ignition. The tractor roared to life.

"Been driving for long?" her companion asked.

"Two or three months," she said.

The other women shrugged. "That's good enough for me. I'm Petunia Brayley-Hawthorn." Beth started, and Petunia laughed. "Horrid name, I know, but it's better than what Mummy calls me."

Beth couldn't resist asking, "What is that?"

Petunia made a face. "Petal."

She laughed. "You're right. Petunia is better. I'm Beth Pedley."

Mr. Jones shouted over to them, "I'm not paying you to socialize, ladies!"

"He's not paying us at all, rotten man. The government is," said Petunia matter-of-factly.

Beth bit her lip, fighting a grin.

Highbury House Farm was, unsurprisingly, the next property over from Highbury House, as it had once belonged to the manor. However, "next door" in the country meant something very different from "next door" in town, and the slow-moving tractor took a good ten minutes to arrive at the fields that edged Highbury House's land.

All of that time gave Beth a chance to learn that Petunia wasn't posh. She was a bona fide blue blood—the daughter of a baron's second son who had taken a modest inheritance from a beloved aunt and grown it to an incredible size.

"Papa was in banking before the war, but he works for the treasury doing something now. War bonds, probably. Mummy used to sit on the board of several charities, but she pivoted to war work as soon as Germany invaded Poland," said Petunia.

"How did you become a land girl?" Beth asked, steering toward the greenhouses at the property line.

"Do you mean why this and not the Wrens?" Petunia laughed.

Beth blushed. "I'm sorry. It's just that the navy's service is—"

"Where all the toffs like me end up," Petunia finished with a kind smile. "I like being outside."

Beth's mind immediately conjured up images of Petunia in a red jacket and jodhpurs, jumping over streams in a hunt.

"And not just riding and hunting," Petunia said, as though reading Beth's mind. "I fish, row, camp, hike. My brothers are to blame for that."

"How many brothers do you have?" Beth asked.

"Three, and they're each as infuriating and wonderful as the others."

"I wish I'd had a brother. Or a sister," said Beth. Things might have turned out differently if that was the case. Her parents would have still died, and she still would have gone to live with Aunt Mildred, but maybe she wouldn't have been quite so lonely.

Petunia was happily nattering away. "If I'm out of doors, I'm happy. Being a land girl seemed like the best way to make sure I could stay outside and still do my service. I think it gave Daddy a moment of pause, but Mummy is just happy I'm out of her way."

They broke through the tree line, and Petunia gasped.

"It's beautiful, isn't it?" Beth asked, a strange sense of pride filling her chest as she gazed out over the view from the edge of the lake up to the house. "I think it might be the most beautiful place I've ever seen."

"It seems a shame to tear it all up for broad beans or whatever they'll put in here," said Petunia.

They stopped behind the other tractor, and Beth killed the ignition. A few patients in bath chairs or using crutches slowly walked the grounds closer to the house, and Beth could feel their eyes on her. They were curious looks—not hostile—and she could understand why. They didn't see women driving huge tractors every day.

She started to climb down from the cab when a man's outstretched hand, an exposed shirt cuff, no jacket, appeared. She looked over her shoulder and found Captain Hastings grinning up at her.

"You look as though you have the matter well in hand, but I thought I would give my assistance. Just in case," he said.

Her work at Temple Fosse Farm had kept her in the barn and out of the fields, so it had been a solid week since they'd last spoken, and she found herself surprised at how pleased she was to see him. Pleased and . . . a little bit guilty because the last time she'd written to Colin she'd reassured him that she hardly spoke to any of the injured soldiers at Highbury House.

But when she returned Captain Hastings's grin, she couldn't help the little tug of attraction low in her stomach. She took his hand, even though she was fully capable of jumping down herself. When she hit the ground, however, he winced.

"I've hurt your shoulder," she said.

"It's nothing."

"Captain Hastings."

"The day I let a pesky injury dampen my gallantry, I shall have to give up, Miss Pedley," he said.

"Well, we can't have that. Petunia," she said, turning to her new friend, "this is Captain Hastings. He sometimes walks out along Mr. Penworthy's fields and stops for a chat."

"Lovely name," he said.

Petunia looked him up and down and then laughed. "It's a terrible name, but it's mine."

"What brings the land girls to Highbury House today?" he asked.

Beth sobered. "We're to tear up the gardens."

His brows shot up. "Really?"

"The land has been requisitioned," said Petunia.

She frowned. "You seem surprised."

He used his good hand to rub at the back of his neck. "Not surprised, per se. It's only that I saw Mrs. Symonds this morning after she returned from London. She mentioned wanting to spend some time in the garden this afternoon after helping some of the men with their letters home."

Beth's brow furrowed. "Landowners are supposed to receive a notice that their land has been requisitioned, aren't they?"

"They are," said Captain Hastings.

"What if Mr. Jones is wrong? What if he's overstepping his bounds? Mrs. Symonds needs to know," she said in a rush, her thoughts racing. But she couldn't slow down. If there was a chance to preserve this beautiful place for just a little longer, she had to try.

"Thank you, Captain Hastings." Beth turned to Petunia. "Do your best to stall Mr. Jones. Ask lots of questions. Be a pest."

"That shouldn't be too difficult for me. Where are you going?" Petunia called after her.

"To find Mrs. Symonds!"

Beth couldn't just burst into Highbury House demanding to see the lady of the manor. Mrs. Symonds didn't know her from Adam.

But one person did.

When Beth flung the kitchen door open, Stella swung around and a wooden spoon clattered to the counter next to her. The cook pressed a hand to her heart. "Goodness me, I thought we were being invaded."

Beth gasped for breath. "You are. We need to find Mrs. Symonds right now."

"Mrs. Symonds?"

"Where is she? I have to talk to her."

"You haven't even met her."

"Stella!" she cried. "The land girls are here to tear apart Mrs. Symonds's garden."

Stella whipped off her apron so fast it tugged her scarf off her hair. "Come with me."

Tugging her by the hand, Stella led her up a flight of servants' stairs and through a door hidden in the paneling, into a large entryway papered in chinoiserie. Plush emerald-green carpet dampened their footfalls as they rushed past a grandfather clock chiming eleven.

"We'll try the wards," said Stella over her shoulder.

"Which one?"

Stella skidded to a stop in front of a nurse and demanded, "Mrs. Symonds, where is she?"

"Ward B," the nurse said, pointing over her shoulder before her eyes fell on Beth's boots. "She can't go in there."

"What if I take my boots off?" Beth asked.

The nurse hesitated just long enough for Beth to clumsily toe the boots off and stumble behind Stella through a large door.

"Miss!" the nurse shouted behind them.

Ward B had clearly once been a drawing room, but it had been stripped of most of its features save a large chandelier. About a dozen men sat in their beds, some in arm slings like Captain Hastings, some with legs propped up in plaster casts. Sitting at a typewriter on a little table was a lady wearing a dark green dress with a black Peter Pan collar.

"Mrs. Symonds," Stella called.

The woman looked up—and so did every soldier and nurse in the ward.

"Miss Adderton, what are you doing in here?" Mrs. Symonds asked, her fingers still on the typewriter's keys. The young man in the bed next to her, whose hand was wrapped in plaster, looked on with interest.

"I'm sorry, Mrs. Symonds, but there is something urgent that Miss Pedley must tell you," said Stella.

Beth stepped forward, all too aware that she was standing in her thick socks.

"Miss Pedley?" Mrs. Symonds prompted, her tone managing to be at once firm and tired.

"I'm sorry to disturb you, Mrs. Symonds. It's just, I'm a land girl," she started.

"Yes, I gathered as much," said Mrs. Symonds.

"This morning, we were told to make our way to Highbury House," she said.

Mrs. Symonds's chin jerked. "Why?"

"Mr. Jones said that your land has been requisitioned. There are tractors at the foot of the lawn right now," she said.

"That's absurd. He can't simply drive over here and start tearing up my gardens. I haven't had a requisition order," said Mrs. Symonds.

"Beth says he has one," said Stella.

"Mr. Jones is going to start any moment, if he hasn't already. He wants the land readied and planted within a week."

"Mrs. Symonds, I can see them," called a man who'd shimmied up in bed to peer out of the window behind him.

"Second Lieutenant Wilkes, sit down!" a nurse bellowed.

"Only trying to help," the man muttered.

Mrs. Symonds pushed away from the typewriter. "Take me to Mr. Jones, please, Miss Pedley."

Relief washed over her. "Yes, Mrs. Symonds."

· DIANA ·

*I*n the months after Murray's death, Diana learned what a powerful motivator fury could be. Mixed with grief, it had propelled
her through those darkest days when the government carted in white-
enameled bed frames and mattresses, surgical equipment and bath
chairs.

As she flew out of the west drawing room, fury fueled Diana again. Behind
her, she could hear Miss Adderton and the land girl rushing to keep pace.

In the grand entryway in the center of the house, she spotted Mrs.
Dibble speaking with Matron.

"Mrs. Dibble," she called. "I need yesterday's post—both deliveries—
and this morning's as well!"

"Yes, Mrs. Symonds. I'll just fetch it," said the housekeeper.

"Now, Mrs. Dibble!" she shouted.

From the scuffle behind her, Diana caught the words "garden" and
"requisitioned." Fists balled tight, she pushed out of the French doors to
the veranda.

The roaring of an engine from down by the lake quickened her pace, and
she raced down the great lawn, past the reflecting pool, to where a crowd
of olive-and-brown-clad land girls were clustered around a tractor. On top
sat red-faced Mr. Jones glaring at a uniformed man with his arm in a sling
who half lay in the mouth of the tractor's huge metal scoop, looking for all
the world as though he was stretched out on a sofa in the midmorning sun.

"Mr. Jones!" she shouted up at the farmer as she approached.

Mr. Jones shoved the brim of his flat cap on his forehead and squinted at her. "Brought the cavalry with you, have you, Mrs. Symonds?"

She glanced over her shoulder to see Miss Adderton, Miss Pedley, Cynthia, and Matron behind her. A dozen yards back, Mrs. Dibble huffed and puffed, waving a white envelope in her hand.

"I think, perhaps, my work here is done," said the officer, who slid out of the scoop gracefully.

"What is your name?" Diana asked.

"Captain Graeme Hastings, at your service, madam," he said, bowing as best he could.

"Thank you, Captain Hastings," she said. "Mr. Jones, I have received no requisition order for my land, so I would like very much to know what you are doing on my property."

The man reached into his jacket pocket, pulled out a folded piece of paper, and held it out.

"Do you expect me to climb up there to fetch it?" she asked.

Chagrined, the farmer came down from his tractor's seat. "There you are, ma'am. You can read it there, clear as day."

He was right. Typed out in orderly lines was the agricultural requisition of all unused land at Highbury House.

Her garden. One of the few things that was still her own—which she'd done her very best to maintain throughout this bloody war—and they were going to take it away from her.

"I'm just following orders," said Mr. Jones.

Mrs. Dibble, out of breath and sweaty, handed Diana the envelope she'd waved across the lawn at her. Slowly Diana broke the flap and pulled out her copy of the order.

"It was in yesterday morning's post," said the housekeeper.

"I see." But then, what difference would twenty-four hours have made? There was no fighting the war effort.

Trying her best to calm her shaking hand, she folded up Mr. Jones's copy of the letter and handed it back to him. "I understand that the great lawn must be sacrificed."

He tucked the order back into his jacket pocket. "Aye, and the garden must go."

"No," she said firmly. "Not the garden rooms."

"Diana, be reasonable. An order is an order," her sister-in-law admonished. "You can keep your kitchen garden, I'm sure."

"I'm being very reasonable. The gardens are useful and are *used*. They are not to be torn up," she said.

"What good are flowers in a war?" Mr. Jones asked.

She pulled her shoulders back. "They're for the men."

"For the men?" he repeated.

"Yes," she said. "They're therapeutic."

"I, for one, could not agree more with Mrs. Symonds," said Captain Hastings, stepping to her side. "I can attest to the healing effects of nature after the battlefield."

"Captain Hastings is right," said Matron. Diana glanced over her shoulder, but the head nurse wore the same stern look she always did—only this time, it appeared they were on the same side. "We are dealing with men who have been through some of the worst things imaginable. They find peace in the garden. It is an escape, if only for a little time."

"Really," Diana heard her sister-in-law mutter.

"You would not want to deprive a healing man of his chance to be at peace, would you, Mr. Jones?" Diana asked.

The farmer frowned and shook his head. "The requisition order—"

"That land is used. The order is for unused land. If a second set comes in ordering me to rip out the gardens, so be it. For now, you may have the lawn," she said.

After glancing at all the expectant faces watching him, Mr. Jones grunted. "I've got my own orders about how much I need to plant. It won't be enough land with just the lawn. I'll need that, too," he said, pointing to the long border.

Diana hesitated, but she knew that if Mr. Jones didn't produce what was expected of him, he'd have to report why, which could bring the government to Highbury House to investigate.

She gave a curt nod. "You may take the long border and the lawn. Nothing more."

After a moment, Mr. Jones shouted over his shoulder, "All right, then. Back to work, ladies!"

As soon as Mr. Jones's back was turned, Diana let out a long breath. The gardens were safe for now.

"Thank you, Captain Hastings," she said.

"It was nothing," he said, dipping his head. "It seemed a shame to lose such beauty, even if the cause is a good one."

"Matron, I appreciate your support as well," said Diana.

"I meant what I said. The gardens do help the men," said Matron.

"Then please, encourage them to use the gardens. And if any of them have a mind to take up a pair of secateurs, I would be happy to put them to work," she said.

Matron nodded. "I'm sure there are some who would be willing and able."

"Miss Pedley, I cannot thank you enough for what you've done today. The gardens mean a great deal to me." Diana paused, fighting down the lump in her throat. "Please feel free to avail yourself of them whenever you choose."

"Oh, I couldn't—"

"Beth is an artist," Miss Adderton cut in.

Diana raised a brow. "Is that right?"

"I just do little sketches here and there. Nothing more than that," said Miss Pedley.

"She did a drawing of me on the back of a piece of cardboard, quick as you like. I couldn't believe it. It looked just like me," said Miss Adderton.

"I only dabble," Miss Pedley insisted.

"I hope you're not going to be one of those women who refuse to believe in her own talents," said Diana.

Don't do what I did.

The younger woman's lips opened a fraction, but she shook her head.

"Good," said Diana.

You didn't refuse to believe. You gave it all up.

"Miss Adderton, I believe you have responsibilities in the kitchen," she added.

She didn't stay to hear her cook's reply. Instead, she made a straight line back up the beautiful green lawn that wouldn't see out another summer to the house. She stuffed her hands in the pockets of her long cardigan. She couldn't stop them shaking.

She was nearly to the sanctuary of the little suite of rooms that were still her own when she spotted Father Devlin on a bath chair, his injured leg stretched out in front of him and his crutches resting nearby.

"You might be able to give a general a lesson or two with that show of force, Mrs. Symonds," he said by way of greeting.

"How do you know what that was all about?" she asked, carefully drawing her hands out of her pockets.

He gestured to the lawn. "It's rather too easy to put two and two together, unfortunately. A vast stretch of lawn like this was bound to be gobbled up for agriculture at some point. The land girls and the tractors confirmed my suspicion."

"Yes, well, most of the gardens can stay. At least there's that," she said.

"It matters a great deal to you," he said.

She could feel her shoulders bunch. "The men use them."

"It's about more than that, isn't it, Mrs. Symonds?" When she didn't reply, he gestured to the empty bath chair next to him. "Please, do sit."

"You realize you're inviting me to sit in my own home," she pointed out.

"Haven't you ever wished that someone would give you permission to rest for a moment?" he asked.

Her chest constricted. Why did a notion so simple cut so deeply? Why did the idea that someone might see straight to the angry, bitter center of her frighten her so much?

"I can't stop," she said as she sat. "Highbury needs me."

"Highbury is a house," he said.

"Robin needs me," she said.

"Robin does need you, but he is far from a neglected little boy."

"He's been sick before."

"And yet I saw him just the other day running with Bobby Reynolds. At this rate, you may one day find him captaining the rugby team at school."

"I'm not sending him away to school."

"No?" the chaplain asked. "Well, either way, I think we both know that Robin is not the reason that you raced down the lawn this morning."

She threw him a hard look. "Then what is it?"

"What do you think it is?"

Murray.

She hadn't been sure that she would love Highbury House, so far away from her few friends, her parents, her beloved harp teacher. But while she'd been hesitant to move, Murray had insisted it would be best to raise their future children in the countryside. He would commute to his surgery in London. She would stay in the countryside, making their home beautiful.

"You won't need to worry about a thing, darling," he'd cooed in her ear, arms wrapped around her from behind, his chin tucked on her shoulder. "Think of all the space we'll have. A nursery for our children. Rooms for guests. And you can have a music room for your harp, all your own. You'll fall in love with it."

She'd twisted at her vanity chair, her hair half unpinned, and kissed him. Then she'd said yes.

He'd been right. She had fallen in love with Highbury House. It had been impossible not to during those first beautiful summer days. They would take a blanket and a stack of cushions into the winter garden to escape the building works. They called it their garden, and she could almost believe that they were the only ones who knew about it. He would lazily comb her hair with his fingers, undoing all of the careful work her pin curls had done the night before, but she hardly cared.

"What do you know of the garden?" she'd ask him once.

"Only what I've found in the papers in the study."

She flipped over onto her stomach, looping her hand around his neck to bring his lips to hers. "Tell me," she murmured against his lips.

He kissed her. She could have lost herself in his kisses. Now she spent her days wishing she had.

When he pulled back, he let his hand linger to the top of her stocking. "Once upon a time—"

She laughed. "Is this a fairy tale?"

"Who is telling this story?" he asked, playfully snapping the ribbon of her garter.

"You are. I apologize."

"Once upon a time," he started again, "there was a woman named Venetia who was a very talented gardener. She was hired by my grandfather . . ."

The story went on, and Diana's attention waned as her husband stroked her hair once again until she was asleep with her head in his lap.

When Murray died, she put away the two keys to the winter garden—their garden—in a dish on the mantel in the library. She couldn't bring herself to enter it. John Hillock, the gardener, or later one of the boys from the village, would ask Mrs. Dibble to retrieve one of the keys so they could tidy it. Then they would lock it up tightly and return the key, and she would once again turn her back.

"Grief can be a powerful thing," Father Devlin said, interrupting her memories.

"I beg your pardon?"

"You are allowed to mourn your husband, Mrs. Symonds," he said.

She looked out over the lawn, to where the land girls' tractors were gouging into the earth. "Do you know how many people told me 'Blessed are those who mourn, for they shall be comforted?'"

"Matthew 5:4," he said.

"So many of those well-meaning people walked up to me at the funeral and said that. The one who didn't was Father Bilson."

"Which, I take it, is why the good vicar is still invited to dinner," said Father Devlin.

She inclined her head.

"What do you remember of your husband's funeral?" asked Father Devlin.

The feeling of being squeezed by her mother and father on one side and Cynthia on the other. Trapped in the pew with everyone watching her, she'd wanted to race out of the church because if she did, maybe she could run fast enough to escape it all.

"We all rose at the end, and I had to walk out first. My father put his hand under my elbow to help me stand. I could barely feel my legs, but somehow I put one foot in front of the other. Then, halfway down the aisle, I couldn't move."

"You were in shock," Father Devlin said softly.

She shook her head. "It happened to me at my wedding as well. I was walking on my father's arm, and suddenly I froze. All of those people were looking at me."

"At your wedding, they were happy for a young bride. At your husband's funeral, they were sad for the pain they thought you must be feeling," he said.

"Those people didn't know anything of how I was feeling." The words came out fierce and bitter. "They wanted to see me break. To see the widow sobbing in her parents' arms, so helpless because her husband is dead."

"I'm sure that no one thought that," said the chaplain.

Her laugh stuck dry in her throat. "Then you have more faith in people than I do, Father. I didn't want to give them the satisfaction of seeing me lose control, but I froze until I felt my mother's fingers dig into my waist. She'd wrapped an arm around me so that it looked as though she was helping, but I could feel the pinch of her grip. 'You're a mother now,' she whispered in my ear. I hated her for it, but she was right. I had Robin to look after. I couldn't fall to bits, because I had my son.

"I've done everything I can to give him a normal life. He attends school with the other boys. He hardly wants, even with rationing. Nothing in this house has changed if I could help it. This will be his home one day."

Even when she'd wanted him during those miserable dinners after the funeral with only Cynthia for company, she didn't send to Nanny for him. She hadn't wanted to place the burden of her grief on her son, so she'd stuck out her chin, blinking back her tears and trying to close the yawning sadness that threatened to split her open.

"We all have to get along with it," she said, somehow unable to stop talking now that she'd begun. "I'm no different from my school friend Marcella, who lost her husband in a U-boat attack, or the wife of my cousin, whose plane was reported missing over France."

"You may well be right about that, Mrs. Symonds, but remember that you do not have to carry the burden of all of Highbury on your shoulders."

She stood abruptly. "I do not need you to tell me what I should or should not do. Good day, Father Devlin."

He didn't protest as she disappeared through the door.

· VENETIA ·

WEDNESDAY, 3 APRIL 1907
Highbury House
Overcast

Matthew Goddard is proving to be a man of his word. Today he drove to Highbury House to take me to visit Mr. Johnston's Hidcote Manor.

My delight at an outing to meet another gardener was dampened by Mrs. Melcourt, who stood at the front door, watching her brother hand me into his old but serviceable gig. Mrs. Melcourt's mouth pinched as Mr. Goddard climbed up and flicked the reins, and off we went.

We rode through the Gloucestershire countryside, where the black-thorn and wych elm were blooming in the hedgerow. At Hidcote Manor, we were greeted by a stable hand who held the horse steady while we dismounted. Another man, older and graying at the temples, explained that Mr. Johnston was with his estate manager but would join us shortly if we would like to begin walking the grounds.

We walked slowly, Mr. Goddard leaving me mostly in silence to study the garden unfolding under Mr. Johnston's direction. But when he asked questions, they were intelligent, pointed. He may have claimed to lack a creative spirit, but he had an eye and seemed to understand the structure of the new garden.

Snow was still mounded in the shade thrown from trees lining the fields as we reached the place where the cultivated garden gave way to countryside. A biting wind whipped the hem of my wool coat, and I settled my knitted muffler a little closer around my neck.

"Are you too cold?" asked Mr. Goddard, a furrow etching in his brow.

"I've weathered worse," I said with a smile before turning at the crack of a breaking twig behind us.

"Hullo, Goddard," called the man in a flat American accent.

"Johnston." Mr. Goddard clasped hands with the man before turning to me. "Miss Smith, may I have the pleasure of introducing Mr. Johnston."

"The pleasure is mine, sir," I said, holding out my hand.

"Welcome to Hidcote Manor, Miss Smith." He seemed impervious to the cold, although his clothing was far too neat for him to have come from gardening, so perhaps he hadn't had the chance to chill to the bone yet.

"What you're building here is beautiful," I said.

"It is quite the change from before. Hidcote had a small garden, but what you see was mostly field," said Mr. Johnston as we began to walk back in the direction of the house. "One day, I hope this area will be a wilderness of sorts. All carefully planned, of course," he added with a smile.

"Creating a fantasy of nature is part of the gardener's role," I said.

"Precisely," said Mr. Johnston. "And you have Goddard, who is more interested in the science of plants than their beauty."

"You judge me too harshly," Mr. Goddard protested good-naturedly. "To study a plant is to understand its beauty fundamentally. Learning how two roses might cross and create something more beautiful and hardier is a revelation."

Mr. Johnston turned to me conspiratorially. "You should ask him to show you his greenhouses."

"Mr. Goddard has already been kind enough to invite me to Wisteria Farm," I said.

Mr. Johnston's eyebrows rose. "Is that so?"

"Miss Smith has taken on the burden of my sister's request to incorporate some of my roses into her design," Mr. Goddard said.

"It's no burden," I said quickly. It's true. I enjoy his company and the way he seems unable to contain his excitement for what fascinates him.

Even more, I enjoy his easy manner. He doesn't treat me as though I'm made of bone china or an oddity playing at being a gardener.

Whether Mr. Johnston thought anything of this exchange, I couldn't tell. Instead, he said, "Tell me about your plans for Highbury House."

I described the grounds to him, and he smiled when I mentioned the reflecting pool.

"And the plantings?" he asked.

"Loose and natural, as though the garden sprung up fully formed out of nowhere," I said, running my fingers over the broad leaves of a hydrangea. "Highbury's rooms will all be characterized by a repetition of plants to create borders, but I don't wish for it to feel too formal. For instance, I would plant this *Hydrangea aspera* Villosa in the poet's garden or around the edges of the water garden, where it might receive a little shade. In twenty years, it should cast its own shade. Who knows what might spring up beneath it?"

"Certain plants that will shoot up like weeds given the right soil," agreed Mr. Johnston.

A man waved to Mr. Johnston from nearer to the house.

"Please excuse me, but I see I'm needed," said Mr. Johnston. "Please feel free to roam at will. I know you're in good hands with Goddard, but I hope you'll find me before you leave."

"I'm very happy you brought me here," I said as Hidcote's owner walked briskly away.

"It's me who should be thanking you, Miss Smith," Mr. Goddard said as he tucked my hand into the crook of his arm.

I laughed. "What do you have to thank me for? I've done nothing."

"You've given me the one thing I wanted."

My breath caught when our eyes met, an intensity I hadn't seen before in his dark blue eyes. "What is that?"

"An afternoon with you."

"Mr. Goddard—"

He covered my hand with his, squeezing it gently. "I just wanted you to know. Nothing else. Now, shall we walk back to the house?"

· EMMA ·

I know, Mum," said Emma, her phone clutched in her hand so hard her knuckles ached.

"I just don't understand. Did you do something wrong?" her mother asked for the third time in ten minutes.

"Eileen," Dad said in that tone he always used when Mum was being particularly outrageous.

"It's a hiring freeze. They happen all the time," she said as she turned onto Bridge Street and crossed the Tach Brook, which was running high from the spring rains.

"Are you upset, Emma?" Dad asked.

Was she? Her pride was wounded, she couldn't deny that. And neither could she ignore the temptations of working for a foundation rather than herself: security, benefits, a regular paycheck, time off for holidays. She had none of those things right now, but she did have Turning Back Thyme.

"Emma?" her father prompted.

She shifted her canvas bag full of groceries higher on her shoulder. "I'm thinking," she said.

"I could phone Bethany," said Mum. "She's very high and mighty these days and doesn't always remember that we grew up on the same block in Croydon, but I think her cousin's husband plays golf with the executive director at the Royal Botanical Heritage Society."

"No thanks, Mum. If they don't have the budget, it's not going to help. Besides, I'm months away from finishing the job at Highbury," she said. And months away from being able to take on more work. If only she could clone herself so that she could work two jobs at the same time . . .

A motorcycle sped by, its engine gunning.

"Where are you?" Dad asked.

"Just walking home," she said.

"Home?" Mum asked.

"Bow Cottage," she corrected herself.

"Good, because for a moment there it sounded like—"

"Oh, leave her alone, Eileen," Dad said with a laugh. Emma could imagine him playfully nudging his wife.

"All I'm saying is that if you're going to settle down, make it somewhere near London or Surrey, Emma. Not the Midlands," said Mum.

"I'm less than ten miles from the M40, which is a straight shot into London," she argued. "It could be Inverness, like my last job."

"Scotland," her mother practically gasped. "This is all Charlie's fault."

She rolled her eyes as the shops of Highbury came into view. "Charlie hasn't lived in Scotland for as long as I've known him. Besides, no one is settling down anywhere."

"She knows she's being ridiculous," said her father, his voice richer now and clearly off speakerphone.

"I am not!" Emma could hear Mum insist in the background.

"She *is* being ridiculous," Emma said.

She could hear her father walking through to another room. "It's just that she remembers what it was like to worry about money. That's why she pushed you so hard to go to university."

"And instead I got my qualifications at the Royal Horticultural Society," she said, remembering those arguments all too well. "I would have been miserable at university."

"I know. Just like I know that your mother means well," Dad said.

She sighed. "I know she does."

"You're a good daughter," he said.

"You two could come up sometime and see Highbury. You might like it," she said.

"I don't know if your mother would feel more or less worried if that happens."

"That would have really bothered me when I was in my early twenties," she said.

"And now?" he asked.

"Now I think that I'm an adult and I can set boundaries, and Mum can respect them." For the most part.

"Smart girl," said Dad.

At a tap on Emma's shoulder, she turned around to see Henry dressed in a black T-shirt with *Jones & Cropper & Steinberg & Jackson.* written on it. He gave her a little wave.

"Dad? Why don't I call you back tomorrow? We can talk more about a visit," she suggested.

"Anytime, love," he said.

"Sorry to interrupt," said Henry as she ended the call.

"I was just catching my parents up on a few things," she said. "I don't understand your T-shirt."

He looked down. "It's Booker T. and the M.G.s," he said, as though it was the most obvious thing in the world.

"Ah." She made a mental note to look it up when she got home.

"Are you close to your parents?" he asked.

"For the most part, although Mum drives me crazy most of the time. She constantly worries I'm putting my entire life into a company that is on the brink of folding."

"Is it?" he asked.

She huffed a laugh. "No, but she wasn't exactly thrilled when I told her I was training to be a garden designer. Or a few years later when I decided to start my own business," she said.

"What did she think you should do?" he asked.

She shrugged. "Not a clue. She worked as a receptionist for a solicitor for a while, so she was pretty hung up on me becoming a solicitor when I was a teenager."

"Children disappointing their parents is practically tradition."

"Isn't farming the same business your father was in?" she asked.

"Have you ever seen that Monty Python sketch where the playwright father rages at his son for deciding to be a coal miner?"

"Sure. It spoofs pretty much every novel D. H. Lawrence ever wrote," she said.

He nodded. "That was Dad."

"So your father wanted you to do anything except for farming . . ."

"Which is why, rebel that I am, that's all I could imagine doing." He gestured behind him. "Are you coming in?"

"Coming in?" She looked up to see the sign for the White Lion.

"I thought that maybe you'd given in to Sydney this week," he explained.

"I would love to," she said, surprised that she actually would. "But I've got these with me." She held up her bag of groceries.

"Anything perishable?" he asked.

"A pint of milk and some Greek yogurt," she said.

"Come with me." He was halfway to the pub door before he turned and said, "If you want."

Emma hesitated a moment. She had a budget spreadsheet to update, sculpture-repair vendors to contact. And she should probably open the email from her accountant she'd been avoiding all day. But when she saw Henry holding open the pub door for her, she realized that going home to an empty cottage simply didn't sound appealing.

Inside, the pub was hot, people all squeezed around round tables and high stools. On each table, a piece of paper and pencil sat waiting amid sweating drinks. She couldn't see Sydney and Andrew through the wall of people.

When Henry reached the bar, he leaned in and shouted over a Little Mix song, "What are you having?"

"A pint, please," she shouted.

He stuck out his hand. "Give me your shopping."

She frowned but handed him the canvas bag just as the bartender, an older woman with a deep tan, heavy black eyeliner, and long black clip-in extensions, sidled over.

"Harry, are you up to no good?" the woman asked.

"I certainly hope so. Dinah, this is Emma Lovell. She's working on restoring Sydney and Andrew's garden," said Henry.

Dinah stuck her hand out over the bar. "Any friend of Sydney and Andrew is welcome at the White Lion, but be careful of this one." Dinah nodded to Henry. "I've been throwing him out of this pub since he was fourteen."

"I'll keep that in mind," said Emma, tucking her hair back behind her ears.

"Give us two pints, would you?" Henry asked.

Dinah picked up a pint glass and began to pull cask ale with a practiced ease. "You're staying for the quiz?"

"Apparently I am," she said.

"Lucy is starting in a few minutes," said Dinah, putting down a full glass in front of Emma.

"Would you mind sticking this in the fridge in the back, Dinah?" Henry asked, handing over the groceries. When Dinah gave him a look, he added, "They're Emma's, not mine."

"For Emma, I'm happy to," said Dinah, depositing another pint in front of Henry. "That'll be eight pounds fifty."

Before Emma could move, Henry had paid for the drinks. She was going to protest, but Dinah said, "Let him. It'll be his penance for when he insists that he has the right answer and costs you the win."

"If you're sure you don't mind," said Emma.

"He doesn't. Don't be shy about asking for your groceries whenever. This lot can wait a few minutes for drinks," said Dinah before peeling off to the back.

"I like her," said Emma, taking a sip of her ale.

"I'm legally required to like her. She's my aunt. I read some P. G. Wodehouse for my A levels. When Bertie Wooster called his aunt Agatha 'the nephew-crusher,' I knew exactly what he meant. Come on, let's see if we can get through this crowd."

Henry dropped his shoulder and pushed through as Emma did her best not to spill her drink or wing someone with her cross-body bag. When the crowd opened up, she found herself in front of Sydney, Andrew, and two others at a low table.

"Hi!" Sydney cried, jumping up and nearly knocking over her gin goblet. "I didn't know you were coming."

"I captured her just in front of the pub and dragged her in," said Henry.

"Welcome," said Andrew.

"Here, take a seat and I'll introduce you around," said Sydney, pulling her bag off an empty seat.

"Thanks," said Emma.

"This is Jaya Singh. She's the head of events for the Priory in Temple Kinton, just down the road," said Sydney.

Emma shook hands with the woman who, despite her youthful appearance, had a striking head of salt-and-pepper hair.

"And this is Colby Powell. He's a professor at the University of Warwick," said Sydney.

"I'm what they call a pinch hitter in the States," said Colby.

"Colby's our resident American," said Jaya.

"It's lovely to meet you both," said Emma.

"Ladies, gentlemen, and others," a voice came over the microphone, "we're ready to begin." The noise in the pub fell to a dull hubbub, and a woman onstage raised her brows. "That's much better. I've had the misfortune of knowing most of you my entire life, but for those I haven't met, I'm Lucy MacFarlane, and I'll be your quiz master." Hoots and hollers from the crowd. "Enough of that now. You all know pub quizzes are serious business. If you'll sharpen your pencils, our first round will be Sport."

Andrew groaned, and Sydney pulled the paper closer to her. "Colby and I have this, unless you have a secret bank of sports knowledge you're ready to unleash on all of us, Emma."

"I watch a bit of football, and Dad pretends to like cricket," she said.

"Excellent. My husband is mad about cricket, but he's away on business," said Jaya.

"I'll do my best," Emma said.

Andrew touched the rim of her glass with his. "With a team name like 'Menace to Sobriety,' that's all any of us can hope for."

* * *

Menace to Sobriety lost.

Badly.

"I can't believe Artificial Intelligence won again," Sydney groused as she, Emma, Andrew, and Henry walked down Church Street. Colby, who'd nursed one glass of wine, had left them at the bar to drive back to his house near the university, and Jaya had waved them goodbye from the front door of her cottage on Heather Lane. Bow Cottage was on the same side of the village as the road to Highbury House, so Emma was getting an escort home. Strangely, she found that she didn't mind.

"You say that every time," said Andrew, pressing a kiss to Sydney's forehead.

"But this time we had Emma. We were *supposed* to win," said Sydney, flashing the soft smile of a tipsy woman at her. "You did *very well*. We wouldn't have made it through the geology round without you."

"That is a fact," said Henry, who had been walking quietly by her side.

"And French literature," Andrew pointed out.

"That was a fluke of my A levels. Anyone who says they like *L'Etranger* is just being pretentious," she said, her lips loosened by a third pint Andrew had insisted on buying her.

Sydney pointed to her husband. "That's Andrew's favorite book."

"Not everyone," she said quickly. "What I meant to say was people who brag about reading it in the original. Like Proust."

"He just finished reading the final volume of *Remembrance of Things Past*. In French," Sydney added.

There was a beat when Emma vowed to whichever saint protected gardeners when Sydney, Andrew, and Henry all burst out laughing.

"Oh, you should see the look on your face!" said Sydney, buckling over.

"The way you said it," Henry howled.

"I'm so sorry, Andrew," Emma said.

"It's all true, and I do brag about it, even though it's pretentious," said Andrew graciously.

She pressed her palm to her forehead. "I feel like an idiot."

"We all say things we don't mean from time to time," said Sydney, slinging an arm over Emma's shoulder.

Even though she knew she should shift out from under Sydney's arm for a number of reasons, ranging from boundaries to professionalism, she didn't. A long dormant part of her craved the platonic touch of friendship.

"Anyway, you're not getting off the pub quiz team that easily. We'll need you next week," said Sydney.

"Jaya's husband will be back," Emma pointed out.

"Which will only be helpful if we get an entire round of cricket questions," Henry countered.

"The last time that happened, half the teams registered complaints," said Andrew.

When Emma glanced at Henry, he explained, "We heckled the quiz master."

Sydney slowed to a stop at a fork in the road. "This is us. Henry?"

"I'm going to walk Emma home," Henry said.

"That's not necessary," said Emma. "It makes more sense for you to go with Sydney and Andrew."

"I insist. Indulge me as I pretend to be a gentleman," he said with a smile.

She thought about protesting but let him have his way.

After Sydney and Andrew waved them off, she and Henry turned in the direction of Bow Cottage.

"You really didn't have to do this," she said, breaking the silence.

"Actually, I had some news for you. I've finally had some time to go through Nan's old papers. I found some of those sketchbooks you were looking for."

"Are there sketches of the garden?" she asked hopefully.

The corners of his mouth tipped up. "Sketches of the garden. Some details of plants. Some of the soldiers as well."

"I'd love to see them."

"I could drop them by your place," he said.

She hesitated, but then nodded. "I'd like that."

"All right, then," he said. "I'll do that."

"This is me," she said when they reached Bow Cottage.

She shifted her groceries higher on her shoulder so she could reach into her handbag for her keys, but as she pulled them out she fumbled them and they fell to the pavement. She stooped to pick them up, but Henry was faster. His hand had already grasped the keys as her own hand covered his. Their eyes met, and for a moment all she could process was the sound of his breath and the slight wave of his dark hair in the nighttime breeze.

"I'm glad you came in tonight," he said softly.

"Even if it was accidental?" she asked.

"Sometimes the best occasions are accidents."

He straightened then, giving her the keys. Her hand trembled a little as she took them.

"Good night, Henry," she said.

She walked up the short garden path to her front door and managed to get it open in one go. She flicked the light on, and when she turned to close the door behind her, she saw he was still waiting, watching that she got in safely. When their eyes met, he gave her a small smile, stuffed his hands in his pockets, and turned to make his way down the lane.

· STELLA ·

*T*hin, cheap paper crinkled in Stella's hands as she read Joan's letter again. The kind postmaster, Mr. Jeffries, had brought it straight to the kitchen door when he delivered the afternoon post.

20 April 1944

Dear Estrella,

Writing doesn't come easy to me and paper's harder to come by now than ever. With the new string of air raids over London, I can't risk having Bobby back here in Bristol. The entire city is still a bomb site from earlier raids.

I need you to take him a little while longer. There's no one to look after him here. I'm working long hours at the munitions factory, and I can hardly get away before dark. Tell him that his mummy misses him very much, and I'll get up to see him quick as I can. And before you ask, no, I don't know when that will be exactly.

You asked in your last letter about money for his things. Didn't you get the money I sent you two weeks ago? Maybe there are light fingers at your post office. I've heard of employees stealing envelopes that look like they might have cash in them. You really should be more careful, Estrella.

I've been bursting to tell you, a few of us girls were invited up to a dance with some American soldiers the other night. The GIs all looked like movie stars with close-cut hair and the best teeth I've ever seen on a man. I danced the jitterbug and . . .

Stella let the letter fall to the counter. She didn't know what she'd expected from Joan, but she'd hoped not this.

It's a wonder Joan's stayed a widow for so long. The thought should have made her cringe with disloyalty to her sister, but it was the truth. Joan wouldn't end this war alone. Stella was certain of that.

But what about Bobby? Joan hadn't sent money two weeks ago, just as there'd been nothing in this letter. Each time her nephew needed something, Stella dipped into her hard-earned savings; the money she'd dreamed of using for a new life dwindled. Books? Gone was train fare to London. He lost his hat on the way to school? There went a week's dinners at a boardinghouse. A new shirt when he'd torn one climbing trees with Robin? Another correspondence course and more precious clothing coupons.

She was trying so hard to do the right thing by her nephew. He was clothed and had food. She made sure he washed up after she and Dorothy cleaned Mrs. Symonds's dinner. She could help him with his schoolwork, although she felt woefully under-equipped to keep up with the steady stream of questions that seemed to bubble out of him these days. She went through all of the motions of motherhood, but motions were all she could muster.

The slap of little shoes down the tiled corridor to the kitchen signaled the approach of her nephew. Stella quickly folded the letter and stuffed it into her pocket.

"Hello, Bobby," Mrs. George called out from the stove.

Beaming, Bobby ran to the other cook and threw his arms around her leg, so different from the frightened little boy who'd arrived at Highbury two months ago.

"Hello, Mrs. George. I saw a hedgehog today," he announced.

"Did you? In the daytime?" asked the cook, ruffling his hair and then gently pushing him away so she could go back to stirring a muddy-looking soup.

"He was walking across the lane."

"And how do you know that it wasn't a lady hedgehog?" Mrs. George asked.

The little boy looked serious. "I know."

"Hello, Bobby," Stella called across the kitchen. When he wandered over but didn't hug her as he had Mrs. George, she busied herself peeking under a tea towel at two loaves of brown bread.

"I had a letter from your mother today. She says that she misses you very much," she continued. Satisfied with the bread, she reached for the end of an old loaf and cut off a thin slice. Onto it went a scrape of margarine. She set the bread and margarine in front of Bobby, who took a huge bite.

"That's all you'll get before tea," she reminded him.

His next bite was slightly smaller. "Where is Mummy?" he asked around a mouthful of bread.

"She has to stay at home because she has a job at the factory," Stella said, feeling the weight of all of her sister's blasé words in her pocket.

"But why can't she work here?" he asked.

"She has a very important job for the war," she said. Joan would love hearing her say that.

"I want to help."

"It's too dangerous even for big boys like you," she said.

His eyes went wide, brimming with tears.

"Will Mummy be hurt?" he asked in a tiny voice.

Oh Lord, she'd put her foot in it now. She reached her arms around him awkwardly. "She's not in danger."

"I want her here!" he wailed.

"She can't be, Bobby," she said.

"But there are bombs!"

She pulled back, shocked. "Why do you think there would be bombs?"

She could sense that Miss Grant and Miss Parker across the room were doing their very best to appear that they weren't paying attention. At least Mrs. George had the grace to watch this exchange openly, her arms crossed under her bosom.

"One of the boys at school said that the Germans blew up London and they blew up Covertee." Bobby sobbed into her chest.

"Coventry," she corrected. When she caught Mrs. George's look of disapproval, she added, "What a horrid thing for that boy to say."

"He said Mummy's going to be bombed." He continued to cry.

Mrs. George shook her head in disgust at the other boy's cruelty, and Stella took comfort in knowing that at least on this front they were united.

"Bobby." She laid a soft hand on his head. "I promise you that nothing bad is going to happen to your mother." *Joan's far too lucky for that.* "In the meantime, you get to live here. Don't you like it at Highbury House?"

His tears soaked her shirtfront as he moved his tiny head in a nod.

"You get to play with Master Robin and all his nice toys." When he peeled himself away from her chest, she nearly winced at the river of tears and snot on her clothes. She wanted to run straight upstairs to change, but instead she pulled out a much-laundered handkerchief and wiped his face.

"He's nice," said her nephew in a whisper.

"I think your mum wants you to have the best time at Highbury House so that when you go back home, you have all of these wonderful memories. Don't you?"

"Yes."

She leaned down so they were eye level. "So there will be no more crying today?"

He nodded.

"Good. Now, would you like another slice of bread?" she asked, although she could hardly imagine that the mealy bread would ever tempt anyone except for a five-year-old who'd never known soft white flour and well-risen loaves.

"Can I have jam, too?" He looked up at her through his lashes.

Despite herself, she snorted a laugh. "Cheeky monkey, yes you can. But just this once."

She went to fetch the jam jar from the high shelf of the pantry—far away from little hands. Bobby knew how rare jam on his bread was. She hadn't had more than a taste of it herself in nearly two years. The sugar was far too dear, and twice she'd found that the small Symonds family's ration coupons didn't add up to enough for the harvest's canning, let alone other needs.

When she came back, she found Bobby quizzing Miss Parker about hedgehogs, befuddling the young woman from Leeds who'd likely never seen one of the creatures before coming to Warwickshire.

Stella cut another thin slice of bread and twisted off the top of the jam jar. She was just looking around for a butter knife when one slid across the worktable to her. She looked up to see Mrs. George, who was . . . smiling.

"That was very well done, Miss Adderton," said the other woman.

I don't know what I'm doing! Stella wanted to shout. *Tell me what to do!*

"It will get easier with time," Mrs. George continued.

"I'm not his mother," she said.

Mrs. George shook her head. "You're the closest thing that boy has right now."

Stella accepted the knife without a word.

As soon as Bobby was finished with his second snack, she shooed him out of the kitchen to go play and set about putting together Mrs. Symonds's tea tray. Although there were fresh tea leaves for the pot, there hadn't been much flour, so Stella had had to resort to oatmeal scones made with drippings. The last time she'd baked scones with butter had been Christmas Day.

Stella carefully carried the tray up the servants' stairs. Really, Dorothy or Mrs. Dibble should bring it, but both were preoccupied with the laundry, which had become impossible to send out with so many washerwomen conscripted and the hospital overwhelming those who remained.

Delicately putting one foot in front of the other, she navigated the corridor past what had once been the double drawing room and the dining room until she stopped at the morning room door. She knocked and then pushed open the door, as Mrs. Dibble had taught her.

"Is that tea, Miss Adderton?" Mrs. Symonds asked from the cluster of chairs where she sat with Miss Cynthia, Matron McPherson, and a priest who was also a patient.

"Yes, Mrs. Symonds," she said.

"You may set the tray there," said Mrs. Symonds, waving a hand to the sideboard next to her. "Would any of you care for tea?"

"I would love a cup." The priest smiled at Stella as she carefully made her way around the breakfast table now serving as the family's main dining set. "What have you baked for us today, Miss Adderton?"

"Oatmeal scones," she said, thankful she'd piled the small plate high.

"How delightful," said the priest.

"Father Devlin, perhaps you'd like to start," said Mrs. Symonds, shooting him a bemused look.

At an almost invisible nod from her employer, Stella bobbed an approximation of a curtsy, feeling painfully old-fashioned and resenting every moment.

Before she reached the door, however, Miss Cynthia stopped her by calling out in her thin voice, "Perhaps you could help us, Mrs. . . . ?"

"Miss Adderton," Mrs. Symonds supplied, in a tone that implied her sister-in-law should know by now who cooked her meals every evening.

"Miss Adderton," said Miss Cynthia.

"If you wish," said Stella, folding her hands behind her back.

"We have rather a dilemma. Some of the nurses have asked for a dance to be held at Highbury House," said Father Devlin.

"I will not have the nurses dancing with the patients in their care," said Miss Cynthia, her tone severe.

"I believe you'll find that it's my responsibility to make that sort of decision on behalf of my nurses," said Matron.

"Surely you wouldn't begrudge the few men who are fit enough the chance to shuffle around the floor," said Father Devlin with a smile.

"It is not the shuffling I'm concerned with." Miss Cynthia crossed her hands primly over her knee. "It would be wholly inappropriate for a nurse to dance with a man under her care. Why, it could create chaos in the wards."

"There is a time and a place for a little fun. Besides, one nurse to every ten patients won't make for a good ratio," said Matron.

"But that is where Miss Adderton might come in handy. Where would we procure some young people to make up a crowd?" asked Father Devlin.

"I would like to point out that I have not yet agreed to host a dance in my home," said Mrs. Symonds.

Stella looked among the four of them, not knowing the right answer.

"You can speak your mind," said Father Devlin gently. "It's only a friendly question."

"Well, there are the land girls," Stella started. "I have a friend who says that they organize dances, and girls come from across the county for it."

The priest clapped his hands together. "Excellent idea!"

"You could also invite the men from the air base. And the WAAFs," Stella added, remembering the women serving in the Royal Air Force's auxiliary branch who worked in support roles at the base.

"If the officers from the base came as well, it would keep the men in line," said Matron.

"It could be a tea dance. There's nothing more innocent than a tea dance," said Father Devlin.

Miss Cynthia squinted at him. "I didn't think the church would approve."

"I know enough about men to understand that they are never so mischievous as when they are restless."

"Women, too," muttered Matron into the edge of her cup.

"A well-chaperoned dance will lift their spirits, and I dare say it will do much the same for your nurses, Matron McPherson," said Father Devlin.

Miss Cynthia shook her head. "No. I don't think it would be proper. I really can't have my nurses cavorting with pilots, either."

"My nurses," Matron reminded the commandant.

"I can understand why the Voluntary Aid Detachment would not want to be seen as endorsing such an activity, Cynthia," said Mrs. Symonds.

Father Devlin sighed.

"Thank you, Diana. I appreciate when someone is able to see reason," said Miss Cynthia.

Stella, who had not yet been dismissed, saw something flicker in her employer's eye when Mrs. Symonds turned to her.

"Now, if I invite the land girls to a dance at Highbury House, would your friend Miss Pedley be able to spread the word?" Mrs. Symonds asked.

Miss Cynthia's cup clattered against its saucer as she jolted. "But you just said . . ."

"I never said there wouldn't be a dance. I said that you, as the head of this convalescent hospital, might not want to endorse it. However, Highbury House is still my home, and I may still choose to organize a dance here," said Mrs. Symonds.

Miss Cynthia sucked in a breath. "I will remind you that the ballroom currently houses Ward C. I cannot authorize the removal of beds for such frivolity."

Mrs. Symonds waved her hand. "The dance will be held on the veranda. We might risk the weather a little bit, but I think the effect will be lovely. Don't you?"

Stella couldn't help the grin that spread across her face. A dance at Highbury. What a thing that would be.

"Miss Adderton, this is more Mrs. Dibble's area, but you wouldn't happen to know the level of our wine cellar reserves, would you?" Mrs. Symonds asked.

Father Devlin laughed. "What of our tea dance?"

"When I was a deb, I never could abide tea dances. Tepid, insipid things. If I'm to throw a party, it will be a good one," said Mrs. Symonds.

Miss Cynthia was beginning to look positively pale. "The nursing staff—"

"If I might, Mrs. Symonds. I think you'll find that you could sell tickets for six pence each and donate the money to a charitable cause. Like the British Red Cross or Queen Alexandra's Royal Army Nursing Corps," said Stella.

Mrs. Symonds cut her a look, and for a moment she thought that her employer would object. Instead, the woman's face brightened.

"I think that's an excellent idea, Miss Adderton," said Mrs. Symonds.

"Very noble indeed, and one I'm sure that everyone at Highbury House would be glad to take part in," Father Devlin agreed.

Miss Cynthia leaned back in her chair, defeated. "If anything happens . . ."

"Patients and nurses are not animals, Cynthia. They will be able to control themselves through a fox-trot or two," said Mrs. Symonds.

"I will be happy to play chaperone. I won't be doing any dancing anytime soon," said Father Devlin.

"I'm sure Father Bilson and Mrs. Bilson would as well, and myself, of course," said Mrs. Symonds. "Does that satisfy you that your girls will all be well looked after, Matron?"

"It does," said Matron.

"There you have it. If you'll excuse me, ladies, some of the patients in Ward A have expressed an interest in studying the Bible together," said Father Devlin as he used his crutches and the arm of his chair to haul himself up.

Miss Cynthia rose as well, still shaking her head. Matron followed her out, a small smile on her usually stern face.

As soon as they were alone, though, Mrs. Symonds said, "You were rather helpful just then, Miss Adderton. I do enjoy a chance to beat the commandant at her own game. I'll have to ring around and find out who to speak to at the base. Please ask Miss Pedley to invite her friends."

"You meant that?" Stella asked.

Mrs. Symonds gave her a look. "Please also remind Miss Pedley that she's to use the gardens at her leisure. She can ask Mrs. Dibble to find me, and I will show her around."

"Thank you, Mrs. Symonds. I think she has been a little hesitant because she did not want to impose, but I will remind her."

A softness started to creep into her employer's expression, but just as quick, Mrs. Symonds schooled it away. "That is all. You may clear the tea tray."

Stella couldn't figure Mrs. Symonds out. The dismissal was issued as easily as the praise.

Stella resumed stacking things onto the tea tray, painfully aware that she was not as graceful or quiet as a proper maid should be. Mrs. Symonds took up a book but didn't open it. Instead, she said, "Your nephew seems to be settling in nicely."

Stella paused, the heavy tray cutting into her palms. "Yes, ma'am. Thank you for allowing him to stay."

"Robin is very fond of him," said Mrs. Symonds.

"Yes," said Stella carefully.

"They performed a play for me the other day that they wrote themselves. It was very clever. Bobby in particular is a very talented mimic."

"Oh, I hadn't realized." Bobby hadn't asked her to watch the play. Or maybe he had and she was too busy to pause. "He'll be getting the mimicry from my sister. Joan always was good at picking up the songs on the radio. She can sing just like Judy Garland or Dorothy Lamour."

"What plans does your sister have for him?"

"Plans?" she asked.

Mrs. Symonds waved a hand. "For his education? His future?"

Stella stared at her employer. Bobby was the son of a builder who'd been killed in action and a mother who seemed more interested in dancing than mothering. What did she expect for Bobby?

"I suppose he'll work after he leaves school," she finally said.

"He's a bright boy. When he's a little older, I may be able to help place him in a good school." Mrs. Symonds paused. "If his mother would like, of course."

"Thank you. I'm sure Joan would appreciate that very much," she lied. While Stella had ended up in service like her mother before her, Joan had run as far from the pull of Highbury House as she could. She doubted Joan would want anything to do with its owner after she no longer needed Mrs. Symonds's goodwill.

"That will be all, Miss Adderton. Thank you," said Mrs. Symonds, opening her book.

Stella pursed her lips, bowed her head, and left the lady to her leisure.

· VENETIA ·

THURSDAY, 25 APRIL 1907
Highbury House
Rain, rain, and more rain

I have never understood "gardeners" who refuse to garden because it is unseemly for a lady or gentleman to dirty their hands. Perhaps they don't know the thrill of plunging a trowel into spring-softened soil to toss up the sweet, earthy scent of leaves and twigs and all manner of matter. By refusing to stain their aprons, they miss the sensation of damp, fresh dirt crumbling between their fingers or breathing the fresh air deeply. They don't know the satisfaction of knocking the dust off one's clothes when retreating into the house for a well-earned cup of tea.

Then again, they also avoid the panic of being caught in a sudden, torrential rain with little cover.

Today I was alone in the poet's garden, staking out the southern border with flags tied to sticks when the heavens opened. Almost immediately, the rain soaked through my shirt and plastered it to my back and chest. I pulled my canvas hat lower on my brow as I did my best to gather up my bundle of sticks. But when a crack of lightning pierced the sky and rattled my very teeth, I dropped everything to hike up my skirts and run for my cottage.

I cut through the ramble, mud weighing down my hemline. A gust of wind tore my hat from my head before picking up my limp hair and thrusting it back in my face.

Around the corner of the cottage, I spotted a figure huddled under the little front porch.

"Mr. Goddard?" I asked, peering through the haze.

He looked at me from under his soaked hat, his grin sheepish. "Good day, Miss Smith. Lovely weather we're having, isn't it?"

"What are you doing here?" I asked.

He lifted a leather bag. "I come bearing gifts." His smile fell. "But you must come out of the rain."

He tried to step out to cede the covered space to me, but I waved him away. "I'm already soaked through. There's no point in you getting wet, too."

I took the cottage key out of my pocket and unlocked the door. "Given the circumstances, I think we would both do well to dry our boots," I said over my shoulder.

Mr. Goddard hesitated, but when I began to ease off my boots, he gingerly put his leather bag down and did the same. As he finished, I went to the woodstove to coax the dying embers back to life. When I turned back, I saw that he'd lined his boots up perfectly with mine against the wall. The sight of it rooted me to the spot. Surely I'd seen Adam's boots lined up next to mine countless times before, but this felt different.

"I could make us tea while you change."

I gave a start. "I do apologize. I'm forgetting my manners."

"I should apologize. I've barreled into your home without warning. Perhaps I should—"

"No. Please stay. And I will make the tea. This is my house, for a time, even if it sits on Mr. Melcourt's grounds." I moved for the door to the small kitchen.

He caught me gently by the elbow, bringing me to a pause in front of him. "Miss Smith, please, allow me. I can assure you, I'm not such a helpless bachelor."

The warmth of his hand through the wet fabric sent a shiver up my arm. I nodded because I didn't think I could say anything without my voice trembling.

In the privacy of my bedroom, I peeled off my wet things and hung them on the iron bed frame before dressing again. Everything felt deliciously dry and soft against my skin, from my chemise and stockings to my shirt and skirt. There was no saving my hair—not that it had been much to look at, jammed up under a hat for hours. Instead, I dragged a comb through it and tied it back with a ribbon to keep it off my face. When I finished, I felt like a girl of eighteen again, fresh and hopeful.

The kettle was whistling in the kitchen when I returned. The fire was beginning to chase off the damp of the day, but rather than sit by it, I went to the large table in the center of the room. Across it lay plans, catalogs, and correspondence.

I put on my spectacles and flipped through the plans for the gardens until I reached the detail of the poet's garden and began noting down an adjustment. A soft clearing of the throat brought me back. Mr. Goddard was standing in front of me, grasping a tea-laden tray with both hands.

"Where shall I put this?" he asked.

I quickly cleared a spot for him. Carefully, he set the tea tray down and drew up a chair.

Automatically, I began to set up cups and handle the strainer. "Do you take milk?"

"Yes, and a lump of sugar, even though Helen thinks it's terribly childish of me," he said.

I dropped the lump in for him and passed the cup over. "You should take your tea however you choose."

"That advice doesn't surprise me one bit coming from you," he said, settling back in his chair and crossing his ankle at the knee to rest the teacup on it.

"What do you mean?" I asked.

"You strike me as the sort of woman who does whatever she's set her mind to without waiting for anyone else's opinion."

I flushed. "That's not true. The very nature of my work means that I have to take a good number of people's opinions into account."

"You forget, Miss Smith, that I've watched you charm my sister and her husband."

"I didn't know that was possible," I said before I could think to stop myself.

He only laughed. "You've seen Helen's drawing room. Gilded and expensive. If she had her way, we'd be living with French knot gardens à la Louis XIV, with enormous Carrara marble fountains at the end of every sight line. And Arthur . . . I don't know that Arthur has a creative bone in his body."

"Despite his poetry?" I asked.

"You are too kind to his poetry," he said. "Arthur's garden would likely be a stretch of lawn with statuary and topiary and nothing else."

"You forget that I've given them a sculpture garden."

He studied me for a moment. "You have, and I suspect, much like the poet's garden, you've done that because you know indulging their pretentions means that you've been able to create exactly what you want otherwise. Did they ask for an all-white garden?"

I smiled into my tea and said softly, "No."

"Do you know, I've been wondering about why you've chosen the rooms that you did, and I think I've finally figured it out."

"What is that?" I asked.

"Each room represents the life of a woman. The tea garden is where polite company comes to meet, all with the purpose of marrying a girl off. The lovers' garden speaks for itself, I should think, and the bridal garden is her movement from girl to wife. The children's garden comes next. I would guess that the lavender walk represents her femininity, and the poet's garden stands for a different sort of romance than the lovers' garden." He sifted through the plans on the table and pulled free the detail of the statue garden. "Aphrodite, Athena, Hera. All of the pieces in the statue garden will be depictions of the female form. Am I right?"

I stared at him, my mouth slightly open. It was a little trick I used sometimes, weaving in a theme to the plantings, but never before had I done anything so blatant. No one had ever noticed before, yet this man had seen right to the heart of it.

"The one thing I don't understand is how the water and winter gardens fit," he said.

"I've always found water to inspire contemplation and introspection. I meant it to represent a woman's interior life."

"And the winter garden?" he asked, leaning in.

"Her death, of course."

He sat back in his chair, his cup nearly empty now. "I haven't shown you what I brought you."

He retrieved a bag stained dark brown with age and rain, and I held my breath when he opened the flap. He pulled out a bundle of muslin and began to unwrap it in his lap. When finally he was done, I could see three plants with their root structures bundled up.

"You brought me hydrangeas," I breathed.

"*Hydrangea aspera* Villosa. I overheard you mentioning that you enjoyed them when we visited Hidcote," he said, handing me one of the plants and taking his seat. "Mr. Johnston was happy to oblige in exchange for the delivery of several 'Shailer's White Moss' he is thinking of planting."

"You brought me hydrangeas," I repeated, touching one of the leaves. "Thank you."

I looked up and found him staring at me with such tenderness, my breath hitched. I'd seen that expression before, between my parents in a quiet moment when they thought no one else was watching. Never before had I thought that anyone would look at me that way, and I knew that I couldn't turn away from it without answering his unspoken question.

Deliberately, I set down the plant and rounded the table until I stood before him. His eyes never left mine as I reached for his hands. His thumb came to rest on the top of my hand, playing tiny circles over my skin. For a moment, we simply stayed like that and then, slowly, he pulled me down until the back of my thigh brushed the top of his.

"Miss Smith . . . Venetia . . ."

His right hand traced up my arm, to my waist. His other hand rose, and he let the pad of his thumb rest against my lower lip.

"I didn't come here to . . ." he said, his voice a whisper. "That is . . ."

I turned my lips into the palm of his hand to kiss his warm skin and whispered, "I know."

He tilted my chin to kiss me in kind.

It had been years since I had been kissed. I could remember the thrill and fission of passion that accompanied one, but I'd forgotten the comfort. The feeling of someone else's skin against mine. The surety of a pair of hands holding me in place.

We danced in silence, his hands spreading against my back as I twisted into him, my arms wrapped around his neck as he kissed me urgently enough to bow my back. When my fingers twined in the damp hair at the base of his neck, I thanked God for the rain.

A falling log crashed against the metal of the stove door, jolting us apart. We both laughed at our foolishness, but still the moment was broken. I slid out of his lap, immediately missing the warmth of him and his comforting scent of wet wool.

"Venetia," he started after a moment.

I sighed. "I understand, Mr. Goddard. You are my employer's brother, and—"

"I wish you would call me Matthew," he interrupted. "I don't want to go back to Mr. Goddard and Miss Smith."

"But why?" I asked as he donned his still-wet coat and slung his bag over his shoulder.

"Because"—he smiled—"I've desperately wanted to kiss you since I set eyes on you."

· BETH ·

5 May 1944

Dearest Beth,

Thank you for your letter. You don't know how much I miss the farm and hearing what you're planting helps.

I've been a thorn in the side of my commanding officer, but I think I may be able to string together enough leave to make it back home to England soon. I want so badly to see you again.

As soon as I have leave, I'll come to Warwickshire and find you. I cannot wait.

With all my affection,
Colin

Beth juggled her box of graphite pencils and her precious sketchbook from hand to hand to wipe her palm on her skirt as she stared at Highbury House's huge iron knocker shaped like a lion's head. She was in civilian clothes today—her day off—and she was determined to finally do what she'd been too intimidated to attempt for weeks. Today she would sketch in Mrs. Symonds's garden.

"You have to come, otherwise she won't believe I told you," Stella had said over a cup of thrice-steeped tea the last time Beth had made her delivery rounds to the big house.

"I can't do that! Mrs. Symonds won't want to be bothered with the likes of me. You said yourself that she's a tough one."

"I don't know about tough. I can't figure her out, really. She's so different than when she first came to Highbury."

"What was she like then?" Beth asked.

"The very picture of a blushing bride. She let Mr. Symonds arrange everything except for her harp."

"Harp?"

"She used to play, apparently. Anyway, she watched the men unload it from the back of their van like a hawk. I don't think she breathed until it was in the music room and set up just so."

"Now that you mention it, I can't imagine her playing any other instrument. She's so grand, a harp suits her," Beth said.

"Yes, well, she wasn't always that way. I was a kitchen maid under the old cook, Mrs. Kilfod. I'll never forget how much Mrs. Symonds fretted over the menu for her first dinner party. Mrs. Kilfod nearly had to throw her out of the kitchen," said Stella.

"Seeing her now, you'd never guess she's ever felt a bit of self-doubt," Beth said, earning a little huff from her friend.

Out of the corner of her eye, Beth saw the flicker of a set of curtains, looking just in time to catch a curious soldier ducking his head. She blushed but picked up the front door's knocker nonetheless. A few moments later Mrs. Dibble opened the door.

"Miss Pedley!" the housekeeper exclaimed. "You're not in your uniform."

"Good morning, Mrs. Dibble. No, I'm not. I hope you don't mind me using the front door, but Mrs. Symonds told me to come around if ever I wanted to—"

"Oh, the garden. Yes, you'd better come in," said the housekeeper, stepping back. "There's been a mix-up somewhere down the line, and four men arrived today from one of the hospitals in Birmingham. Only there are no more beds for them. The whole household is in a dither. Even us, and we're not supposed to have a thing to do with the hospital. Although, how I'm meant to stay out of it, I'd like to know."

"I can come back another time," she said, edging back.

"No, no, you stay there," Mrs. Dibble called before disappearing down a corridor to the left of the grand stairs.

Beth shifted from foot to foot as a nurse rolling a patient in a wheelchair cast her a curious look. A part of her wished that Captain Hastings would materialize, but she suspected that at this time of day he would be out for one of his long, rambling walks.

He seemed to have an instinct for knowing when Mr. Penworthy would be out in the fields, for he stumbled across them a couple of times a week. The farmer would often laugh and tell Beth to amuse the captain so that he could finish his work.

It didn't take much to amuse Captain Hastings, she was learning. She'd never thought of herself as the sort of girl who had much to say or many opinions, but maybe it was just that no one had cared to ask her before. Captain Hastings wanted to know how she was finding her work, of course, but also what she thought of the progress of the war. What she would have done if she hadn't been a land girl. How she felt about being orphaned. What life in her aunt's house had been like. What her favorite films were and the last books she'd read.

For a girl who had grown up mostly in silence, this onslaught was electrifying, uncomfortable, shocking. But the more questions she answered, the more she wanted to share. It was like Mrs. Penworthy's suppers or Ruth's whining, Mr. Penworthy's grunts of approval when she did something correctly, the way that a cluster of land girls would shout her name when she walked into a dance or the cinema.

She hadn't realized how lonely she'd been until she'd found all of these people.

When Mrs. Dibble reappeared, she looked no less harried than before.

"Come on, then." The housekeeper gestured to Beth. "Mrs. Symonds will see you in the library."

Beth jogged to keep up, even as she passed the open doors of converted wards. In the middle of Ward C, under a chandelier that dripped with crystals, two women argued in whispers.

"That's Matron McPherson and Mrs. Rhys, the quartermaster who's in charge of operations. They've been like that all morning," said Mrs. Dibble.

"What will they do about the extra patients?"

"I don't know. I want to support our men just as much as anyone else, but it isn't my job to take care of a house and a hospital." Mrs. Dibble stopped in front of an oiled oak door. "Stay here. I'll announce you."

Left in the corridor, Beth felt like a schoolgirl waiting on the headmaster. She could hear the housekeeper murmur her name, and then the door opened wider so Mrs. Dibble could beckon her in.

"Hello, Miss Pedley," said Mrs. Symonds from across the room. The woman had pinned her thick, dark hair up, presumably to protect it from dust as she worked on what looked like a large project to rearrange the books in the library.

"Good morning, Mrs. Symonds. I hope I'm not bothering you," she started.

"Not at all. I'm glad you've decided to make use of the gardens. They start to come into their own this time of year."

"Thank you," she said.

"You plan to draw?" Mrs. Symonds asked.

She looked down at her art supplies that she held up to her chest and immediately dropped her hands. "Yes."

"I never had much talent for it myself, much to my mother's disappointment. She was rather Victorian in her belief that a lady should be proficient in drawing, painting, dancing, singing, and at least one instrument. As an all-around student, I was a bit of a disappointment."

"I can't imagine that, ma'am," said Beth.

"Oh, I had talent. It was just taken over completely by the harp. I had a foolish notion once that I might play professionally, but of course that was impossible."

"The harp is such a beautiful instrument. Do you still play?"

Mrs. Symonds's lips tightened. "I gave it up after I married. Would you care for a tour?"

The sudden snap from one subject to the next knocked Beth back a bit, but she managed to say, "Yes, I'd like that very much."

Mrs. Symonds plucked a large iron key out of a bowl on the mantel. "Come along."

Beth followed the lady through the corridors, awed at the way she seemed to glide rather than walk. She supposed it made sense: Mrs.

Symonds was from a class in which being a gentleman's daughter still mattered. Elegance would have been trained into her from an early age.

"Little has changed in this garden since it was first planted," said Mrs. Symonds as they strolled through a garden room planted in sweet, pale colors that Beth had only stolen a glimpse of once. "My husband could have told you about its creation in more detail. I'm afraid he was the family scholar. I do know that this is the tea garden. It has a sweet little gazebo, although it's looking rather in need of a coat of paint. I shall have to speak to Mr. Gilligan about that."

"It's beautiful," said Beth as they passed into a space filled with rich red tulips that stood tall among the spring foliage.

Mrs. Symonds seemed to relax as she looked around. "It is, isn't it? It smells divine when the jasmine is in full bloom. I'll take you to my favorite part."

They wound their way through the different rooms until they reached the crushed gravel walk leading to the iron gate that Beth had seen on her first visit.

"This is the winter garden," said Mrs. Symonds.

Beth stole a glance around as the other woman unlocked the winter garden, but the toy she'd spotted the first time she'd visited was nowhere to be seen.

Inside the winter garden's walls, things seemed quieter, as though the dial of the volume of the entire world had been turned down. A copse of bloodred trees that lined the north wall of the circular garden were covered in pale green new leaves. Everything was still, including the pool of water in the center.

"I like the peace of this place," said Mrs. Symonds, looking around.

"Why do you lock it?" she asked.

"When I began to work in the gardens after Murray went away to war, I learned that there are a few nastier plants that look beautiful but that you wouldn't want a toddler putting in his mouth. I worried about Robin getting in." Mrs. Symonds hesitated. "But I suppose I really started locking it after Murray died. We spent many days in here when we first moved to Highbury."

"It's special to you," she said.

Mrs. Symonds looked down at the key in her hand, her forehead creased. "Yes. It is."

A silence stretched between them, weighted down, no doubt, with Mrs. Symonds's memories. When the older woman looked up, Beth saw that she'd schooled her features into the expression of aloof perfection she usually wore.

"I will leave you to your drawing, Miss Pedley. If you wish to use the winter garden, ask Mrs. Dibble for the key. There are two, so she should be able to retrieve it even if I have one. You can return it to her when you're through. And if the boys venture in, do watch them, please," said Mrs. Symonds.

"Are you certain?" she asked.

Mrs. Symonds handed her the key with a crisp nod. "Somehow, Miss Pedley, I feel that if anyone will appreciate the winter garden's beauty, you will."

Beth had drawn and rubbed out a sketch of what she thought was monkshood—although she couldn't be sure without seeing its purple flowers in bloom—twice, when she heard children's voices. She lifted her head in time to see a flash of blue and black race by the winter garden's gate accompanied by a shrill "It's open! It's open!"

Seconds later, two little boys came crashing into the still of the garden. Immediately Beth recognized Bobby, Stella's nephew, from a rare Saturday delivery when Bobby hadn't been in school. The second boy, also dark-haired, although a little taller, must be Robin Symonds.

"Hello," she called, folding her hands over her sketchbook.

The two boys froze like they'd been caught doing something naughty.

"Who are you?" asked Robin.

"I'm . . ." She cast around for the words, settling on, "An acquaintance of your mother's. Who are you?"

"I'm Robin, and this is Bobby. We're best friends," the boy announced.

Bobby grinned, and Beth's heart ached. She remembered wanting a friend so badly during those lonely years after her parents died. Colin had been such a lifeline, his letters and the occasional meeting in town precious to her. However, now when she got his letters, she couldn't shake the slight nagging feeling of dread that she'd have to answer them and try her best to match the things he said.

Shaking her guilt off, she stuck out her hand for each of the boys to shake. "I'm Beth Pedley."

"What are you doing?" Bobby asked after solemnly shaking her hand like a grown-up.

"I'm drawing. What are you doing?"

"Playing pirates. There's buried treasure here," said Robin.

"What's this I hear?" a voice boomed from the other side of the wall. "Talking to pretty ladies already? You're far too young for that."

"Oh!" She scrambled up from her spot on the grass, spilling her sketchbook and box of pencils just as Captain Hastings came through the gate.

"We'll help!" Robin called, surging forward. The boys fell to her feet, fighting to scoop up the pencils.

"Hello, Miss Pedley," said Captain Hastings. "It seems as though you have acquired a couple of Prince Charmings, whether you want them or not."

"They are true knights in shining armor," she agreed with a laugh.

"What are you drawing?" Robin asked.

She tilted her sketchbook down to show the boys. "I'm doing a very poor job of sketching that monkshood."

"I want to draw!" Robin exclaimed.

"Yeah!" Bobby echoed.

"Boys," Captain Hastings warned. "Miss Pedley might not have any paper to share."

Their faces fell.

"Oh, it's fine," Beth hurried to say. "Really it is. I can share."

She flipped open the back of her sketchbook, where she kept Colin's envelopes and bits of paper that had only been printed on one side. It would be a shame to waste good paper on bad ideas, so she often tried a quick drawing on scrap before she committed to her sketchbook. Only the occasion of drawing in a grand house's garden had made her upend her routine.

"Here you are," she said, handing each boy a piece of paper and a pencil. "You'll have to find a flat surface to draw on, I'm afraid, as I don't have any board with me."

Both raced to the stone path that circled the garden and crouched down with their borrowed pencils.

"They were excited about the gate being unlocked. If I had realized that you were sketching, I would have told them not to disturb you," Captain Hastings said.

"They're not disturbing me at all. I like children, and I'd been hoping that I would have the chance to meet Robin for some time."

"Then you knew Bobby already?" he asked.

She settled again onto the shawl she'd spread over the grass, and after a moment's hesitation, he followed her. "His aunt is Miss Adderton, the cook for Highbury House. I met her when I started making the weekly delivery."

"When you were giving paper to the boys, I couldn't help but notice that you have several envelopes with a service number on them. Do you have someone special?"

Heat rose in her cheeks, but she held his gaze. "A friend who looks forward to a kind word from back home."

The corners of Captain Hastings's mouth pulled up.

"Should I expect to see the boys with you when you go walking in Mr. Penworthy's fields now?" she quickly asked.

He laughed and shook his head. "Will you think less of me if I say I hope not? They're good boys, but the two of them have enough energy to power all of Birmingham."

They sat a moment watching the boys jab at their paper, their hunt for buried treasure temporarily forgotten.

"How is your shoulder healing?" she asked. He still wore the sling, but he seemed to be far less ginger with it than when they'd first met.

He looked down at his arm, resting half out of the flap of his jacket. "It's funny you should ask. Just yesterday the doctor was trying to decide if I need another surgery."

"I'm sorry," she said, even though she was selfishly relieved. He was the person she looked forward to seeing most mornings. She liked the way he listened to her and how he once reached out to lift off her face a stray bit of hair that had escaped her pins. When he healed, he would leave, and she wasn't ready for that.

"I was never in danger of losing my arm like some poor devils, but the surgeon is worried that I might lose some mobility. I told him that I don't need to throw hay bales or climb mountains. I just need to be able to rejoin my men."

"Rejoin them?"

He tilted his head to study her. "They patch us up at Highbury to send us back."

"But you've been hurt."

He shrugged his good shoulder. "I'd ask to go back regardless. I've been a solider for eight years. I've never known another profession. Men who served under me are still risking their lives out there. I can't abandon them."

"But surely there are other people who need you as well," she pushed.

"I don't have a wife. My parents worry, but I suspect they'd worry regardless of what I was doing in the war. Are you all right? You've gone pale."

She pressed a hand to her temple. "I just hate to think that you might be hurt again."

He took her hand, time slowing like golden syrup poured from its tin. "Miss Pedley, before I picked up those ruffians, I had hoped that I would find you today, even though it's your day off."

"Why were you looking for me?" she asked.

"I enjoy the days when I see you much more than those when I don't." He brushed his thumb over her knuckles. When she didn't move, he let his large hand cover hers.

"Miss Pedley—Beth—I wondered if you would do me the very great honor of allowing me to accompany you to the charity dance in two weeks' time."

"You want to take me to the dance?" she asked.

"If you intend to go," he said, almost shy. It was the first time she'd seen him unsure of himself. As though he didn't think she'd say yes.

"I would love to go with you," she said.

His hand tightened around hers. "Splendid."

They sat like that until the boys began to lose interest in their drawings and found a pair of sticks to swashbuckle with.

"I should step in before Captain Hook puts Blackbeard's eye out." He let go of her hand and used his good side to push himself up. "We'll leave you in peace."

She murmured a goodbye as Captain Hastings rounded up the boys. Robin and Bobby returned her pencils and thanked her before Captain Hastings shooed them out of the garden. She thought he would leave, too, but he stopped on the threshold of the gate and whipped around quickly, returning to her in a few long strides. Her lips parted when he leaned down to kiss her on the cheek. His lips felt soft against her skin, and her eyes fluttered closed for a moment. But just as quickly, he was pulling away.

"Right," he murmured. He pulsed toward her, but at the last moment he seemed to pull himself back. "Right."

Then, he was gone.

Beth sat there a moment, stunned. She'd never been kissed before. A little laugh of disbelief escaped her lips, and she shook her head before taking up her sketchbook once again and beginning to draw two boys, their heads bent diligently over scraps of paper.

· EMMA ·

MAY 2021

*E*mma let her head fall against the woven back of the patio chair she'd dragged from the shed in Bow Cottage's garden.

"You're going to fall asleep if you sit like that for too long," said Charlie.

She opened one of her eyes and squinted at him through the late-day sunshine. The days were stretching toward summer now and becoming longer, and when she and Charlie wrapped up an inventory of the plants, she'd invited him over for a drink.

"It's tempting," she said.

He laughed. "Now you know why I bought those deck chairs last year."

"I still don't understand how you can live on a narrow boat. It's so . . ."

"Narrow?" he asked with a grin. "I like it. I don't have to worry about getting stuck next to neighbors I hate."

"Free to roam the open waterways?" she asked.

"So long as I can find a mooring space. You should come out again. We'll take the boat up the Avon through some of the locks," he said.

"At least you're mentioning the locks up front. The last time you conned me onto your boat with promises of sun-drenched picnics on the roof and a slow jaunt down the river, you had me working the locks every twenty minutes. And it poured."

"The risk of an English summer," he said, tilting his beer bottle toward her before taking a sip. Then he paused. "What are we listening to?"

She picked up her phone and glanced at the home screen. "'Ain't That Terrible' by Roy Redmond."

"Not your usual thing," he said.

"Soul's kind of growing on me. It's happy music," she said.

"I've known you for almost ten years and worked for you for five, and in all that time I've heard you listen to three things." He held up his fingers. "Indie rock like the Killers and Razorlight, oldies, and terrible pop music."

"Lady Gaga is not terrible pop music. And my musical tastes are evolving. You should be happy."

"You're usually too stuck in your ways to change. Something's up," he declared with all the annoying certainty of a best friend.

She closed her eyes again. "I don't know what you're talking about. Anyway, you're wrong. I change all the time. That's the beauty of not having a house."

"Do you hear knocking?"

She sighed and sat up, listening. There *was* knocking.

"No one knows I live here," she said.

Charlie snorted. "You're in a village. Everyone knows where you live."

She shot him a look, set her beer down, and hauled herself to her feet. The muscles in her legs, back, arms—everywhere really—screamed in protest. She'd helped the crew carry in hundreds of plants from the loading site so that they would be able to start digging and planting tomorrow. She'd also helped set the posts for the gazebo, turned the compost, tied in the clematis and roses in the bridal and lovers' gardens, and on and on and on. The list never seemed to stop, and now her body was feeling the effects.

Coming in from the patio, she squinted into the dark of the cottage, bumping her shin on a coffee table that seemed to be in the way no matter where she put it. Cursing, she half hopped to the front door, pulling it open just as the person on the other side started to knock again.

"Oh, it's you," she said, bending to rub her shin.

Henry grinned. "It is me. Are you all right?"

"Sorry. I'm glad you're here, it's just that I gave myself a knock on the coffee table," she said.

"Coffee tables are the most vicious of all the furniture. They have a tendency to leap out at you when you least expect it."

She gave a little laugh. "Something like that." She spotted a messenger bag slung over his shoulder. "Are those your grandmother's sketchbooks?"

He patted the bag. "Guilty as charged. Can I come in for a moment?"

"Sorry. Yes."

He looked around as he walked into the entryway. "I haven't been in here since Mr. and Mrs. Mulligan sold Bow Cottage. It's looking good."

"It's just a rental, so I took it as is." She glanced at his shirt, which read *Lou Rawls* in Coca-Cola font. "Who is Lou Rawls?"

"Try 'Stormy Monday' or 'Love Is a Hurtin' Thing.'"

Two more for the playlist. "We're in the back garden. Do you want a beer?"

"I wouldn't say no to one. Who's 'we'?"

"Charlie. Best friend and right-hand man. He was my first hire at Turning Back Thyme."

"Sounds like a good friend to have."

"I don't know what I'd do without him," she said. And it was true. If Charlie ever told her he was moving on, she'd be happy for him and devastated in equal parts.

They stopped in the kitchen long enough for her to pull a beer out of the fridge, pop the top, and hand it to him.

"We have company," she called to Charlie as she stepped out of the French doors. "Charlie, this is Henry Jones. He's got Highbury House Farm, right next door to the Wilcoxes."

"I think you filled in for me at a pub quiz. Nice to meet you in person, mate," said Henry.

"What brings you over this way?" Charlie asked. The way he relaxed back into his chair might have fooled most, but Emma knew him too well. He was on high alert, scoping out the man. She scowled, and Charlie smirked.

"Emma thought I might have some things that would be useful for her research. Nan was here during the war," said Henry.

"Oh, you're the one with the sketches," said Charlie, glancing at Henry's shirt as though something had just dawned on him. He swigged the last of his beer and stood. "Well, I'll leave you two to it, then."

"You don't have to go," she said.

Charlie smiled. "I know. Let me know what you find out, hey?"

After Charlie said his goodbyes, she glanced back at Henry.

"I always wondered what a gardener's garden would look like," he said.

She cringed at the patchy grass and the few drab shrubs. "It's a rental, so I haven't done anything with it."

He nodded. "It must be strange being away from your home base for so long."

"I don't have one. Once a job is wrapping up and I'm getting ready to transition it over to a team of regular gardeners for maintenance, I've usually lined up my next job and am looking for a new place to live."

"That's nomadic," he said.

She shrugged. "I haven't really had a reason to stay in one place."

He raised a brow. "What if someone gave you a reason?"

The word "yes" started to form on her lips, but she stopped it before it could be more than an idea. Yes to what exactly? Flirtation was all well and good, but what else could there be with a man she hardly knew?

She cleared her throat and gestured toward the bag. "The sketchbooks?"

"The sketchbooks. There are three." He dragged his chair closer to hers, and she tried to ignore his heat invading her space as he pulled the sketchbooks out. "The paper's not great quality."

"There was a paper ration on during the war."

"History A levels?" he asked.

"And spending too much time around archivists."

"Well, you might be happy to know that Nan dated her sketches." He opened the cover of one of the books. "Like in the bottom right-hand corner here."

"Very helpful."

"There are some sketches of people's faces and hands. I would guess some of them are the patients who were sent here to recover from their injuries. It looks like Nan took a shot at drawing some landscapes—this plane might be from the airfield not too far away. But mostly, it's drawings of the garden," he said, flipping to a full-page sketch of what had to be the great lawn, planted with neat rows of vegetables.

"Part of the garden had been requisitioned for agricultural land. I've seen pictures of it," she said, running her finger just under the first row of graphite-sketched plantings.

"My grandfather was to blame for that, I'm afraid, although Dad always said Granddad helped reseed the lawn in the fifties."

"We're rebuilding the reflecting pool that used to be right here," she said, tapping a blunt fingernail on the drawing.

"If you continue, there are a lot of details of plants," he said.

She saw drawings of velvet-soft sage, reaching hazel trees, elegant lavender, bowing meconopsis, and cloudlike hydrangeas.

"She was very talented," she said.

They were nearly through the book when he turned a page, and she gasped. A beautiful garden with curving brick walls, tall dogwoods stretching up to the sky, and lush foliage beneath. In the center was a shallow pond made from a gently sloping clay dish of water. And above the drawing, Henry's nan had written "The Winter Garden."

"That's what it was supposed to look like," she breathed.

"What is it?" he asked, leaning in.

"We haven't been able to get into this garden yet. We don't have access through the gate, so we need to spend some time cutting a path in, but there are no detailed plans. I didn't want to damage something irreplaceable, so it keeps falling to the bottom of the list."

"And this helps?" he asked.

She nodded. "Now I know what it was supposed to look like when it was mature. It's not the exact same garden Venetia planted—nothing is ever quite as intended because some plants fail and some thrive. But this at least guides the way."

He sat back. "Good. I'm glad it helps."

She studied the page. She wanted to stand in the middle of it, the shallow dish of water in front of her, and put it to rights once again.

She shook her head, bringing herself back to the moment. "Is there much else in this one?"

"Just this." He reached over and flipped to the last page of the sketchbook. One sketch dominated it. It showed two boys sitting against a background of shrubs. Their heads were bent, the hair falling across one of their brows while he watched the other play with a toy lorry.

"The detail is wonderful," she said, admiring how the dashed pencil lines came together to form such a sure image.

"I wondered who they were."

"Sydney's grandfather and one of his playmates, I would think. I could ask Sydney when I'm next up at the house. She probably has some photographs," she said.

"You should take these for as long as you need. It'll save you time," he offered.

"I appreciate you trusting me with them."

The song switched, and Otis Redding's voice filled the back patio.

"I'm happy to, but I'll warn you, my interest's piqued," he said.

She hesitated, and then said, "You know, if you have the urge to see them, you could drop by."

"Be careful, I might not be able to resist an offer like that from a woman with such good taste in music." He nodded to the portable speaker sitting on the patio table. "'These Arms of Mine.' Great song."

"There's this guy who keeps coming around in these band shirts. He's got me listening to all of this music I wouldn't normally. It must be the power of suggestion."

"I hope he isn't bothering you," he said.

She smiled. "No. He's not bothering me."

"Good," he said before standing. "I should get out of your way."

"You don't have to," she said.

"How tired are you right now?"

"On a scale of one to ten?" she asked. "Probably an eleven."

He laughed. "Then I should go."

She rose and took his bottle from him as he looked around again.

"Pots," he declared.

"I'm sorry?"

"You could get some pots and do a container garden. Then you could take them to your next cottage in your next village for your next job," he said.

"I thought you were going home, Henry." She laughed.

"I am. I am."

She walked him to the front door, leaning against the jamb as he stepped out onto the porch.

"Thanks for the beer," he said.

"Anytime."

She went still when he put his hand on her arm and leaned in to kiss her, once on each cheek. He pulled back slightly, his voice low, and said, "I'm looking forward to seeing you again soon."

Then he flashed that smile she liked so much and strolled off.

Arms crossed, Emma watched the hive of activity in the poet's garden. Vishal and Zack were laying plants out following the details she'd sketched from Venetia's plans. Charlie and Jessa followed, methodically unpotting and planting. Someone had brought a radio, and the tinny sounds of a BBC1 jingle drowned out the sounds of a crew hard at work.

Emma had spent her day going over the sketchbooks. Henry's grandmother had done an excellent job of recording the garden as it had been in 1944. All of the details of the plants, carefully labeled, were invaluable. Plants she wouldn't have guessed, like jasmine tobacco and monkshood, likely kept interest during the summer season. For the first time since she'd arrived at Highbury House, Emma felt as though the winter garden wasn't some impenetrable challenge but a manageable task.

Of course, to tackle a task she had to actually start it.

"Charlie!" she called from the poet's garden entrance.

He looked up and adjusted his ball cap. "What?"

"Give me a hand, will you?"

He planted his spade into the ground and hauled himself up, brushing his knees as he approached. "What do you need?"

"I want to try to get into the winter garden today."

He gave a low whistle. "Today?"

"Not all of it. I just want inside. I think I've figured out where we can cut without damaging anything important." She showed him Henry's grandmother's sketch. "No roses, clear of trees. And if this drawing is right, no sculpture up against the wall."

He rubbed the back of his neck, peering up over the yew to the unruly mess shooting out of the winter garden. "You sure?"

She nodded. "I'm sure."

"Then let's get the ladders."

In no time, Charlie and Emma had pulled two ladders, a hedge trimmer, a pair of lopping sheers, and a machete out of the old gardener's cottage, where they stored some of their more expensive or dangerous tools. She and Charlie leaned one of the ladders up against the winter garden wall, and she began to climb.

"Watch out for that rose cane about six inches from your head," he called out, holding the base of the ladder steady.

"Got it!" she shouted down. Less than thirty seconds later, she bumped her head into the rose and cursed as she detangled herself.

"Very slick."

"I'd like to see you try," she called down.

"You're doing great, boss," Charlie called up. She rolled her eyes.

She battled her way up into the overhanging tangle of branches, cutting as she went. If he stood on tiptoe, Charlie could just barely hand her the tools she needed, with the exception of the machete, which she kept strapped to her right hip Indiana Jones–style.

Finally, she reached the lip of the wall, Charlie carefully passed the other ladder up to her. She dropped it down as best she could, trying to stay away from the foliage. Twice as she climbed down a branch stabbed her, and she managed to put her hand straight around a rose. If she hadn't been wearing work boots and gloves, she would have been in a world of pain.

When finally her foot touched the ground, she looked up through the foliage and found she could only see slivers of sky through the overlapping leaves.

"How are you doing?" Charlie called, his voice coming through the thicket.

"Are you at the gate?" she shouted back.

"I just ran around. How does it look?"

She gazed around her, the scent of damp, rotting undergrowth perfume-like. "Like we're going to need a pulley system to get whatever we cut over the wall."

"Breaking the lock is still an option," he said.

She peered around. "No, it's not. I can't explain it, but it just feels wrong."

"Fair enough. See if you can cut a spot big enough for the both of us down there, and I'll do what I can to bring the tools over," he called.

She drew her machete, grasped a branch, and gave it a good whack. A half hour later, Charlie gingerly stepped from the top of one ladder to the other.

"I hate heights," he muttered.

"I know, I know."

He passed down a lopper and stepped down to join her with a sigh of relief. "So this is the winter garden."

"Or Celeste's garden."

"Still wondering who Celeste is?" he asked.

"Everything gardeners do is intentional. We create order out of nature. If she called this Celeste's garden, there was a reason," she said.

"Wasn't it written in someone else's handwriting?" he asked.

"Yes, but Celeste must mean something for someone to add it to the drawings."

"You could reach out to Professor Waylan," Charlie suggested, naming an academic who had helped her in the past with some of her trickier research questions.

Emma's forehead furrowed. "I think he's still on his annual sabbatical north."

Something of an eccentric, the professor cut off all communication when on sabbatical except for once a month when he picked up letters on a supply run into the nearest village.

"He won't mind a letter from you. Everyone else, maybe, but not you," said Charlie.

She nodded. "I'll send him a letter and ask if he knows of a Celeste connection."

Charlie looked around again, hands on his hips. "This is quite the jungle."

"A fun challenge," she said with a raised brow.

"We have different definitions of fun, you and I. For instance, ask me what I'm doing this weekend," he said, pushing down a branch to make a cut.

"Let me guess. You're taking the boat down one of the canals and then going to the pub."

He shot her a look. "Okay, fine. What are you doing?"

"Hand me the loppers." When he did, she chopped away a branch that had been jabbing her in the back. "There we go."

"Emma, what are you doing this weekend?" he asked again.

"I was thinking about going to a garden center."

He laughed. "This isn't enough for you?"

"Actually, I was thinking about getting some pots. For Bow Cottage."

He stopped. "You'll just have to take it with you when you leave," he said.

She smiled. "Then it's a good thing that you own a pickup truck, isn't it?"

· VENETIA ·

FRIDAY, 17 MAY 1907
Highbury House
Warm with clear skies

*S*o much has happened today—tonight. I'm shaking with excitement like a girl.

I've never had a great sense for fashion. I have dresses for dinners in the evening. However, a ball gown is quite another thing. That is why, when I tugged a little at the lace sleeves of my best evening dress earlier this evening, a touch of worry flared up. I'd been to countless dinners, but this was not just dinner. There would be dancing afterward, the ballroom filled with women dressed in their very best.

I might have given an excuse and begged off Mrs. Melcourt's dance had it not been for the promise of seeing Matthew. In the three weeks since he kissed me, we have seen each other only briefly and never alone. He takes tea with his sister every first Thursday of the month and he makes a point to walk the developing garden with her. Twice I thought I'd caught him watching me as I worked on the long border and he smoked cigars with Mr. Melcourt on the veranda, but I couldn't be sure.

I wanted to not worry about Matthew and what he might think of me after our interlude, but I did care. Each kiss in my life had been a calculated risk, yet I was glad for the risk I'd taken with him. I could only hope he was as well.

He would be in attendance that evening, along with some of Warwickshire, Gloucestershire, and Oxfordshire's finest families. At dinner the night before the ball, I met three couples—all prominent men of industry and their wives—who had come down from London, necessitating three trips to collect them from the station. This morning, when I went to the village bookseller's, I'd heard several women chatting excitedly about what they would wear.

As I approached the house, I gave one last tug to my sleeve and adjusted the white gloves that stretched up my arms before stepping through the French doors off the veranda. Mrs. Creasley was occupied helping a group of four guests with their wraps and hats, so I left my shawl on a sideboard and slipped in unnoticed. My invisibility was not to last, however. A mere three steps into the drawing room, Mrs. Melcourt rushed forward, her hands outstretched.

"My dear Miss Smith," she said, all smiles and light, "you are just the woman I wanted to see. Lady Kinner, may I introduce Miss Smith?"

I curtsied and looked to the other woman, hoping for some prompt that would help me understand why Mrs. Melcourt had dropped her usually frosty manner. Lady Kinner was clearly a woman of distinction. She bore herself as though graciousness and good manners were as fundamental to her being as blood and bone. She wore her carefully styled silver hair in a cloud of curls, and her dress was an understated mauve covered in a black net overlay. Despite her diminutive height, her eyes shone with an uncommon intelligence. I liked her immediately.

"Miss Smith, when Mrs. Melcourt told me that you were the woman Mr. Melcourt had selected to transform Highbury House's gardens, I was delighted. My dear friend Mrs. Bartholomew has not stopped singing your praises about the magic you performed on Avenlane," said Lady Kinner.

I gave a little laugh. "Thank you, Lady Kinner. I appreciate Mrs. Bartholomew's accolades, especially considering Avenlane's situation." I spared Mrs. Melcourt a glance. "The house sits high on the Dover cliffs, and the sea wind whips across the garden. Many plants will never thrive in that sort of environment, so it was vital to select each one carefully.

We also created wind breaks of walls and tree lines across the property, and none of them obscured the views of the sea from the house."

Never mind the exacting nature of Mrs. Bartholomew herself. A stubborn woman who was unafraid to speak her mind, she knew nearly as much as I did about native British trees. We also argued fiercely at various points during the project, and by the end, we'd both received a stellar education in coastal flora, if only to prove the other wrong.

As though reading my thoughts, Lady Kinner said, "I'm certain that Mrs. Bartholomew proved to be a spirited client."

"One might say that," I said.

"Laura has been that way since we were girls," said Lady Kinner with affection. "Did you back down?"

"Not when I was right. Our most strenuous fight was over a row of great hedges of 'Common Lavender.' I told her that they would make no sense in a coastal garden, but she insisted, so we planted one to see how the lavender fared. It died after five weeks."

"What did she do?" Lady Kinner asked.

"She asked if I was happy I had proven my point. I told her yes, and she threw up her hands and said, 'The problem, Miss Smith, is that you and I are far too alike, and that means I can't hardly dislike you.'"

All through this exchange, Mrs. Melcourt watched us, her head cocked to one side as though weighing how far up the social ladder this easy conversation with Lady Kinner should put me.

Now the lady inserted herself, saying, "Lady Kinner, it is such a shame that your niece was not able to come. It would have been a delight to have such an English rose at our little dance tonight."

"Theresa was very sad to miss the occasion, but she does not return from Boston for another three weeks. She has been spending time with her maternal aunt," Lady Kinner told me.

"Matthew will miss her. I know that he enjoyed her company greatly when they met last autumn," said Mrs. Melcourt.

Whatever Lady Kinner thought of that, I was never to know, for Mrs. Melcourt received the signal that dinner was ready to be served, so she took the hand of the highest-ranking gentleman—Lady Kinner's husband, Sir Terrance Kinner—and led the way to dinner.

All around me, gentlemen paired off with the ladies Mrs. Melcourt had no doubt discreetly informed them they would be escorting into dinner. I stood there, smoothing my skirts and feeling more than a little lost, when Matthew appeared at my side.

"Miss Smith, I believe I have the honor of taking you in," he said, elbow outstretched to me.

I bit my lip and slipped my hand into the crook of his arm. "That is very kind of you, Mr. Goddard. Thank you."

As we approached the dining room, I ventured, "I would have thought that, as the brother of our hostess, you would have been paired with a woman of greater repute. Perhaps Lady Kinner's niece?"

He huffed a laugh. "Helen has been pushing Miss Theresa Orleon, a woman fifteen years my junior and with no more interest in me than I in her, for a full year now."

"Is she not a good match?"

His hand covered mine just before we passed through the doors and into the view of all of the guests. "She is an excellent match, but I do not have the same ambitions as my sister."

"Surely you've thought of marriage. It must be expected of you," I said.

He slanted a look my way. "Surely *you've* thought of marriage. It would be expected of you."

My mouth stayed firmly, resolutely shut.

He squeezed my hand. "I'm glad that Miss Orleon is not in attendance tonight. I would rather walk you in to dinner."

I rolled this over in my mind as he guided me around the table to an empty chair and pulled it out. I looked up to thank him for his attention when I saw him grasp the carved wooden frame of the chair next to me. From the top of the table, Mrs. Melcourt frowned.

"Your sister seems displeased," I said as I watched him sit.

He leaned in. "Earlier tonight, I persuaded one of the footmen to switch the place cards. I'm meant to be between the vicar's wife and Mrs. Filsom."

"Mr. Goddard," I said in mock horror but could hardly keep the laugh from my lips.

"I promise you, Miss Smith, there is no one I would rather sit next to at the dinner than you."

I want to write more, I do, but I think I shall need a day to think on everything that happened after dinner and see just how brave I am. For now I will put down my pen and say good night. Good morning. Good day.

SATURDAY, 18 MAY 1907
Highbury House
Clear skies

I have been studiously avoiding my diary, but I know that I must write down what happened after Mrs. Melcourt's dinner if only so that one day I might look back at it and remember it was not a figment of my imagination.

After the final course was cleared and the ladies retired to the drawing room to allow the gentlemen time with their port, the guests who had been invited just for the dancing began to arrive. I am not a particularly distinguished dancer, so balls hold little interest to me. I would stay for an hour and then slip away, I promised myself as I was swept up in the crowd headed for the ballroom.

Yet even I couldn't deny that when couples began to step into the swirling circle of the waltz, there was an undeniable romance in the air. From the safety of the dance floor's edge, my foot tapped along to the music pouring from the violin. The tinkle of laughter danced over the top of the hubbub, and everyone seemed to sparkle under the electrified lights of the chandelier. Mrs. Melcourt had pulled off a triumph of a country ball.

Four dances in, I spotted the lady herself at the head of the room. Her husband stood next to her and, a few feet off, dancing with his arm around a woman in green, was Matthew. As soon as the music started, he had been waylaid by his sister and had spent the past twenty minutes dutifully taking out to the floor every young lady placed in front of him.

I closed my eyes, wondering whether this was a sign that I should melt away, collect my shawl, and walk back to the gardener's cottage. I had tasks to complete in the morning. (It hardly seems possible to complete all of it by the end of the year.)

I turned on my slippered heel and made for one of the open doors leading from the ballroom to the veranda. I would retrieve my shawl the next morning when the residents of the house were still fast asleep. The music had stopped, and ladies and gentlemen were shuffling between partners.

I was out the door when a man's voice stopped me.

"You're not going, are you?"

I looked over my shoulder, squinting at the figure silhouetted against the light of the party. "Mr. Goddard?"

He stepped down from the threshold. "I liked it better when I was Matthew."

I glanced around, fearful that someone might have heard. Luckily, we were quite alone, yet there were so many reasons we shouldn't be. We were standing in the home of my employers. Moreover, I was a woman working and living alone. Only my status as a gentleman's daughter and my irreproachable reputation allowed me that privilege.

And yet . . .

"You aren't for bed yet," he said.

"I cannot imagine that dancing with me holds much appeal for the gentlemen inside," I said.

"I should like to dance with you." He traced a finger down my bare arm and over my wrist. "Ever since supper I've been trying to make my way back to you. My sister seemed determined to occupy me."

"I wonder why," I said, brow lifted.

He held out his hand. "Come."

I hesitated only a moment before allowing him to pull me out of the view of the ballroom's tall windows, past the lime walk, and into the tea garden.

The gate closed behind us with a soft metallic click, but still he led me deeper into the garden.

"Matthew . . ."

"Just a little further," he said.

We stopped in the lovers' garden. I watched him turn a full circle, searching in the silvery light from the half-moon for something.

"What are you looking for?" I asked.

"Anyone else." A smile tipped the edge of his lips. "It appears we're alone."

He slipped his hand up my arm to my shoulder and over my neck. He cupped my cheek tenderly. Then he kissed me, fully and deep. And I kissed him back.

Kissing him feels like turning my face up to the spring sun and luxuriating in the warmth spreading over my skin after months of winter. Kind and inquisitive and passionate—they feel fundamentally him. A revelation each time.

When at last he pulled back, I leaned against his chest, and his arms wrapped around me. I knew I should step away. If I had done that, I might have been able to wake up the next morning and go back to my life as it was before. I might have pretended that I am passionate only about my gardens. Yet I knew what it was to be touched—longed for—and I ached for this long-neglected part of me.

This time I was the one who kissed him. I slid my hands into his hair. I breathed in the smell of him. I angled myself into the warmth of his body.

A laugh from somewhere nearby broke the spell, and both of us stumbled back a step.

The laugh came again, further off than we realized. Both of us breathed a sigh of relief.

He lowered his forehead to rest against mine, and he took my hand again, his thumb playing circles along the back of it.

"Venetia." He said my name like a prayer.

It was that reverence that made me whisper, "Come to my cottage."

"Someone might see us together."

"Wait here for ten minutes before following me. No one will be suspicious about you visiting the greenhouses."

"In the dead of night?" he asked.

"It will only add to your reputation as an eccentric horticulturalist."

He huffed a laugh and shoved a hand through his hair. "I will follow you after ten minutes."

My heart was in my throat as I followed the winding path through the garden rooms and across the ramble. Once in my cottage, I went to my vanity and began unwinding my hair from the elaborate knot the maid had dressed it in earlier that evening. I dropped pin after pin into a little china dish, each ping punctuating my wait.

A soft knock sounded at the door—exactly ten minutes after I left him. When I reached the front room, he was already inside, his jacket off and his necktie hung in two long strips against his shirt.

Without a word, I offered him my back. Chin resting on my shoulder, I watched him undo each and every button of my dress with a steady, patient hand.

· BETH ·

21 May 1944

Dearest Beth,

I know it's been too long since I've written to you last. It's just that this war . . . it weighs so heavily on the mind.

The men in my unit don't talk about these sorts of things, but I can tell. Just the other day, Parker came out of a fog he'd been in for weeks because he got a letter from his wife. He's a proud father to a little girl he will not meet for weeks or months if he manages to survive this war at all.

I sometimes wonder if I was unfair asking you to be mine. The truth is, I've always wondered what would have happened if your aunt had lived closer to the farm. What if you hadn't moved away when we were children or if I'd said the right things to you the few times we saw each other last year.

That is too many ifs for one letter. Just know that I look forward to your letters always.

With all my affection,
Colin

"Stop fussing your hem." Ruth knocked Beth's hand away from, once again, tugging at her borrowed dress.

"You look fine," said Petunia with a laugh as they walked up the long crushed lime drive of Highbury House.

Six land girls had all come together to the dance, moving like a pack of excitable parrots in all their finery. Christine and Anne had ridden on a pair of old bicycles to Temple Fosse Farm to pick up Beth and Ruth. Petunia and a girl named Jemima, who was new to South Warwickshire and still growing the calluses on her hands, had joined as well.

Captain Hastings—Graeme he'd asked her to call him—had tried to insist on picking Beth up at Temple Fosse Farm.

"It's the proper thing to do," he'd said just the day before.

She'd laughed. "What's proper during this war? Besides, it doesn't make any sense for you to go all that way only to come right back to where you started. I'll walk over with the other girls, and you can meet me there. I'll feel like Cinderella entering the ball."

He'd grudgingly agreed, and she was glad, for it had been fun getting ready together. Almost like having a mismatched band of sisters all rushing around her. Ruth had taught Christine how to pin up her curls at each temple, and Anne had tried a swatch of every single lipstick in the farmhouse before deciding on a coral. Beth wouldn't have traded anything for the moment when they'd all cheered because Mrs. Penworthy'd convinced her husband to drive them to the big house in the horse and cart.

"I wonder if there will be soldiers," said Anne in her breathy voice when the house came into view.

"Pilots. Many, many pilots," said Ruth with the sort of determination that almost made Beth feel sorry for the men.

She smiled at her usually sullen roommate. It was hard not to be caught up in the excitement. The dance was a proper one, with decorations pulled from the house's huge attics and a band from the local air base. Rumor had it that Mrs. Symonds had opened up the wine cellar, although Stella had told Beth she would believe it when she saw it.

And the best part of all was that a man she liked was waiting for her.

Maybe she should feel a bit more guilty. Just that morning, another letter from Colin had arrived in the post. She'd read it and tucked it into the box by her bedside to deal with later.

She couldn't continue this way. She'd said yes to being his girl because she hadn't known how to say no, but their correspondence had never sat comfortably with her. Now that her world had grown, she was another person from that girl he'd telephoned before shipping out. Now his letters were not enough.

Petunia squeezed her hand as they approached Highbury House's front door. "Are you excited to see your captain?"

"I am," she said, brightness glowing past her guilt.

"Then let's go find him."

The entryway was already heaving with men and women in a mix of uniforms and civilian clothes. The dance would start at six o'clock to take advantage of the lengthening late-spring days and to avoid violating the blackout. No one here cared that six would have been unthinkably early in peacetime. They would all squeeze as much joy out of the night as they could.

Beth floated through the brightly lit entryway toward the French doors thrown open to the veranda and the sound of "I'll Be Seeing You." Sister Wharton collected their tickets, and they handed off their coats to Dorothy, a maid who looked desperate to be asked to dance.

Fighting her niggling fears, Beth's eyes swept the crowded dance floor as she looked for Graeme. What if he'd fallen ill? Or perhaps he'd been discharged earlier than he thought, and he couldn't get word to her. Or maybe he'd changed his mind about her.

"There you are."

She spun on her heel with a smile of relief. There he stood, tall in his dress uniform, a spray of orchids in his right hand.

"You look beautiful," he said, leaning down to kiss her on the cheek.

She pressed a hand to her chest, still not used to its flutter every time he drew that close. "Thank you."

He held up the flowers. "For you."

"They're beautiful," she said, smelling them. A pin secured the ribbon wrapping the stems: a corsage. The man had managed to find her a corsage in the middle of rural Warwickshire during a war.

"Thank you," she murmured as she pinned the orchids to her navy dress.

"Shall we dance?" he asked, gesturing to the floor.

She realized then that he wasn't wearing his sling. "It's gone!"

"The doctor changed his mind about surgery. He told me I could remove it just this morning. I've been warned every way from Sunday that I can't do much with it, but he didn't disapprove of the idea of me leading a beautiful woman around on the dance floor, so long as the song is slow."

"Then we should dance to celebrate," she said, taking his hand.

They pushed into the crowd of RAF men, army officers, WAAFs, land girls, nurses, and doctors. When they found a patch of dance floor, Graeme slipped his arm around her waist, pulling her to him. "Here we go," he said.

"Where did you find orchids?" she asked.

"I have my methods," he said, a twinkle in his eye. When she laughed, he added, "Highbury House isn't the only big house in the area. I happen across Lord Walford of Braembreidge Manor walking his dogs from time to time. His house was requisitioned for a school, but he refused to leave because he has a prizewinning collection of orchids. When I explained the situation, he gave me a few."

"He gave you his prizewinning orchids?" she asked.

He grinned down at her. "I told him that they would be worn by the most beautiful woman in the world tonight. Lord Walford is a bit of an old romantic underneath it all."

He pulled her closer to him, and it seemed the most natural thing to rest her head lightly against his shoulder.

"This isn't hurting you, is it?" she asked, glancing up at him.

"Not even the littlest bit," he said.

"Good," she murmured into the warm wool of his jacket.

When the song ended, she reluctantly began to step away, aware of the couples breaking apart all around her. But although he dropped her hand and let his arm slide from around her waist, he twined his fingers in hers. "Do you fancy a walk in the gardens?" he asked.

She cast a glance around. "Are we supposed to?"

"I don't think Mrs. Symonds will mind," he said, jerking his chin to where the mistress of the house was laughingly protesting being led out by a senior officer.

184 · JULIA KELLY

"I've never seen her look that happy before," said Beth in awe.

"I don't think she laughs often. It's a shame." He tugged her hand. "Let's go."

She let him pull her toward the lime walk. New green leaves fanned out above them in the soft light of the early evening.

"Have you thought of the end of the war?" he asked her as he tucked her hand into the crook of his arm.

"Haven't we all?"

"I mean, have you thought about what you'll do? Or where you'll go?" he asked.

She paused. "I thought that maybe I could ask Mr. and Mrs. Penworthy if they could afford to have me stay on. If they need me, that is." She paused. "I can't go back to Dorking."

"Why not?"

"I don't have a home there any longer. My aunt made it clear that she'd done her duty by me. I'm on my own."

"I'm sorry."

"I'm not. When she took me in, I didn't have anyone in the world, and I would have likely ended up in an orphanage otherwise. But she made it clear from the beginning that she didn't want me."

He shook his head. "How could anyone not want you?"

She didn't demure at the compliment. She liked hearing Graeme say these things. Colin had written sweet things to her, too, but she couldn't help feeling it had been a pantomime of a happy couple.

"What would you want to do if you could do anything with your life?" Graeme asked.

"I would want to be around people who care about me," she said automatically. "I might stay in Highbury. I know the people at the neighboring farms. Shopkeepers recognize me when I go into the village. The librarian holds books for me just because she thinks that I might enjoy them, and Stella always has a pot of water on for tea when I come to make my weekly delivery. Even Mrs. Symonds is kind to me. I've never had that before."

"You're not dreaming of a life in London?" he asked.

She shrugged as they turned onto the path at the top of the sculpture garden. "What is there for me in London?"

"I thought all women wanted fashion and theater and restaurants and glamour," he said with a laugh.

She paused, resting a hand on his arm to stop him, the heady scent of the first lavender blooms drifting over. "If I wanted those things, there would be nothing wrong with that, but I don't. I want other things."

"There are so many things I want to ask you. A thousand questions. I don't want to spend one day with you, but a thousand days." He grew serious now. "I wonder, Beth, if I could ever hope that you would spend those days with me by your side."

Her grip tightened. "Graeme, what are you asking me?"

She watched as he lowered himself to one knee, grasping her hand as he went.

"I don't know when this war will end, but I do know that when it does, I want to come home to you." He swallowed then and asked, "Elizabeth Pedley, would you do me the greatest honor and say you'll be my wife?"

"Graeme, we hardly know each other," she breathed.

"If this war has taught me anything it's that life is too short to wait when you know what you want," he said.

"You're certain?" she asked.

"I thought I was going to be the one asking the questions."

"Be serious. This is marriage we're talking about. Forever."

He lowered his forehead to the hand he held clasped in his hands. "You're right. I just . . . Those days when I see you out in the fields or in the garden have been the happiest of my life. You're a beacon in the night sky, Beth. Please be mine."

There were so many reasons to say no. She'd known him for only a few short months. She hadn't met his family. She had to sort out the mess with Colin. And yet, when she stared down at the man whose eyes were fixed on hers, none of that mattered. He was the one she wanted.

"Yes," she said in a quiet voice.

"Yes?" he asked.

She laughed. "Yes!"

He surged up, catching her around the middle with his good arm and pulling her into a kiss. A proper kiss. Their first. She sank against him as he cradled the back of her head in his hand, his lips moving slowly over hers. She clung to the lapels of his jacket, desperate not to let this moment go.

When finally he broke away breathless, he stroked a thumb along the line of her jaw. "I was so certain you were going to say no. But since you didn't . . ." He pulled out a slim package from the inside pocket of his uniform jacket. "I will get you a ring, but until then, perhaps you'll accept this."

She pulled the twine and brown paper from the package. It was a long, slim metal case with "Derwent" painted on the top. "You bought me pencils?"

"For your drawings."

She threw her arms around him and kissed him. "You wonderful man!" She laughed and kissed him again. "Why would you ever think I would say no?"

He gently tapped the pad of his thumb against her lips. "Because I've never been the luckiest man."

"That can't be true," she said softly.

"I was never academic. I never had a head for business. I joined the army because I didn't know what to do with myself, but I was good at soldiering. I liked leading my men, knowing that what I was doing mattered. But then I was shot."

"And now you're better," she said.

He kissed her again but didn't respond, and understanding dawned in her.

"You're leaving Highbury?"

"The Pioneer Corps needs officers."

"But we just got engaged—"

"I have to go where the army sends me, Beth. I'll write to you, and I'll take every bit of my leave to come back to Highbury," he said.

It was Colin all over again, only this time Graeme had asked her face-to-face and now they were *engaged*.

"What if you're sent back to fight again?" she asked, gripping his hand.

He shook his head, testing his shoulder slightly and wincing. "I still have a ways to go before they'll let me fight."

"You said you were better. We shouldn't have danced," she said.

He smoothed a hand down her hair. "It was worth it. I'll do everything I can to make you happy. I promise. And until we can live together properly, I'll make sure you're taken care of. My parents would love it if you would live in Colchester with them."

"I can't. I'm a land girl here," she said.

"Not now. After the war," he said.

"But you'll be done with the army then," she said.

He offered her a rueful smile. "It's all I've ever been good at."

"And what will I do then?" she asked. "Where will we live?"

"If I'm stationed at a permanent base, we can live there together."

"*If*," she said.

"My mother always wanted a daughter."

Does your mother even know about me? Does your father?

"Now, shall we go back and share our happy news?" he asked, offering her his arm.

She stared at him, reservations creeping in. To Graeme, everything was all settled. Yet his proposal had thrown her life into chaos. She needed to write to Colin. She needed to explain what had happened while he'd been away fighting. Her stomach squeezed tight and sour. She dreaded him opening her letter, thinking that it would be filled with little stories about Highbury and cartoons of the people around her and instead finding that she'd chosen another man.

I don't love you, Colin.

She glanced at Graeme from under her lashes. Did she love him? Did he love her? Men were supposed to talk about love when asking a woman to marry them, weren't they? So why had he never mentioned it?

And yet now that she was engaged to Graeme, the thought of *not* becoming his wife was inconceivable.

She took a deep breath. They would figure everything out, one thing at a time.

· DIANA ·

A drink for the hostess of this fine party?"

Diana smiled at Father Devlin as she accepted a glass of white wine from Nurse Holt. "You have the nursing staff carrying your drinks now, Father Devlin?"

"The crutches make it rather difficult to be self-sufficient, I'm afraid. Nurse Holt was kind enough to humor me when I told her that the wine was for you," said Father Devlin.

"Thank you," Diana said to the younger woman, who dipped her head and scurried away. She slanted a look at the chaplain. "The nurses are all afraid of me, you know."

"How could they be when you're always so warm?" he asked.

She snorted, and then immediately covered her mouth. "Excuse me. That was hardly ladylike."

"It's good to see you laugh," he said.

"I laugh."

"Not enough."

"Is that the advice of a spiritual adviser?" she asked.

"That is the advice of a man who hopes you consider him a friend, otherwise he's sure that he's been a terrible nuisance since he arrived at Highbury House," said Father Devlin.

"No, you're not a nuisance," she said, surveying the party. "It is good to see a bit of fun in the house. This is what Murray wanted."

"You've brought joy to a great many people tonight, and raised a good deal of money by the looks of it," said Father Devlin.

The notion was all rather . . . satisfying. When she and Murray had moved into Highbury House, it had been run by a skeleton staff for far too long. Murray had started on the renovation with enthusiasm, but his practice in London had pulled his attention away, and it had become Diana's responsibility. Diana's home. She'd worked hard to return it to what it had been when the Melcourts lived there: a place where people gathered. A place for parties and flirtations and joy and friendship. Even though the dance floor was filled with injured men and women in uniform, it felt as though it might be that sort of place again.

She tilted her glass in the direction of the dance floor. "It's all worth it to see Matron discuss the Voluntary Aid Detachment with that American Air Force major. He's been trying to edge her out onto the dance floor for a half hour now."

Father Devlin tipped his head to study the pair. "They would cut a rather fine figure, don't you think?"

"Mmm," she hummed in agreement. "Now, if Cynthia comes out of her office and dances this evening, I'll never say another ill word against her again."

A couple of nurses standing nearby guffawed.

"You'd better hope that doesn't make its way back to her before the end of the evening," said Father Devlin.

"She's still angry I overruled her. Do you know, I've never been a great lover of parties and gatherings?" When the chaplain raised his brows, she continued, "Oh, if you're forced to do it for long enough, you learn how to dance and talk and laugh. That is being a debutante. But it doesn't come naturally to me.

"One of the reasons I fell in love with Murray was because he was everything I wasn't. If I was happy watching people from my corner of the room, he was right in the center making everyone laugh. I was more interested in staying in the safety of the music room."

"How did you meet?"

"At a dance, actually. He'd been harangued into asking me by some relative who knew my mother, and he was so gallant about it. We danced, and then he talked with me for the rest of the evening about music. I later learned that the poor man had a tin ear and couldn't carry a tune at all, but he saw that I liked talking about it. Three months later, we were engaged, and I found I didn't mind the dances and suppers nearly as much. Not if he was with me."

"You loved him very much," said Father Devlin.

She squared her shoulders even as grief pressed down on her. "I did. He gave me a different world."

The old Diana had lived under her parents' roof, her mother making well-meaning decisions for her. Marriage had been freedom from that.

"Have you given any more thought to what the next stage of your life looks like?" Father Devlin asked.

She cradled her glass into her chest, the cool of the condensation soothing her. "Perhaps after the war when there are no more battles to fight."

A tall man with jet-black hair approached the pair.

"I hope you don't mind me being so forward," he said to Diana. "But I understand that you are the hostess."

Diana raised her brows, but before she could say anything, Father Devlin helpfully piped up, "She is."

The man placed a hand to his chest and gave a neat little half bow. "I'm Wing Commander Edmund Grayson, and I wanted to thank you personally for tonight. There aren't many opportunities for my men to let off a little steam, and this has given them something to look forward to."

"Anything for the Royal Air Force," she said, knowing she sounded a little flip, but not caring.

Wing Commander Grayson paused and then said, "I also wondered if you might care to dance."

She lifted her glass. "I'm afraid my hands are occupied."

Father Devlin shuffled his crutches so he could pluck the glass from her. "Enjoy your dance, Mrs. Symonds."

She nearly objected, but then stopped herself. What harm was there in one dance? She took Wing Commander Grayson's extended hand and let him lead her onto the floor.

"It's been a very long time since I've danced. I hope you won't find me too clumsy," he said.

She laughed. "I can promise you that however long, it's been longer for me."

"That can't be the case. A beautiful woman like you must dance all the time," he said.

Was he flirting with her? "The last time I danced, I had come up to London to meet my husband on leave. We went to the Dorchester."

"You'll have to ask him to take you again," he said.

"My husband won't be coming back from the war."

Wing Commander Grayson's arms stiffened around her, but he didn't stop dancing. "I'm very sorry to hear that, Mrs. Symonds. I can't imagine what I would do without my wife, Flora, and I never want to think about what it would do to her if something happened to me."

Then why are you fighting? She wanted to scream the question, but she knew the answer just as well as he did. Still, that didn't make being left behind any less brutal.

"When did your husband die?" Wing Commander Grayson asked her.

"August of 1941," she said.

"I can't imagine how hard it's been for you."

"It's been a long time," she said, even though it didn't feel that way most days. "He volunteered to serve. He didn't wait for conscription. I . . ."

"Didn't want him to?" Wing Commander Grayson offered.

"No."

"Sometimes a man feels a responsibility to his country that is too great to ignore."

"He said something to that effect once. I told him that his responsibilities were to our son. To me. I don't think I've ever really forgiven him." She looked up at the officer. "I don't know why I'm telling you this."

"Sometimes it's easier to talk to a stranger," he said.

She glanced at Father Devlin over the officer's shoulder, certain her newfound candor was the result of his meddling. She'd spent so much time closing doors behind her, making sure no one had a key. Yet the chaplain seemed determined to pick open each of those locks and let the sunlight stream in again.

"Perhaps you're right," she said.

They danced in silence until Wing Commander Grayson spun her a quarter turn so that she could see Mrs. Dibble at the end of the veranda, waving wildly at her. "I think someone might be trying to catch your attention."

"What on earth has come over her?" she asked, brow furrowed. But when she saw who was standing next to the housekeeper, her heart sank.

"What's wrong?" Wing Commander Grayson asked.

"That's Mr. Jeffries, the postmaster. He only comes out after hours with urgent news."

"Like a telegram," said Wing Commander Grayson.

The postmaster raised his hand to show a folded slip of paper.

They stilled. Slowly a hush fell over the veranda as around them couples began to notice. Even the band stopped playing. Mrs. Dibble made her way through the parting crowd, Mr. Jeffries following solemnly behind her. When they stopped in front of Diana, the postmaster handed her the telegram.

"I didn't think it should wait for the morning," he said.

Diana looked down at the name on the paper, and her breath caught in her throat. "No." Her voice cracked. "You're very right, Mr. Jeffries. Thank you."

"I'm sorry, Mrs. Symonds," murmured Mrs. Dibble, shuffling backward.

The housekeeper clearly did not want to be the one to dispense the news, but Diana couldn't blame her. She didn't want to, either, but she was the mistress of Highbury House. It was her responsibility.

"Please excuse me, Wing Commander Grayson," she said.

He gave a nod of sympathy and a little bow.

She squeezed her eyes closed, took a breath, and then scanned the veranda. She saw Miss Pedley and Captain Hastings walk up the steps and stop in confusion at the silent scene, but she kept looking. Finally, near the French doors to the double drawing room, she spotted the telegram's recipient.

She walked a straight line, watching as realization flashed on the woman's face. Then hope that maybe she was wrong. And finally understanding that Diana would not be veering away to face someone else.

"Miss Adderton, I think we should find some privacy," she said.

Miss Adderton's hand shot out to grip Diana's arm. "No. Please. Not Joan."

Joan. The mother of the little boy who had become such fast friends with Robin.

From behind Diana, Miss Pedley and Captain Hastings rushed forward to hold Miss Adderton up. "Come on, Stella," Miss Pedley said. "Let's step inside, away from all of these people."

Diana watched as Miss Adderton nodded, letting herself be steered by the land girl.

"Take her two doors down the corridor to my morning room. It will be more private," Diana whispered to Captain Hastings.

They set Miss Adderton down on the sofa while Diana lingered nearby, awkward in her own house. Miss Pedley sat next to the cook, rubbing her back and murmuring reassurances in her ear. The slow but steady thud of Father Devlin's crutches on the corridor's carpet announced the chaplain's approach while Captain Hastings poured out a finger of brandy from one of the sideboard's decanters.

When all was settled, Diana held out the telegram.

Miss Adderton looked up at her, eyes brimming with tears. "I can't read it. Will you? Please?"

Diana looked around at the other faces in the room. "Surely there's someone more well suited for this. Father Devlin?"

Miss Adderton's hands trembled the brandy in her glass. "Please."

With her own shaky fingers, Diana unfolded the telegram and began to read the typed letters:

We regret to inform you Joan Reynolds's building was hit during a raid yesterday evening STOP She was killed instantly STOP

Miss Adderton's body collapsed against Miss Pedley's, sobs racking her. The men stood back, grim-faced and solemn.

Diana looked down again at the telegram in her hands, and all she could think was: *That poor little boy.*

SUMMER

· VENETIA ·

*U*ntil Matthew, I never understood how a woman could lose her head over a man. It is as though, after years of practicality, I'm unable to see straight. He has blinded me with affection, tenderness, and touch. To be held by another person is deeply intoxicating, and whenever we part, I find myself craving more.

I know that it was a mistake to kiss him and lead him back to my cottage that first night. But it felt *right*. It's been easy to open the door to him again and again whenever darkness and quiet falls over Highbury House. Each time, we extinguish the lights in my cottage and wind our arms around one another in the dark. He leaves only when orange-pink dawn streaks across the sky.

We agreed that if we're to avoid being caught, we would have to become more careful. And so, feeling like the heroine in a penny dreadful, I began to leave my lover notes in the twisted trunk of a tree a mile down the road from Highbury House. I can now safely say that I am an expert at excuses to venture into the village.

Earlier this afternoon, however, I visited Wisteria Farm for reasons that were not entirely contrived. I needed yet more roses. A variety called

'Belle Lyonnaise' was to climb over arches at four points of the bridal garden, and *Rosa foetida* 'Bicolor', 'Souvenir d'Alphonse Lavallée', and 'Rosearie de l'Hay'—a new favorite of mine—would be interspersed with artful casualness throughout the poet's garden, lest we ever forget that love is like a red, red rose.

With Matthew's housekeeper out visiting her sister, I knew we would have nearly an entire afternoon to ourselves. We enjoyed it as best two people sneaking about can.

As four o'clock grew closer, we forced ourselves to dress again. I fumbled with my corset, the stays even more restraining than usual.

"This summer heat is dreadful," I moaned.

Matthew laughed. "Let me play lady's maid."

He gently dealt with my laces and then eased on my corset cover, skirt, shirt, stockings, and boots.

As I watched him, I wondered at how thoroughly he'd changed me since that first kiss. I read books and thought what he might say about them. When I heard a horse ride into the courtyard at Highbury, I held my breath, waiting to see if it was him.

When he was done lacing my boots, he kissed the inside of my knee. "When can I see you again? Like this. When the sun is shining."

"When can you once again arrange for everyone in the vicinity of your home to be otherwise occupied?" I asked with a laugh.

He sighed. "Venetia, I don't want to keep stealing moments like this."

All at once, a wave of exhaustion hit me, and my every nerve felt oversensitive. He'd written those words in every hedgerow letter, but he'd never said them before.

"No good will come of people finding out," I countered. No matter how he might try to share the responsibility, there was only one reputation on the line—*mine*. I had overstepped the boundaries of proprietary the moment I walked in the gardens at night with a man to whom I was not affianced. And I'd thoroughly and indisputably fallen when we'd stripped each other of our clothes and made love.

"I wouldn't let anything happen to you," he promised, forehead against mine, arms around my waist.

"I know you will try." That was all he could do. If his sister and her husband found out, I would be turned out of Highbury House.

Yet it wasn't just this job that was at risk. I could lose *everything*. The annuity my father left was barely enough for Adam to live on, let alone me. I might think of myself as an artist, but I also worked because I had to. Now my brother and I both relied on my income.

It was easier for Matthew. Even with the hint of eccentricity that hung about him like perfume from one of his roses, he had options. He could marry or not. He could start a business or not. He could simply *be*.

"I wish that you would allow me to show you that you can trust me," he said, as though he could read my thoughts.

"I don't need to trust you," I said.

He slipped his arms around me. "We all need trust, Venetia."

I twisted, unable to watch him look at me with such open, earnest hope. Still, I let him coax another kiss out of me when he led me outside to my cart.

"You'll write to me?" he asked. "I check our hedgerow every day."

My cheeks flushed, and all I could do was nod before snapping the leads. But as my horse and cart bumped its way out of the courtyard, I couldn't resist looking back at him, eyes fixed on me at the entry to his drive.

SATURDAY, 29 JUNE 1907
Highbury House
Hot

I lied to Matthew. I did not write to him this morning as I promised. I woke up intending to, but as soon as I donned my gardening apron and stepped out of my cottage door, I heard raised voices and braying. I hurried to the gate between Highbury House and the farm and found the usually unflappable Mr. Hillock in a dither. One of Adam's orders must have been misread, because instead of four carts of gravel, nine donkey-drawn carts were neatly pulled up.

After sorting out the gravel debacle, an issue arose with the reflecting pool, and then Mr. Hillock's son, Young John, and another of the gardeners, Timothy, flew at each other in an argument while bending canes for arches. (I gather that the disagreement had more to do with a young lady in the village than it did building garden arches.)

All in all, an exhausting day, and the reason why I couldn't even put pen to paper to write in this diary yesterday evening. Instead, I'm stealing a few moments over the cup of tea and toast that the maid brings me each morning to write a few lines. Then, a letter to Matthew.

· STELLA ·

JUNE 1944

Stella should have been watching Bobby to make sure he wasn't tearing things off the shelves of Mrs. Yarley's shop, but all she could do was stare at the two suitcases on the shelf before her. They weren't particularly beautiful, but she used to come in just to look at them and dream that one day they'd hold her belongings.

Even now, she wanted to pull one down and take it back to Highbury House, the case slapping against her leg as she walked the dusty, sun-baked road. She would throw it down on her bed and fill it to the brim with clothes and her magazine cuttings of all the places she wanted to travel and her coursework. Then she would take that case to the train station and *leave*.

She would leave everything behind. Warwickshire. Highbury House. The fights with Mrs. George. Men's shouts filling the house in the dead of the night. The smell of antiseptic and clatter of the medicine cart too close to her kitchen for comfort.

But mostly, she would leave Bobby.

A low, deep guilt rolled through her.

Even before Mrs. Symonds had read the telegram out, Stella was certain what it would say. She knew the moment she saw Mr. Jeffries out on the veranda that the news was for her, but she'd hoped and prayed that the evening's tragedy would be someone else's.

When Mrs. Symonds read out the final "STOP," Stella had fallen apart, at the loss of her sister, yes, but also at the death of the life she'd longed for. She would never leave Highbury. Never move to London and put to use any of her studies. Never see the places in her pictures.

Beth had told her later that Mrs. Symonds had gone up to Stella's attic bedroom to tell Bobby. Apparently the mistress of Highbury had cradled the boy to her when he'd begun to sob.

Bobby had not been able to sleep on his own since, so neither could Stella, with him softly snuffling into his pillow. After one week of simultaneously burnt and underdone meals, Mrs. Symonds declared that Bobby would temporarily move to the night nursery with Robin, under the watchful eye of Nanny.

"Are you planning a trip?"

The familiar voice sent Stella's eyes rolling to the ceiling of Mrs. Yarley's shop.

"Miss Adderton?" came her employer's slightly short tone.

She fixed as pleasant a smile as she could muster on her face and turned to the woman who paid her wages. "Hello, Mrs. Symonds. I didn't realize you were coming into the village or I would have taken a list for you."

Mrs. Symonds's brow furrowed. "I enjoy a little time away from the house from time to time. Are you quite well, Miss Adderton?"

My nephew is an orphan. I hate my life, and now I can never change it. But other than that . . .

"I'm fine," said Stella.

"How has Bobby been settling into his new routine?" Mrs. Symonds asked.

Stella searched the other woman's face, looking for malice or judgment, but there didn't seem to be any edge to her employer's tone.

"Nanny tells me that he sometimes wakes up in the night, but he seems to be sleeping well in the cot next to Master Robin." After a moment, she added, "Thank you for allowing it."

"Don't worry too much," said Mrs. Symonds. "Children are resilient."

A great crash of breaking glass erupted behind them. Both women spun around to see Bobby standing next to a pile of glass shards and what looked like fat quince fruit.

"Bobby!" Stella gasped, rushing forward. "What happened?"

He started to cry.

She looked around in despair at all of the broken glass. At all of the fruit and sugar—oh, the sugar!

"Were you tugging on the shelf, Bobby?" she asked, desperate for him to say no.

The question only made him cry harder.

"Bobby, please," she said, growing increasingly conscious of the small crowd around her and the extremely red face of the shopkeeper. "Please don't cry."

"Stop yelling at me!" he wailed.

"I'm not yelling!" Except she was. She pushed her hair back from her forehead, at a loss for whether to shake him or hug him to her. Maybe both? She didn't know. She didn't *know*.

"Bobby," Mrs. Symonds said in a soft voice. The elegant lady had picked her way through the glass and was now standing in a syrupy puddle of quince juice. "Are you hurt?"

Goodness, Stella hadn't even thought to ask. Should she check him over for cuts? See if he was beginning to bruise?

"Are you hurt, Bobby?" Mrs. Symonds asked again, placing a gentle hand on the boy's shoulder.

Sniffling, Bobby shook his head.

"That's good, isn't it? We wouldn't want for you to be hurt because then you might not be able to play with Robin," said Mrs. Symonds. "Now, can you tell me what happened? It will be all right. Just tell me."

"I thought there was chocolate," he said in a voice as small as a field mouse.

"I must say, that would be something. Chocolate is a treat these days. Did you try to climb on the shelves to get to it?" asked Mrs. Symonds.

Another nod.

Clucks and tuts from the other shoppers. Stella shot a fierce glare at them, and one or two took a step back.

"Mrs. Symonds, that was a dozen jars of quince in syrup," said the shopkeeper, wringing her hands.

A dozen jars? Think of the cost, let alone the sugar coupons.

"I'll take care of it, Mrs. Yarley. First, however, I think it's probably best if we see to this mess, don't you?" asked Mrs. Symonds.

Stella watched in amazement as the shopkeeper actually retreated and returned with a broom and dustpan.

"Here," said Stella, holding out her hand.

As she swept up the glass to allow Mrs. Yarley to get at the syrup with a mop and bucket, Mrs. Symonds checked Bobby over for cuts. Stella couldn't help but watch how gentle she was with him, wiping away his tears as she went.

When the mess was cleaned up, Mrs. Symonds said, "Now, Bobby, do you remember learning about consequences at school?"

He hesitated.

"Everything we do has an impact on something or someone. You knew that you weren't supposed to climb on the shelves, didn't you?"

His lip trembled, but to his credit he didn't begin crying again. "Yes, Mrs. Symonds."

"Good. I'm glad you aren't hurt, but you will have to have a punishment, with your aunt's permission." Mrs. Symonds glanced up at her, and Stella nodded, unsure. She'd never punished a child before.

"Now, I need an assistant for a big project in the library. Every afternoon for the next two weeks, you're to come to the library right after school and help me. Do you understand?"

"Yes, Mrs. Symonds," he murmured.

"Good." Mrs. Symonds turned to Mrs. Yarley. "Please send the bill to Highbury House, and I will settle it."

"A good amount of sugar went into those preserves," said Mrs. Yarley.

"I will account for the loss of sugar as well," Mrs. Symonds promised before turning to Stella. "Now, shall we walk home?"

"Come on, Bobby," Stella beckoned after murmuring another apology to Mrs. Yarley.

The little boy walked by her side through the village, but as soon as they were clear of Church Street, he began to twist at her hand.

"Bobby, why don't you run ahead and see if you can catch Mr. Gilligan in the lane? He was coming into the village to see about buying some more twine for the climbing roses," said Mrs. Symonds.

As soon as Stella released his hand, Bobby was off like a shot. She watched him run away, the edge of his shirttail coming untucked.

"I thought that Mr. Gilligan went out this morning," said Stella.

"He did," said Mrs. Symonds.

They walked in silence for a while, Stella aware of the great divide between them.

"I prayed for a girl."

Stella cast her a glance. "I'm sorry?"

"When I was carrying Robin, I prayed for a little girl. I thought it would be easier because at least I knew what it was like to be girl. But the moment I heard Robin cry, I knew he was what I wanted. That doesn't mean it hasn't been hard, though."

"When Mr. Symonds passed—"

Mrs. Symonds gave a little hollow laugh. "Long before that. Even before the war, Murray was back and forth to his London surgery. On Nanny's Wednesday afternoons off, I would spend the hours wondering how I was going to make it through another moment of being alone with Robin. I would turn my back for one moment and he'd climb the nursery curtains or hop from sofa to end table."

"What did you do when it became too much?" Stella asked.

"I once took him to the winter garden and locked us both in just so I could keep him from wandering off while I tried to finish embroidering Murray's handkerchiefs."

"Did it work?"

Mrs. Symonds's laugh was genuine. "Of course not. If I looked away for one moment, he'd be trying to grab a rose or eat a worm he'd found."

The moment should have been light—even filled with a warmth she'd never shared with her employer before—but Stella couldn't laugh. Instead, she finally said the words that that been stuck in her throat for days. "I don't know how to do this."

"How to do what?" Mrs. Symonds asked gently.

"Be a mother to him."

She knew she should feel something—and she did feel things. She missed her sister. She was furious at the bomb that had fallen on Joan's flat. She was angry that Joan had died and scampered out of yet another responsibility. But mostly she felt an absence of love for this little boy.

Aunts weren't supposed to pour their lives and souls into a child the way mothers did. Were they?

"You don't have to be a mother to Bobby. That was your sister's role," said Mrs. Symonds.

"He's all alone in the world," she said.

"Doesn't he have family on his father's side?" her employer asked.

"No. None that Joan talked about, anyway."

"Well, your nephew is not alone. He has you," said Mrs. Symonds.

"I don't know if I'm enough," she confessed.

"None of us is. I believe that Father Devlin would say that that's why we meet so many people in our lives," said Mrs. Symonds.

Stella frowned. Never in all her years of working at Highbury House could she imagine that she would have a conversation like this with her employer.

As the empty brick pillars that had once held the gates of Highbury House came into view, Stella spotted Bobby leaning against one of the brick columns that framed the drive. He was huffing and puffing, as though he'd run a great race. Stella had a sneaking suspicion that when they got inside, she would also find him streaked with dust from the road that had stuck to splatters of syrup from the store.

"It will not always be this difficult. It will become easier," said Mrs. Symonds.

"Thank you."

As they over into the drive, Mrs. Symonds nodded crisply. "Miss Adderton, I wanted to speak to you about the tea. You really must find another solution for the scones. The last two batches have been hard as rocks. I refuse to believe that there's no good flour to be had in all of Warwickshire."

Any bond that Stella felt to Mrs. Symonds beyond that of employee and employer crumbled.

Balance had been restored.

· BETH ·

My darling Beth,

Already I miss you, and I've only just arrived on base. The journey from Highbury was long and slow and made more difficult by the fact that I knew that every mile traveled was a mile further away from you. You won't forget me, will you, all the way up in the Midlands while I'm staring at the sea?

Love,
Graeme

My dearest Graeme,

I still can't quite believe that you're gone, but every time I worry about when we might see each other again, I can't help but feel grateful that you're in Southampton and not in Italy. You must forgive me if that sounds selfish. I know there is nothing you want more than to be with your men again, but Stella tells me that a newly engaged woman is allowed to be a little bit selfish.

I am not too proud to admit that I cried the entire afternoon you left. Mr. Penworthy took pity on me, dear man that he is, and sent me to Mrs. Penworthy. She just shook her head, told me she was sorry to see two young people separated, and set a stack of onions in front of me to slice for soup, since I couldn't possibly cry any more than I already was. Petunia stopped by as well and sat with me awhile, and even Ruth is being very kind about the whole thing.

But don't worry. I've decided to be very brave. I will keep to my duties on the farm and go to the cinema with Petunia and continue to sketch in Mrs. Symonds's garden. Everyone has been incredibly kind to me—even Mrs. Yarley in the village shop has stopped eyeing me when I come in to buy drawing pencils. (I am saving yours for something special, don't worry.)

Enclosed in this letter is a drawing of the garden where we first kissed. Maybe it's a little sentimental to send you such a thing, but I want you to remember what it's like here with the flowers in bloom and the summer sun heating the pathways. I don't think there is a place more beautiful on this earth.

Love always,
Beth

Saturday, 3 June 1944
Highbury, Warwickshire

Dear Colin,

I still have not heard from you, and I fear that my letter may have been lost. Or maybe you simply don't want to talk to me. I could understand that.

I have no excuse for Graeme. Know that I didn't intend it to be this way. I didn't want to hurt you.

All I can ask for is your forgiveness.
Please try to understand.

Affectionately,
Beth

Monday, 5 June 1944
Highbury, Warwickshire

My dearest Graeme,

I hope you will not mind me sending you another letter when I haven't had one back from you yet. I know that it must be difficult for you to write as you settle into your new role. I remember how long it took me to learn how to do all of my tasks under Mr. Penworthy's supervision.

Today I wasn't just a land girl but also a shepherd. Ruth and I were sent over to Alderminster, where Alice is assigned to help Mr. Becker, the shepherd, with the last of the shearing. Petunia was there as well. (She says hello and asks when she can expect to be a bridesmaid.) It took some time to learn how to hold the sheep down and use the clippers. Ruth was nearly kicked in the face, but instead the hoof hit her shoulder. I know I've told you that she whines terribly sometimes, but she had good reason today. When we came home, her entire shoulder was black-and-blue. If we had any beef to spare, Mrs. Penworthy would have made her hold a steak to it, I'm sure.

For all of the hard work it was, however, I enjoyed it. We helped weigh and draft the lambs into different fields. It's hard not to be charmed by them. They are such dear things, and my hands feel the softest they've been since I became a land girl thanks to all of that wool.

I've been thinking about our wedding. There is no point of having it in Dorking. I don't know if you would prefer Colchester, but maybe it would be possible to marry here in Highbury. I've only been to the church a handful of times, but the vicar seems a very decent sort of man. Also, so many of my friends are in Highbury, and I know that the doctors and nurses from the hospital would be delighted to wish us well on the day.

I'm getting too far ahead of myself now. I should set this letter aside and go help Mrs. Penworthy with dinner.

> Love always,
> Beth

> Tuesday, 6 June 1944
> Highbury, Warwickshire

My dearest Graeme,

Another day without a letter in the morning post. I've told myself not to worry, but I can't help it. There is so much for us to learn about each other . . .

Forgive me my shaking pen. I wrote the above just before heading to the fields, intending to pick it up again if nothing came in the afternoon post, either. Instead, I've learned of the invasion underway. Mr. Penworthy carries a wireless radio in the tractor, and we were listening to the BBC while having lunch in the field when John Snagge read out a special bulletin. I will never forget how my stomach dropped when I heard the words "D-Day has come."

I cannot help now but worry that you were sent to the beaches of Normandy. That this is why you haven't written to me in days, when you promised you would write every other day at the very least. I will listen to the king's broadcast tonight—as the entire country will—and pray that you are safe.

I love you. I should have told you that in the garden, but I was so shocked and happy and stunned that you wanted to marry me.

> I love you, I love you,
> I love you,
> Beth

Tuesday, 6 June 1944
Highbury, Warwickshire

Dear Colin,

Please write to me and tell me that you're safe.

Affectionately,
Beth

Wednesday, 7 June 1944
Highbury, Warwickshire

My dearest Graeme,

I do not expect a letter back from you. I can only hope that you are
not in Normandy, but I fear from your silence that you are. I can
only pray for you and your men.

I love you,
Beth

Thursday, 8 June 1944
Highbury, Warwickshire

My dearest Graeme,

We are all praying for you. Everyone.

Mrs. Symonds was in the kitchen when I made my delivery to
Stella, and when she asked for word of you, I could hardly speak
through my sobs. She wrapped her arms around me and held me
close to her, saying nothing.

Come back to me, Graeme. Come back to me.

I love you,
Beth

"I hate laundry day," Ruth groaned.

Beth hauled up a basket of wet sheets and balanced it on her hip. "Open the door for me, will you?"

Ruth rushed forward. Since D-Day, everyone seemed to be tripping over themselves to be kind to her. Beth appreciated it—she did—but she would happily work doubly hard to trade away the constant worry for her fiancé's safety.

Every morning she scoured the newspapers that Mr. Penworthy drove to the village to buy for her. Everyone in the farmhouse gathered around the wireless, hoping for some scrap of information. None of them expected to hear Graeme's name on the radio, or even much detail about the Pioneer Corps he had been assigned to after being discharged from Highbury House, but it gave them something to do. Something to hope for.

Setting her washing down in the sweet-scented grass under the clothesline, Beth pulled a bunch of pins out of her pocket and clipped them to the arm of her blouse. Ruth picked the top sheet off the stack and unpeeled the wet fabric from itself. Together, they tossed one end over the line, and Beth pinned it in place.

"There's a dance in Leamington Spa tomorrow evening," said Ruth.

Beth made a noncommittal noise.

"Petunia will be there," Ruth tried again. Now that was a sign of how worried Ruth was about her. Her roommate hated Petunia and had once called her one of those horsey girls who couldn't talk about anything but breeding lines and county hunts. Beth suspected that the truth was that, for all of her resentment of the Women's Land Army, Ruth liked being the poshest local land girl. When Petunia was around, it was hard to compete.

"If I went, none of you would enjoy yourselves," said Beth.

"You can't just sit on your bed and mope."

"I can, and I will if I want to," she said.

"Fine," said Ruth, throwing the next sheet over the line so forcefully that it would have ended up on the ground if Beth hadn't dived to catch it.

"I appreciate what you're trying to do," said Beth, softening. "I really do."

"Beth! Beth!" Mrs. Penworthy came running out of the house, flapping her hands about.

"What is it?" Beth asked, her hands stilling on the washing.

"You have post! Two letters!"

The sheet slipped from Beth's hands and pooled in the grass as she ran toward Mrs. Penworthy. Meeting her halfway, she snatched up the letters, recognizing the handwriting on the top one.

"Graeme," she breathed, dropping the other letter to tear it open.

Monday, 19 June 1944

My darling Beth,

I cannot tell you where I am or what I am doing but know I'm safe.

> *Yours forever,*
> *Graeme*

P.S. I've loved you since I saw you on top of Mr. Penworthy's tractor.

Beth's knees gave out. "He's safe." *He's safe, and he loves me.*

Ruth and Mrs. Penworthy dropped into the grass next to her, engulfing her.

"I'm so glad, pet. I'm so, so glad," said Mrs. Penworthy.

The three women stayed like that, rocking gently back and forth, until finally Beth loosened her grip on them both.

"The second letter," she said.

The other women let her go, and Ruth reached behind her to pluck it up off the ground. Beth's heart sank when she saw the handwritten address.

"It's from Colin," she said.

"You need to open it," said Ruth.

Beth nodded.

"Come on, let's give her some privacy," said Mrs. Penworthy, wrapping an arm around Ruth's shoulders and guiding her toward the house.

With trembling hands, Beth opened Colin's envelope and drew out the letter. There was only one word written there: *No.*

· EMMA ·

JULY 2021

*E*mma pulled off her hat and used a handkerchief to wipe her brow, a habit she'd picked up from helping her father in the garden. He would stand, wipe the sweat from his neck, and declare that it was time for a cool drink. She would bound up the garden path to the kitchen, where Mum, who liked to sit at the window while they worked, was already pouring tall glasses of lemonade.

What she wouldn't give for a lemonade.

All of England and Wales and most of Scotland was in the grips of a heat wave. They'd become a certainty in recent years, and everyone suffered for it in this country with so little air-conditioning. Bow Cottage had remained hot all last night, and she'd hardly slept, even with the rotating fan. When she'd greeted Charlie that morning, he'd told her he'd slept on the roof of the narrow boat, under the stars, and woke up to his mooring neighbor's dog licking his face.

Still, she was glad to be in the wilds of the winter garden today. It was peaceful here, which certainly had its appeal, but it was more than that. Different garden rooms had different feelings. The children's garden was playful with its wildflowers and delicately blossomed cherry trees. The tea garden felt formal and proper. But the winter garden held a sobriety that gave her the same sensation as walking into a church. No matter what she encountered outside, she could hitch her leg over the wall, climb down the other side, and the weight of the place would press gently, comfortingly on her shoulders.

Charlie felt it, too, but he wasn't drawn to it the way she was.

"There's something about it I just don't like," he'd say, shivering as soon as his feet hit the ground. "It feels sad."

Reverential maybe, she'd decided, thinking of the faint penciled-in name. Celeste's garden. A remembrance.

"Knock, knock!"

Emma spotted Sydney at the top of the ladder. "Hi."

"I hope you don't mind me climbing this, only I wasn't sure if you would be able to hear me from the gate," said Sydney.

"So long as you don't fall off. My insurance couldn't afford it," she said.

Sydney laughed. "I promise I won't."

"Do you want to come down and see it?" Emma asked.

"I'd love to."

Sydney scrambled over the top of the wall before Emma could warn her to be careful. She breathed a sigh of relief when her employer's feet were firmly on the ground again.

Sydney pushed her hair out of her face and gazed around. "It's like a jungle in here. If I didn't know better, I would think I was in a forest."

"I'm afraid forests do a lot better at regulating themselves. This is completely overgrown," she said.

"I think it's spectacular. Look at all that you've already done."

"Thanks," said Emma, genuinely appreciative. "Was there something you needed in particular or were you just curious?"

"Nosy, more like it. No, I actually did have something to ask. Andrew and I were talking, and we wanted to know if you would consider doing the kitchen garden."

"The kitchen garden?"

"I know it's not as historically significant as this one, but we'd really like to get it up and running again. We just don't really know where to start," said Sydney.

"A kitchen garden that size was designed to feed the house's family and staff, food for a dozen or more. Are you sure you want something that large?"

"It wouldn't just be for us. I've been talking to a teacher at the local primary school, and she said that the kids would get so much out of spending a term in the garden as they learn about plants. I thought it could be part functional garden, part teaching tool."

It was a fantastic idea. The younger that children got into the garden, the more passionate they were likely to remain when they grew up.

"What would you do with the extra produce?" she asked.

"Henry's offered to take it on. In addition to his main distributors, he does some community farming initiatives, sells directly to restaurants, things like that."

She had walked through the kitchen garden only a dozen or so times, but already she could envision what to do with the space. They'd need to rebuild the raised beds and rig up a durable system of netting to keep cabbage butterflies and wood pigeons out. Succession planting to make sure that there was always something ready for harvest, and—

No. She was getting way ahead of herself. She'd already booked her next job after Highbury House—a contemporary bonsai garden for an influencer in Berwick-upon-Tweed—and there would be no room in the schedule to add the kitchen garden in, no matter how tempting the extra money would be.

"I'm really sorry, Sydney, but I don't think I can extend the job. Besides, kitchen gardens aren't really my specialty. Charlie has some experience in urban farming, though," she said.

Sydney's face fell for just a second before her bright smile popped up again. Still, Emma clocked it.

"I can refer you to a few colleagues who are very good at that sort of thing," Emma said quickly.

"That would be great," said Sydney graciously. "Sorry to barge in while you were working. I did try to text."

"Did you?"

Emma dug her phone out of her back pocket. She saw she'd missed Sydney's message as well as a string of texts on her family chat:

Mum: We've decided to come visit in two weeks! We're driving up on the Saturday.

Dad: If that's okay with you.

Mum: We want to see the garden you're working on.

Dad: Eileen, you can't invite yourself to other people's gardens.

Mum: Emma will arrange it.

She groaned.

"What's wrong?" Sydney asked.

"Would you mind if my parents drop by to see the garden in a couple weeks? They're curious, and it's been a while since I've worked on one close enough for them to see," she said.

"Of course they should come! Why don't you all stay for tea as well?" Sydney suggested.

"Are you sure? Mum will grill you about every aspect of the house. She's not the most subtle woman in the world," she said.

"I think I can handle that." Sydney turned to the ladder but stopped herself. "Charlie isn't a partner in Turning Back Thyme, right?"

"No. Why do you ask?"

"If Charlie has experience with veg gardens, do you think he might be interested in doing the kitchen garden as a one-time contract?" Sydney asked.

"Oh. I really don't know," she said, surprised.

"Would you mind if I asked him?"

"Of course not. He can do whatever he likes," she said, realizing as she said it that Charlie would probably jump at the chance to do a favor for Sydney.

"You're sure you don't mind?" Sydney asked.

She shook her head. "Go for it. And thank you again for the invitation to tea."

"I'm glad you'll be able to come," said Sydney.

Alone once again, Emma picked up a pair of loppers and resumed attacking the underbrush.

Sydney's questions about Charlie bounced around her brain all afternoon and evening. Did he want to take on his own jobs? She'd never really thought about that before, but maybe she should have. He could design, but he'd always told her he was more interested in the physical side of their work.

Selfish though it might be, she couldn't stand the idea of Charlie striking off on his own, not because he would be competition but because she'd miss him. She'd met every one of his girlfriends and drank in pubs across the Home Nations with him. She'd been at his mother's funeral, and he'd been the one to drive her to the hospital when she'd broken her arm falling off a ladder. Charlie was her right-hand man, her confidant, her best friend.

That was why, the morning after her conversation with Sydney, she'd shown up at work armed with a pair of coffee cups.

"Here," she said, thrusting one at him.

"What's this?" he asked.

"Coffee," she said.

He rolled his eyes. "Why?"

"Can't a friend buy a friend coffee?"

Suspiciously he took the cup. "Did they do the extra pump of hazelnut?"

"Yes. You drink the most frilly drinks," she said.

"Nothing wrong with a little frill," he said, opening the top of the disposable cup to let the steam off. He took a sip. "That is good."

"I'm glad."

He held up the cup and pointed at the green-and-white logo. "The closest location is a ten-minute drive, and you live within walking distance of your job. Why did you drive twenty minutes to get me coffee?"

She lifted her chin. "Do you ever think about leaving Turning Back Thyme?"

He shrugged. "Sure, all the time."

"What?" she sputtered.

"Well, last week, you dropped a shovel on me."

"That was an accident," she muttered.

"And then there was the time you didn't tie up my boat properly, and we nearly drifted into a riverbank."

For that she had no defense other than having had a few Pimm's on a boat trip with the Turning Back Thyme crew, none of whom should have been lashing boats to docks in their state.

"So you want to leave?" she asked.

"There are times when I think about it. Five years working for the same company is a long time—even with you as my boss. There are projects I've wanted to try, but our schedule hasn't let me." He paused to sip his coffee. "But I like what we have here. It's a good little company."

"It's not that little," she grumbled.

He shot her a smile. "What's with all of the questions? What happened?"

She sighed. "Sydney's thinking about redoing the kitchen garden. We're supposed to move up to the Berwick job after this, and I've run out of grace period given the delays when we found Venetia's plans. I can't squeeze it in."

"And you don't do vegetables," he said, finishing her thought.

"She thought about asking you."

He cocked his head. "How does she know I'd be interested?"

"I told her you had experience with veg."

"That's good of you."

A long pause stretched between them until finally he said, "I'm not in a rush to leave, Emma. But I'd be a pretty rotten friend if I didn't level with you that I'm not going to be happy on your crew forever. I've other skills."

"I know you do. I'll figure something out."

"I'm sure you will." He lifted his coffee. "Anytime you feel like bribing me to talk again, go right ahead."

· VENETIA ·

MONDAY, 1 JULY 1907
Highbury House
Hot, dry. This summer will never end.

*S*o many things have happened since I last wrote. I hardly know where to start.

After midday, when the afternoon was thick with heat and laziness, I took the note I'd written Matthew out of my writing box. Being only a passable horsewoman, I decided to walk the distance to our secret hiding place in the hedgerow. It would be good to stretch my legs, which too often are cramped under me as I dig.

As the hot road stretched before me, though, I began to regret my ambition. A dry, grassy scent enveloped me as insects danced in the sunlight. A dairy cow lowed in a field, watching me with disinterest, but most of the herd had sensibly sought the shade of a small group of trees.

It was a relief when I reached the bend in the road where the hedgerow was split by a dying English oak. It would be years before it came down, unless a storm tore it up at the roots, and a kestrel had made her nest in a hollowed-out bit of the trunk far higher than I could reach. However, it was a knot lower down I was after. The casual passerby would never have noticed it, but I could not walk or ride by without eyeing it, for it was my postbox with Matthew.

As I always did, I reached in, hoping for a letter. My fingers touched paper, and when I drew them out I found two notes. I winced. He'd written twice since we'd last seen each other, and I had only just penned my message that morning.

I slid the notes into my left pocket and was just reaching into my right when a voice hailed me.

"Good afternoon, Miss Smith."

I squeezed my eyes shut tight, knowing that when I turned around, I would find Mrs. Melcourt in the open-topped carriage, her driver, Michaelson, pretending that he was not listening to every single word.

Easing my hand back into my pocket and wrapping my fingers around my handkerchief, I pulled it out and made a show of dabbing my forehead as I turned.

"Good afternoon, Mrs. Melcourt," I said.

The other woman frowned. "Are you quite well?"

"I must confess, I may have misjudged the summer afternoon. I went for a walk, only to find myself overtaken by the heat."

"There are far more pleasant walks than this road," said Mrs. Melcourt.

"That is true, but Mr. Hillock's son, John, said that he spotted a crested cow-wheat not far from here," I said, the first lie I could think of.

"What is that?"

"It's a rare flower," I said.

The woman stared at me for a moment. But then she nodded to the carriage. "If you've had enough of hunting for flowers, perhaps you would enjoy a ride back to the house. And your *work*."

The word stung, just as she'd intended. There was nothing that I wanted less than to ride even a mile with this woman who seemed to barely tolerate my presence in her house these days, but to insist on walking home was foolish. I would only spite myself and my swollen feet in the process.

I nodded, and Michaelson climbed down to open the door for me. Drawing up my skirts, I climbed into the carriage with his help.

As soon as I was settled across from Mrs. Melcourt, she said, "I have just been visiting Lady Kinner. You will remember her from the ball."

"Yes, I recall. I hope she is in good health."

"Any woman with that much money and so few obligations should be. Her niece is returned from Boston."

My awareness sharpened, even as I fixed my gaze on the countryside passing us by.

"Miss Orleon is such an accomplished young lady and quite charming. Matthew was taken with her when he went up to London for the Season last year."

I couldn't help it when my brows shot up.

"Is it so amusing that Matthew would have done the Season?" asked Mrs. Melcourt.

"He seems so content at Wisteria Farm with his roses."

"Life is about more than flowers, Miss Smith. He has a duty to marry, and I am determined to see him marry well. He cannot continue to live on the generosity of Mr. Melcourt for much longer."

"Generosity?"

"My husband provides Matthew with the use of Wisteria Farm as well as other necessities."

We slipped into an uncomfortable silence until the gates of Highbury House came into view. I glanced at Mrs. Melcourt, thinking to thank her for the ride back, when she leaned in. "You occupy a peculiar position in this household, Miss Smith."

"I do not think of myself as 'in this household' at all, but rather a guest of it," I said.

Mrs. Melcourt tilted her head. "And yet my husband pays you a wage for your work. Payment is not customary for guests."

I was about to reply when my heart began to pound and my head became light. My hand went to my chest.

"Miss Smith, are you quite well?" Mrs. Melcourt asked me for the second time that afternoon, that voice of hers freezing the very air.

But just as soon as the sensation had overtaken me, it fled. I shook my head slightly and said, "I'm fine, thank you," resolving to apply a cool cloth to my neck and loosen my corset as soon as I could retire to the gardener's cottage.

Mrs. Melcourt squinted at me. "You look a little pale."

"Nonsense," I said as Michaelson drew the carriage to a stop. A boy ran out from the stable and caught the lead horses to hold them.

I had risen when Mrs. Melcourt said, "You'd do best to let Michaelson help you down."

"I'm made of sturdier stuff than most," I said. I put one shaky food down on the carriage's short ladder. My head swam again, but I sucked in a deep breath. One step. Two steps. Three steps.

When my boot touched the ground, the world rushed closed to a pinpoint and then everything went black.

When I opened my eyes again, I was looking into the face of a man in a black coat with an impressive set of muttonchops, last in fashion during the previous century.

"There you are, Miss Smith," he said, sitting back.

"Who are . . . ?" I tried to push myself up only to realize that I didn't know where I was or how I'd gotten there.

"I'm Dr. Irving," he said.

"What happened?"

Dr. Irving looked over his shoulder, and I realized that Mrs. Creasley filled the doorway, her arms crossed over her chest.

"You're in my sitting room. You fainted in the courtyard," said the housekeeper.

"Do you remember fainting?" Dr. Irving asked.

I squeezed my eyes shut, trying to recall. "I remember climbing down from the carriage."

"Mrs. Melcourt said you fainted," said Mrs. Creasley.

I frowned at Mrs. Creasley's icy tone. The woman had always been courteous, but in that moment I couldn't help but feel like a maid who'd scorched the mistress's linens.

"Miss Smith would appreciate a cup of tea, I'm sure," Dr. Irving said. "Not too strong, but with plenty of sugar."

There was a slight narrowing at the housekeeper's eyes, but she nodded nonetheless.

As soon as the door closed, the doctor's cheerful expression fell. "Miss Smith, have you experienced fainting spells before?"

"No."

"Does your mother have a habit of fainting?" he asked.

"I was not aware of such a habit. She's dead."

He pursed his lips. "And have you been experiencing any other symptoms?"

"I don't understand. Symptoms of what?"

He sighed. "Have you felt unable to eat or drink?"

"No."

"Light-headed?"

"Other than this afternoon, no."

"I beg your pardon for being so forward, but have you noticed that your clothing no longer fits as it once did?" he asked.

I frowned. "I have some things that fit me better than others, but you must understand, Dr. Irving, there are aspects of my work that require a degree of physical exercise that most ladies do not engage in."

"I cannot find fault in your desire for exercise, Miss Smith. In fact, I wish more ladies and gentlemen would engage in activities in the fresh air."

"Then you agree that there is nothing wrong with me."

"I do apologize for the intimacy of this, Miss Smith, but when was the last time you experienced your courses?"

I looked up sharply. "What?"

"When were your last courses?" he asked slowly as though translating for someone who spoke another language.

I did a quick count in my head, trying my hardest to remember back to the last time I'd needed the bundle of rags I kept in a plain box in my wardrobe. Surely it was just a few weeks ago. When the arbors went in between the poet's garden and the water garden. I remembered needing to excuse myself to check for—

That was two months ago, before the Melcourts' party.

"Dr. Irving"—my voice high with rising panic—"surely you are not suggesting—"

"That you might be with child? I'm afraid when a hale and hearty lady faints, and then the housekeeper who is called to help ease her corset finds that the lady in question has been wearing her laces looser than the notches in them might suggest, I must ask the obvious question."

"It is hot. No lady likes to wear her corset close when the weather is as it has been," I insisted.

The doctor looked on with some sympathy.

Shame collapses on me. It is one thing for the doctor to suggest that I might be with child, but if the housekeeper knew . . .

I buried my face in my hands. I needed time to think. Time to figure out what I could do, for I mustn't lose the garden at Highbury or my livelihood.

After a moment, the doctor said, "I take it, then, that you were not aware of the possibility of your condition."

It hadn't even crossed my mind.

"I'm thirty-five years old," I said.

"A great many women older than you have borne healthy children safely," he said.

I swallowed. "Dr. Irving, I'm unmarried."

"Ah. Yes. Well, I gathered as much when Mrs. Creasley called you Miss Smith."

I grabbed his hand. "I cannot have this baby."

He pulled back, his avuncular jocularity gone. "Miss Smith, think very carefully what you say next. There are things in this world that are not only an affront to God but a crime."

I sank back, miserable knowing that this doctor wouldn't help me even if he knew how.

He began collecting his things and placing them carefully into his brown leather medical bag.

He was halfway to the door when I stopped him. "Dr. Irving, please would you do me the courtesy of not telling Mr. and Mrs. Melcourt."

The doctor pressed his fingers to the bridge of his nose. "Mr. Melcourt will ask me for my bill."

"If you could tell them you treated me for a nervous condition . . ."

"I would not betray the confidence of a lady. But Miss Smith, you do know that at some point it won't matter what I do or do not tell the Melcourts. They will know. Everyone will."

"Thank you, Doctor," I said weakly.

He left, plunging the room into silence and leaving me in despair.

· DIANA ·

*D*iana's trug bounced against her side as she snipped another long-stemmed bloom and placed it into the shallow basket. All around her in the tea garden bees hummed fat and lazy in the summer sun, going about their industrious days a little slower than usual.

She'd always loved this time of year. She could cope with the dreariness of winter, but she craved sultry air. She enjoyed late nights on the veranda with a glass of something cool and sweet in her hand. In her parents' home, she'd never have dared to wear anything but the cotton nightgowns her mother selected for her. In her own home, however, she'd learned the delicious freedom of sleeping nude in the summers.

No longer sharing a bed with a fever-hot man at night was one of the few aspects of widowhood that she'd allowed herself to enjoy. She might long for the weight of Murray's hand on her back as she fell asleep, but she didn't miss the way his mere presence would stifle her. Now she went straight from the cool of her bath into bed.

Passing into the lovers' garden, she heard a woman's voice from over the hedge.

"Remember, it's important that you stay still," the woman said, followed by little boys' giggles.

Curious, Diana poked her head into the children's garden. Sitting shoulder to shoulder with their backs against one of the cherry trees were Robin and Bobby. A few feet away sat Miss Pedley with her sketchbook.

"Mummy!" Robin shouted as soon as he saw her. He was up like a shot, throwing himself at her legs. Her heart swelled just looking down at the top of his little blond head. Some days she thought it was a miracle he was here; others he reminded her of Murray so much it was almost painful.

"Hello, darling. Are you playing artist's model for Miss Pedley?" she asked.

"She's drawing us," said Robin.

Bobby hovered nearby. "Miss Pedley's teaching us to draw, too."

"Well, that is very kind of her," said Diana, eyeing the abandoned pencils and pieces of paper covered with children's scribbles. "However, the teacher shouldn't also have to provide the supplies. I'll ask Mrs. Dibble to root around the attics to see if she can find Cynthia's old sketchbooks from when she was a girl. There must be some unused paper in there."

"Thank you," said Miss Pedley, her hands crossed over her sketchbook, pressed against her stomach.

"Might I have a look?" Diana asked.

"Oh, yes." The young woman hesitated before opening the cover of the book. "It isn't much. Just little scribbles."

Miss Pedley turned the book to show the half-finished sketch of the two boys. Robin's head was resting back against the tree, and Bobby's was canted slightly to the left. Both had spindly limbs sticking out of shorts, the way that boys do. Yet for all they looked alike, there were distinct differences. Robin was confident, almost arrogant. Bobby shyer, looking out from underneath his lashes.

"Very pretty. They could be cousins posed like this," Diana said.

"Mummy." Robin tugged on her hand. "Mummy, I want to go show Bobby my pirate's cave."

"You know that you're not allowed in the winter garden without me."

He toed the ground. "But my pirate's cave."

She couldn't help but soften. "And a very good one, I'm sure. Once I'm done with the flowers, I'll fetch one of the keys and take you both."

A chorus of cheers.

"I've been meaning to ask, Miss Pedley, if you and Captain Hastings have discussed the plans for your wedding any further," she said.

"Yes. That is, we've written about them."

"Is he still in Normandy?" Diana asked.

"He's been attached to the Pioneer Corps, so he's been back and forth, although he's stationed in Southampton. I don't know when he'll have leave, but we'll marry then," Miss Pedley said.

"That's hardly helpful for planning," she said.

"No." Miss Pedley sighed. "And I fear it'll get worse. He's trying to rejoin his original unit."

"The man's shoulder was nearly taken apart by a bullet," said Diana.

Miss Pedley chewed her lip. "I had hoped that he would take to being a supply officer. I don't want him back in combat."

"Have you told him that? Asked him to put in a transfer that will keep him in Britain?"

Miss Pedley dipping her head was all the answer Diana needed.

"And what of you? Will you remain a land girl?" she asked.

"Yes," breathed the young woman, as though the backbreaking labor was a relief and not a burden. "Conscription means that I'll stay on unless I become pregnant."

"What would you do then?" she asked.

"Graeme tells me that he could make arrangements for me to stay with his parents."

"Where are his people from?" Diana asked.

Miss Pedley's shoulders sagged a little further. "Colchester."

"Colchester is quite far from Highbury, and you seem to have so many friends here."

"I know." Miss Pedley lifted her head, and Diana was surprised to see tears glistening in her eyes. "I'm sorry. It's silly to become upset, but it's just that Highbury is the first place I've ever been happy."

This poor girl. That she needed help was clear, but by the looks of it, Miss Pedley had few women to guide her.

"And you wish to stay?" Diana asked.

Miss Pedley nodded. "But that's just as silly. This isn't my home, either. I just don't know what to do."

"Are you certain that you want to marry this man?" Diana asked.

Miss Pedley's answer was immediate. "Yes. I've known him for so little time, but yes."

Perhaps if she were a different person, Diana would have embraced this young woman. She'd hugged Miss Pedley once, when they'd all waited with bated breath for news of Captain Hastings from the invasion, but she couldn't break through years of "correct" behavior quite so easily again.

Instead, she said, "Well, that brings us back to the question of your nuptials. If Captain Hastings can secure leave, I suppose you'll want to marry here. If you like, I'll send word to the vicar, and he can help you arrange a date around Captain Hastings's leave."

"Oh, thank you, Mrs. Symonds. That's very kind," said Miss Pedley.

"What were your plans for a wedding breakfast?" she asked.

"I hadn't thought, yet. It all seems so daunting, especially with rationing on," Miss Pedley said.

"You must have a wedding breakfast. You'll have it at Highbury House," Diana said before she could second-guess her offer—or consider how Miss Adderton would feel about it.

"At Highbury?" Miss Pedley asked.

"On the veranda, if you like, or in the morning room if it's raining. Highbury House might be a convalescent hospital, but I think it's proven it can still manage a party when called upon."

Miss Adderton would be in a foul mood at the idea of having to magic a wedding breakfast out of thin air and thin rations—or maybe not. She'd seen the way Miss Pedley had stayed by Miss Adderton's side when the telegram came.

Cynthia would be another matter.

"Are you sure it wouldn't be a bother?" Miss Pedley asked.

"None at all," Diana lied through a smile. Miss Pedley's wedding breakfast was sure to become another battleground on which Diana and her virtuous sister-in-law squared off. "Well, I should leave you to your drawing."

She was halfway across the garden room when Miss Pedley called out, "Am I giving up too much if I agree to move to Colchester after the war?"

Slowly Diana looked over her shoulder. "Love can make women do ridiculous things. Intelligent women become silly. They give things up they never intended . . ." She trailed off. "Just know that you can tell him what you want. You can demand what you need."

"What did you give up for Mr. Symonds?" asked Miss Pedley.

Diana adjusted the trug so it sat higher on her arm before answering, "Everything."

That afternoon, after she'd made her rounds to visit with the soldiers, Diana stood in front of the music room that had been reduced to storage when the hospital moved in.

She smoothed her skirt and then set her shoulders back. It was just a room. It didn't think ill of her.

And yet, when she opened the door, the air felt thick with regret, like taking tea with a now-distant acquaintance who'd once been a dear companion.

Softly she closed the door behind her. The maid, Dorothy, must come to air the room out every once in a while; it smelled fresh and there was hardly any dust floating in the light through the gap in the navy curtains. And standing in the corner, just where she'd left it, was her harp.

She approached it as a rider might a shy horse. Her fingers grazed over the felt cover. She'd wanted this instrument with every ounce of her being when she was fifteen. She'd been talented. Her teacher had even encouraged her to study at a conservatory. She'd asked her parents for permission. *Begged* for it. Shortly afterward, she'd been sent to Switzerland to be "finished" instead.

Reverently Diana removed the cloth cover. The folds fell away, revealing the harp's deep walnut soundboard and brass pedals. Pulling up a chair, she eased the instrument back against her shoulder, stopping to hitch her skirt up a little. With a deep breath, she placed her thumb to middle C and plucked.

A discordant twang rang out, making her jump.

"Of course it's out of tune," she murmured.

She nearly set the harp upright again, ready to cover it and leave the room, but then she spotted her son's sheet music on the piano. If Robin could have music, why couldn't she?

She retrieved her tuning fork and tuning key from the bookcase, then worked methodically, slowly bringing the harp back to life.

When at last the final string had been tightened to the right tone, she placed her hands to the strings and began a Leduc piece that she could have played in her sleep when she'd been practicing seriously. However, although she could still remember the notes, her hands had lost much of their agility.

She finished the piece, making a note to herself to oil the pedals, and then switched to a Schubert piece she'd once loved. Halfway through, she stopped to shake out her aching hands. Her fingers were moving at half the speed they had when she'd last played years ago.

When an hour later she covered her instrument and let herself out of the music room, she knew she didn't want to wait that long again.

· VENETIA ·

I have neglected to write these last weeks, but could anyone fault me for it?

Being with child, I have learned, is a misery. Ever since Dr. Irving's diagnosis, I have been struck down by nausea and fatigue, as though my body has now been given permission to betray me each day.

This morning, I found myself on my knees behind a buddleia in the children's garden, trying to bring up the morning's meager breakfast of tea and toast. I understand the irony of planting a garden meant to bring children joy when I am so miserable with my condition, but that is reason to move swiftly. I will show before my work at Highbury House is complete.

To think that I will never see this garden completed makes my heart ache, but an aching heart and an intact reputation is better than disgrace. I have a plan. Sometime in September, I will begin to feign an illness—what type I have not yet decided. It must be serious but not too grave, only requiring a period of uninterrupted rest and, if I'm lucky, a doctor's recommendation of warmer climes. I will leave plans, detailed drawings, and plant lists for Mr. Hillock to finish the garden. Then I will take myself away for six or eight months to a place where I know no one and hire a discreet woman to help me with the birth. After arranging for the child to be placed with a family who will love her, I'll return to England.

It is the only way.

Everywhere I turn, sacrifices arise. I have given up Matthew. There was no argument. No grand tragedy played out. Instead, I've stayed close to Highbury House. I no longer venture to the hedgerow, and if I must pass it, I keep my eyes resolutely on the ground in front of me.

I swiped my handkerchief over my mouth and stood from my floral hiding spot, brushing off my skirts. *This too shall pass*, I told myself, as I did every day.

"Miss Smith," a girl's distant voice called.

I cleared my ragged throat. "I'm here."

One of the maids I didn't recognize poked her head through the break in the hedge from the bridal garden. "Miss Smith, Mr. Melcourt's asked to see you in the drawing room."

My stomach lurched. He knew.

Stiffly I nodded, tidied my gardening gloves and tools into their wicker basket, and gathered up my skirts to follow the maid to my reckoning.

She showed me to the double drawing room. How fitting that my termination should take place in the same room where I had been hired.

When I looked around, I saw that Mr. Melcourt was not alone. He was standing with a small man with unusually tanned skin, which contrasted sharply against the brilliant white of his shirt.

"Miss Smith. I'm sorry to take you away from your work," said Mr. Melcourt pleasantly—not at all the tone of a man who was about to dismiss his garden designer.

"Not at all," I said cautiously.

"May I present Mr. Martin Schoot? The director of the Royal Botanical Heritage Society." Mr. Melcourt smiled at his guest. "He expressed a desire to make your acquaintance."

The Royal Botanical Heritage Society—a prestigious and pompous organization that refused to admit women to its ranks.

I fought a frown as I said, "Mr. Schoot, you'll have to forgive me for not shaking hands. I've just been in the garden."

His hand remained outstretched. "A little dirt cannot hurt me, Miss Smith. Quite the contrary. I imagine you are happiest when you are out in nature rather than confined indoors."

Reluctantly I took his hand.

"I have been corresponding with Mr. Schoot ever since I had the idea to give new life to the gardens at Highbury House," said Mr. Melcourt.

"I wanted very much to meet the woman behind such a large project," he said.

"Does it surprise you that a woman should be given charge of a garden like Highbury's, Mr. Schoot?" I asked.

I'd expected him to react as so many men do when faced with a woman's thinly veiled scorn—poorly—but instead Mr. Schoot began to laugh. "Well met, Miss Smith. I see from the loose, natural structure of your plantings that you hold William Robinson's designs in high regard."

"And Gertrude Jekyll. My father gave me her book *Wood and Garden* not long before he died," I said.

"It's interesting that you mention Miss Jekyll's work—"

Before Mr. Schoot could finish his thought, Mrs. Melcourt glided in, followed by her brother.

Matthew stumbled over the Turkish carpet when he saw me. His eyes widened, his lips opened, and then he smiled. He *smiled*. My stomach lurched.

"Miss Smith, you're not in the garden," said Mrs. Melcourt.

"I'm to blame. I expressed an interest in meeting Miss Smith, and your husband kindly obliged," interjected Mr. Schoot.

Mrs. Melcourt's lips pursed into a tight line before spreading into an imitation smile. "Of course. Has Miss Smith told you what she has done to work a rose or two from my brother Matthew's collection into the garden?"

A rose or two? The garden was overflowing with Matthew's roses now, so much so that it was impossible to turn a corner without being confronted with a reminder of him.

Matthew bowed his head. "My contribution is nothing compared to Miss Smith's creation."

236 · JULIA KELLY

"Come now, Matthew. You are too modest. My brother is a gifted botanist, you see," said Mrs. Melcourt.

"My sister flatters me. I'm merely a man whose hobby has taken over his life," said Matthew good-naturedly.

"No, that's not right," I said sharply. All eyes snapped to me. I shouldn't have said more, but I won't stand for a man with Matthew's passion and dedication downplaying his achievements.

"Mr. Goddard has a great talent with breeding roses," I continued. "He is far more knowledgeable than I am in the intricacies of crossing and grafting them. It has been a pleasure to watch him work."

I caught Matthew's smile just as Mrs. Melcourt's eyes narrowed. "Watch him work?" she asked.

"Miss Smith has visited Wisteria Farm on several occasions to select roses for the garden. And she's crossed a rose or two herself. I should be harvesting the seeds soon," said Matthew.

"Several occasions?" Mrs. Melcourt asked with a thin laugh. "I hadn't realized Miss Smith had taken such an interest."

"Miss Smith's opinion is invaluable to me," said Matthew, his eyes on mine.

A deep, taunting ache ripped through me. I wanted to reach out to him—to have the right to touch him in front of all of these people. It was impossible.

"My dear, perhaps you could ring for tea," said Mr. Melcourt, breaking the tension in the room with his innocuous request.

His wife nodded. However, before she reached for the bellpull, she called to her brother. "Matthew, you must tell me where to hang this new landscape painting Arthur bought when he was last in London."

Matthew dipped his head. "Yes, Helen."

The tension in my shoulders eased a little bit as he drifted off, but still I started when Mr. Schoot said, "You mentioned before that you're an admirer of Miss Jekyll, Miss Smith. Have you considered writing yourself?"

"I keep a garden journal, but that isn't meant for the public," I said.

"Do you have a mind to try your hand at an article? Or maybe more. The society is starting a journal. I should like it very much if you would consider writing for it."

From across the room, I watched Matthew's eyes flick from Mr. Schoot to me and back again.

"That is incredibly flattering," I said.

"Then you'll consider it?" the director asked.

"I'm afraid I must decline, Mr. Schoot. It would not sit well with my conscience to write for an organization that would not allow me to join its ranks."

Mr. Melcourt shifted from foot to foot. "Miss Smith . . ."

Mr. Schoot put up a hand. "The lady is correct. There have been rumblings questioning the exclusion of women for some time now. I'm afraid, however, that changing the mind of the board has proven to be a challenge. I'm sure you understand, Miss Smith."

I did not. Not at all.

"To turn down such an opportunity . . . And with the possibility of writing about a garden such as here at Highbury," Mr. Melcourt floundered.

Ah. It was not enough that I was giving Mr. Melcourt a beautiful garden for his family. He wanted a *famous* one.

"Nonetheless," I said carefully, "I must decline until the day that women are admitted as full members."

Mr. Schoot rocked back on his heels. "You may find that day comes sooner than you think, Miss Smith."

I gave him a small smile. "I hope so, Mr. Schoot."

I escaped from the Melcourts' drawing room as quickly as I could, striding across the great lawn, past the reflecting pool that had been completed the previous month, and down to the lake's edge.

When I could be sure that trees shielded me from view, I pressed my hand to my forehead, willing away my headache. I needed time to think. I needed space. I needed to be alone.

My plan to carry this child until the time I chose and then go away had seemed so clear when I was alone. Now, having seen Matthew again, it was anything but.

If only he'd been cold and distant or furious and indignant. If only he hadn't looked happy to see me. No, not happy. Overjoyed. Shame and want twisted in me. I didn't want to let him go, even though I had no other choice.

I gulped in breaths, my back slumped against a tree, desperate for air and fearful I might faint again. I squeezed my eyes shut.

"Venetia?"

I opened my eyes. Matthew stood a few feet away, his hand out-stretched. When he met my gaze, it dropped as though he knew that to touch me would be too much.

"You shouldn't have followed me," I said.

"You left before I could speak to you. I . . . I wanted to know what I've done."

I inched around the tree, the bark catching on the fabric of my shirt. "This was a mistake."

"A mistake?"

"We both knew that what we were doing was wrong."

"How could what we feel for each other be wrong?" he asked.

"Matthew, I'm carrying your child."

His lips fell open. I watched him, desperate for some sort of sign of . . . what, I don't know. The life I'd created—that I loved—was crum-bling around me.

Slowly he asked, "Is this why you've been avoiding me?"

"The affair has to end, for both our sakes. Surely you see that."

He scrubbed a hand over his face. "How long have you known?"

I fixed him with a look. "Since the beginning of this month. I fainted and the doctor was called."

"You fainted?" he murmured in disbelief. "I should have been with you."

"No, you couldn't have been. You can't be. If the Melcourts were to find out—"

"I don't care what my sister and her husband would say. They have far too much hold over my life as it is."

I drew myself up to my full height. "And they have the power to ruin mine. If I leave Highbury House in disgrace and people find out why, I will never be able to work again. This is my livelihood, Matthew. The jobs that I take don't just support me. They give Adam employment as well. I cannot leave my brother without means."

"Your brother could find another position," he said.

"But could I? If I have a child out of wedlock, all of my respectability goes away. I know that you wouldn't condemn me to that sort of life."

"I want the world for you, Venetia," he whispered.

When he stretched his hand out over the gap between us this time, I let our fingers brush, knowing that it might be the last time we touched. "Then don't think too harshly of me for what I am about to tell you."

And I laid out my plan for him. Every detail except for where I would go for my confinement. He listened, as I told him in no uncertain terms that I intended to cut him out of my life. The longer I spoke, the more the distance between us felt like an insurmountable chasm.

I wouldn't have forgiven me.

When I'd finished, Matthew looked down at our hands lightly touching fingertip to fingertip. "I've sat at Wisteria Farm these past weeks, trying to think of what I might have done. Why you might have pulled away from me, when you are all I think of." He lifted his eyes to mine. "There is another way, Venetia."

I shook my head. "I've considered everything."

"No you haven't."

"Yes, I ha—"

"Marry me."

I jerked back. "Marry you?"

"Marry me, please," he repeated, his voice cracking as he grasped for me.

I tried to twist my wrist out of his grip. "You don't have to do this. I have a plan."

"Stop talking about your plan. I don't like your bloody plan one bit!" His voice rang out the harshest I'd ever heard from him.

I stepped back. "I cannot marry you."

"Why not? Can you honestly say that you feel nothing for me?" he asked.

I couldn't, and both of us knew it.

He brushed a bit of my hair from my forehead. "I know that what we have has not been a passing fancy for you—you took an incredible risk." When I said nothing, he tried another tack. "You spoke of your respectability."

"It's the one thing I have," I said.

"You have me. You have our child," he said tenderly.

My resolve nearly faltered. I wanted so badly to believe in the words he offered me, but they were just words.

"Your sister won't stand for it. She dislikes me," I said.

"Helen is not my keeper, Venetia."

"I know that the Melcourts are your landlords. You would lose Wisteria Farm."

His jaw tightened. "And the income my brother-in-law gives me each year as part of my sister's marriage settlement. But what dignity would I have as a man if I let that keep me from my responsibilities?"

"Even if we did marry, people would talk," I pushed.

"People want to believe in love."

"People want to believe in the fallacy of others," I countered.

"Are you always so cynical?" he asked with a smile.

I planted my hands on my hips. "Are you always so idealistic?"

Rather than responding, he wrapped his arms around me.

"I've found the woman I'm going to marry. What man wouldn't be idealistic?" he murmured into my hair.

In spite of my better judgment, I melted into him. I craved his reassurance.

"How would we do it?" I asked.

He gave a short laugh. "Well, I expect that we probably won't be wed in All Soul's in the village, if that's what you mean."

"There's only so much longer that I can keep the child a secret."

"Then we'll follow your plan. Together," he said.

"Go away?"

"Yes. We'll marry quietly and go on a tour of Italy or Spain. It will look like our honeymoon, and it will allow you to go into your confinement. After a month, we'll write home and tell everyone that we fell in love with the countryside and have decided to stay a little bit longer. You'll have the baby. We'll announce the birth nine months after the wedding. When we return in a couple of years with a child who is a little taller than other two-year-olds, who will know the difference?"

There were still risks. One false move, one spilled word. The scandal could destroy both of our families. If I were a better woman, I would have walked away right then and there. Instead, I swallowed and nodded. "Then we'll marry."

He caught my face up in both of his hands and touched our foreheads together. "You will not regret it. I promise you." He stepped back. "I should return to the house. Helen will be looking for me."

I watched him walk away, ducking his head under tree branches, until I could see him no longer.

Sitting here, writing these words, I know I should be happy. A good, honorable man will marry me. I will not be forced to have a child alone. For the first time in my life, someone will walk with me, side by side. But for all of that, I cannot help the sinking feeling that we are naive to think that we can outrun a ticking clock and the inevitable ruin that will follow.

· BETH ·

Saturday, 12 August 1944
Southampton

My darling Beth,

Every time I receive one of your letters, the sun shines again. They are what sustains me and makes me know that this brutal campaign will be worth it if I can come home to you.

You asked how I feel about working behind the line. I cannot tell you much, as you know, for fear that this letter will become entirely black strikethroughs, but I will say it's not the sort of visceral existence that I felt when I was fighting. Nothing can replace that, but I can see the good that we're doing. Whenever a lorry full of petrol rolls onto the road, I know that that is going to move us forward. Whenever supplies for the bakeries or butcheries arrive, I know that the men will eat.

How is the farm? How are Mr. and Mrs. Penworthy? Has Ruth finally found herself a flyer? These little details are what holds me close to you and Highbury.

One thing you can do for me is call on Lord Walford at Braembreidge Manor. I know you'll not want to bother the man who owns such a grand place, but he's a lonely sort and I worry about him.

Only promise me you won't let him charm you into marrying him instead. He may be seventy-three, but he is an earl.

I love you.

Yours forever,
Graeme

Beth eyed Ruth, who sat on the edge of her bed, squinting in the fading light of the late-summer sunset. Ruth was attempting to apply a recipe for homemade nail varnish to her toes, but the paint was too clumpy to make a clean line.

"Do you think that one is better?" Ruth asked, sticking her foot up for Beth to examine.

"I don't want to look at your feet, Ruth," she said, raising her book in front of her nose. "Could you please go back to your own bed?"

"Yours is closer to the window. Besides, I need your opinion," her roommate whined. "I'm half-blind as it is."

"You wouldn't be if you would wear your glasses," she pointed out.

"That's easy for you to say, you're nearly a married woman. I can't be out and about in glasses."

"Nearly married is not the same thing as married," she reminded Ruth.

In the weeks following D-Day, she'd been able to settle. A little bit. Graeme's letters had been few and far between in the three weeks directly after the invasion while the supply lines were being established, but when he began to escort goods between Normandy and Southampton, she'd begun to receive letters nearly every other day. He couldn't tell her much of what he was doing, but it seemed as though he was as safe as a soldier could be.

Each time he wrote, he told her he loved her. Each time she read those words, she knew that she'd chosen the right man. But constantly running in the back of her head were Mrs. Symonds's words:

Love can make women do ridiculous things. Intelligent women become silly. They give things up they never intended . . .

Day after day, Beth turned those words over in her head. She wasn't naive. She knew that things would be different between her and Graeme after the war. For starters, she wouldn't be a land girl any longer. All of her friends—Petunia, Alice, Christine, even Ruth—would go off to their respective homes. If not for Bobby, Beth would have counted on Stella leaving Highbury House as soon as possible.

Despite all of that, she wanted to stay. There were plenty of people who had made her feel welcome. The Penworthys, Mrs. Yarley, the Langs who kept sheep down the road. The sour Mr. Jones could be a welcome sight on days he grunted to her in greeting. Even Mrs. Symonds said hello in the village, although friendship seemed a laughable aspiration.

She could be happy in Highbury—she was convinced of it—and she wasn't going to let that go on the vague promise of a life uprooting and resettling at army bases across the country. She refused to feel orphaned again.

"Come on." Ruth shook her foot in front of Beth's face.

She sighed and gave a cursory glance at the other woman's toes. "Congratulations, it looks like you've painted them with red currant jelly."

Ruth made an exasperated sound. "I don't know why it's not working."

"Maybe because you're not meant to be able to make nail varnish in Mrs. Penworthy's kitchen sink," she said.

Ruth flopped back on Beth's bed. "Is it so much to ask for just a little bit of glamour?"

Despite herself, Beth smiled. Her first impression of Ruth—that the well-dressed, spoiled woman would be miserable no matter where she'd been assigned—stood. However, Ruth understood what it was to fall asleep before her head hit the pillow because she'd been baling hay all day. She had suffered through blistered hands, cracked heels, and chapped lips. They were both land girls, and that connection counted for something.

"Why don't we go into Leamington Spa tomorrow and see if we can find you a new lipstick," said Beth.

Ruth rolled over on her side. "Really?"

"Yes. It's our day off. It will be fun."

Ruth squealed with delight, and Beth settled back into her book with a laugh.

* * *

It *was* fun. In Leamington Spa, where there were shops and people and not a tractor in sight, Ruth came into her own.

Beth had let her roommate drag her around the shops, looking for a new dress for a dance. Beth was pleasantly surprised when, not having found anything up to Ruth's standard, they headed for the fabric section of a department store.

"I think I'll fit it through the bodice with little cloth-covered buttons marching up the front, and I'll leave the skirt as full as I can with such a measly fabric allowance. But that cobalt blue will look divine against my hair," said Ruth, touching her long red curls.

"It will," said Beth as they walked by the train station, "but I didn't know you could sew."

Ruth grinned. "How do you think I have such a fabulous wardrobe when fashion is so dreary now? I only do it late at night after everyone's gone to bed."

"I had no idea."

"You're a heavier sleeper than you think." Ruth stopped Beth with a hand on her arm. "I'd like to buy a flower for my hair."

"All right," said Beth, glancing at her watch. They could always catch the next bus.

They wove through the crowd of people exiting the train station, aiming for the little flower stand near the front.

"The London train must have just come in," said Beth.

"I wonder if there are any new airmen. I heard that some are already making their way back from Normandy," said Ruth, scanning the crowd.

"Ruth, if we're just here to . . ." Walking out of the station door was Graeme.

Beth broke into a run, pushing through people to get to him. She was almost to Graeme when finally he saw her. His kit bag fell from his shoulder, and he opened his arms, sweeping her up into a kiss.

"You're here. How are you here?" she murmured against his lips.

"When my commanding officer granted me leave, I was on the first train up from Southampton. You are the only place I want to be."

Right there, in the middle of the train station with all of Leamington Spa watching, she kissed him as though she'd never kiss him again.

Finally, when they pulled apart a little breathless, Graeme touched his forehead to hers. "That is exactly how a man imagines his homecoming will go."

"I can't believe you're here," she whispered.

"Captain Hastings, it's good to see you," called Ruth from somewhere behind Beth.

"Go away, Ruth," said Beth, earning a laugh from her roommate.

"Beth?"

Her bubble of joy popped. Both she and Graeme turned, and, for the first time in nearly a year, Beth saw Colin. He looked taller, but he was maybe just thinner than she remembered. His uniform looked clean, but worn. But the most remarkable change was his face. He was gaunt, his eyes hollow, and he seemed somehow . . . gone.

"Colin," she said as she felt Graeme's arm go around her.

"Is this him?" Colin asked.

"Who are you?" Graeme countered.

Beth glanced at Ruth, whose mouth was hanging wide open.

"Respectfully, Captain, you've got your arm around my girl," said Colin through gritted teeth.

Graeme tensed. "You're mistaken, Private. This is my fiancée."

"Beth, tell him—"

"Stop," she said sharply, cutting off Colin midsentence. "Both of you, stop."

"I didn't expect you to be the type, Beth," Colin said.

"The type?" she asked.

"The backstabbing type," he spat.

Graeme surged forward, but Beth clamped a hand on his arm. "You stay right there."

She stepped up to Colin then, facing him squarely. "What are you doing here?"

"I applied for a transfer right after I received your letter, but it only just came through. I managed forty-eight hours' leave to come see you."

"You should have used it to see your parents. We tried, Colin, but I never loved you and you didn't love me, either."

"And now you're engaged." Colin's expression darkened. "I didn't think you meant it. Lots of girls write things they don't mean."

She shook her head. "Colin, I'm sorry if I've hurt you. I could have told you more about Graeme and how I felt about him, but things moved so fast. But you also have some blame here, Colin. You ambushed me on the phone, asking me to be your girl just as you were leaving to fight. That wasn't fair."

He deflated a little. "I thought . . . I thought we were friends."

"We were, but that's all. You just wanted a woman waiting at home for you, and that might have been enough for me in Dorking, but it isn't enough for me now. I have a *life* here. I have people who love me."

"I love you," he said, but she could see that even he didn't fully believe it.

"No, Colin, you don't. You love the idea of having someone."

"Your letters got me through. Knowing that someone other than Ma was writing helped me," he said.

"I'm glad for it. I will always care for you, but I don't love you. I love Graeme," she said, looking up at her fiancé, who'd edged closer. "I'm going to marry him."

When Colin didn't say anything, Ruth patted him on the arm.

"Come on, Private . . ."—Ruth peered at Colin's uniform badge— "Colin Eccles. Let's go buy me a flower."

Still looking stunned, Colin let Ruth guide him away to the stand.

"Poor chap," said Graeme.

She raised a brow. "Poor chap? You were about to fight him in the middle of the train station."

"When I thought he was trying to steal you away."

"I'm not something to be stolen. I'm a woman whose mind is made up," she said.

He smiled. "I'd marry you today if you'd have me, Elizabeth Pedley."

"How long is your leave?" she asked.

"Four days."

"We'll marry on Monday, the day after tomorrow." The moment the words were out of Beth's mouth, she knew that was what she wanted.

"Do you really mean that?" he asked, touching his hand to her cheek.

She didn't want to wait for Graeme any longer. She didn't know what their life would look like, but they would figure those things out. Together.

"I'll marry you, Graeme, but I want you to know that I'm not going to be happy picking up and blindly following wherever the army sends you," she said.

"We don't have to talk about this right now," he said.

"Yes, we do. I want to be your wife, but I won't do it unless you promise me that I can have a home. A permanent home."

He looked down at their joined hands and brushed his thumb over her knuckles, just as he had when he'd first touched her in the winter garden. "Okay."

"Okay?"

"If this matters to you, then we will figure out how to make that happen," he said.

She let out a breath. "Thank you. Now, we have a wedding to plan."

"We could go into Warwick," he said.

She shook her head. "I don't want a town hall wedding. I want to be married in Highbury."

"Are you certain?" he asked.

"I think we'll find the vicar sympathetic."

"You have Highbury village wrapped around your little finger, don't you?" he asked.

"No," she said. "It's just home. That's all."

He gave her a little smile and then nodded. "Understood."

And she hoped he truly did.

· EMMA ·

AUGUST 2021

*E*mma sat around a large outdoor table with Mum and Dad on her right and Sydney and Andrew on her left. Charlie should have rounded out their group, but he'd begged off because he had plans to take the boat up to Birmingham that weekend. Instead, Henry—wearing a burnt-orange shirt with an image of the late Bill Withers silk-screened on it—occupied the space across from her and kept grinning as her mother said things like "I suppose the house has some presence, doesn't it?"

A few times, Emma wanted to bury her head in her hands and moan with teenage-like embarrassment. But it turned out, Mum's backhanded compliments were no match for Sydney's bright optimism.

"Any bigger and I'd lose Andrew in it," Sydney laughed as she patted Clyde's silky back. Bonnie was content to lay in the sun a few feet off, the perfect picture of a very good dog.

"It is a lot of space for two people," said Mum in an odd reversal that still managed to feel judgmental.

"That's entirely my fault. I've always loved it, and I practically begged my parents to let me buy it off them," said Sydney. "It was a bit of a white whale for a long time."

"And"—Andrew picked up his wife's hand—"we're hoping that it won't just be the two of us for too many more years."

Emma watched love spread sweet and glowing to Sydney's eyes.

"Good luck to you both," said Dad. "Do you have plans for the garden beyond Emma's restoration?"

Sydney and Andrew glanced at each other. "Actually, we'd thought about reopening it to the public for the season in a few years when it's matured."

"Really?" Emma asked, sitting up. "What about the community kitchen garden project?"

"We'd like to do that, too, but it seems a shame to have all of this beautiful space and not share it." Sydney paused. "I didn't know how you'd feel about that."

"It's your garden. I'm just the person who gets to work on it for a little while. If you don't mind managing it yourself, you could look at what Kiftsgate Court has done. They're still family run, and they're close by," she said.

"Wouldn't that be a lot of work?" said Mum.

Emma lifted one shoulder. "Yes, but if you charged a small admissions fee, it could help offset the cost of some of the work it will take to keep the garden up."

"That will be good for Turning Back Thyme, won't it, Emma?" Dad asked.

"It will. If you don't mind talking about the restoration in your materials and press releases when you're ready to open," she said.

"I wouldn't dream of leaving it out. I'm glad you like the idea." Sydney flashed Emma's parents her winning smile. "The work Emma's doing is incredible. You should have seen the place before she got here."

"It's looking a little patchy, don't you think?" Mum asked as she craned her neck to look at the long border.

Sydney's eyes flashed, but Emma gave her a tiny shake of her head. She was used to this.

"It will grow in," she said.

"Do you mind if we take another turn around the garden rooms? It's almost overwhelming how much there is," Dad said, always one to defuse an awkward situation.

She wasn't sure if he intended to split off their groups or not, but all of them rose from the table. Sydney, Andrew, Henry, and Dad all hung on to their mugs as they trooped through to the tea garden.

"The gazebo looks great since Jessa and Vishal painted it," Andrew remarked.

"What is the pale pink rose that's growing up it?" Dad asked.

"I don't know. We moved it from another part of the garden. I've never seen it before, and there doesn't seem to be any record of its name." She'd scoured Venetia's plans, but the rose seemed to pop up in places she wouldn't have expected, never labeled.

They spread out around the tea garden, Andrew and Henry wandering off into the lovers' garden with Bonnie while discussing a farm-to-table delivery service that had approached Highbury House Farm. Watching them, Emma hadn't realized that Mum was on her heels until her mother said, "They're nice enough people."

She started and turned. "They are."

"Not too stuck-up. And that Henry is good-looking in a farmer sort of way."

She sighed. "What is a farmer sort of way?"

"You know what I mean."

"I don't."

"Sunburned face, dirty hands. He looks as though he spends his time out of doors," Mum said.

"His hands are not dirty, and if you say things like that about him, you might as well say them about me," she said, giving Clyde's ears a scratch when he pushed up into her hand.

Her mother pursed her lips in the way that told Emma she probably did say them about her.

"I'm surprised Sydney's so familiar with you. Usually toffs like her are too high-and-mighty to talk to the help," said Mum.

She rolled her eyes. "'The help'? Really, Mum? It's not 1860. And Sydney's a nice person."

"You didn't have to be the help, you know. You could have taken your place at the University of Bristol and been just like Sydney and Andrew," said her mother. "All of your teachers said that you had the talent for law, or even business."

"I know I have a talent for business because I run a business."

"It's hardly setting the world on fire, though, is it?"

"Mum, this has to stop!" The words burst out of her all at once. Mum stared at her, stunned that her quiet daughter had talked back, but Emma wasn't going to stop. Not now. "I made my choices. I decided that I wanted to train rather than go to university. If I had failed, you could tell me 'I told you so,' but I didn't. I built something from the ground up. Something that is successful and that I'm proud of."

"Then why are you always phoning up, worrying about payroll or tax payments or whatever it is that day?" asked Mum.

"Because doing this by myself is hard." It was so very hard.

"You don't think about all of the things your father and I gave up so that you wouldn't have to risk so much like we did," said Mum.

"I didn't ask you to give anything up! Mum, I'm never going to be the kind of woman who goes on skiing holidays in the winter or plays golf on the weekends. I like being in the garden. I like having a pint in the White Lion after work and saying hello to the people in the shops."

I like it here in Highbury.

Mum stared at her for a moment. "I worry about you."

"I know you do, but I need you to stop judging everything that I'm doing as a failure because I didn't pick the life you wanted for me."

"You shouldn't have a hard life. Your father and I struggled so much before you were born," said Mum.

"I have a good life, Mum. One that I chose. It just looks different than the one you picked out for me. I may never have a job in the city and a house in the old neighborhood, and I need you to be okay with that.

"And no more giving my information to people who you think might help my career. Unless they have a garden that needs designing, I don't want to hear about it," she said. "So, are we okay?"

Mum gave an almost imperceptible nod. "All right. Fine. Yes, I understand and will not try to help you in your career anymore."

That wasn't quite what Emma had said, but it was a start.

"What else?" Emma asked.

"I will stop worrying so much."

"Good. You could also be a bit more supportive," she said.

Mum hesitated. "What do you want me to do?"

"Ask me how Turning Back Thyme is going. Ask after Charlie, Jessa, Zack, and Vishal. They always ask about you."

"I could do that."

She slung an arm around her mother's shoulders and hugged her close. "I love you, Mum. Now, if you ask her, I'm sure Sydney will show you the construction in the house. She's very proud of the work they're doing here."

Her mother nodded and then kissed Emma on the cheek.

The Tuesday after her parents' visit, Emma stumbled through the door of Bow Cottage, dodging a seed catalog and a letter on the entryway rug. She was exhausted. One of the pipes to the water garden had broken and had required digging up their hard work to find the breakage and repair it. They'd spend the next two days replanting, which would put them behind schedule. Again. It would also mean she would have less time to work on the winter garden.

She'd begun to stake out the areas that she would replant based on Henry's grandmother's drawings. Charlie had ceded this project to her fully, and she was okay with that. Every time she went up and over the wall, she felt somehow calmer, as though this were her own space.

Yes, she wanted to get back to it, but first she needed a square meal, a long bath, and about fifteen hours of sleep.

She dropped her workbag on the kitchen table, pulling out her phone to plug it in. The thing had died sometime around midday. She'd thought about running up to the house to ask Sydney or Andrew if she could charge it, but the repair project had distracted her.

Emma moved to the fridge, pulled out a tub of hummus, and tore into a bag of pita that sat on the kitchen counter. She popped the pita into the toaster, and set about hunting around for cheese, chorizo, and some fruit or vegetable that would serve as a nod to health. It was too hot to cook, and she'd learned that if she ordered too often from the Golden Swan Chinese takeaway in Highbury, her meal would come with unnecessary commentary about how often they saw her.

She was cutting up an apple when she remembered the post she'd walked over. Setting down her knife, she retrieved it. She had been wrong; it was two seed catalogs—one stuffed inside the other—and a letter with her address handwritten on the front but no return. Slipping her finger under the flap, she ripped it open and pulled out a sheet of heavy cotton writing paper.

A grin spread across her face. Professor Waylan had written.

20 August 2021

My dear Miss Lovell,

I trust you are well. I was delighted to receive your letter. I do so enjoy the little challenges you send me and your rapacious interest in the past. If only more of your generation had such reverence for the gardens of our great forebearers.

I'm thrilled that you thought to bring me this little challenge about our beloved Venetia Smith. This one was a tricky one. (How very clever of you!) I did not recall a Celeste ever being associated with Venetia, but then I have forgotten more about the great gardener than most will ever learn. When none of my searches in books at home proved fruitful, I broke my happy isolation and took the ferry to the University of the Highlands and Islands, where they are kind enough to allow me access to their research facilities. Finally, after three days of exhaustive hunting, I believe I may have found something for you.

The name Celeste appears in none of Venetia's archived papers. I had thought that perhaps she was a relation of one of Venetia's clients, yet that path proved a false end. In Adam Smith's letters, however, was a clue. He was long engaged to a young woman whom he later married after Venetia left Britain for America. In 1903, not long after the start of his sister's career, he wrote a letter to his future wife. I have enclosed the pertinent parts below:

You asked me if I miss my parents now that I am an orphan. Simply, yes. Sometimes, when I sit in my chair in front of the fire, I recall my father looking over at my mother with such love as she worked a little bit of needle-point, completely unaware of his gaze. At those times he would call her his "Celeste" because being married to her was heaven itself.

Quite the romantic, Venetia's father, Elliot, was!

The second reference appears years later and may be too labored a stretch for your purposes; however, I know you like to leave no stone unturned. Venetia's eventual husband, Spencer Smith, wrote a letter to her in 1912 from their home outside of Boston while she was overseeing the construction of the Plinth Garden in Minneapolis. In it he writes, "Sometimes when you are away I think back to the celestial connection that forever binds me to you. The joy that slipped through our fingers led us to where we are now. I hope you do not hate me for having no regrets, because now I have you." He then goes on to describe in quite some detail just how ardently he loves his wife.

I do hope that these little tidbits prove helpful in your search, my dear. All I ask in return is that one day you tell me about what it is that has prompted your quest. I know you are unlikely to give me even the tiniest of hints until you are ready, but when you are, I beg you to remember . . .

Your faithful servant,
Walter Wayland

She shook her head in bemused exasperation at the professor's over-wrought letter and the fact that he'd found something while on a university campus and hadn't emailed her. But then again, what did she expect from a man who locked himself away from the world in an isolated house on a remote island on an annual basis?

She read the letter again, lingering on the passage from Adam Smith to his beloved. Celeste. The heavenly one. Perhaps all those months ago, Charlie had guessed correctly. The garden was named for Venetia's mother. It seemed the only connection to make sense.

Emma snapped a photo of the letter and texted it to Charlie before swiping through her phone. She frowned when she came to a voice-mail notification from an unknown number. She hit play and put the phone on speaker.

"Hello, Miss Lovell. This is May Miles from the Royal Botanical Heritage Society. I realize that this call might come as a bit of a surprise, but we underwent a budget review earlier this year, and I'm happy to say that our hiring freeze has now ended. If you are still interested in the head of conservancy position, please do give me a ring back, as we were very impressed with your initial interview."

The woman rattled off a phone number before Emma even thought about grabbing for a pen or pencil. The foundation job was open again.

· STELLA ·

"Come on, Bobby. We haven't all day," Stella said as she stood in her attic bedroom, holding out her nephew's little navy jacket. She'd just brushed it clean that morning, but she'd waited to dress him until the very last minute, lest he dirty it. The problem was, now they were at risk of being late for Beth's wedding.

"But, Aunt Stella, I'm about to win the war," he said, looking up from a set of tin soldiers he must have borrowed from Robin.

"Bobby," she said sharply.

"We're invading Tahiti!" he whinged, pointing to a postcard of the tropical island she'd found in a charity shop and stuck to the wall with Sellotape.

She planted her hands on her hips. "You're being a very naughty boy."

As soon as the words were out of her mouth, she wished she could pull them back. Her nephew seemed to close in on himself, become somehow smaller.

She pushed her hair back from her forehead. She was rubbish at this. Pure rubbish. Despite trying her hardest to do right by her nephew, every time it was just the two of them, she seemed to put a foot wrong. Just last week, she'd tried to explain that he must wait to be asked up to the nursery because Robin might not wish to play with him now that he was sleeping in the cot beside her bed once again. Rather than chasing after him when he ran crying from the room, she'd slumped in her chair, defeated. All she'd wanted to do was warn her nephew that at some point the divide between servant and master would be too wide to overcome.

Yet she hadn't been able to rid herself of the guilt that had split her in two at the sound of his crying.

"We have to get to the church, Bobby. Remember, Miss Pedley is getting married today, and you're invited just like a big boy," she said.

He looked up from under a flop of hair she could never get to lay down quite right. "I like Miss Pedley," he said softly.

"Me, too," said Stella.

He held his arms out for his jacket.

Stella blew out a slow, steady breath and slipped the sleeves over his arms and shoulders. Then she gave it another good once-over with the clothing brush.

"That's you done, then," she said, picking up her handbag. "Let's go see Beth married."

Stella found a spot in the third pew from the front. The wedding had all come together so quickly, she didn't know who had been invited. She nodded a hello to Mrs. Penworthy and several of the land girls. Two nurses sat on Beth's side, too, with two others for Graeme, as he'd told Stella to call him. The pair of nurses not in attendance were back at the hospital tending to the patients who were too sick or unable to make the short walk to the village church for the ceremony. Even Mrs. George was there with her little band of minions—a relief, because Stella hated to leave the kitchen defenseless while the woman was around.

She stole a glance at the front of the church where Graeme stood in his uniform. Her friend had caught a handsome one, Stella would give her that.

She felt a little tug on her arm, Bobby pulling the sleeve of her pale yellow dress.

"Can I sit with Robin?" the little boy asked.

"Robin is sitting with his mother today," she said just as the boy in question turned around from his spot in the first pew to stick his tongue out at Bobby.

Bobby broke out into a laugh that turned several heads. Fortunately, everyone who caught Stella's eye looked like an understanding sort.

"He wants me to sit with him." Bobby shifted in his seat. "He does!"

"There will be plenty of time to play after the ceremony," she said. There would be no stopping him because, although she was a guest, she'd also made the wedding breakfast her present to the couple. It would be the very best that rations could offer—some donated by Mrs. George and the convalescent hospital—with the crowning achievement a two-tiered cake, made with real eggs and butter. She just hoped that it would be enough to give everyone a little slice.

Bobby settled into his seat with his arms crossed over his chest, but he didn't fight her anymore. She was, she'd found, impervious to a pouted lip and could ride out a temper tantrum with the best of them.

"Bride or groom?"

Stella turned to the woman who'd asked the question, taking in her fiery-red hair and meticulously tailored dress.

"Bride," she replied.

"I am as well." The woman gave a carefree laugh. "How do you know Beth?"

"We met when she began making deliveries to Highbury House."

"Those deliveries . . ." the other woman muttered before shaking her head.

"Beth also comes up to sketch in the gardens."

"And visit her captain, I'm sure. Who knew she would be the smart one, taking on deliveries."

A light coating of bitterness coated the words. "And you?" Stella asked, trying to steer the conversation onto safer ground.

"I'm also in digs at Temple Fosse Farm."

So this was Ruth. Now that Stella could put the face to Beth's stories, the affected boredom made sense.

"It's a pleasure to meet you," she said.

"I still can't believe they were able to get this all arranged so quickly," said Ruth.

"It's my understanding that Mrs. Symonds made the arrangements, and the vicar was happy to help a couple who are both doing their part," said Stella with a note of censure in her voice.

"I do my part," Ruth said tartly. "What do you do?"

"I was declared medically unfit to serve by the ATS, the WRNS, and the WAAFs. The Women's Land Army wouldn't take me, either, so I couldn't have done what you're doing now." The back of her neck grew hot, so she added, "I volunteered with a Civil Defense unit, but then I became my nephew's guardian a few months ago."

The other woman's mouth snapped shut as the organ began to boom from the opposite end of the room. Stella let out a sigh of relief.

The scrape of shoe leather against stone resounded as the guests all stood. Outlined against the sunlight was Beth in a navy-blue dress. She wore a hat with a white net—a little bridal nod when clothing rationing made wedding dresses impossible. Stella touched the spot above her heart when she saw Mr. Penworthy holding Beth's arm, looking proud as punch.

Stella glanced up at the altar, where Graeme stood beaming. As soon as Beth reached the top of the aisle, she looked down at her bouquet of flowers, a blush pinking her cheeks.

Father Bilson adjusted his glasses, smiled, and began to speak. "The grace of our Lord Jesus Christ, the love of God, and the fellowship of the Holy Spirit be with you."

"And also with you," echoed everyone in the church.

After the sermon and the readings, Mrs. Symonds stepped forward to take Beth's bouquet when it came time to exchange the rings, and Stella frowned, still in awe of how her polite friend had managed to establish such ease with the imperious Mrs. Symonds.

When the vicar declared Beth and Graeme husband and wife, Stella felt something lurch inside of her. Not jealousy or envy, but an awareness that she was witnessing something she may never experience. May never *want* to experience.

The congregation rose a final time to cheer the couple as they walked down the aisle and out of the church. Stella caught Beth's smile as Beth passed her by; she'd never seen her friend so happy.

A little elbow hit her arm. Stella looked over and realized that Bobby had climbed up onto the pew.

"Bobby, get down from there," she gasped. "We're in church."

"I can't see," he said.

"We're going outside right now," she said.

"I'm hungry," he complained as she tugged his jacket into place.

"You'll have to wait until we're back at the house." Then she would hand him off to the maid, Dorothy, tie on her apron, and get back to work. Even with Mrs. George's help, a thousand things needed doing for the wedding breakfast.

"No!" Bobby shouted right in the middle of the aisle.

Dozens of heads swiveled to them.

"No!" Bobby screamed again.

"Bobby, stop it," she hissed.

"No!" He hung on the "o," dragging it out so that it echoed up to the arches and rose above the organ. Then he threw himself on the floor.

Stella knew she was supposed to react, but all she could do was stare. She didn't know how to make him stop this tantrum. All she knew was that she didn't want to deal with any of it.

I don't want to do this. Her guilt dropped through her like a stone through water. She hadn't asked for this child, even if he was blood.

Bobby began to writhe on the floor as people murmured, their eyes darting from the child to her and back again. As though they expected her to somehow stop this display.

"Bobby, get up," she said, her voice weak, defeated.

He continued to squirm, hot tears rolling down his face.

"Bobby—"

"Bobby Reynolds, you will stand up this instant!"

The sharp voice of Mrs. Symonds brought Stella's nephew to a stop. He peered up at the mistress of Highbury House with wide eyes, as though just realizing that he had an audience. He'd likely never heard Mrs. Symonds use anything but the soft, ladylike voice she employed as either a pat or a slap.

Mrs. Symonds put her hand on Bobby's shoulder and crouched down until she was almost on her heels. "You will pick yourself up off the floor and apologize to Father Bilson. Do you know why?"

"I was yelling," he said softly.

"Yes, you were yelling in church. That is not acceptable behavior. Do you understand?"

He nodded, and Stella watched him pick himself up off the floor. His coat was dusty and his eyes were rimmed red, but he was standing, which was more than Stella had been able to accomplish.

"I'm sorry, Father Bilson," Bobby said to the vicar, who stood, his arms crossed over his chest.

"I accept your apology, young man. All of us have moments of weakness that we must fight against," said Father Bilson.

"Now, will you tell me why you were throwing a tantrum?" asked Mrs. Symonds.

"He was—"

"Robin, that question was not for you," said Mrs. Symonds, not even glancing at her son where he stood next to her.

"I'm hungry, and my jacket itches, and I'm hot and—"

Mrs. Symonds held up a hand. "I think that I have a good idea of the situation. I'm afraid you must put up with all of these inconveniences until we are home. Can you be a brave boy and do that?"

Another nod.

"Good, then go with your aunt, and she'll see that everything is sorted out," said Mrs. Symonds.

As her employer straightened, Stella gritted her teeth and murmured a thank-you.

"There's no reason to thank me," said Mrs. Symonds.

"You made him stop crying," she said.

Mrs. Symonds offered her a little smile. "It isn't a matter of stopping a child crying. Often it's a question of listening to what it is that they want. If they are hungry, tell them that they will be fed. If they are hot, let them know that they will soon be somewhere cool. Bobby is a smart boy. He understands these things, but he is only five."

"I'll see to it that he doesn't disturb the wedding breakfast," said Stella.

Mrs. Symonds waved a hand. "He'll be even more bored there than he was here. Send him to play with Robin. They can amuse each other."

Stella hesitated but nodded. She had a wedding breakfast to finish, and it wouldn't do to argue with a kindness on today of all days.

· DIANA ·

When Diana first met Cynthia Symonds, she had been convinced that her future sister-in-law was perfect. Although not particularly pretty, Murray's petite, delicate sister had pale blond hair and peaches-and-cream skin that never seemed to blemish. Cynthia could speak eloquently in four languages with anyone from a duke to a diplomat. She was remarkably well-read, and she could ride to hounds without letting the veneer of calm slip from her face. She went to church, but not too often. She flirted, but only a little. She was just as a lady should be.

Perhaps that was why it had been so satisfying when cracks began to show in Cynthia's facade. It had started when Cynthia and Murray's mother ran off to Africa with the man who was now her husband with hardly a goodbye to her own children. This forfeited Murray's mother's right to Highbury House. Diana had witnessed the moment Cynthia heard that the family property would pass to Murray and seen the flicker of jealousy flash over her sister-in-law's eyes.

Then, one day at a party, Diana had realized that Cynthia had been out for quite a few Seasons, and the number of times Cynthia found herself partnered to dance had shrunk. An engagement to a baron's son in 1936 never materialized. Then, in the spring of 1939, the National Service Act passed, and the young men who'd once flirted with the only Symonds daughter left for officers' commissions.

Cynthia had changed after that. As the nation entered war, her purpose in life seemed to transform overnight from marriage to the war effort. She'd become almost dictatorial in her passion, hardened in her determination to win the war from Highbury House. That, and Diana's own stubbornness about the transformation of her home, had sparked much of their discord.

Now, however, Diana sat studying her sister-in-law, who wore a lazy smile on her face thanks to the champagne coupe in her hand and the wedding breakfast they'd just enjoyed.

"Do you know, I'd forgotten what this tasted like," said Cynthia, raising her glass.

"You mentioned," said Diana.

"It tastes like happiness," Cynthia said.

It, Diana realized, was quite possible that Cynthia was drunk before the four o'clock hour.

"That's Bollinger for you." She'd opened up the wine cellars again today, a move that had made Mrs. Dibble look positively queasy. But what was a wedding without something to toast with? Miss Adderton had done her best with the food, but there was no changing the fact that rationing was still on. It felt good to air out the well-stocked wine cellar for a celebration.

"The bride looks pretty," said Cynthia, squinting in the direction of the new Mrs. Hastings.

"Brides are always pretty on their wedding day. It's a rule," said Diana.

"You were lovely."

Only Diana's long-trained control kept her from recoiling at the compliment. "Thank you."

"I remember thinking you were beautiful and my brother was handsome. What a funny thing it was that you two married."

"Funny?"

"Oh yes, don't you think? I doubted you would be married at all when I first met you," said Cynthia.

"I was already engaged to Murray when we first met."

Before Cynthia could reply, Robin pounded across the veranda to Diana.

"Mummy! Mummy! Do you want to see how fast I can run?" he shouted between excited breaths, Miss Adderton's nephew close on his heels.

"Robin, now isn't a good time," she said, her eyes sliding to her sister-in-law.

"But, Mummy! Bobby and I have been practicing," he whined.

"Go play in the garden," she said while Cynthia tried to sip from her already-empty glass.

Her son skipped over to Bobby and whispered something in his ear. The pair of them giggled and ran off together.

"Yes, I didn't see how a marriage between you and Murray would work at all," Cynthia continued, unprompted.

"Why?" Diana fought to keep the edge out of her voice. She shouldn't have asked—nothing good would come of digging up old feelings—but she couldn't help herself.

Cynthia laughed. "Isn't it obvious?"

"My family is just as good as yours."

Cynthia gave an uncharacteristic snort. "Oh, better if you asked your mother."

She inclined her head, acknowledging her mother's snobbery. Truthfully, the Eddings family had made its money in the Napoleonic Wars, and the Symondses had only acquired their wealth when Murray and Cynthia's mother had married into the family, bringing the Melcourt soap fortune and Highbury House.

"Then what was it?" she asked.

Cynthia leveled a look at her. "I thought my brother was going to swallow you alive. You were such a quiet, serious thing, and my brother was a bully."

"Murray was not a bully," she said automatically.

"Oh, Diana, he was, though. Even you must see it. He wasn't cruel, but he had to have his way, and he wielded kindness to get it," said Cynthia.

"I won't stay here and listen to this," she said, pushing herself out of her seat. "I cannot believe you'd speak about your late brother that way."

"And I cannot believe that you can't see that he did it to you, too." Stunned, Diana slowly dropped back into her chair, and Cynthia leaned in closer. "When was the last time you went to a concert?"

Diana swallowed around a lump of emotion. "We moved to Highbury. It's not like London."

"You could have found something in Leamington Spa or Birmingham, or you could have taken the train down with Murray. He was always in London. Without you."

"Are you're implying—"

"No, nothing like that. For all his faults, he had a moral compass, but that doesn't mean he didn't leave you up here to rot."

"I became a mother. I had to put music aside," she said.

Cynthia snorted. "No, you didn't, and you have a nanny."

"There was so much to do . . ."

"Besides, you stopped doing things you enjoyed long before you became a mother, didn't you?" asked Cynthia.

"Concerts can be so tedious—" She stopped abruptly.

"My brother hated anything where he had to sit quietly and let something or someone else be the center of attention. Concerts, opera, theater—none of it was for him, so he convinced you that you didn't want to go, either.

"I'll bet fifty guineas that he was the one who pushed to move to Highbury—a place where you didn't know a soul—so that he could play at country gentleman. I'm sure he told you that you two would be happier without the distraction of parties and friends."

"I didn't like parties all that much," she whispered. And she hadn't, but she'd tried her hardest because, when they were first married, it had mattered to Murray that they were liked. Popular. She'd begun to gather a small group of women around her. She'd started to look forward to seeing them regardless of whether Murray was by her side. She began to have a life, and then Murray had inherited Highbury House and uprooted them. There had been no discussion, no question. London wasn't a suitable place to raise children, he'd argued. Highbury was a home. She'd let him convince her. It seemed so obvious that it's what she should want. But had she?

It felt as though all of these years she'd been watching her memories from behind glass, and Cynthia had just swung a hammer.

"In fairness to Murray, he probably thought that what you wanted and what he wanted were conveniently in step. He had Highbury House and an important London practice, a big house and a wife to make it beautiful. You built a life to his exact specifications," said Cynthia.

But that wasn't true. Highbury House was her creation because Murray had become bored of it. *She'd* dealt with the builders, decorators, and gardeners, answering their questions about what brass knobs to buy and how high to hang the pictures. *She'd* argued with the vendor who'd delivered the wrong bathtub for the master bathroom. Twice. *She'd* been the one exhausted at the end of each night, constantly covered in a fine layer of construction dust.

"And whatever happened to your harp?" Cynthia asked.

Her stomach fell. In her heart of hearts that she'd given up playing for Murray, and she'd resented him for it. Why else did her daily hour in the music room bring her so much joy and guilt all at once? Why else would she feel so furious when she thought about the time he'd come home from London and found her crying on Nanny's day off because Robin had croup and she hadn't even had time to bathe, let alone practice. He'd suggested she put away her harp, so she'd packed up her greatest joy because that was what a wife did when her husband was thinking of her best interests. She loved her husband, but when she thought of that day, she hated him, too.

"Why didn't you say anything?" Diana asked.

Cynthia shrugged. "Would you have listened?"

"I might have."

That earned her a hard laugh. "The scared little girl my brother paraded in front of all of us, not for approval, but to show that he'd won an Eddings? I think not. You hung on his every word."

"I loved him," she said.

Cynthia sobered. "I'm glad for that. For all of my brother's faults, I'm glad that he was loved."

Diana looked down at her hands, clenched in her lap. She didn't know if Cynthia was playing a game or speaking truthfully, but she did know one thing with a certainty that seemed to penetrate her very bones.

Slowly she unknotted her fingers and smoothed them out over her skirt. "I am not a scared little girl any longer. No matter what you think of me, I will not be dictated to about how I run my household or raise my son."

"I know."

Diana's chin jerked. "You know? You swept into my house and took over."

"Because you were useless. The day the requisition order came through, Mrs. Dibble telephoned me because she said you barely looked at the order."

"I was grieving."

"I came here because if I hadn't stepped in, who knows what would have happened to the house. Look at Sir Parker's home in Suffolk: It was practically burned to the ground thanks to the troops using it as a training ground," said Cynthia.

"But the way you speak about the house . . ."

"How do I speak about it?" Cynthia asked.

"As though you think it should be yours!" she exclaimed.

Cynthia's expression darkened. "I'm a Symonds by birth, and this was my home long before it was yours. I hate that after this war, this hospital will dissolve, I'll be gone, and you'll still have Highbury House."

Diana opened her mouth to say . . . *what?* That Cynthia could visit anytime? Neither of them would be comfortable with that arrangement.

"I thank you for stepping in to Highbury when I was unable to," Diana said, careful to control her voice as she lifted her drink like a shield.

"Who else would have been commandant? You?" Cynthia gave a bitter laugh.

"Mrs. Symonds!" a shout came from the lawn. Her head shot up to see a young solider hobbling, frenzied on his crutches. "Mrs. Symonds!"

"What's the matter?" she asked, as people behind her began to murmur.

"Come quick! Your son."

Her wineglass fell. It shattered, but she was already pushing through the crowd.

"What is it?" she asked, racing toward the soldier. "Where is he?"

"The garden in the middle. The one with the gate," he said, wincing.

The winter garden. Terror coursed through her. Something had happened to Robin. She had to get to him.

"Diana!" Cynthia shouted behind her, but Diana was already racing down the stairs and across the grass.

He will be fine. He will be fine. He must *be fine.*

She ran around the soldier and across the lime walk to the pathway leading to the winter garden. A child's sobbing cut through the sound of her blood roaring in her ears.

He is fine. If he's crying, he's fine.

When she saw the gate was open, she slid to a stop on the crushed limestone. A nurse knelt on the ground next to a prone figure—Robin.

"No!" she shouted, racing forward and dropping to her knees next to her son. Vomit at the corners of his mouth, his eyes were closed. She took his little shoulders, so fragile, and shook him. "Robin!"

As though through a fog, she heard Bobby trying to speak around hiccuping sobs. "We were playing and—and he said the plants were magic."

"I'm so sorry, Mrs. Symonds." The nurse's voice cracked. "I can't wake him up. I think he ate that."

The nurse pointed to several stalks of pretty purple flowers. Monkshood. So beautiful and so deadly.

"Find a doctor!" she shouted at the nurse. "Now!"

The woman was up like a shot, racing out of the winter garden. Diana picked her son up in her arms, cradling him as she had when he'd been an infant.

Something brushed her arm. Bobby had shuffled over to her.

"It's going to be okay, Bobby. Robin will be okay," she said.

"He said it was magic," Bobby wailed, throwing his arms around her.

"It's going to be okay," she said. "It's going to be okay."

They sat like that, Diana rocking her son and Bobby clinging to her, as what was left of her world fell apart.

AUTUMN

· VENETIA ·

THURSDAY, 12 SEPTEMBER 1907
Highbury House
Overcast with the scent of rain
in the air. Autumn is coming.

*T*his morning I lay in bed, Matthew's arms wrapped around me so his hands could rest on the slight swell of my belly. I am fortunate. Even four months into my pregnancy, I am hardly showing.

"We could marry at the village church in Wilmcote," Matthew said, drawing lazy circles on my side. "The priest at Saint Andrew's is an understanding man and will hardly give a thought to a small ceremony with only two witnesses."

"The church will fall down around my ears given my current state," I said.

He kissed the side of my neck. "Then we'll go to London, or somewhere no one knows us."

I twisted around to face him. "Are you certain you've made peace with the fact that the Melcourts could turn on both of us for this?"

"Helen's been after me to marry for years, remember?" he asked with a smile.

"Not to me." Mrs. Melcourt would have wanted a virginal bride for her brother—one who came with money and status. Marriage was a

274 · JULIA KELLY

game of strategy to women like Mrs. Melcourt, and I don't even come close to contending.

"The sooner we marry, the sooner Helen and Arthur will come to love you," Matthew said. "You needn't worry."

"We should both be worried."

He nudged me. "We won't be caught."

"That's not the only thing to fear, Matthew."

He sank back onto his side of the bed. "Then what?"

"Our lives will change."

"For the better," he said.

"What happens if I can no longer work?" I asked.

He shifted on the pillow to look at me. "That won't happen. I won't let it."

"You might not have a choice. *I* might not have a choice."

He didn't say anything then.

Now that we share a life raft, I can't imagine how I ever would have enacted my original plan. However, to wed under the veil of lies and deception . . . I haven't considered marriage for a long time, but this would not have been the way I would have wanted it to start.

And then there was another issue. I'm embarrassed to write about it, but I do not truly know how Matthew feels about me. I know that he is affectionate. I know that he is kind. I know that he is optimistic that we can create a life together, but we were pushed into this arrangement by our child. I can't help but wonder if part of him doesn't feel as trapped as I do.

I do not know if he loves me, and I cannot bring myself to ask because I do not want to know the answer.

· DIANA ·

SEPTEMBER 1944

*P*eople. She was never without people, now. Staring at her or—even worse—sitting next to her. They all wanted to hold her hand, but she didn't want that even if she hadn't the energy to push them away. Instead, she simply sat with one of Robin's little jumpers spread over her lap and stared at a spot on the wall.

It was ink, she was almost certain. She'd become intimately acquainted with its shape over the last three weeks. In another time and place, she might have asked Mr. Gilligan to scrape that bit of wallpaper and replace it, but now she found the spot made things easier. When she focused on it, she didn't have to think.

She needed space away from all of it—but a heavy fog hung around her, squeezing her so tightly sometimes she struggled to breathe. It made the world so very slow.

Somewhere from the depths of that fog, Diana registered the opening and closing of the nursery door. China rattled on a tray. The scent of toast and eggs drifted to her. Two women whispered to one another.

"Diana, Miss Adderton is here with your tray."

Diana looked up from her spot and found her sister-in-law standing over her, hands clasped and face pinched.

"I have some eggs for you, Mrs. Symonds," Miss Adderton said with forced cheeriness. "Real eggs."

"Isn't that a treat?" Cynthia asked.

Diana let her eyes fix back on the spot, her hands knitting into the yarn of the jumper again. "I am not a child."

Her sister-in-law straightened in surprise. "No, you're not a child." When Diana didn't respond, Cynthia continued, "However, you are acting like one."

Diana's fists clenched tighter.

"You've suffered a great loss, and everyone understands that. However, many people are suffering as well. Some at this very hospital. You have a duty—"

"I had a duty to my son. I was supposed to keep him safe," she said.

"What happened to Robin was a great tragedy," Cynthia tried again.

"He died because of my garden. Because I was too lax about hiding the keys. He died because I didn't rip out the monkshood, even though I knew how deadly it could be. He died because of *me*."

The room fell silent.

"You aren't yourself, Diana," Cynthia said.

No, and she might never be again. Robin had been what was good in her life—a reminder of before the war, but also a harbinger of the future. She'd poured her love into him. She told herself she kept him close to her because Murray had hated his time at school, but her reasons went deeper than that. She'd thought that if she was near, he would be safe.

In the end, there'd been nothing she could do.

Robin never regained consciousness. The doctors hadn't been able to do anything to save him. Neither could a manor full of nursing staff. Her beautiful boy had died with her head bent over him, keeping silent vigil through the night.

"I would like to be left alone, please," she whispered to the nursery wall.

She heard Miss Adderton set down the tray, but only one set of footsteps left the room.

"This isn't going to be like Murray all over again, is it?" Cynthia asked.

Diana slowly turned her head. "Like what?"

Her sister-in-law huffed out a breath. "The way you go about your grief, Diana, is really too much. All of this haunting the nursery like Miss Havisham. Miss Adderton tells me that you haven't eaten a proper meal in weeks, and if the state of your hair is anything to go by, you clearly are no longer caring for your appearance."

"Weren't you the one trying to push us all to make do and mend for the war effort?"

"This is unseemly," said Cynthia.

"I'm mourning my son," she said.

Cynthia threw her hands up. "And just as selfish about it as ever!"

Diana shot to her feet, Robin's jumper nearly sliding to the floor before she caught it up and brandished it before her. "He's gone!"

"And so is my brother, and Private Welthrope's sister, and Mrs. George's son, and the loved ones of a whole number of people," Cynthia argued. "It isn't natural the way you lock yourself up for weeks when something bad happens."

"You do not get to tell me how I should mourn my son," she bit out.

"I'm not—"

"Murray should be here." Diana's voice broke. "He had no right to go join up without discussing it with me first. He didn't give Robin or me one moment's consideration, and by the time he told me what he'd done, there was no changing it.

"My husband had so little regard for my opinion that he went off to fight and then got himself killed. And now my son is dead, and you think I'm being selfish because I'm taking time to grieve? How dare you."

"I didn't realize Murray hadn't spoken to you before he joined up," Cynthia said quietly.

Diana lifted her chin. "If you had once bothered to ask, I would have told you."

"I'm sorry for Murray's sake and for Robin's sake." The words sounded drawn out and painful on her sister-in-law's lips, but they were there. "I will leave you."

Diana turned away to the window.

The fog of grief again hugged her in too close. A few moments later, she heard the open and close of the door once again.

✳ ✳ ✳

"Good evening, Mrs. Symonds," said Miss Adderton as the hallway clock chimed half past seven. So regular was the cook's habit of bringing up a tray that Diana normally hardly noticed, except this time she couldn't keep Cynthia's words from echoing in her head.

Selfish.

"Thank you."

She looked over in time to see Miss Adderton's shoulders stiffen under her blue dress. It was, Diana realized, probably the first she'd spoken directly to the cook in weeks.

Miss Adderton folded her hands behind her back and then turned, a pleasant enough smile fixed on her face but one that showed pain around the edges.

"Dinner is a pork medallion with beetroot and potatoes," said Miss Adderton.

Diana didn't care about dinner. She cleared her throat. "How is your nephew?"

The cook's gaze dropped immediately to the floor. "Bobby is as well as can be expected."

"Given what he has been through, I would assume that means he isn't very well at all," she said.

"He doesn't sleep very well. He often has nightmares," Miss Adderton admitted.

"I see."

The cook hesitated but then said, "He's quiet now, too. Like when he first arrived, before he started playing . . ."

Diana's heart squeezed as Miss Adderton trailed off. *Before he started playing with Robin.*

The other woman was looking at her, waiting for her to say something. She knew she should. This was when a lady was meant to offer some sort of platitude. But Diana couldn't find it in herself to be dignified any longer. Instead, she said, "Thank you, Miss Adderton. You may go."

The cook nodded, and when the door closed softly behind her, Diana began to weep.

· VENETIA ·

MAYBE OCTOBER
Highbury House

I don't know the day of the week or the date because I do not care any longer. I haven't written for days because how does one record the worst day of their life?

I knew that my time at Highbury House was coming to a close. I felt it acutely when I stood on the dew-softened soil with Mr. Hillock to discuss planning for next spring; the days had become shorter.

"The daffodils will be ready to plant next week if we receive shipment of them," he said.

"I wrote to my brother four weeks ago to ask for the bulbs. I'll write to him again tonight and see why there has been a delay," I promised.

"O'Malley told me this morning that the ground is prepared for the winter garden," he said.

I recall sighing then. "I will have the sketches ready for you shortly."

Mr. Hillock squinted at me. "If you don't mind me saying so, Miss Smith, it seems as though you're not wanting to work on that winter garden."

"Nonsense," I said, even though I knew he was right. It was the last of the gardens to be planted, and I had taken to tweaking and changing it almost daily. It would be my farewell to Highbury House, but I was not yet ready to say goodbye.

We parted ways, and I took myself off to the children's garden, where I had begun to spend much of my time. On my hands and knees, I weeded and tidied as best I could. It was becoming harder and harder to find the energy to garden like that. My knees and back protested as soon as I stood. However, after a while, I took out secateurs to begin cleaning up a buddleia.

I grasped a thin branch of the silvery-green plant and made the first cut close to the base. A twinge tweaked my back, and I hissed in a breath. I did not stop. Instead, I chopped the buddleia branch into three neat pieces and dropped each into the large canvas bag that one of the gardeners will haul off to the compost pile later.

I worked like this for a few minutes, methodically cutting the plant back to half its height. When I reached for a thicker branch, my back spasmed more violently this time. I dropped the secateurs and grasped at my back, my fingers digging in to the stiff fabric of my corset. Another pain gripped me, but this time it squeezed deep inside.

I knew something was wrong. I needed to sit down. Catch my breath. Think. I lifted my skirts to step gingerly over gaura and asters and saw it—a trickle of fresh blood snaking down the side of my shoe.

I lost my child—a daughter, Dr. Irving informed me, although I had not asked and had not wanted to know.

It took hours from those first pains in the children's garden to when Young John found me crouched on the ground, my arms clutched around my stomach and my skirt soaked with blood. I'd tried to stop him, but he ran straight to Mrs. Creasley. She helped me to the cottage, Mr. Hillock supporting my other side. She sent for Dr. Irving.

And then she went straight to the Melcourts and told them everything.

Mercifully, I saw no one but the doctor from the moment I was laid in bed. By midnight, it was done.

Dr. Irving spent an eternity tidying his instruments and washing his hands. When finally he was finished, he cleared his throat. "Miss Smith, I'm very sorry—"

I didn't reply. I didn't want his sympathy or his pity.

"It is possible that you may have other children in the future."

I squeezed my eyes shut. I had lost my daughter, and my grief shocked me. Until that moment, I had convinced myself I could be dispassionate. Now I could see that all of my hours planning and worrying had been for her as much as for myself. I had wanted to give her the best life that I could.

But she was Matthew's daughter as well, and it would only be a matter of time before everyone else knew it. And so I mourned not only for her but for my life as it had once been. For my ruined professional and social reputations. For the loss of my income and my independence. And for Matthew. There was no reason for us to marry now. I would be forced to leave, and Matthew's life would resume as before.

"Thank you for your assistance, Doctor," I said, trying my best to keep the shake from my voice.

Dr. Irving hesitated, but then nodded. Before he opened the door, he gave me a little bow. "Try to rest. It is the best thing."

As soon as I was alone, I turned my face away, knowing sleep was not for me tonight. Instead, I thought of Adam and the little house I owned and loved. I thought of my own beautiful garden that I poured love into when I was not living away. How simple things had seemed then when there was little to worry me other than my next project and whether the seeds ordered from this catalog or that one could be counted on to germinate. So much had changed since I'd come to Highbury House. *I'd* changed.

From somewhere outside the cottage, I heard distant shouts. I pushed myself up on my elbows, wincing at the deep soreness in my body.

"Be reasonable!" I heard Mrs. Melcourt shout.

A great pounding came at the door, and then it crashed open. "Venetia! Venetia!"

"Matthew," I murmured, shrinking down and pulling the coverlet up around my chest.

A second later, Matthew burst through my bedroom door and dropped on his knees to the floor.

"Dearest, what happened? What is the matter?" he asked, clasping at my hands.

His sister and her husband rushed through the door after him, both gasping for breath. They had chased him all the way through the house, desperate to keep him from me.

"Matthew Goddard, what are you thinking busting into Miss Smith's cottage like this? It's most unseemly."

"Venetia, what's wrong?" he asked, ignoring his sister.

I glared at his sister and her husband. "You haven't told him?"

"Told me what?" Matthew asked.

"It's none of your concern, Matthew," said Mrs. Melcourt primly.

"Venetia, what is the matter? Mrs. Creasley sent word to me that you had taken ill and the doctor was sent for," he said.

A strange lump of hatred and gratitude for the interfering house-keeper lodged in my throat. He had a right to know. He had been the father.

He squeezed my hands tighter. "Is the baby all right?"

I heard his sister gasp and Mr. Melcourt utter "I say," but they didn't matter.

"No."

His hands slipped from mine. His face was pale, his expression blank. I'd lost him.

"Matthew, this is highly inappropriate. I must insist you leave," said Mrs. Melcourt, her voice high. She knew, I could tell she did from the way she looked at me, but she was trying valiantly to unknow.

"It is none of your business, Helen," he said.

"Now, Matthew—"

"None of yours, either, Arthur," he snapped at Mr. Melcourt.

"If Miss Smith has engaged in indiscretions under our roof, then I don't see how it will be possible for her employment to continue. I will have to ask you to leave the property immediately, Miss Smith."

Matthew shot to his feet. "She has just lost a child, Arthur. Have you no sympathy?"

"Matthew, please . . ." his sister started.

"It is the middle of the night," Matthew argued.

"Then in the morning," said Mr. Melcourt, as though this was a great concession.

Mrs. Melcourt placed a hand on his arm. "Arthur, I think we can show Miss Smith a little more courtesy than that. Miss Smith, you may stay through the duration of your recovery. You will not see anyone. You will not leave this cottage, although I doubt that would be possible given your condition. Do you understand?"

I nodded wearily, for what else could I do?

"Now, we should leave Miss Smith to rest. You, too, Matthew," said Mrs. Melcourt.

Matthew cast a pained look at me. "Venetia, if you wish me to stay . . . ?"

I shrunk back. "I want to be alone."

I could not lean on this man for comfort when I knew that so soon he would be gone from my life. Once again I would be alone in the world, unsure if even my brother would want anything to do with me once he found out why I had been dismissed from Highbury House.

"I will come back tomorrow," Matthew promised.

"No, please don't."

"Matthew," his sister said sharply from where she held the bedroom door wide for both men.

My lover cast a last look at me from over his shoulder, and then he was gone.

I expected Mrs. Melcourt to follow, but instead she closed the door softly behind them. She drew up a little needlepointed chair and sat on the edge of it.

"I find myself in an extraordinary position, Miss Smith," she said, her tone losing all of the coaxing sweetness she'd deployed with her husband. "Even though the Lord has blessed us with three healthy children, we should have had more. Arthur may not dwell on it, but I will never forget all the children we lost."

"I'm sorry," I murmured.

"I do not seek your sympathy," Mrs. Melcourt snapped. "I merely want you to understand why I stopped my husband from casting you out of this cottage at dawn. You lost a child. You also betrayed my trust when you seduced my brother."

"I didn't seduce your brother."

She carried on as though she hadn't heard me. "Matthew is a good man, but he can be naive. He skates over some of the more difficult realities in life because he does not want to engage with them."

"Why are you telling me this?" I asked.

"He will not marry you."

I swallowed. "I don't expect him to marry me."

She nodded. "I'm glad we understand one another. You may recuperate here in the gardener's cottage until Dr. Irving believes that you are fit for the train journey back to London. I ask that you not contact my brother for the duration of your stay."

"If he comes here, that will be his choice alone," I said.

"Matthew will fall in line with my wishes. He always has, because he lives at Mr. Melcourt's pleasure."

"He doesn't want your husband's money," I said.

She leaned in. "Then why does he continue to take it?"

I had no reply.

"Perhaps you are right. It is high time that Matthew find himself a bride who will bring a good settlement to the marriage. I will see that it happens by the end of the year. I will also see to it that my husband comes to his senses about this scandal. We cannot dismiss you, as too many people know about your work here. Instead, you will finish any designs remaining and instruct Mr. Hillock on the details he will need in order to complete them himself."

The horrid woman had come to the same plan to exit Highbury House as I had. Somehow that sank me into an even darker despair.

"Thank you, Mrs. Melcourt," I said quietly.

She arched a brow. "I'm doing what is necessary to take care of my family. I am protecting my brother from being tricked into marriage by an unsuitable woman."

Some spirit rose in me. "Unsuitable? I am a gentleman's daughter, just as you are."

"We both know that we are not the same, Miss Smith. I have position and wealth such as you could never imagine. You dig in the dirt and play with plants for *money*," she said.

"I have talent and artistry."

"And I have a husband. I hold all of the cards, Miss Smith. Now, I suggest you rest. The sooner you recover, the sooner that we can be rid of one another."

My fists clenched in the sheets to keep from lashing out with a blow. Instead, I fixed her with a look and said, "Mrs. Melcourt, I can assure you that nothing would give me greater pleasure than knowing I never have to see you again."

I will leave this place, never to see Highbury House again. I risked my livelihood and my life here, and I may pay the consequences for years to come.

· EMMA ·

SEPTEMBER 2021

*E*mma wiped her palms against the fabric of her black pencil skirt. It had been chilly that morning in Highbury when she'd forsaken her regular gardening clothes and put on the skirt and a thin, three-quarter-length cashmere jumper she'd set out the night before. On went a pair of black patent leather heels—just high enough to have a bit of polish but not so high that she teetered. Now she was glad she'd left her maroon coat in her car. She would be sweltering in it.

As she sat in the reception area of the Royal Botanical Heritage Society's building, she fiddled with the strap of her handbag. She'd gone back and forth about this interview so many times. If she got the job, it would mean selling Turning Back Thyme and working in an office job for the first time in her life. It would mean stability and security. She would have a regular salary, a bonus, private health care. She'd never have to handle another client and their demands. She could make plans for holidays. She could *take* holidays—when was the last time she'd done that?

But mostly it would mean less stress. She'd shouldered an entire business on her own for six years. She was exhausted.

But who said you had to do it on your own?

A message from Charlie pinged her phone:

Mulch delivery is short 40 bags. Don't worry. I already called and sorted it. Enjoy your day off!

She stared at the phone until an older woman in a twin set and buff-colored slacks approached from the elevator bank. "Miss Lovell?"

"Yes?"

"I'm Mr. Rotheby's assistant, Amy. Will you come with me?"

Emma clicked her phone to silent, slid it into her bag, and followed Amy to her interview.

Emma pulled up to the small car park on the side of the road in a village called Cropredy and killed the ignition. She opened the back door and sat on the seat to swap her heels for mud-splattered wellies. Then she hid her purse under the driver's seat, locked up, and set off across the bridge to the canal side.

She walked for about ten minutes over the dusty ground until a familiar yellow-and-blue stern with *Darling Mae* painted in white came into view.

"Ahoy, Captain!" she called up, shielding her eyes from the low-hanging sun.

Charlie, who was sitting on a deck chair with a glass of wine in his hand, looked down. "Look at you all dressed up. Date?"

"Since when have I been able to keep a date from you?" she asked.

He laughed, the gold light from the sunset catching the highlights of his brown skin as he threw his head back. "Better question: When was the last time you had a date?"

"Oh, thanks. May I come aboard?"

"Can you climb aboard in that skirt?" he asked.

She gave it a try, succeeding on her second attempt after hiking the skirt halfway up her thigh.

"You're going to have the entire canal gossiping about me by sundown," he said as she settled into the other deck chair. "Wine?"

"Please, but just the one. I drove over."

"From where?"

She arched a brow. "You didn't ask why when I told you I was taking the day off."

"I was giving you space. Hold on." He ducked down into the cabin and reemerged with a wineglass. "Here you go."

"Thanks." She took a long sip. "I was in London."

Her friend let the silence stretch until finally he said, "Are you going to make me ask?"

She took a deep breath. "I had a job offer."

"You're not really dressed like a gardener today," he pointed out.

The head of conservancy position . . . it didn't really feel like a job for a gardener. She would have a team—not a crew. She would set policy for the Royal Botanical Heritage Society. She would consult on high-profile, special projects and have some media responsibilities. She would need to speak to donors.

She sat there in William Rotheby's office listening to him speak enthusiastically about the guidance her real-world experience could bring to the organization and the conservation education program they wanted to start for small garden-design businesses like Turning Back Thyme. She could mentor members of staff, even teaching some of the professional courses herself if she liked. There would be a generous salary, perks, and benefits.

But she wouldn't be a gardener any longer.

"I was at the Royal Botanical Heritage Society."

"Loraine Jeffers told me they're interviewing again. They called her after the hiring freeze thawed," he said, naming one of their competitors. "If Loraine was up for it, I knew you must be in the mix."

"I was headhunted for it just after the New Year."

"Why didn't you tell me?" he asked.

"I didn't want to worry you or the crew if nothing came of it. We had the big job at Highbury, and Turning Back Thyme was my main priority. I didn't want all of you to worry about where your next paycheck was going to come from."

"Emma, I work for Turning Back Thyme because I *like* working here. I could get another job if I wanted to. People have offered."

"They have?" she asked.

"You numpty, of course they have. I can run a crew. That's valuable."

"I'm sorry. Of course you can. I guess I was afraid that if I said anything, it might ruin our friendship."

"I'd be a bloody awful friend if I was more worried about my job than your happiness. If the head of conservancy job is the right move for you, take it. I want you to be happy."

"You're serious?"

"Yeah, but it's going to take me a couple weeks to get over the fact that you didn't think I would be."

"That's fair." She went quiet for a moment before saying, "I should take the job. They're offering so much and it would be much less stress than running the business. It would be dumb not to."

"But . . . ?" Charlie prompted.

She looked out over the water and the field dotted with cows on the other bank. "Those people in the office said such nice things and told me about the staff I'd have and what I could do. And do you know the only thing I could think of? How I wanted to be back in the winter garden, digging up the main bed."

Charlie grinned. "You can take the girl out of the garden—"

"But you can't get the dirt out from underneath her nails. I told them I didn't want to move forward with the hiring process," she said.

"Then you're still in business?"

"Actually, I thought it's time that *we* went into business. Together."

Charlie's chin jerked up. "What do you mean?"

"I should have asked you to become a partner years ago. You're as much a part of Turning Back Thyme as I am."

"Are you asking me to business marry you?"

She grinned. "I think I am. If you'll have me."

"You just want me to take care of the clients you don't like," he said.

"And payroll and a good seventy-five percent of the logistics and planning," she said.

"You don't enjoy it. I do," he said.

"I was also thinking, we could run two jobs at once if we expanded to a second crew. It would mean twice the revenue and help protect against lean years. That is, if you want to do it. You can have some time to think on it."

"As though I'd need to think on it, you numpty."

She made a show of putting one hand on her hip. "You really need to stop calling me a 'numpty' if we're going to stay friends, you deranged Scotsman."

"Stuck-up southerner," he threw out.

"I'm from Croydon."

"Still the South. As business partner and best friend, can I give you some unsolicited advice?" Charlie asked.

"Doesn't asking if you can give it make it solicited?" she asked.

"Shut up, Emma." He laughed.

"Tell me," she said.

"There's been something different about you this year."

She nodded. "I have pots."

"You have pots. I've seen you going up to the house for a cup of tea with Sydney or talking about the remodel with Andrew. You like them, and you like that village and that little house. You feel at home in Highbury."

Home. The word seemed to expand to fill her chest. She didn't know why, but she fit in Highbury. She loved the little cottage with the wood-burning stove and the huge beams on which she accidentally hit her head if she wasn't careful. Somehow Lucy's pub quiz had become a weekly habit, and the owners of the small grocery on Bridge Street knew her by name. And when she sat in her garden these days, she spent most of her time redesigning it a dozen different ways in her head.

"I think I want to stay in Highbury," she said. "It feels right."

"That's the way I feel about the *Darling Mae*," he said.

"But you're mobile," she said.

"The stretch of canal might change, but the boat stays the same."

She set her glass down. "I'm going to head back to the cottage. I'm exhausted. Thanks for the wine."

"Thanks for the business deal," Charlie replied.

He waited until her leg was hitched over the railing of the *Darling Mae* to call out, "You know, if you did want to set down some roots in Highbury, you might start by asking that farmer out."

She just saved herself from slipping. "I swear to God, Charlie, if I fall into the canal, I'm going to kill you."

"Henry came by the gardens looking for you today."

"Charlie!"

She just managed to hop off the bow onto the safety of solid ground, her blush fierce and her friend's laughter following her back down the canal path.

· DIANA ·

OCTOBER 1944

*D*iana was lying on Robin's bed when Father Devlin came to her.
"Mrs. Symonds, I thought I might sit awhile," he said, as
though it was the most normal thing in the world to greet a woman lying
in a child's bed, a jumper pillowed under her head.

She lifted her head to look up at him. "I've learned, Father, that there
is little that I can say that will stop you if you wish to say something."

He laughed. "That is true. Pushiness and interference are both quali-
ties for which I'm certain to be judged at the gates of Heaven."

With a sigh, she pushed herself up and took her usual chair, angling
it slightly so it wasn't facing the wall. He took Nanny's chair—always
vacant now. Someone must have sent the woman away.

"I assume you wish to speak to me," she said, her words thick. "Or
check on me. Everyone seems to be these days."

He folded his hands over the Bible propped against his leg. "Should I
be checking on you?"

"I thought it was the prerogative of priests to console grieving mothers."

"I could say a number of things. 'Let the little children come
to me and do not hinder them, for to such belongs the kingdom of
heaven.' Or maybe Matthew 18:14 would better suit: 'So it is not the
will of my Father who is in heaven that one of these little ones should
perish.'"

"If you did, I would tell you to leave my house."

He smiled. "I thought as much. You once told me that you still speak to Father Bilson because he didn't offer you such platitudes when you were widowed."

"The death of a child is different," she said.

He inclined his head. "As I am not a father, I can only imagine the pain that you must be feeling. And the rage."

Rage. Yes. Layered underneath the sadness and self-pity and pain was a white-hot iron of rage. She could see it—feel it—as though hearing that one word had brushed the fog of everything else.

"This war," she spat out. "This bloody, stupid war fought by men who don't care a thing about the cost. My son. My husband. I have no one left."

He simply sat there, so she pushed on. "I was promised a good life, if I only behaved myself. I twisted myself into knots to be a daughter, a debutante, a bride, a wife, a mother. I was supposed to be cared for. And now all is gone."

"And now you don't know what to do with yourself," he said.

She sagged forward. He was right. She didn't have a purpose. She was nothing, just a woman with her husband's name and a house shrouded in grief.

"Robin gave you a reason to continue as you were before," said Father Devlin. "You kept this house for him as best you could. You sent him to school. You tried to give him a normal life."

"And now none of that matters," she whispered.

His eyes bore into hers. "Does it not? You are still here. You, who had a life of your own, once."

"My life before was merely waiting to be married."

"That may be so, but now you are a woman of independent means. You may choose to live the life you want to lead. You could play the harp at every hour of the day, or you could run this hospital," said Father Devlin.

"Cynthia is the commandant."

"Miss Symonds is not the mistress of Highbury House," said Father Devlin.

She pursed her lips. A new start. It was tempting—more so than any-thing she'd felt since Robin's death. But it was daunting, too. Moving toward an uncertain future meant walking into the possibility of yet more pain.

Finally, she said, "I wouldn't know where to begin."

He stood. "Will you indulge me a moment and come with me?"

She looked at his hand outstretched as though it was the most alien request she'd ever heard. But, after a moment, she let herself be gently pulled to her feet. Father Devlin released his grip on the back of the chair that balanced him and retrieved his crutches. They began a careful walk out of the room.

Down the stairs, Diana held her head up high as nurses and patients looked up and stared. She must appear to them as a ghost, the unwanted reminder of senseless tragedy.

Still Diana walked on, following the priest through the French doors and down the steps into the tea garden.

She squinted in the afternoon sun. This was her first time out of doors since Robin's death, and the garden was in the midst of its au-tumnal transformation. Roses were going to hips, and tall grasses were beginning to throw up their willowy buds. The air was crisp, layered with the damp scent of rotting leaves. In a matter of weeks, the trees would begin to change and all of Highbury would begin to go to sleep except the winter garden.

The winter garden.

"Where are we going?" she asked.

"I think you know," said Father Devlin.

Reflexively, she put out a hand to stop him. "No. I can't. It's too soon."

The priest shifted his crutches to pat her hand. "I would not do any-thing that I didn't think you were strong enough to handle. Trust me."

She did trust him, so she forced her breathing steady. When they rounded the winter garden's brick wall, she stopped. On the pathway just inside the winter garden's gate sat Bobby. He held one of Robin's tin lorries, silently driving it across the path.

"It's meant to be locked," she said.

"I imagine some well-intentioned person put the keys back where you usually keep them. He comes here every afternoon after school and sits in this same spot. When it begins to become dark, he locks the gate again and goes in to his aunt."

Diana didn't say anything, watching the little boy. Miss Adderton had been right. All the spark and life that would flash across his face when he and Robin would play at marauding pirates or soldiers was gone. He was too quiet, eyes too solemn.

"I asked Bobby why he comes here, and he says that it's because Robin told him that this was their special place." Father Devlin paused. "Do you know what I see when I look at him? I see a little boy who has lost his best friend. He is too young to understand it isn't his fault. He's seen far more than his fair share of tragedy already. He has no father, no mother, and now no best friend. His aunt seems overwhelmed by the responsibility of taking care of him. If someone doesn't do something, this little boy might just grow up thinking that he doesn't have a place. A purpose."

She watched Bobby in silence for a moment, rubbing at her left forearm. She thought of what she would hope for Robin if he were the little boy playing alone on the pathway. She thought about what she'd told Father Devlin about her own life. It's purposelessness.

Slowly she crossed the path to Bobby. The grass must have muffled her steps because he didn't look up until she was right in front of him, his hand still clutching the red lorry.

"Hello, Bobby," she said.

"Hello," he muttered, and went back to rolling the lorry along its invisible path.

She frowned and crouched down. "What are you doing?"

"Playing lorries," he said softly. She remembered this little voice from when she'd first met him in the kitchen. He'd seemed so small and meek, nothing like Robin's best friend.

"How did you get into the garden?"

Fearful, he looked up at her. "I didn't steal the key. I put it back."

She placed a gentle hand on his shoulder. "It's all right, Bobby. I'm not angry. I just want to know why."

"When me and Robin were pirates, we would go into Blackbeard's lair and take the key and then come here to look for buried treasure.

Only we never found it. We had to take the key back or we might get in trouble."

She smiled. "That's very clever of you making sure to put it back exactly where you found it. And did you ever find buried treasure?"

He shook his head.

"Why aren't you looking for your treasure now?" she asked.

He looked up at her, his big hazel eyes filling with tears. "Robin had the map."

The little boy began to cry heaving sobs. The pressure in Diana's own chest built, pushing against her heart until her own tears flowed free. Her first instinct was to run, but then she looked at the child laying prostrate on the ground. She couldn't leave him.

She began to see a path with such clarity it seemed incredible she hadn't thought of it before. But right now, the only thing that mattered was comforting her son's best friend.

"Bobby," she choked out, "I would like a hug. Would you like one as well?"

The little boy half crawled into her lap and buried his face in her chest.

· VENETIA ·

FRIDAY, 18 OCTOBER 1907
Highbury House

*T*his morning, Mrs. Creasley told me unbidden that it is the eighteenth, which means I have been a prisoner for two weeks.

Each morning, she comes with a tray. Then she helps me dress and sits me in a chair, facing the window. I stare at the garden for hours, the birds and insects flitting around before me as they do their autumnal work. I do not sketch. I do not read. I am buried too deep in the pain of the loss.

I had no other visitors, just Mrs. Creasley and the doctor. Mr. and Mrs. Melcourt do not come, which is a relief.

Matthew does not come.

MONDAY, 21 OCTOBER 1907
Highbury House

I awoke this morning and felt different. My grief is still here, but it seems different somehow. It no longer presses down on me so hard I cannot move.

When Mrs. Creasley came this morning, I said, "I should like to take a bath today, please."

She nearly dropped her tray from the shock of hearing me speak, but she pulled herself upright and set the table just as she always does. I pulled my dressing gown on and sat down to eat a proper meal for the first time in weeks. Two maids came with a hip bath a half hour later.

In the bath, I scrubbed at days, hours, minutes of grief and came out feeling a little lighter for it. I let my hair dry before pinning it up and dressing. Then, I rejoined the world.

Mrs. Melcourt had banned me from the gardens, but I didn't care. I needed the outdoors.

My steps were slow and deliberate. My body was punishing me for the neglect I'd shown it, yet as I walked through the ramble, I could feel myself returning in the scent of the autumn leaves crunched underfoot and the cool of the misty rain that touched my forehead.

I could not bear the thought of the children's, lovers', or bridal gardens. I did not want to see Matthew's roses in the poet's or tea gardens. Instead, I went straight to the winter garden and pushed open the gate Mr. Hillock had installed, a key already sitting in the lock with a spare hanging off its ring. Inside, the earth stood bare but freshly turned, awaiting my instructions. I sat down on the stone path and began to cry.

That was how Mr. Hillock found me, my skirts smashed under my weight and my eyes raw. He didn't rush up to me or try to calm me. Instead, he closed the garden gate behind him and sat down next to me.

He extended a handkerchief. "It is a terrible thing to lose a child. Mrs. Hillock and I know better than some but not as much as others," he said in his quiet, steady voice.

"I'm sorry," I said, dabbing at my eyes.

"So am I."

He let me sit in silence while I collected myself. When finally I handed his handkerchief back, he said, "Has Mr. Goddard been to see you?"

My heart clenched at the mention of Matthew. "No."

He shook his head. "It doesn't matter how old a man grows, he will always have the foolishness of a boy."

"What do you mean?"

"He's been to see me, your Mr. Goddard," said Mr. Hillock.

My heart skipped. "Why?"

The gardener lifted his flat cap and ran a hand over his balding head before replacing it. "That's a story he'll have to tell you himself."

I stared out over the unfinished garden. Matthew had been to see Mr. Hillock but not me. His sister had been right. He was ruled by her, by her husband's money, all of it.

"It's a shame about this place," said Mr. Hillock. "It's the heart of the garden."

"And you're worried that I'm leaving it unfinished," I said.

After a long pause, Mr. Hillock replied, "I don't worry about the garden, Miss Smith, but if you don't finish your work at Highbury House, there are things that will never be complete."

"None of the sketches I've made for the winter garden feel right, and the Melcourts won't allow me the luxury of time."

"You have measurements and a feel for the place. And I've heard tell that the post works well these days. It even comes to gardener's houses in little villages of no real consequence."

When I looked up, I saw he was wearing the faintest hint of a smile.

I twisted to slowly gaze from one side of the garden to the other.

"Silver birches alone would be too obvious, don't you think?" I asked.

Mr. Hillock tilted his head to the side. "Maybe."

"Dogwoods, too, then. There"—I pointed to one side of the gravel path—"and there. The red bark will bring depth to the garden on the worst days of January. And grasses. We'll need grasses for height."

"If we plant them soon, they'll have time to establish," said Mr. Hillock.

"We'll need Christmas rose," I said, beginning to see possibility. "And sage and holly and hart's-tongue fern and bellflowers. I'll write to Adam and . . ." I trailed off, remembering abruptly that I was no longer employed at Highbury House.

"I will find the plants," said Mr. Hillock firmly.

My shoulders relaxed. "Thank you."

"The garden needs a focal point."

"What did you have in mind?"

"A pool would look well in the center."

"Maybe a sculptural one, different than the water garden."

His cap came off again, but this time he held it between his hands. "It could be a memorial. If someone felt they needed to remember something," Mr. Hillock said.

"The Melcourts would never stand for that."

"The Melcourts never need to know."

"You are a good man, Mr. Hillock." I reached for the man's grizzled, callused hand. He flinched, but then relaxed, and we sat there together in silence on the hard ground for some time.

· STELLA ·

Stella lay staring at the ceiling. Bobby was finally fast asleep in the cot next to her, exhausted from crying. He seemed fine during the day—quiet but dry-eyed—but as soon as she tucked the blankets around his chin at night, he would begin to weep.

At first she'd tried to comfort him. She'd laid a light hand on his chest. She'd tried singing and reading to him. She'd grown angry and stern. None of it seemed to stop the flood of hot tears that rolled down his face. One day she'd simply gotten up, announced that she had to finish her duties downstairs, and left. When she'd come back, she'd found Bobby asleep, curled around his slightly damp pillow.

She glanced down at him. His hair had fallen over his brow, and he looked peaceful. She knew that some instinct should probably have compelled her to reach forward and brush his hair back or tuck the covers a little closer around him, but she felt nothing except unadulterated fear. She'd barely been able to take care of him when he'd been just another boy, but now he'd lost his mother and father, and he'd seen his best friend die. Surely it was all too much for a child.

Stella pressed the heels of her hands to her eyes, forcing starbursts to explode in the black. The truth had been pressing on her for months now. She'd tried to escape it but couldn't.

"I can't do this," she whispered.

She opened her eyes and looked around the room. Her neat little magazine clippings and tear-outs from travel brochures seemed to mock her. Hawaiian beaches she would never see. Mountain peaks in the Alps she would never climb. She wouldn't know the feeling of sultry air on her skin in South America, nor would she experience the dry, scorching heat of the Sahara Desert. She was going to be stuck here in Highbury for the rest of her life.

A sourness rose in her stomach, burning her throat. She pushed herself off her bed and went to the nearest wall. *Rip!* She tore Niagara Falls off the wall. Bobby snuffled and shifted in his sleep, but he didn't wake.

Rip! Down came the pyramids of Egypt.

Rip! The Great Wall of China fell.

Rip! The sandy beaches of Tahiti washed away.

She worked methodically, piling the pages on top of her bed. When the walls were bare, she turned to her tiny desk and removed booklet after booklet from her correspondence courses. Onto the pile the guides to shorthand and typing went. She pulled out the magazine articles she'd saved about modern girls.

When her desk was cleared, she gathered up the mound of paper and walked out. Down, down, down the back stairs she went, descending into the basement of the house. A clock struck one in the morning. Good. No one would be in the kitchens.

For once, it was silent in the room where she spent most of her working hours. She dropped her papers on the wood worktop and went to the iron range. Heat radiated off it from when she'd banked the fire after supper. Stella opened the front hatch, stirred up the remains of the embers, and began to feed in little bits of wood until she saw flame. She wouldn't need a big fire.

The correspondence coursework was on top, but she hesitated as she reached for it. How many hours had she hunched over her desk after her work was done, writing in her exercise books? She'd hung everything on those classes, scraping and saving to pay for them. She'd turned down trips to the cinema on her day off and went without new shoes one year. She'd been so focused on her plan, so sure that this would finally free her from Highbury once and for all.

She put the course materials aside and grabbed the Tahitian beach. When she fed it into the stove, the paper caught and curled with green and blue flame. In seconds, the image burned away. She pursed her lips and let out a long breath. Then she reached for an image of Switzerland.

"Miss Adderton, what are you doing up so late?"

Stella whipped around at the sound of Mrs. Symonds's voice, banging her knee into the stove's open door as she did. She cried out, grasping at her right leg. A firm set of hands gripped her by the shoulder, and she found herself half hopping to a chair.

"Do you need a compress?" Mrs. Symonds asked.

She bent her knee a couple of times, testing it. "No," she managed.

"I'm sorry I frightened you," said Mrs. Symonds.

Stella looked up at the other woman from under her lashes. *I'm sorry.* It was so odd to hear those words from her employer.

"It's nearly a quarter past one," said Mrs. Symonds.

"I had some things I needed to take care of."

She watched Mrs. Symonds's gaze drift to the pile of papers on the worktop. "Are you burning these?"

"Yes," she gritted out.

"Nice, San Sebastián, Cape Town, Bombay . . . Are these all places you dreamed of going?" Mrs. Symonds asked.

Shame suffused Stella's body. "They were on the walls of my room. It was silly," she said.

Mrs. Symonds sifted through the papers. "I've been to a few of these places—Paris, Rome—but you're far more adventurous than I am. I didn't know that you wanted to travel."

Stella sat, lips firmly shut, watching her employer's hand fall on the correspondence coursework.

"You're taking shorthand dictation courses?" Mrs. Symonds asked.

"Another silly thing." Another dashed plan.

"I didn't realize that you wanted to do anything besides cook," said Mrs. Symonds.

Stella's heart twisted, and she nearly gasped.

"I hate cooking." The words that had been building up in her for years flew from her lips.

Mrs. Symonds looked stunned. The lady carefully put down the exercise book. "I'm sorry you feel that way."

Look what you've done now, Stella. "I'm sorry. I'm grateful for my job here."

Mrs. Symonds pulled her quilted satin dressing gown closer and took the wooden chair across from Stella. Finally, she said, "There are things that I wished I could have done. Regrets that I have . . . May I ask what you would do with your life if you weren't a cook?"

She knew that she shouldn't answer honestly. But she was simply too tired to lie. "I was born in Highbury," she said.

"Yes, I know. Murray said that your mother worked as a housemaid until her arthritis became too taxing," said Mrs. Symonds.

"That's right. Mum's cooking lessons helped me catch Mrs. Kilfod's eye when I was fourteen. She made me her helper and taught me what Mum couldn't."

"What did you want to do instead?" Mrs. Symonds asked.

"I wanted to leave," she said in a burst. "Joan was the lucky one. Mum thought she was too bold to be in service, so she was sent to work at one of the department stores in Leamington Spa. She met Jerry when she was sixteen, and he married her three months later. When she moved to Bristol, I was so jealous I could hardly stand to look at her. I've spent my whole life two miles from the cottage I was born in. I wanted to go to London. To work and then maybe to do more. Would you want to spend all your days in the basement of a house that's not yours, cooking for a family that's not yours?"

Mrs. Symonds inclined her head. "So that's what all of these correspondence classes are about."

"Yes."

"You thought to go to London and become a secretary, I take it?" Mrs. Symonds asked.

"Yes."

"And one day you want to travel."

Stella looked miserably at the pile of unburned papers on the table. "I thought if I worked hard enough, I might be able to save. It was a silly idea."

"You've done that three times now," said Mrs. Symonds sharply.

"What?"

"Used the word 'silly.'"

Stella's back straightened.

"How did you find the time for both?" Mrs. Symonds asked.

"After I finished in the kitchen every night, I would go to my room and study. Sometimes, I would wake up early in the mornings as well."

"Can you not continue to do that?" Mrs. Symonds asked.

She shook her head. "With Bobby, it's too difficult. Besides, there's no point now."

"No point?"

"I used most of the money I'd saved on him," she said.

Mrs. Symonds looked shocked. "Your sister didn't provide for him?"

"Joan could forget about money like that," she snapped, "when it suited her."

"You could have asked if Robin had any clothes he'd grown out of. He was a little taller than Bobby, but with a little hemming they would have worked," said Mrs. Symonds.

This time Stella kept her proud mouth shut.

"No, I see. That wouldn't do," said Mrs. Symonds.

"It isn't just the money. What am I supposed to do with him? If I move to London, I'll have to find some place to stay that allows children. I'll have to find a job with an employer who doesn't mind that I have a child, even if he isn't my own son. It doesn't matter that my story about Joan dying is the truth. I know what it sounds like. And what happens when he is ill and needs to be nursed?"

"You and Bobby will always have a home here," said Mrs. Symonds.

No. Stella felt the word in every bit of her body. What Mrs. Symonds was offering was a kindness few domestics could hope for, but it felt wrong. She couldn't stay here.

Still, she wasn't thinking only for herself and it was time to accept that.

"Thank you," she said, shoulders drooping under the heavy weight of her future.

Mrs. Symonds toyed with the cover of one of Stella's exercise books. "If you still do wish to move to London, there might be a way."

"How?"

"Let Bobby stay here."

"What?"

"He is already settled at Highbury. He can move back into the nursery, and I can recall Nanny or hire on someone else. I can care for him, and you could go to London."

"I have no money," Stella said.

Mrs. Symonds arched a brow. "I could arrange that, too."

"It wouldn't be too painful for you after Robin?" Stella asked.

Mrs. Symonds set the book down and folded her hands on top of each other before looking up, her eyes solemn but determined. "It would give me a great deal of pleasure."

There it was, her plan held out on a silver platter to her, funded by this woman she'd worked for, for so long. She could go to London. She could work her way into a job that, one day, might let her see those places she'd planned to go for so long. But it would mean turning her back on the one responsibility she should hold most dear.

"I don't know if I can do that," Stella said.

"I am going to London at the end of the week. You may think about it until I return," Mrs. Symonds said. "Now, I think I'll have that warm milk I came down for."

Stella stood automatically. "It'll just be a moment."

"No, Miss Adderton, you take your things and go back to bed."

When she shot Mrs. Symonds an uncertain look, the mistress of Highbury laughed. "I can warm a pan of powdered milk. I'm not completely helpless."

Stella had never seen the great lady do anything of the sort, but who was she to argue with the mistress of the house? Instead, she picked up her things and began the long climb upstairs knowing she wouldn't sleep a wink.

· VENETIA ·

SATURDAY, 26 OCTOBER 1907
Highbury House
Cold with the first frosts already threatening

My conversation with Mr. Hillock brought me back to life. I stood, brushed off my skirts, and returned to the desk I'd neglected since my miscarriage. Opening my sketchbook, I began to work out a plan for the winter garden.

For four days, I hardly left my desk, falling asleep over my pencil. But every morning I woke up, peeled the paper from my face, bathed, and then went back to work.

Twice in four days, Mr. Hillock came to the house bearing bread or cakes from his wife's kitchen. I ate like a starving woman while he looked at my drawings, asking questions and familiarizing himself with the design he would have to execute.

I have not yet told Adam what happened at Highbury House. If he thinks anything of the lapse in my correspondence, he hasn't mentioned it in the letters that are delivered with my breakfast tray. I will tell him in my own time what had happened. Or I won't. It is no one's business but my own.

And Matthew's.

Matthew, who has yet to reappear. I cannot deny that I had hoped he would, if only to share a little bit of the burden of grief. If I let myself think back to that horrible evening when everything went wrong, I can see the expression of rage and desperation and grief stretched across his face. But then every doubt I ever had of his feelings—about the proposal, the baby, everything—creeps back in.

Back to my garden.

· STELLA ·

Thwack! The cleaver went straight through bone and hit the wood butcher's block, solid and satisfying. Beth, who was sitting well out of the range of chicken's blood, watched Stella, wide-eyed.

"How you don't chop your own hand off I'll never know," said Beth. Behind her, Mrs. George and her minions banged pots and pans.

"More years of practice than I'd like," said Stella, setting the neatly severed thigh to the side of her board. Her cuts had to be precise because every bit of this chicken would be used. She would pound the breasts thin, coat them with margarine and herbs, roll them in the last brown bread crumbs from the morning's loaf, and then fry them for something approximating chicken Kiev for Mrs. Symonds's dinner tonight. She would roast the thighs separately, pulling the meat from the bone to use in a pie. And the carcass would go into a pot for stock, Stella retrieving any remaining meat to shred for a soup with the vegetables Beth had just delivered.

"I suppose I'll have to learn how to cook properly at some point," said Beth.

Stella looked up. "You can't cook?"

Beth shrugged. "Basic things, but I haven't had much practice with it. My aunt never let me in the kitchen with her. She said I was a distraction. You can teach me if I'm still in Highbury."

If I'm *still at Highbury,* Stella thought.

"Have you heard from your Graeme?" she asked.

"I get a letter most days," said Beth.

"And have you talked any more about where you'll live?" she asked.

Beth sighed. "No. Every time I bring it up, he keeps telling me that he will take care of it, but I have to wait. What if his plan is to move to Norfolk or Scotland or somewhere even further?"

"When does he return on leave?" she asked.

"In two weeks," said Beth. "Forty-eight hours this time, and he was only able to get that because he's been dispatched to support with some work in London. He can't tell me anything else."

"You can talk to him then about where you want to set up your home," said Stella.

"Oh yes, I'm determined to," said Beth.

Stella gave a half smile, but she found herself struggling to focus. All she could think about was Mrs. Symonds's offer. Could she leave Joan's son behind and start her new life? Mrs. Symonds's trip to London was only two days away. She would have to make up her mind.

The clatter of little shoes down the corridor leading to the kitchen made Stella's stomach clench. Sure enough, Bobby burst through the door, a grubby hand clutching an exercise book.

"Aunt Stella! Look at my handwriting!" He shoved the book at her.

"Bobby, what did we discuss?" said Mrs. Symonds, gliding into the kitchen behind him.

Bobby took a step back. "Hello, Aunt Stella. How was your day?"

She stared at her employer. "It was very good, thank you."

"The 's's are hard, but the teacher said I did well," Bobby said, thrusting the exercise book at her again.

"That's very good," she said, patting him awkwardly on the head.

"Bobby, would you run up to the morning room and fetch me my shawl, please?" said Mrs. Symonds.

Without questioning why, Stella's nephew raced off.

"He did do well," said Mrs. Symonds. "I spoke with the headmaster today, who thinks that this week has been better."

"Thank you," said Stella. She knew she should ask for more details, but she was at a loss.

"No surprises for the menu tonight, I take it?" Mrs. Symonds nodded to the chicken.

"Supper will be as we discussed," said Stella.

Mrs. Symonds nodded. "I'll leave you to it, then."

As soon as Mrs. Symonds was gone, Beth said, "She's good with Bobby."

"I still don't understand why she wants to spend time with him when she just lost her son. It must be painful to be around children."

Mrs. George turned around from her stove. "Did you ever think that taking care of that boy could be just as much for her as it is for you or for him?"

"What?" Stella asked.

The older woman put her hands on her hips. "Mrs. Symonds needs someone to care for. I'll reckon she's been missing the feeling of being needed."

Stella dropped her gaze to the butcher's block and picked up her cleaver again. "Enough talking. I have work to do."

· BETH ·

1 November 1944
Temple Fosse Farm

My Lord,

Please forgive me for being so forward, but I believe you are a friend of my husband, Captain Graeme Hastings. He asked me to let you know how he is faring because he misses your conversations. I apologize that I have been remiss in not writing to you earlier, and I hope you do not think it forward of me to express my hope that our paths might cross one day.

Yours faithfully,
Mrs. Graeme Hastings

2 November 1944
Braembreidge Manor

Dear Mrs. Hastings,

There are few good things about this war, but one of them is that we are not so bound by politeness as we once might have been. I would be delighted to make your acquaintance any time that would suit.

Don't bother to call at the house. I spend a good portion of my day in my greenhouse with my orchids.

Yours sincerely,
—A.W.

7 November 1944
Braembreidge Manor

My dear Mrs. Hastings,

It was a great pleasure to make your acquaintance, and I enjoyed hearing your report of how Captain Hastings is faring. I must confess, it makes an old man wish he could be of some use.

I hope you will give thought to my offer. Regardless of your decision, please come again. I will ask my cook to keep back some tea leaves so that we might have fresh for your visit.

Yours sincerely,
—A.W.

She looked up at the screech and grind of metal on metal, pulling her shoulders back under the jacket of her best hunter-green suit.

People began to stream down the steps from the platform. Two RAF officers walked by in their navy uniforms followed by a pack of four WAAFs, their heads bent together so close that their caps nearly touched. A woman in a worn tweed coat tugged at the hand of a little boy who'd outgrown his trousers so that his knobby ankles peeked out.

Beth went up on her tiptoes, eager to see her husband for the first time since their wedding. They'd spent their honeymoon in bed, clinging to each moment they had together. Too soon, they'd had to say goodbye in the Temple Fosse Farm farmyard. She'd watched the lorry carrying him to the train station pull away, and as soon as he was out of sight she ran to Stella's kitchen door. Her friend had taken one look at her tearstained face and put the kettle on.

She was not going to waste one moment of Graeme's first forty-eight-hour leave, but there were the many things she needed to speak to him about, as well. She was determined to have that conversation before they did all of the things he'd dared scandalizing the military censors to write her.

She was just beginning to worry he hadn't made his train when there he was. A grin widening his mouth as soon as he spotted her. He raced down the stairs as she surged forward, all of her concerns pushed aside. He caught her up in his arms and kissed her.

Beth was sure that one of the passing WAAFs sighed when he broke apart enough to say, "It's good to see you," and kissed her again.

She let her body soften to his as he cradled the back of her head. She wanted to stay like this, in this moment kissing him in the lobby of the train station, for as long as she could. But that would be dodging all of the things she'd practiced saying to him.

She pulled back, breathless. "I've missed you."

"I've missed you. Eight weeks is a long time."

He tucked her hand into the crook of his arm and made for the bus station that would drop them a half mile from Temple Fosse Farm. Since Beth's wedding, the Penworthys had given her her own room.

"You'll want your own space when Captain Hastings is on leave," said Mrs. Penworthy, laughing when Beth spluttered her tea.

Ruth had moved into an old storeroom Mrs. Penworthy had helped her do up. Beth had been surprised when Ruth hadn't objected, though the privacy meant all of them gained something.

It was so tempting to just let Graeme come home with her and hole themselves up in her bedroom until he had to go back to his unit.

So tempting and so cowardly.

The bus rolled up to the stop, and the metal doors clanked open.

"Come on," she said, never letting go of his hand.

They boarded and paid the fare, the driver nodding at the sight of Graeme's uniform. They settled into a pair of seats toward the back, his hand laced with hers and resting on his lap.

As the bus pulled onto Old Warwick Road, Graeme said, "I want to hear everything about what you've been doing."

She laughed. "I write to you every day. You're better than keeping a diary."

But still she told him everything. Stories from the farm, what the Penworthys were planting, how Bobby was doing in school. But there was one thing she didn't say. She would keep that to herself for just a little while longer.

He leaned over and kissed her temple. "When there aren't other people around . . ."

She pushed gently on him and reached around him to tug on the cord to ask the driver to stop. "We're here."

"This is too early for Temple Fosse Farm, isn't it? It's two more stops."

"It is. We're not going to the farm," she said.

Graeme followed her off the bus, looking around as he went. "This is Braembreidge Manor."

"It is," she said, pulling him toward the drive of the grand country house.

"You didn't mention you'd spoken to Lord Walford."

"We've had tea a few times. He wants to see you straightaway," she said.

"Lord Walford can wait. I want to spend time with my wife," he said, slipping his hands around her waist.

She went up on her tiptoes to kiss him. "We can't keep the earl waiting."

With a good-natured groan, Graeme offered her his arm.

They crossed the gate she'd found so imposing on her first visit. If Highbury House was grand, Braembreidge Manor was palatial. Yet now that she'd been here a few times, she'd come to enjoy the sight of the old manor house. It was landscaped, not planted in gardens the way Highbury House was, and there was something charming about seeing children from the Coventry school spilling out of the doors whenever they were released from classes.

When they were halfway down the drive, a man in shabby tweeds and a pair of gum boots appeared around a bend. Three spaniels trotted along next to him until they saw Beth and came running.

"Good afternoon, my lord," she called, using her free hand to pat the dogs each in turn.

"Good afternoon! Captain Hastings, it is good to see you hale and hearty," said the older man in a gruff but polished voice.

"The pleasure's mine, Lord Walford. I'm pleased to hear you've met my wife," he said, placing a hand on the small of her back.

"I'm angry with you, Hastings, that you'd kept such a delightful woman from me."

Beth smiled at the earl. "The earl has been tutoring me on the finer points of raising orchids."

"And Mrs. Hastings has been pretending to enjoy it because she's a good sport," said Lord Walford. Then he dug into the pocket of his waxed jacket and pulled out a brass key. "I'll let my housekeeper know that we'll have tea in about a half hour. If you need me, I'll be in the stables."

"Thank you," said Beth, clutching the key.

As Lord Walford walked off, his dogs dancing around his feet, Graeme asked, "What is that?"

Beth simply smiled. "This way."

A few yards away, the path they were on branched off the main drive. Beth led Graeme along until, through the trees, a cottage of good size came into view.

"Here we are," she said.

"Here we are what?" he asked. "You have the better of me."

"Our home. If you want it," she said.

His brows popped up. "Our home?"

"When I went to visit Lord Walford, he asked me where we planned to live. When I told him I didn't know but that I wanted to stay in Highbury, he offered us this cottage. I haven't accepted yet," she said quickly. "I thought we could decide. Together."

She watched him stare at the beautiful yellow stone house with its thatched roof. A chimney bracketed either side, and she could almost smell the smoke that would curl out of them if this house were hers. A rose grew up and over the porch, and she wondered what color the flowers would be in June.

"Are you angry?" she asked.

"No."

"I know that you suggested living with your parents, but—"

He brought one of her hands to his lips and kissed the back of it. "I'm not angry. Not at all. I am surprised."

"Would you like to go inside?" she asked.

He nodded.

She unlocked the door and stepped aside to let him walk into the entryway laid with multicolored tiles. Two doors banded with iron greeted them on either side, and ahead was a flight of stairs leading up to a set of bedrooms.

"The earl told me that a few of the cottages were updated about ten years ago because his land manager refused to live at Braembreidge Manor unless he had hot water, central heating, and working bathrooms," she said.

He pressed a kiss to her hair. "Have you seen this house yet?"

"No. Lord Walford wanted to have it cleaned first, and I thought it would be best to see it together."

She let herself through one of the doors and into a sizable sitting room. Light streamed in through leaded glass windows as she turned to take it in. Although there wasn't a scrap of furniture in the place, she could see how the room might be laid out around the iron fireplace, topped with a wide mantel.

"There's a snug through there for the winter, and Lord Walford says the dining room and the kitchen are at the back of the house. There are three bedrooms upstairs and a smaller room for a study," she said.

She turned to find him leaning against the doorframe, watching her.

"Or a nursery," he said.

She smiled. "Or a nursery."

"I want to see the rest of the house, but first, I should tell you something." He rubbed a hand on the back of his neck. "I wrote to my mother asking if you could stay with my parents if you became pregnant before the war ended or if I was dispatched abroad after the war ends. She very bluntly pointed out that you were a new bride and you might not want to live with your mother-in-law in a strange home that you've never visited before. She also asked me if I had ever considered how lonely you might be in Colchester, where you know no one. She told me that I was being selfish."

"Your mother sounds like a woman of strong opinions," said Beth as neutrally as she could.

"She has a clear sense of what is right and wrong. In this case, I was in the wrong."

"I could also have told you all of that. In fact, I did," she said.

"I'm sorry I didn't listen. I'm going to be apologizing for that for years, I'm sure," he said sheepishly.

"Not years. Maybe days," she said.

"I promise I will become better."

"All I want is for us to make decisions together." She crossed the room and kissed his cheek. "You promise you're not angry that I spoke to Lord Walford?"

"How could I be angry at such a resourceful wife?"

They walked from room to room, Beth exclaiming when she found little delightful details. Though modest, someone had put a remarkable amount of thought into its construction. By the time they had walked over each inch of it, including the cool, dry root cellar, she was charmed.

"Could you see us living here? I know it's not right in Highbury, but we can cycle in," she said.

"When the petrol ration is lifted, we could save for a car," he said.

"You're so certain that the war will be over soon," she said.

"Things have been changing since D-Day." He hesitated. "I was going to wait until tonight to tell you this, but I've requested that my position with the Pioneer Corps become permanent."

She sucked in a breath. "You're not trying to return to your regiment anymore?"

He shook his head. "I put in for a transfer to a posting in London, and my commanding officer seems to think I'll be approved. I will still need to stay in digs, but I can come up whenever I have leave. It's possible that the role might continue after the war."

"Are you certain?" she asked. "You were so set on returning to your men."

He smiled. "If this transfer goes through, it will mean starting our life together all the sooner."

She slid her hands down his arms so their fingers interlaced. "I want this house, and I want this life with you."

"Good. Shall we tell Lord Walford?" he asked.

"Yes, but first . . ." She tilted her head back and kissed her husband in their future home.

· VENETIA ·

I awoke this morning to the pale autumn sun streaming through the bedroom window. I had neglected to draw the curtains last night, and I could see the corner of one of the greenhouses and yellowing leaves of the ramble. All at once, I missed the smell of the freshness and the crisp, heavy morning air.

Dressing quickly, I swept up my sketchbook and pencil. I knew the Melcourts would be at church, servants in tow. I would use the time to check my final drawings for the winter garden against the physical space. Then I would pack my things.

Outside, the weak sun felt warm when I tilted my head back to sample it. A goldfinch chirped, and leaves whispered as they floated to the earth. Underground I knew that the hundreds of bulbs Mr. Hillock's men and I had spent hours planting would be beginning their life cycle, emerging from dormancy before the first green stem burst out of the ground in defiance of the winter.

I took my time, enjoying the solitude as I made my way through the sculpture garden with its slow-growing topiaries. I turned the corner to round the hedge between the water and poet's gardens and walked straight to the winter garden's gate. They key was in the lock, so I let myself in.

I breathed deep.

Starting on the right edge of the circular garden, I began a slow progression around the space, letting myself dream. Although meant to look its best at the bitterest time of the year, I wanted it to be beautiful in spring, summer, and autumn as well. Mr. Hillock and I had agreed on a climbing rose that would spread over the wall, a tribute to Matthew. Echinops' silver spikes of leaves would rise up and show off their pale purple flowers in the summer, and by winter they would have died back to perfect pom-poms of seed heads swaying in the wind and scattering their bounty. I made a note with my pencil to ask Mr. Hillock to be sure to leave the seeds for the birds as long as he could.

I don't know how long I stayed. I was lost, absorbed by my task and compelled to finish. To be done with Highbury House so I could try to move on.

My concentration was broken when I heard the squeak of the gate. I looked up from where I'd crouched to scribble a note. Matthew.

He paused, his right hand resting on the iron gate, his eyes locked on me. "Venetia."

My name drifted to me on the autumn breeze.

Hesitantly I rose. "Why are you here?"

"I hoped to find you alone." He took a step forward. "I needed to see you."

My hand flew up. "Stop! Please don't come any closer."

He froze midstep, his expression agony. But so was mine. I could leave this place behind. The pain and loss may never completely leave me, but they would fade. But I could not do that if Matthew kept opening the wound.

"But, Venetia—"

"Whatever you've come to say, I don't need it. I don't want it." My voice cracked, and I looked down at my shaking hands. "Why did you have to come now, when I'm finally ready to leave?"

"I wanted to come earlier," he said.

"Then why didn't you?" I hurled the words at him, aiming to wound.

"Helen told me that you didn't want to see me," he said.

"Your sister said that? And you believed her?"

322 · JULIA KELLY

His shoulders sagged. "Why shouldn't I? You didn't return any of my letters."

"You wrote? The only correspondence I've received is Adam's."

He shoved a hand through his hair and gripped the roots. "They kept us apart."

"And we believed them," I murmured.

"Why wouldn't we? If we no longer have a child, you are freed of your obligations to me."

My obligations to him? I was the one who was being cast out.

"Matthew, I appreciate that you were trying to do the noble thing when you asked for my hand."

He stared at me so long that I began to shift from foot to foot under his scrutiny.

"You think I was doing the noble thing?" he finally asked.

"With no child, there is no scandal. If you're worried that I will hold you to your offer of marriage, don't fear. I'll absolve you of all responsibility."

"Then you don't wish to marry me?" he asked.

I turned away. "I have accepted that what I want and what I can have are two different things. I'm leaving Highbury House today. I cannot stay any longer knowing that our daughter died here."

He hinged at the waist, gasping out, "A daughter? We had a daughter?"

"You didn't know?" I asked.

Tears shone in his eyes. "My sister said that it was impossible for the doctor to tell."

My free hand balled up into a tight fist. "Your sister lied. We had a girl. I thought to call her Celeste."

He dashed tears from his eyes. "It's a beautiful name."

"It was what my father called my mother sometimes."

"Then I know what to name these." He dipped his hand into his jacket pocket and pulled out a small brown paper envelope. He offered it to me. Hesitantly I took it and opened it. A half dozen seeds fell out into my hand.

"What are they?" I asked.

"Our rose. The one that we crossed in the spring. It took, and now we have these. A new breed, with any luck."

"But you don't know for sure?"

"I won't until I can plant these and see what grows, but I'm fairly confident." He cleared his throat. "I had been saving them for a wedding present. I had thought to name the new breed 'Beautiful Venetia', after you. Now I wonder how you might feel calling them 'Beautiful Celeste'."

Tears welled up in my eyes, and I closed my hand around the seeds. "I think that's a fine idea. We can ask Mr. Hillock to plant 'Beautiful Celeste' here."

I hugged my stomach as tears began to fall. I squeezed my eyes shut, but all at once I was no longer alone. Matthew's arms came around me, one of his large hands cradling my head to his chest. My sketchbook and pencil fell to the soft earth as I clung to him and cried.

"I'm so sorry," he murmured into my hair.

"I lost her and now I've lost you, and I don't know if I can stand it any longer."

He pulled away a little, the pad of one of his thumbs wiping at my tears. "You never lost me."

I shook my head. "I became with child. Neither of us wanted—"

"I wanted you, Venetia. That's all I wanted at first, and then when I found out that we would have a child . . . That day by the lake was the happiest of my life. I thought that finally I would have all that I wanted."

"You didn't think I'd trapped you?"

He laughed, sharp and a little bitter. "Far from it. I feared that you felt trapped by me, and what's worse, I was glad. I had you and I never wanted to let you go."

"What could you possibly want with me?"

He jammed his hands onto his hips, shaking his head. "You are the most stubborn, infuriating woman. I love you."

"You hardly know me."

He sighed. "I know that you have a sharp, determined mind, and arguing with you is like trying to break through concrete with a toothpick. I know that when you smile deeply, there is a dimple next to your right eye that creases just so. I know that you're more comfortable in your gardening clothes than in a gown, and that when you fall asleep you turn to your right side. But mostly I know that I want to learn something new about you every day. I understand if that is asking too much. I don't have much to offer, but I can promise that I do love you, truly and deeply, and will more with each passing day."

"I don't know if I'll be able to have another child," I said.

"Then we will be happy with just each other."

"Your family won't accept me."

He hugged me closer, wrapping the ends of his coat around us both. "You are my family. Will I be met with resistance from your brother?"

I shook my head. "Adam will probably thank you for being brave enough to marry me. Although you might wish to avoid telling him of our affair, in case he has developed an old-fashioned taste for dueling."

He smiled. "I'm a novice with dueling pistols, so I will take your advice."

I paused. "Between the Melcourts, the doctor, and the servants, too many people know about what happened here."

"We'll move."

"Are you sure you can give up Wisteria Farm?" I asked.

I could see the tightness at the corners of his mouth. I hated to think he would regret giving the property up, but I didn't see how we could stay when the life we lived was so tied to the Melcourts' goodwill.

"The roses are not exactly easy to transport at the moment, but we will think of something. Where do you want to live?"

I thought for a moment and then asked, "What do you think of America?"

"So long as I'm with you, I don't care where we are. Now, why don't we see about your things? Much as I don't want to let you out of my sight, you can't stay at Wisteria Farm until we're married. There is a respectable boardinghouse for women in Royal Leamington Spa."

"I'll go there until the banns can be read," I said, nodding at the practicality of his suggestion.

"Good. There's just one more thing."

When I looked up at him, he cupped my face and kissed me.

"Say again you'll be my wife?" he asked, his lips brushing against mine.

"I'll be your wife," I murmured.

He kissed me swiftly again and then scooped up my pencil and sketchbook. "Your drawings."

And, hand in hand, we left Celeste's garden.

· DIANA ·

*D*iana peeled off her gloves and lifted the little gray hat from her hair, careful not to catch the net in the wave at her temple. It had been a long journey back from London, where she'd ensured that all of the loose ends were tied up. But now it was done, and in the crocodile handbag she kept firmly on her arm, she had her future.

"Thank you, Mrs. Dibble," she said, handing her things off to the housekeeper but retaining her handbag. "Do you know where Miss Adderton is?"

"She was in the kitchen garden with Mrs. Hastings. I believe Mrs. Hastings was casting an eye over the potato crop to see if they're ready to be lifted," said Mrs. Dibble.

"Could you please ask them to join me in the morning room?"

Mrs. Dibble bustled off to the cabinet to hang up Diana's coat.

In the large, gilt-framed entryway mirror, Diana gave her hair a couple of pats to mold it back into place.

"You're looking very smart."

She glanced up to see Cynthia and Matron McPherson approach. "I've just come back from London."

"I thought you were only going for a day," said Cynthia.

"My business delayed me longer than I expected. It necessitated a stay overnight," she said.

"Where did you stay?" Cynthia asked.

Diana dropped her hand and turned, plastering a smile on her face. "The Harlan Club. I've retained my membership."

"Matron was just remarking on your absence. You've missed your usual round of letter writing," said her sister-in-law.

The pop of Matron's eyebrows told Diana that the conversation hadn't quite had the judgmental tone that Cynthia implied.

"I only said that several of the men had letters in this afternoon's post," said Matron.

"I'll be sure to make my way through the wards as soon as I'm finished with some urgent business," she reassured the head nurse.

Cynthia sighed. With measured calm, Diana unsnapped the clasp of her handbag and pulled out the thinner of two envelopes she'd carried from London.

"It might interest you to know that I saw some old friends in London, including a Mrs. Delmonte, who was a fellow student of my old harp teacher. She began volunteering with the British Red Cross before the war, and she's found herself rather high up in the Voluntary Aid Detachment. She was particularly interested in the work that you've done with Highbury House Hospital, Cynthia. So interested, in fact, that she thought it would be helpful to use your expertise as commandant in a convalescent hospital opening in Wales."

"I'm needed here," said Cynthia.

Diana smiled wider as she handed her sister-in-law the envelope. "I think you'll find all of the details in Mrs. Delmonte's letter."

Cynthia snatched the envelope from her and ripped it open. A strange calm settled over Diana as she watched Cynthia scan the letter, then lift a glare to her.

"You're to become commandant of Highbury House Hospital," Cynthia spat.

"I am," she said.

"That's ridiculous."

"When the hospital first arrived, I would have agreed with you. I thank you for all of the hard work that you've done," she said.

"This is my family's home," said Cynthia.

"You may have spent your childhood here, but this is *my* home. And it will remain so when the war is over. You would do well to remember that."

Cynthia paled, but still she pushed. "You don't know the first thing about running a convalescent hospital."

Matron McPherson stepped forward. "I have no doubt that, given Mrs. Symonds's experience managing a house of this size and its staff, she will fit smoothly into the role."

Diana shot Matron a grateful look, and the other woman returned a small smile.

"I think you'll see that you are due in Wales in a week's time, so it's best if you begin packing your things. I'll be needing use of your office immediately." As Cynthia sputtered, Diana inclined her head toward Matron. "I would appreciate it if you could find some time to share a cup of tea and counsel this afternoon. I'm sure I will have many questions."

"It would be my pleasure," said Matron.

"Now, I have an appointment to keep, and then soldiers' letters to write. If you'll excuse me."

A rush hit her as soon as she left the entryway. For the first time in a long time, she felt ebullient. In one fell swoop, she had eradicated her sister-in-law and taken back her home.

When she reached the morning room, she saw the door was already ajar. This conversation would be more of a risk, less likely to succeed. But, still, she must try.

She pushed open the door and smiled at Miss Adderton and Mrs. Hastings. "I'm sorry to have kept you waiting."

"Good afternoon, ma'am. Mrs. Dibble said that you wanted to see both of us," said Miss Adderton.

Carefully Diana set her handbag down on her writing desk and drew out the fat, heavy envelope her solicitor had drawn up. "I would like your answer to my question, Miss Adderton."

"What question?" asked Mrs. Hastings.

"Mrs. Symonds would like to take charge of Bobby's care so that I can go to London," said Miss Adderton.

Diana held her hand up. "Actually, I would like to do more than that. I want to adopt your nephew."

Mrs. Hastings's hand flew to her throat in shock.

"You never said anything about adopting him," said Miss Adderton.

"Because I did not know whether it was possible. I needed to speak to my solicitor first." She paused. "I would be more than Bobby's legal guardian. I would be his parent. He would be my son.

"Think about it, Miss Adderton. I can do for him things that you'll never be able to do. You could never afford to send him to the right schools or give him the right clothes. When he's older, I can introduce him to the best path in life. I can teach him what he needs to know to succeed. One day, Highbury House will be his. I can make his life extraordinary."

"You can't just trade one son for another," said Mrs. Hastings.

Diana's eyes narrowed. "No one can replace my son, and nothing can bring him back. I wish with every fiber of my being that I had secured the keys to the winter garden better or that I'd pulled up every dangerous plant in this garden. I will never stop regretting that my last words to him were to shoo him away. He was my *son*," her voice cracked. "He was the very best part of me, and only one other person here comes close to understanding what that feels like to have lost him," she said.

"Bobby is a five-year-old boy," said Mrs. Hastings.

"And I am the mother of his best friend. Bobby and I will always be connected by our loss."

"I could understand you wanting to adopt Bobby if he didn't have a family, but he does. She's standing right here." Mrs. Hastings gestured to Miss Adderton, pale as a ghost.

Diana closed her eyes. How could she convince these women? For the first time in a long time, she could see her life beyond the walls of this house. She didn't want to collapse in on herself in grief. She wanted to spread her arms. She wanted to give all the love she had to this child.

"Can you even do this?" Mrs. Hastings was asking.

"Miss Adderton, if you would take a moment to look at the documents my solicitor has drawn up—"

"I'll do it," Miss Adderton cut her off, and swept up the papers from the desk. "I sign these and Bobby is yours?"

"Yes," Diana breathed. "My solicitor will take care of the rest."

Miss Adderton looked down at the papers covered in black type.

"Stella . . ." Mrs. Hastings began.

Miss Adderton turned to her. "I can't be Bobby's mother, Beth."

"No one is asking you to be," said Mrs. Hastings.

"But you are, even if you don't use those words. I can take him to school and remember to feed him and make sure he takes a bath, but those are all items to check off a list. I can't love him the way I should. I've been trying to make myself since Joan died, and I can't," said Miss Adderton.

"But you're his family," Mrs. Hastings pushed.

"I would have thought that you of all people would know how terrible it is to live with someone who is obligated to care for you."

Mrs. Hastings's eyes widened. "What happened with my aunt was completely different."

"Was it truly, though? Wouldn't you have wanted a chance to be raised by someone who loved you?" Miss Adderton asked.

"I can love Bobby," Diana interjected. "I already love him for who he was to my son. In time, I can love him as my own."

Miss Adderton nodded, her eyes still fixed on the papers in her hands. "I sign these and you'll give me the money to move to London?"

"Yes," breathed Diana. "I'll give you the money for a room in a board-inghouse or flat, if you prefer. I'll help you with a wardrobe and pay for your courses—not correspondence courses but an actual secretarial college. I can ask my friends in London to help find you a placement. You can travel. Let me help you live the life you'd always wanted."

"It hardly seems like a fair trade," said Miss Adderton with a hollow laugh.

Mrs. Hastings looked from one to the other. "I can't believe that you're actually considering this."

Miss Adderton whirled on her friend. "I hate it here. I hate being in service. I hate that my sister left Warwickshire and I stayed behind. You have the life you want, Beth. Let me try to have mine."

Mrs. Hastings, who looked as though she was about to argue, snapped her mouth shut.

"You can see Bobby whenever you wish. I would be happy to bring him up to London if that's easier," said Diana.

Miss Adderton crossed her arms over her stomach and hugged herself closely. "Mrs. Symonds, please understand: If I sign these documents, I will never see my nephew again, but I do want to know how he is. Will you write to me?"

"Of course," she said.

The cook reached for a pen. "Where do I sign these?"

"There are three copies, one for you, one for me, and one for my solicitor to register the adoption," she said, easing the papers out of Miss Adderton's hands so she could show her the spaces to sign. Then she bent down to put her own signature to the pages.

Straightening, she held out the pen to Mrs. Hastings. "We require a witness."

Mrs. Hastings stared at the pen, and for a moment, Diana thought that the woman would refuse.

"Beth, please," Miss Adderton whispered.

Mrs. Hastings snatched the pen out of her hand. "Fine."

"Please keep an eye on him, Beth. You're going to be so close," Miss Adderton said.

When Diana lifted her brow, Mrs. Hastings said, "My husband and I have an agreement to let a house on the grounds of Braembreidge Manor. We'll move there when the war is over."

"It sounds as though we're all beginning anew," Diana said.

Mrs. Hastings pursed her lips but nodded.

Diana blotted the signatures and stood back. It was done.

"What now?" Mrs. Hastings asked.

"I'll speak to Bobby and tell him he's to live here. Unless you want to, Miss Adderton," she said.

"No. I'll make arrangements to leave by the end of next week," said Miss Adderton as she took her copy.

"I'll write to my banker. He'll see to it that you have what you need," she said.

Miss Adderton turned to leave, but then she glanced over her shoulder.

"You can't call him Bobby any longer. It's far too common a name for the heir to this house. Robert would be better."

Diana squeezed her eyes shut. "That was Robin's given name, as well."

"It's a good name," offered Mrs. Hastings.

Diana gave her a weak smile, grateful for the olive branch. The other woman might never understand—most wouldn't—but Diana knew that she'd done what was right for the three people who mattered.

"We'll see what Bobby thinks, but later," she said. "Right now, one change at a time."

· EMMA ·

OCTOBER 2021

*E*mma stamped her boot down onto her spade and levered more earth out of the hole she'd been at for the last five minutes. Beth's drawings had shown two beautiful stands of hydrangeas up against the winter garden's wall. Usually hardy plants, the ones she'd revealed when cutting back foliage had been diseased beyond the point of preservation. A couple of calls and a few favors, and she managed to secure two huge pot-grown plants to replace them at a deep discount.

Normally, she'd only dig down about a foot and plant out the shrubs, but the surrounding roots were so dense she was digging down further to give the hydrangeas a fighting chance. Twice already she'd had to pull out the handsaw to get through a dense thicket of roots, and she'd already shed her jumper.

"Hi!"

Emma looked up, squinting against the glare of the overcast day. At the top of the ladder into the garden stood Henry. His hair was, as always, a mess, and he wore his usual crooked smile—the one that made her heart flip.

"Hi. Are you looking for Sydney or Andrew?" she asked.

He came by looking for you. Charlie's teasing words pinged around in her brain.

"Actually, I'm looking for you." Henry hitched a long leg over the wall, and she watched him climb down. She was a little disappointed that his T-shirt was covered up by a black cable-knit jumper.

As soon as Henry was off the ladder, he looked around. "This is going to be beautiful."

"Thanks. It'll be another full year before you can really start to see things come together, but it'll get there," she said.

"I heard that Sydney's got you re-creating the kitchen garden and doing some work on the orchard," he said.

She laughed. "I took Charlie on as a business partner, and his first act was to overrule my decision to pass on the kitchen garden. It was a coup."

"I didn't take Charlie for a despot, but maybe all he needed was a little taste of power. How are you feeling about the project?"

"It won't be historically accurate—we're planting more disease-resistant vegetables, for instance—but it should be fun. Zack and Vishal are measuring for raised beds right now."

"I saw. Sydney walked me through." Henry gestured to her spade. "Have you got another one of those?"

She nodded and retrieved the one Charlie had been using earlier. When she passed it over to him, their fingers brushed. Another flip.

"How deep?" Henry asked, seemingly oblivious to what just the thought of seeing him did to her. Or maybe it had always been this way, and she'd just tried her best to ignore it.

"About a foot more," she said.

He grunted and sank the spade into the ground. After a moment's hesitation, she did the same on her end of the hole.

"What did you want to see me about?" she asked, tipping her head to keep her ponytail out of her face to watch him.

"I just wanted to see you. It's been a while, and I wondered where you'd gone. I thought maybe you'd started to think about what you might do after Highbury."

A smile twitched her lips. "I have another garden job lined up, but I thought I'd keep Bow House for a little while."

He looked up sharply. "Really?"

"Really. I'll be working up in Berwick-upon-Tweed, but I'll commute back on the weekends."

"What about your nomadic lifestyle?" he asked casually.

"I've realized there might be some merits to staying in one place for a while," she said, thinking about the appointments she already had lined up with a local real estate agent to see properties around Highbury.

"You know, we never did have those welcome-to-the-neighborhood drinks," Henry said.

She laughed. "We've gone to pub quizzes together."

"Welcome drinks needs to be one-on-one. It's a rule," he said.

She drove her spade into the earth again, but this time it didn't budge.

"You okay there?" he asked.

"I must have hit a taproot or a rock," she said. But when she wiggled the spade, she heard the scrape of metal against metal. She pointed. "Hand me that trowel, please."

He did, and she crouched on the ground, bringing up trowels full of dirt.

"Can you work on the other side?" she asked.

Shortening his stroke so as not to hit her, he cut away to expand the hole while she dug around. It took some effort, but in a few minutes they'd exposed the top of a tin box studded with nails.

"What is that?" he asked.

"I don't know. It's loose enough over here. I think I can lift it."

"Got it," he said.

They both heaved, and the rest of the box broke free from the earth. A padlock hung from a rusted loop.

"Let's see that trowel?" Henry said.

She handed it over, and he used it to knock the loop clean from the box in a few strokes.

"I know a few historians who would be livid with you right now," she said.

"Good thing they aren't here, then, isn't it?" he asked cheerfully. "Do you want to do the honors?"

She nodded and slowly opened the lid.

Inside was an oil cloth. She lifted it and found dozens of old photographs of a young boy. In some he was alone, but in others he stood with an elegant woman, posed formally for the camera.

"Who's this?" Henry asked.

"No idea," she said, lifting one of the pictures.

"We should show this to Sydney," said Henry, pulling out his phone, dialing, and putting it on speaker. "Hey, Syd?"

"You all right?" Sydney asked.

"You're going to want to come to the winter garden. Emma and I found something," he said.

"What is it?" Sydney asked.

"Come and see," he said.

"Okay, but bring it over the wall. I'm not up to climbing ladders today," Sydney said.

"Will do."

While he hung up, Emma replaced the photos and closed the lid. They lashed the box closed, and Henry climbed up and over to the top of the outside ladder. Emma threw him a rope she'd tied around the box, and he hauled it up as she climbed, using one hand to steady the box with every rung she took. When she reached the top, Henry climbed down, and she lowered it to him.

Emma was just coming down the outside ladder when Sydney strode up. "What did you find?"

Emma opened the box again and took out one of the photographs. "Do you know who these two are?"

Sydney frowned. "That's my Great-Grandmother Diana, so that must be Granddad Robert." Sydney began to sort through the photos, flipping them over as she went. "Here, look at this. Someone's written 'Robin, age three' on the back."

"There are so many baby pictures in here. Who would bury these?" asked Emma.

"There's more in there," said Henry.

Sydney collected up the photographs to set them aside, revealing what looked like the contents of a child's toy box. A set of tin army men, a toy lorry, a couple of books, a pair of baby boots with a robin stitched onto each heel, a jumper . . .

"What is all of this stuff?" Sydney asked.

"Look, there's an envelope," said Emma.

Sydney opened it and pulled out several papers. On top was an official document with an application number at the top and *Certified Copy of an Entry* written in red across it:

Date and county of birth: 12 March 1939; Bristol
Name and surname of child: Robert REYNOLDS
Name and surname: Diana SYMONDS
Address: Highbury House, Highbury, Warwickshire
Occupation of parents of adopted child: Housewife
Date of adoption order: 16 November 1944

"This can't be right," said Sydney. "My grandfather wasn't adopted. His name is in the family Bible in ink just above his father's recorded death, and I just found his birth certificate earlier this year when I was going through his papers."

But when Sydney shuffled to the next page, the adoption papers were clear as day.

"Who signed them?" Emma asked, pointing to the bottom.

"Diana Symonds, Stella Adderton—"

"And Beth Hastings?" Henry asked. "Why would my nan have been a witness?"

"You said she was a land girl near here. She must have known either Diana Symonds or this Stella. She must have been allowed on the grounds to do the sketches you showed me," said Emma.

Sydney stared blankly into space. "I don't understand."

Emma watched Sydney turn on her heel and start back toward the house with the box in her hands. Emma and Henry glanced at each other and immediately followed.

Sydney hurried through the house, down the corridor, and into the library. They were right behind her when she went straight up to a large book on a carved wooden stand.

"This is the family Bible. It goes back seven generations on Helen Melcourt's side." Sydney flipped open the front cover and traced her finger down a page of handwritten names in various shades of black ink. "Here, Robert Symonds. That's my grandfather."

Henry peered over Sydney's shoulder. "Born 14 May 1939."

"The dates don't match, Sydney," said Emma quietly.

"But if Robert Reynolds was adopted, then who is this boy?" Sydney asked, jabbing a finger at the Robert in the family Bible.

"Henry, remember that sketch of your grandmother's of the two boys under the tree?" Emma asked.

"You think that there were two boys here during the war. One was Robin and the other was Sydney's grandfather, Robert," said Henry, reading her mind.

"Yes. I have the sketch at Bow Cottage. I can get it," said Emma gently.

"That would be good," said Sydney quietly.

"Are you okay?" Emma asked.

Sydney crossed her hands over her stomach. "Why would Diana have had one son and adopted another only to never mention the first boy again? The only thing I can think is that Robin must have died."

The three of them looked down at the photograph of three-year-old Robin.

"I suspect that the war wasn't the only thing that brought tragedy to families during those years," said Emma quietly.

"If this date of birth and adoption are correct, Robert was only five when he was adopted. He might not have remembered much of his life before his adoption," said Henry.

"And every family has their secrets. Maybe they just didn't talk about it," said Emma. "Maybe Diana thought it would be easier for him to grow up without worries. I don't know who he was before, but life was probably easier as the son of a wealthy family."

"Sydney?" Henry pushed a hand through his hair. "I think I've met Stella Adderton. My nan used to go up to London every once in a while to see dealers about getting her paintings into shows. She would stay with her friend, Stella. I don't remember her last name, but Stella was what we would call an executive assistant now. She used to travel a lot for her job, so she left Nan the key to her flat. Nan took me up with her once when I was maybe ten. We went to the London Zoo."

"Do you think Beth would tell Stella about how Robert was getting on?" Sydney asked.

"I'd like to think so."

Emma was half listening, her gaze fixated on something in the family Bible. No. It couldn't be . . . She couldn't believe that an answer to a more than one-hundred-year-old question had been sitting in plain view this entire time, if only someone knew to look for it.

"Do you mind if I take a picture of this?" she asked.

"Hmm?" Sydney murmured as she began to sift through the box again.

"The family tree. Do you mind?"

"Go ahead," said Sydney, already turning her attention again to the buried artifacts of a boy's life.

"Hey, there's something else in here," Henry said.

Emma's phone camera clicked, and she turned to see him holding a large iron key.

Sydney squinted "Is that—"

"The key to the winter garden's gate. Let's go find Andrew and Charlie," said Emma.

Thirty minutes later, they stood in front of the winter garden gate. Sydney was practically vibrating with excitement, key clenched in her hand, but Emma hung back. She kept glancing at her phone, unsure if she should believe the photograph she'd taken.

"Emma," Sydney prompted her.

Her head shot up, and she slipped her phone back into her pocket. "What can I help with?"

Her friend held out the key. "I think you should open it."

"No, it's your garden," said Emma.

Sydney shook her head. "You're the one bringing it back to life."

Emma glanced at Andrew, who nodded. She swallowed but took the key nonetheless. She slid it into the lock and turned it. It resisted, but with a little effort, she managed to get the tumblers to grind open.

"Give me a hand, will you?" she asked, gripping the bars.

Henry and Andrew both shoved against rust and age, opening the gate for the first time in decades. Then, one by one, they walked through the gate and into the winter garden.

Sydney turned around, slowly taking in what Emma had done. "It's going to be beautiful."

"You're sure you want to keep restoring it, even after finding the box?" Emma asked, hoping that her friend would say yes.

Sydney nodded. "It's already been a garden for the lost. Now I want it to be a place where we can make new, happy memories."

Andrew looped an arm around his wife's waist and kissed the top of her head. "I think we should start now."

Sydney smiled up at her husband. "In about seven and a half months, we're going to be three running around this big old house."

"Not running right away," said Andrew, paling a little bit.

"Oh, Sydney!" Emma gasped, pulling her friend into a hug. This was what she'd been looking for. To be a part of joyful beginnings. To have a home.

Sydney whispered to her, "And you'll be around to see it."

Emma pulled back. "How did you know?"

"There are no secrets in a small village, remember? I ran into your real estate agent at the grocery store the other day."

"I haven't told anyone else except Charlie that I'm looking to buy, but I may have mentioned I'll be staying on for a little longer," said Emma, glancing at Henry, who was crowding around Andrew with Charlie, shaking his hand and clapping him on the back.

"I'd tell you to take all the time you need, but I'm pretty sure he's one trip to the White Lion away from finding out." Sydney stepped back and announced to everyone, "I think I need to sit down. I never took it seriously when people told me that pregnancy was exhausting, but I believe it now. Why don't we all have a cup of tea?"

"You don't have to ask me twice," said Charlie.

"Let me just get this hydrangea into the ground," Emma said.

"I'll help you," said Henry.

Sydney and Charlie exchanged looks but left without a word, followed by Andrew.

"Well," said Emma.

"Back to work," he said.

Emma moved toward her spade but snuck a look at her phone again.

"What do you keep checking?" Henry asked.

She turned her phone around to show him the photo of the Bible page.

He stepped close to lean in, resting his hand on the small of her back. "What am I looking at?"

She read out, "Helen Marie Goddard marries Arthur Melcourt in 1893."

"I'm still not seeing it," he said.

"The family tree shows that Helen's brother is Matthew Spencer Goddard. There's a gap in the correspondence between Venetia Smith and her brother, Adam, who handled all of the operations of her business, during the autumn of 1907. Then Venetia reappears seemingly out of nowhere in America in 1908, married to a man named Spencer Smith. The same middle name as Matthew Spencer Goddard, Helen Melcourt's brother."

"You think Spencer Smith is really Matthew Goddard?" he asked.

"Think about it. Venetia was a single woman working for his sister's family. She leaves the country without any explanation and never comes back. I think she was running because she and Matthew fell in love."

"But why not just marry?" he asked.

"It must have been more complicated than that. I think she and Matthew had an affair and her reputation was on the line."

"And so Matthew marries her and takes on a different name so no one could trace the affair back to her work at Highbury House," he said.

"And look at this," she said, excited as she flicked through the pictures on her phone to the image of Professor Waylan's letter she'd texted to Charlie. "A professor who helps me sometimes found this letter from Spencer Smith to Venetia in 1912. 'Sometimes when you are away I think back to the celestial connection that forever binds me to you. The joy that slipped through our fingers led us to where we are now. I hope you do not hate me for having no regrets, because now I have you.' Someone wrote on the final garden plans 'Celeste's garden' under the name for this space. What if the celestial connection is this garden?"

A little smile tipped his mouth. "I love how excited you are by this."

She grinned. "I like the idea that maybe I know a secret about Venetia Smith that no one else in the world knows. Except you."

Henry picked up his spade and began pushing dirt to level off the bottom of the hole they'd pulled the box out of. "You know," he said as he worked, "I never did get an answer to my question."

She crossed her arms as she watched him. "What was that?"

"When are we getting drinks?"

"Are you asking me out to be neighborly or because you want to ask me out?"

He huffed a laugh. "If you have to ask, I'm not doing a very good job of sending signals."

Emma crossed the short patch of ground between them, and kissed him. She could feel his surprise as his lips opened, but then he cradled the back of her neck, deepening the kiss. She traced her hands up his arms, gripping his hair and pulling him closer to her, finally letting herself do what she'd wanted to since he'd taken her groceries from her at the pub and pulled her into his world.

When finally she pulled away, he kept her anchored to him, his hands on her hips.

"Let's skip drinks and go straight to dinner," he breathed.

She laughed, wrapping her arms around his waist. "I thought you'd never ask."

· DIANA ·

DECEMBER 1944

*D*iana watched Bobby pick up the red toy lorry with its chipped paint and place it in the tin box. It had been three weeks since Bobby's aunt had left Highbury House carrying a battered suitcase and her handbag. While quiet, Bobby was a sweet little boy. With time, he would once again grow into the vibrant child who'd played with her son.

Sometimes Diana fretted that she had used her money and her position to force Miss Adderton's hand, just as she'd forced Cynthia out. But then why did Miss Adderton shake her hand before walking down Highbury's drive? And why had the only letter that had arrived from London been addressed to her, not to Bobby? Miss Adderton wrote that she had enrolled in a secretarial college full of other women deemed unable to serve for whatever reason. She'd taken on hours with a volunteer ambulance unit in Willesden, where she'd found a flat. She was already making friends.

There was not one message for Bobby in the entire letter.

No. Diana may have made many mistakes in her life, but adopting Bobby was not one of them.

"Are you certain you don't want to keep it, Robert?" she asked, nodding to the toy.

He shrugged in a way that she was learning meant he was embarrassed. "It was Robin's favorite."

Tears stung at the bridge of her nose. "Then you're right. It should go into the box."

Silently she packed the rest of the items on the table into the box. A red jumper she'd knitted for Robin two Christmases ago. A couple of his baby photos she had duplicates of. A set of tin army men who'd fought brave battles over the grass of the children's garden. The spare key to the winter garden.

Her hand hesitated over a sealed envelope that lay to her right. Perhaps it was unwise for her to hide away the adoption papers, but she didn't want them in the house where Bobby might come across them. He was her child now.

Carefully she placed the envelope inside the box, closed the lid, and latched it shut.

"Come along now. It's time to bury our treasure," she said, offering her hand to Bobby.

The two of them made their way out of her new office. In the hallway, a nurse and a soldier who had been flirting parted at the sight of her, making her smile. When she'd assumed the title of commandant, she'd ceased to be an object of curiosity who'd thrown a party and a wedding and had become an authority figure to be tiptoed around—with respect. With Matron's guidance, she would show them that she could be trusted.

As they walked, soldiers making their way up and down the hall stopped to say hello to Bobby. He hugged close to Diana's side but said a polite "Hello" to every one of them. When Father Devlin called to her from where he was sitting with a patient in Ward B, they stopped.

"Off to defeat the Nazis?" the chaplain asked.

"That was yesterday," said Bobby.

After luncheon, Diana had taken him to the ramble for hide-and-seek. She hadn't cared about the stained elbows of his shirts. Bobby had laughed. She'd laughed. It had felt like catharsis.

"So what is it today?" Father Devlin asked.

"We're burying treasure," Bobby said.

"Is that right?" asked Father Devlin. "What sort of treasure does a pirate hide in Warwickshire?"

"A lorry and playing cards and a top and pictures," Bobby rattled off.

Father Devlin lifted his eyes to Diana's. "Ah. Treasures, indeed."

She crouched down, still holding the box. "Robert, be a good boy, go ask Mrs. Dibble to find us the trowel, please. And my gardening gloves."

He skipped off—skipped!—and she straightened. "I thought it might help him to bury some of Robin's things."

"Him or you?" asked the chaplain.

"Both of us."

He nodded.

"I don't think he understands. He knows that his aunt has gone away, but I don't know if he's absorbed it," she said.

"Be gentle with him."

She nodded, thinking about the new nanny's stories of how Bobby thrashed in the night.

"Where are you going to bury the box?" he asked.

"In the winter garden. I never understood why it was Robin's favorite place," she said with a shake of her head.

"Nothing is more tempting to little boys than a locked gate."

She gave a little smile. "I suppose you're right."

"Remember, I was a little boy once, too, difficult though that is to imagine." He nodded behind her. "Your pirate returns."

Bobby was brandishing two trowels and a set of gardening gloves. He stuck them out to her.

"Thank you very much, Robert," she said, her tone brighter. She collected the gardening things on top of the box and ignored the loose dirt that fell from her gloves onto her cashmere sweater. "Now, shall we go?"

The rain that had been threatening all day held off for them as they moved through the garden rooms. When they reached the winter garden, she pulled out the key she'd slipped into her pocket and unlocked the gate.

"Now, where would a pirate bury this treasure?" she asked.

"Here!" Bobby shouted and ran toward the dogwood trees.

She handed him a trowel, and together they dug a hole for the box. Most of Bobby's dirt slid back in, but he worked diligently with his tongue sticking out of the corner of his mouth. When it was almost a foot deep, he looked at her and asked, "When is Aunt Stella coming back?"

The question hit her right in the heart. "I'm sorry, Robert. Your Aunt Stella couldn't live at Highbury anymore, and she couldn't take you where she was going." There, that stuck closely enough to the truth that a child could understand.

"Is she dead?" he asked.

Another pang. "Why do you ask that?"

He dragged his trowel through the soft dirt. "When Dad died, I couldn't go visit him. Or Mummy, either."

"No, she didn't die, Robert. She's happy and healthy, just busy working, and you live here at Highbury with me now. We should get this treasure buried before it begins to rain."

She placed the box in the earth, and she and Bobby pushed dirt over it until a shallow mound of disturbed earth was all that was left.

Silently they left the winter garden, stopping only to lock the gate behind them for the final time. Then Diana took Bobby by the hand and led him down to the lake's edge.

There was a small outcropping of rocks that jutted out into the water. The key felt heavy in her hand as she turned it over and over again.

"Are you ready to say goodbye?" she asked.

Bobby nodded.

Taking a deep breath, she threw the key as far as she could. When it hit the water, it sent ripples spilling out after it.

"Mrs. Symonds?" he asked.

She glanced down at him. "Yes?"

He hesitated before looking up at her. "Can I call you Mummy?"

"Why would you want to do that?" she asked.

"Because you do all of the things that mummys do."

The sob broke from her before she could stop it, and she clapped her free hand over her mouth.

"Yes," she whispered. "Of course you can."

"Mummy," he said as though testing the name out, "could we have cocoa?"

She gave a watery laugh and swung him up into a hug. "Let's go see what's in the larder."

· EPILOGUE ·

MARCH 1908

*S*he steps off the boat, glad to be on solid ground. The Atlantic crossing hasn't been as arduous as she's been warned, but five days on the water was enough.

A gentle hand on her elbow makes her look up. He is smiling down at her. "Are you ready?"

"I think so."

Her heart still aches to think of all she's left behind in England—her brother, her home, her memories—but she finds that the ache dulls a little bit each day.

They'd stolen back there one frozen January Sunday when they knew that the Melcourts would not be at home. They crossed Highbury House Farm's fields and let themselves in through the gate by her old cottage.

They crossed the lavender walk to the yew path that went straight to Celeste's garden. He hung back a little, but she went to the gate. The head gardener—dear, dear man—had written to tell her where she might find the key. It was under the rock just as he'd described. She let herself in, slipping it into her pocket as she went.

Much of the garden was still freshly planted, but she could see how it would grow and fill the space. Already the grasses looked tall and noble against the red brick. The hellebores bloomed an impossible white, and the green stalks of snowdrops and crocuses stood strong with tight buds that would open in the coming weeks and days.

A part of her heart will always remain in Celeste's garden.

But now she turns her sights to her new home. I will do great things here, *she thinks as she touches the letter of introduction a Mr. Schoot has sent her with a note enclosed: The Royal Botanical Heritage Society had voted to begin admitting women to its ranks this May. And so she will write for Mr. Schoot and his journal as she establishes herself and starts a new life with the man she loves. Matthew.*

Only she mustn't call him that any longer. He'd told her as they lay in their cabin on their first night at sea that he thought it best to go by his middle name, Spencer. They cannot cultivate speculation about what happened between the gardener and the brother of her employer.

"I thought about changing my surname, too. I have little attachment to it," he said, cupping her face.

"Who will you become?" she asked as the boat rocked back and forth under them.

"I thought perhaps I will be a Smith. There are so many Smiths, what is one more?" He paused. "And it's your name. What more could I wish for?"

She kissed him, grateful to have such an unconventional husband.

Over the painful autumn months, she has learned to collect perfect moments of hope and joy to hold close. That night in the cabin was one of those moments, and she will think of it when grief and pain became too much.

When finally the ship pulls up to the dock and the deckhands lash it in place with thick ropes, a gangway is put down. The crowd of passengers eager to stand on land again surges ahead. She slips her hand into her husband's and prepares to walk off into their next adventure together.

AUTHOR'S NOTE

The Last Garden in England grew out of a garden. For years I carried around with me the idea that I wanted to write a book about several different generations of women, all connected by a single garden. I didn't know where it was, what it looked like, or why any of the characters felt pulled to it, but I knew that at some point it would mature into something special.

I found the key to that story when I began to learn about requisitioned houses. Just as in World War I, during World War II the British government needed space for training grounds, hospitals, barracks, and administrative headquarters. Some of the country's great estates that would have served as perfect backdrops for *Downton Abbey* played host to schools, orphanages, and maternity wards for expectant mothers evacuated from the country's urban centers for fear of bombing raids. But it wasn't only the huge houses with dozens of bedrooms that were requisitioned. Even dower houses, village houses, and inns were snapped up for use, and my parents' home served as a WAAF barracks for a period of time.

This was all allowed thanks to the Defence (General) Regulations 1939 under the Emergency Powers (Defence) Act 1939. When orders came, some homeowners tried their best to fend off the invading strangers, as detailed in Julie Summers's excellent history, *Our Uninvited Guests: Ordinary Lives in Extraordinary Times in the Country Houses of*

Wartime Britain. Some had good reason to be fearful of the military coming into their homes. Sir William and Lady Hyde Parker's home at Melford Hall in Suffolk burned down in 1942 after the officers stationed there let their nighttime revelries escalate dangerously. However, others, like Lady Mabel Grey at Howick Hall in Northumberland, embraced their contribution to the war effort.

Lady Grey, who was the model for the best parts of Cynthia Symonds, served as the commandant for a military hospital in her home during two world wars. At the start of the war, the War Office estimated that it would require twenty thousand beds. It found them in convalescent hospitals like Howick Hall, where women like Lady Grey, who were used to running large country houses and staffs of dozens, made the ideal commandants. She would have had a quartermaster to handle operations as they worked with the doctors, matron, and other senior staff of the hospital to ensure everything ran smoothly. It was a vital bit of war work, as the facilities in requisitioned homes allowed casualty hospitals to treat injured servicemen and women and then move them along to convalesce in the countryside.

While researching this book, I paid a visit to Upton House and Gardens in Warwickshire. Lord Bearsted housed his family's bank and its staff on the beautiful grounds of his country residence, which is now a National Trust property. However, it wasn't just Upton House's wartime history that drew me in but its gardens as well, which combine beautiful, classically English borders with a wild-seeming Bog Garden. All the better that it was designed by a young woman named Kitty Lloyd-Jones, who, according to her biographer, was hired by clients in the 1920s and 1930s to lend a sense of good taste to the grand gardens they'd acquired with their new houses bought with new fortunes. Venetia became an amalgamation of the talented female gardeners of the past like Lloyd-Jones and the far more famous Gertrude Jekyll, whose influence on gardening was so deep that many of her principles are still used today.

Not far off from Upton House is Hidcote Manor in Chipping Campden, the product of the real-life Lawrence Johnston, who Venetia and Matthew pay a visit to in the early days of their courtship. It was after a visit to Hidcote on a hot August day that I decided to focus Venetia's vision for Highbury House around a series of garden rooms. Hidcote is laid out in much the same way, with hedges dividing the rooms in which Johnston focused on a single color or theme. The red borders were in full bloom when I visited and served as inspiration for the lovers' garden in this book. In fact, it was when I saw the red borders that I started to see the possibility of what Highbury's fictional gardens could be.

I learned to love gardens as a little girl when I would dig in the dirt next to Dad. Living most of my adult life in New York City and central-ish London meant that, when I was writing this book, I hadn't yet had the pleasure of creating my own garden—except for the little set of container-bound plants that bloom in front of my house. If there are any errors in the plantings, they are all my own. However, my very limited experience with my own plants has taught me that there are no real mistakes when it comes to gardening. Sometimes perfectly well-suited plants that are fussed over and tended to die for no good reason. Other times I've found that a neglected plant will take off like a weed, defying all expectations even when it is in the wrong soil, sun, or situation.

I believe that, much like books, gardens are organic, unpredictable things, revealing their beauty how and when they choose. It is up to us to remember to pause and enjoy that beauty every day.

ACKNOWLEDGMENTS

Whenever I write the acknowledgments for a book, I am always awed thinking back on the generosity of my friends and family.

Thank you to Alexis Anne, Lindsay Emory, Mary Chris Escobar, Alexandra Haughton, and Laura von Holt, my friends and writing retreat companions who encouraged me to press on with this book when I needed it most.

Thank you, Sonia, Eric, Zara, Jenn, Jackie, Ben, Mila, Sloane, Jemima, Mary, Beatrice, Christy, Kather, Sean, Amanda, Liam, and Andy, for keeping me grounded from near and far.

Thank you to my wonderful agent, Emily Sylvan Kim. I still laugh when I think about that long pitch session of not-quite-right ideas that was just wrapping up when I said, "There is this one idea I had about writing a book set around a historic garden that crosses a few time periods." I'm glad we got there in the end!

To Kate Dresser, Molly Gregory, Jen Bergstrom, Aimée Bell, Jen Long, Abby Zidle, Michelle Podberezniak, Caroline Pallotta, Christine Masters, Jaime Putorti, Anabel Jimenez, Lisa Litwack, and the entire team at Gallery Books: I'm so grateful that I've been able to work with you on this book.

My family has been my biggest group of cheerleaders since long before a reader ever held one of my books in their hands. Thank you, Mum, Justine, and Mark, for listening to my frustrations, helping me work through plot points, reading early drafts, and generally being the most wonderful people I could ever have asked for.

I could not have written this book without a lifetime of inspiration from Dad, who let me play around in the dirt and deadhead the roses next to him when I was a little girl. Thank you for lending me your knowledge, playing research assistant, and letting me ransack your gardening books for inspiration. I can't wait to keep learning from you in your own beautiful garden.